Praise for
WATERMELON

"Watermelon introduces readers
to the trials and tribulations of an irresistible,
and suddenly single heroine."
The Houston Chronicle

"A lot of laughs and sassy girl talk."
Kansas City Star

"Hilarious interior monologues...
puts this first novel on the Gen-X 'must-read' list.
It will appeal to mainstream, women's fiction,
and romance fans, too. Highly recommended."
Library Journal

"A rollicking novel about survival
and retaining one's sense of humor
under the worst of circumstances."
The Monterey County Post

"Endearing...*Watermelon* does prove itself
as a delightful light read...It is lightly humorous
and keeps the reader turning pages."
Copley News Service

"Watermelon laughs along with its narrator
on her journey homeward
and her search for who she is."
Booklist

WATER MELON

MARIAN KEYES

AVON BOOKS
An Imprint of HarperCollins*Publishers*

This is a work of fiction. Names, characters, places, and incidents either are the product of the author's imagination or are used fictitiously. Any resemblance to actual events, locales, organizations, or persons, living or dead, is entirely coincidental.

AVON BOOKS
An Imprint of HarperCollins*Publishers*
10 East 53rd Street
New York, New York 10022-5299

Copyright © 1995 by Marian Keyes
Interior design by Kellan Peck
Excerpt from *Lucy Sullivan Is Getting Married* copyright © 1999 by Marian Keyes
Inside cover author photo by Michael Edwards
Library of Congress Catalog Card Number: 97-49670
ISBN: 0-380-79609-0
www.avonbooks.com

First Avon Books Paperback Printing: July 1999
First Avon Books Hardcover Printing: July 1998

Avon Trademark Reg. U.S. Pat. Off. and in Other Countries, Marca Registrada, Hecho en U.S.A.
HarperCollins® is a trademark of HarperCollins Publishers Inc.

Printed in the U.S.A.

WCD 10 9 8 7 6 5 4

For Mam and Dad

WATER MELON

prologue

February the fifteenth is a very special day for me. It is the day I gave birth to my first child. It is also the day my husband left me. As he was present at the birth I can only assume the two events weren't entirely unrelated.

I knew I should have followed my instincts.

I subscribed to the classical or, you might say, the traditional role fathers play in the birth of their children. Which goes as follows.

Lock them in a corridor outside the delivery room. Allow them admittance at no time. Give them forty cigarettes and a lighter. Instruct them to pace to the end of the corridor. When they reach this happy position, instruct them to turn around and return to whence they came.

Repeat as necessary.

Conversation should be curtailed. They are allowed to exchange a few words with any other prospective father pacing alongside them.

"My first," (wry smile).

"Congrats . . . my third," (rueful smile).

"Well done," (forced smile—is he trying to imply that he's more virile).

Feelings do tend to run high around this time.

Or they are allowed to fling themselves on any doctor who emerges exhausted from the delivery room, covered in blood up to his elbows, and gasp "Any news, Doctor???" To which the doctor might reply "Oh God no, man!—she's only three centimeters dilated." And your man will nod knowingly, while understanding nothing other than the fact that there is still a fair bit of pacing to go.

He is also allowed to let a spasm of anguish pass over his face when he hears the agonies of his loved one within. And when it's all over and mother and child have been cleaned up and mother is in a clean nightgown and is lying back against the lacy pillows looking exhausted but joyful and the perfect infant is suckling at her breast, then, and *only* then, should the father be permitted to enter.

But no, I gave in to peer pressure and agreed to be all new age about it. I was very doubtful, I can tell you. I mean, I wouldn't want any of my close friends or relatives at the removal of . . . say . . . my appendix. Humiliating! You'd be at such a disadvantage. All these people looking at you, at places of yourself you'd never even seen before, not even with a mirror. I didn't know what my large intestine looked like. And by the same token I didn't know what my cervix looked like. And nor did I want to. But half the staff of St Michael's Hospital did.

I felt at a great disadvantage. That I wasn't doing myself justice.

To put it simply, I was not looking my best. As I say, a humiliating kind of a business.

I'd seen enough macho inarticulate truck drivers on the TV, a tear in their eye, a catch in their voice, struggling to tell you about how being present at the birth of their child was the most pro . . . prof . . . pr . . . pr . . . deep! thing that ever happened to them. And I'd heard stories about beer-slugging jock rugby players who invited the entire team over to watch the video of their wives giving birth.

But then again, you'd wonder about their motives.

Anyway, James and I got all emotional about it and decided he should be there.

So that's the story of how he was there at the birth. The story of why and how he left me is a bit longer.

I'm sorry, you must think I'm very rude. We've hardly even been introduced and here I am telling you all about the awful things that have happened to me.

Let me just give you the briefest outline of myself and I'll save details like, for example, my first day at school until later, if we have the time.

Let's see, what should I tell you? Well, my name is Claire and I'm twenty-nine and, as I mentioned, I've just had my first child two days ago (a little girl, seven pounds, four ounces, totally beautiful) and my husband (did I mention his name is James?) told me about twenty-four hours ago that he has been having an affair for the past six months, with—and get this—not even his secretary or someone glamorous from work, but with a married woman who lives in the apartment two floors below us. I mean, how *suburban* can you get! And not only is he having an affair but he wants a divorce.

I'm sorry if I'm being unnecessarily flippant about this. I'm all over the place. In a moment I'll be crying again. I'm still in shock, I suppose. Her name is Denise and I know her quite well.

Not quite as well as James does, obviously.

The awful thing is she always seemed to be really nice.

She's thirty-five (don't ask me how I know this, I just do; and at the risk of sounding very sour grapes and losing your sympathy, she does *look* thirty-five) and she has two children and a nice husband (quite apart from my one, that is). And apparently she's moved out of her apartment and he's moved out of his (or ours, should I say) and they've both moved into a new one in a secret location.

Can you believe it? How dramatic can you get? I know her husband is Italian, but I really don't think he's likely to kill the pair of them. He's a waiter, not a Mafia stooge, so what's he going to do? Black pepper them to death? Compliment them into a coma? Run them over with the dessert trolley?

But again, I seem flippant.

I'm not.

I'm heartbroken.

And it's all such a disaster. I don't even know what to call my little girl. James and I had discussed some names—or, in retrospect, I had discussed them and he had pretended to listen—but we hadn't decided on anything definite. And I seem to have lost the ability to make decisions on my own. Pathetic, I know, but that's marriage for you. Bang goes your sense of personal autonomy!

I wasn't always like this. Once I was strong-willed and independent. But that all seems like a long, long time ago.

I've been with James for five years, and we've been married for three years. And, my God, but I love that man.

Although we had a less than auspicious start, the magic took hold of us very quickly. We both agree that we fell in love about fifteen minutes after we met and we stayed that way.

Or at least I did.

For a long time I never thought I'd meet a man who wanted to marry me.

Well, perhaps I should qualify that.

I never thought I'd meet a *nice* man who wanted to marry me. Plenty of lunatics, undoubtedly. But a nice man, a bit older than me, with a decent job, good-looking, funny, kind. You know—one who didn't look at me askance when I mentioned *The Partridge Family*, not one who apologized for not being able to get me a birthday present because his estranged wife had taken all his salary under a court maintenance order, not one who made me feel old-fashioned and inhibited because I got angry when he said that he'd screwed his ex-girlfriend the night after he screwed me ("My God, you convent girls are so *uptight*"), not one who made me feel inadequate because I couldn't tell the difference between Piat d'Or and Zinfandel (whatever that is!).

James didn't treat me in any of these unpleasant ways. It seemed almost too good to be true. He liked me. He liked almost everything about me.

When we first met we were both living in London. I was a waitress (more of that later) and he was an accountant.

Of all the Tex-Mex joints in all the towns in all the world, he had to walk into mine. I wasn't a *real* waitress, you understand, I had a degree in English, but I went through my rebellious stage rather later than most, at about twenty-three. Which is when I thought it might be a bit of a laugh to give up my permanent, wellish-paid job in Dublin and go off to the Godless city of London and live like an irresponsible student.

Which is something I should have done when I *was* an irresponsible student. But I was too busy getting work experience during my summer holidays then, so my irresponsibility just had to wait until I was good and ready for it.

Like I always say, there's a time and a place for spontaneity.

Anyway, I had managed to land myself a job as a waitress in this highly trendy London restaurant, all loud music and video screens and minor celebrities.

Well, to be honest, there were more minor celebrities on the staff then amongst the clientele, what with most of the staff being out-of-work actors and models and the like.

How I ever got a job there at all is beyond me. Although I might have been employed as the token Wholesome Waitress. To begin with I was the only waitress under eight feet tall and over eighteen. And although I might not have been model material, I suppose I had a certain, shall we say, natural kind of charm—you know—short shiny brown hair, blue eyes, freckles, big smile, that kind of thing.

And I was so unworldly and naive. I never realized when I was coming face to well-made-up face with the stars of stage and television.

More than once I'd be serving (and I use the word in its loosest possible sense) some table of people (and I also use that word in its loosest possible sense) when one of the other waitresses would elbow me (sending scalding barbecue sauce into the unfortunate groin of a customer) and hiss something like, "Isn't that whatshisname from that band?"

And I might reply, "Which guy? The one in the leather dress?" (Remember, these were the eighties.)

"No," she might hiss back, "the one with the blond dreadlocks and wearing the Chanel lipstick. Isn't he that singer?"

"Er, is he?" I would stammer, feeling untrendy and foolish for not knowing who this person was.

Anyway, I loved working there. It thrilled me to the middle-class marrow of my bourgeois bones. It seemed so decadent and exciting to wake at one in the afternoon every day and go to work at six and finish at twelve and get drunk with the barmen and busboys afterwards.

While at home in Ireland my poor mother wept bitter tears at the thought of her daughter with the university education serving hamburgers to pop stars.

And not even very famous pop stars, to add insult to injury.

I had been working there about six months the night I met James. It was a Friday night, which was traditionally the night the OJs frequented our restaurant. "OJ" standing, of course, for Office Jerks.

At five o'clock every Friday, like graves disgorging their dead, offices all over the center of London liberated their staffs for the weekend so that hordes of pale, cheap-suited clerks descended on us, all wide-eyed and eager, looking for the stars and to get drunk, in any order you like.

It was de rigueur for us waitresses to stand around sneering disdainfully at the besuited clientele, shaking our heads in disbelieving pity at the attire, hairstyles, etc., of the poor customers, to ignore them for the first fifteen minutes or so of their visit, swishing past them, earrings and bracelets jangling, obviously doing something far more important than attending to their pathetic needs, and finally, after reducing them near to tears with frustration and hunger, to sashay up to the table with a huge smile, pen and pad at the ready. "Evening, gentlemen, can I get you a drink?"

It made them so *grateful*, you see. After that it didn't make a blind bit of difference if the drinks orders were all wrong and the food never came at all, they still left a huge tip, so lucky did they feel to get our attention.

Our motto was "Not only is the customer always wrong, he is likely to be very badly dressed into the bargain."

On the night in question, James and three of his colleagues sat in my section and I attended to their needs in my normal irresponsible and slapdash fashion. I paid them almost no attention whatsoever, barely listened to them as I took their order and certainly made no eye contact with them. If I had I might have noticed that one of them (yes, James, of course) was very handsome, in a black-haired, green-eyed, five-foottenish kind of way. I should have looked beyond the suit and seen the soul of the man.

Oh shallowness, thy name is Claire.

But I wanted to be out back with the other waitresses, drinking beer and smoking and talking about sex. Customers were an unwelcome interference.

"Can I have my steak very rare?" asked one of the men.

"Um," I said vaguely. I was even more uninterested than usual because I had noticed a book on the table. It was a really good book, one that I had read myself.

I loved books. And I loved reading. And I loved men who read. I loved a man who knew his existentialism from his magicrealism. And I had spent the last six months working with people who could just about manage to read *Stage* magazine (laboriously mouthing the words silently as they did so). I suddenly realized, with a pang, how much I missed the odd bit of intelligent conversation.

Because I could raise the stakes in any conversation on the modern American novel. I'll see your Hunter S. Thompson and I'll raise you a Jay McInerney.

Suddenly the people at this table stopped being mere irritants and took on some sort of identity for me.

"Who owns this book?" I asked abruptly, interrupting the order placing. (I don't *care* how you want your steak done.)

The table of four men were startled. I had spoken to them! I had treated them almost as if they were human!

"I do," said James, and as my blue eyes met his green eyes across his mango daiquiri (even though he had, in fact, ordered a pint of lager), that was it, the silvery magic dust was sprinkled on us. In that instant something wonderful happened. From the moment we really looked at each other, even though we knew almost nothing about each other (except that we liked the same books) (oh, yes—and that we liked the look of each other), we both knew we had met someone special.

I maintained that we fell in love immediately.

He maintained nothing of the sort and said that I was a romantic fool. He claimed it took at least thirty seconds longer for him to fall in love with me.

Historians will argue.

First of all he had to establish that I had read the book in question also. Because he thought that I must be some kind of not-so-bright model or singer if I was working there as a waitress. You know, in the same way that I had written him off as some kind of subhuman clerk. Served me right.

"Have *you* read it?" he asked, obviously surprised, the tone of his voice actually implying "Can you read at *all*?"

"Yes, I've read all his books," I told him.

"Is that right?" he said thoughtfully as he leaned back in his chair, looking up at me with interest. A lock of his black silky hair had fallen across his forehead.

"Yes," I managed to reply, feeling slightly nauseous with lust.

"The car chases are good, aren't they?" he said.

Now, I should tell you here that there were no car chases in any of the books we were talking about. They were serious, profound books about life and death and similar matters.

"Jesus!" I thought in alarm, "handsome, intelligent *and* funny. Am I ready for this?"

And then James smiled at me, a slow, sexy smile, a knowing kind of smile, totally at odds with the pinstriped suit he was wearing, and I swear to you, my entrails turned to warm ice cream. You know, kind of hot and cold and tingly and . . . well . . . like they were dissolving, or something.

And for years afterwards, long after the initial magic had worn off and most of our conversations were about insurance policies and dry rot, all I had to do was remember that smile and I felt as if I had just fallen in love all over again.

We exchanged some more words.

Just a few.

But they were enough to let me know that he was nice and clever and funny.

He asked for my phone number.

It was a fireable offense to give a customer my phone number.

I gave him my phone number.

When he left the restaurant that first night, with his three cronies, a blur of briefcases and umbrellas and rolled-up copies of the *Financial Times* and somber-looking suits, he smiled good-bye at me, and (well, I say this with the benefit of hindsight; it's very easy to foretell the future when it's already happened, if you know what I mean) I knew I was looking at my destiny.

My future.

A few minutes later he was back.

"Sorry"—he grinned—"what's your name?"

As soon as the other waitresses found out that a suit had asked for my phone number and, worse again, that I had actually given it to him, I was treated like a pariah.

But I didn't care. Because I had really fallen for James.

For all my talk of independence, I was actually a very romantic person at heart. And for all my talk of rebellion, I was as middle-class as you could get.

From the first time we went out together, it was wonderful. So romantic, so beautiful.

And I'm sorry to do this to you but I'm going to have to use a lot of clichés here. I can see no other way around it.

I'm ashamed to tell you that I was walking on air. And I'm even sorrier to have to tell you that I felt like I'd known him all my life. And I'm going to compound things by telling you that I felt that no one understood me the way that he did. And as I've lost all credibility with you I might as well tell you that I didn't think it was possible to be that happy. But I won't push it by telling you that he made me feel safe, sexy, smart and sweet. (And sorry about this, but I really must tell you that I felt that I had met my missing other half and now I was whole, and I promise that I'll leave it at that.) (Except perhaps to mention that he was funny *and* great in bed. Now I mean it, that's *all*, positively *all*.)

When we first started going out together I was waitressing

most nights, so I could only see him when I finished work. But he would wait up for me. And when I came around, exhausted, after hours of dishing up char-grilled whatever to the people of London (or the people of Pennsylvania or Hamburg, if I'm to be more accurate), he would—and I can't believe it to this day—he would bathe my aching feet and massage them with Body Shop peppermint foot lotion. Even though it was past twelve and he had to be at work helping people fiddle their tax returns, or whatever it is that accountants do, at eight the following morning, he still did it. Five nights a week. And he would bring me up-to-date on the soaps. Or go to the twenty-four-hour garage for me when I ran out of cigarettes. Or he would tell me funny little stories about his day at work. I know that it's hard to believe that any story about accounting could be funny, but he managed it.

And my job meant that we could never go out on Saturday nights. And he didn't complain.

Weird, huh?

Yes, I thought so too.

And he would help me count my tips. And give me great advice about what to invest them in. Government bonds and that kind of thing.

I usually bought shoes instead.

Shortly after this I had the good fortune to be fired from the waitressing job (a silly misunderstanding involving me, several bottles of imported lager, a "dinner-in-lap" scenario and a totally unreasonable customer who had absolutely no sense of humor; anyway, I believe his scars faded almost completely).

And managed to secure another position with more regular hours. So our romance proceeded on a more traditional timetable.

And after a while we moved in together. And after a bit longer we got married. And a couple of years later we decided to have a baby and my ovaries seemed to be game and his spermatozoa registered no complaint on that score and my womb had no objection so I got pregnant. And I gave birth to a baby girl.

Which is where you came in.

So I think we're pretty much up-to-date here.

And if you were hoping for, or expecting, some kind of awful gory depiction of childbirth, with talk of stirrups and forceps and moans of agony and vulgar comparisons with excreting a hundred-pound sack of potatoes, then I'm sorry to disappoint you.

(Well, all right then, just to humor you, take your worst period pain ever and multiply it by seven million and make it last for about twenty-four hours and then you have some idea.)

Yes, it was scary and messy and humiliating and quite alarmingly painful. It was also exciting and thrilling and wonderful. But the most important thing for me was that it was over. I could kind of remember the pain, but it no longer had the power to hurt me. But when James left me I realized I'd rather go through the pain of a hundred labors than go through the pain of losing him that I felt then.

This is how he broke the news of his imminent departure to me.

After I held my baby in my arms for the first time, the nurses took her away to the baby ward and I was brought back to my ward and went to sleep for a while.

I woke up to find James standing over me, staring down at me, his eyes very green in his white face. I smiled up at him sleepily and triumphantly. "Hello, darling." I grinned.

"Hello, Claire," he said formally and politely.

Fool that I was, I thought he was being grave and serious as some kind of mark of respect. (Behold my wife, she was delivered today of a child, she is woman, she is lifegiver—you know, that kind of thing.)

He sat down. He sat on the edge of the hard hospital chair, looking as if he was going to get up and run away any second. Which, as it turns out, he was.

"Have you been to the baby ward to see her?" I asked him dreamily. "She's so beautiful."

"No, I haven't," he said shortly. "Look, Claire, I'm leaving," he said abruptly.

"Why?" I asked, snuggling back into my pillows, "you've only just got here." (Yes, I know, I can't believe I said that either, who *writes* my lines?)

"Claire, listen to me," he said, getting a bit agitated. "I'm leaving you."

"What?" I said slowly and carefully. I must admit he had my attention now.

"Look, Claire, I'm really sorry, but I've met someone else and I'm going to be with her and I'm sorry about the baby and everything and to leave you like this, but I must," he blurted out, as white as a ghost, his eyes bright with anguish.

"What do you mean by you've 'met' someone else?" I asked, bewildered.

"I mean that . . . well . . . I've fallen in love with someone else," he said, looking wretched.

"What do you mean, another woman, or something?"

"Yes," he said, no doubt relieved that I seemed to have grasped the basics of the situation.

"And you're *leaving* me?" I echoed him disbelievingly.

"Yes," he said, looking at his shoes, at the ceiling, at anything other than my eyes.

"But don't you love me anymore?" I found myself asking.

"I don't know. I don't think so," he replied.

"But what about the baby?" I asked, stunned. He couldn't possibly leave me but he especially couldn't leave me now that we had had a baby together. "You've got to take care of the two of us."

"I'm sorry, but I can't," he said. "I'll make sure that you're taken care of financially and we'll sort something out about the apartment and the mortgage and all that, but I have to go."

I couldn't believe we were having this conversation. What the hell was he talking about, apartments and money and mortgages and crap? According to the script we should be cooing over our baby and gently arguing about which side of the family she got her looks from. But James, *my* James, was talking about leaving me. Who's in charge around here? I'd like to complain about my life. I distinctly ordered a happy life with a loving husband to go with my newborn baby and what was this shoddy travesty that I'd been served up instead?

"Jesus, Claire," he said, "I hate to leave you like this. But if I come home with you and the baby now I won't ever be able to leave."

But wasn't that the whole idea? I thought, bewildered.

"I know that there's no good time to tell you something like this. I couldn't tell you when you were pregnant, you might have lost the baby. So I have to tell you now."

"James," I said faintly, "this is all very weird."

"Yes, I know," he agreed hurriedly. "You've been through a lot in the last twenty-four hours."

"Why were you at the birth, if you planned to leave me the minute it was over?" I asked him, holding his arm, trying to get him to look at me.

"Because I promised," he said, shaking my hand off his arm and not meeting my eyes, looking like a chastised schoolboy.

"Because you promised?" I said, trying to make sense of this. "But you've promised me lots of things. Like to cherish me and to love me till death do us part."

"Well, I'm sorry," he mumbled. "But I can't keep those promises."

"So what's going to happen?" I asked numbly. I didn't for a second accept a single word of what he was saying. But the band keeps playing even though no one is dancing. I was having what to all intents and purposes might appear to the impartial outside observer to be a conversation with James. But it wasn't a conversation at all because I didn't mean anything that I said and I didn't accept anything that he said. When I asked him what was going to happen, I didn't need an answer. I *knew* what was going to happen. He was coming home with me and the baby and there would be no more of this nonsense.

I think I almost felt that if I kept him talking and with me he would realize how silly he was being.

He stood up. He stood too far away for me to be able to touch him. He was wearing a black suit (we had often joked in the past about his wearing it to oversee receiverships and liquidations) and he looked grim and pale. And in a way he had never looked more handsome to me.

"I see you're wearing your undertaker suit," I said bitterly. "Nice touch."

He didn't even attempt a smile, and I knew then that I had lost him. He looked like James, he sounded like James, he smelled like James, but it wasn't James.

Like some fifties science fiction film, where the hero's girl-friend's body is taken over by an alien—it still looks like her on the outside (pink angora sweater, sweet little handbag, bra so pointy it would take the eye out of a spider, etc.)—but her eyes have changed.

The casual observer might still think it was James. But I knew from looking at his eyes, my James had left. Some cold unloving stranger was in his body. I didn't know where *my* James had gone.

Maybe he was in the alien spaceship with Peggy-Jo.

"I've moved most of my things," he said. "I'll be in touch. Take care of yourself."

He turned on his heel and quickly left the ward. In fact, he almost broke into a run. I wanted to run after him but the bastard had taken advantage of the fact that I was bed-bound courtesy of several stitches in my vagina.

He was gone.

I lay in my hospital bed, very still for a long time. I was stunned, I was shocked, I was horrified, I was disbelieving. But in a very odd kind of way, there was something I did believe about it. There was something almost familiar about this feeling.

I know it couldn't be a feeling of familiarity, because I had never been deserted by a husband before. But there was defi-nitely something there. I think there's a part of everyone's brain, certainly mine, that keeps a lookout on some rocky out-crop high in the hills, waiting for signs of danger. And it sig-nals back to the rest of the brain when trouble is afoot. The emotional version of "the injuns is coming." The more I thought about it, the more I realized this part of my brain had probably been flashing mirrors and sending up smoke signals like crazy over the past months. But the rest of my brain was with the wagon camp down in the pleasant verdant valley of pregnancy and didn't want to know about impending danger. So it completely ignored the messages it was sent.

I'd known that James was miserable for most of the time that I was pregnant, but I had put that down to my mood swings, my constant hunger, my raging sentimentality, where I cried at everything from *Little House on the Prairie* to *The Money Program*.

And, of course, our sex life was drastically curtailed. But I had thought that as soon as I had the baby everything would be back to normal. Except better, if you know what I mean.

I thought that James's misery was just a result of my being pregnant and its attendant side effects but, looking back, maybe I had ignored things that I shouldn't have.

So what was I to do? I didn't even know where he was staying. But some instinct told me to leave him alone for a while. Humor him. Pretend to go along with it.

I could hardly believe it.

Leaving me, indeed! My normal reaction to feeling hurt or betrayed was to go on the warpath, but somehow I knew that it wouldn't do me any good at all in this situation. I had to stay calm and sane until I could decide what to do.

One of the nurses squeaked past me in her rubber-soled shoes. She stopped and smiled at me. "How are you now?" she asked.

"Oh fine," I said, willing her to go away.

"I suppose your husband will be in to see you and the baby later," she said.

"I wouldn't bet on it," I replied bitterly.

She gave me a startled look and moved away quickly, over to one of the nice, civil, polite mothers, clicking her pen and throwing me nervous glances.

I decided to call Judy.

Judy was my best friend. We'd been friends since we were eighteen. We had come over to London together. She had been my bridesmaid. I couldn't cope with this on my own, and Judy would tell me what to do.

I cautiously and gingerly levered myself out of bed and, as quickly as my episiotomy would permit, I made my way to the pay phone.

She answered the phone immediately.

"Oh hi, Claire," she said. "I was just on my way over to see you."

"Good," was all I said.

God knows, I *wanted* to bawl and tell her about James's allegedly leaving me, but there was a line of women in pink terry cloth robes behind me waiting to use the phone (no doubt to call their devoted husbands) and, against all the odds, I had *some* pride left.

"Smug bitches," I thought sourly (and irrationally, I must admit) as I limped back to bed.

As soon as Judy came I knew that she knew about James. I knew because she said, "Claire, I know about James." Also because she didn't arrive with a huge bunch of flowers, a bigger smile and a card the size of a kitchen table with storks all over it. She looked anxious and nervous.

My heart sank to my boots. If James was telling other people, then it *must* be true.

"He's left me," I said dramatically.

"I know," she said.

"How could he?" I asked her.

"I don't know," she said.

"He's fallen in love with someone else," I said.

"I know," she said.

"How do you know?" I demanded, pouncing on her for the information.

"Michael told me. Aisling told him. George told her."

(Michael was Judy's boyfriend. Aisling was a girl who worked with him. George was Aisling's husband. George worked with James.)

"So everyone knows," I said quietly.

There was a pause. Judy looked as if she would like to die.

"Then it must be true," I said.

"I think it is," she said, obviously embarrassed.

"Do you know who this other woman is?" I couldn't believe my best friend knew that my husband was cheating on me and hadn't told me. I was pissed off at her, but the highest priority was extracting information, at this point.

"Er, yes," she said, even more embarrassed. "It's that Denise."

"*What!*" I shrieked. "Not nice Denise from downstairs?"

A miserable nod from Judy.

It was just as well that I was already lying down.

"That *bitch!*" I exclaimed.

"And there's more," she mumbled. "He's talking about marrying her."

"What the hell do you mean?" I shouted. "He's *already*

married. To me. I hadn't heard that they had made polygamy legal in the last day or so."

"They haven't," she said.

"But then . . ." I trailed off, bewildered.

"Claire," she sighed despondently, "he says he's going to divorce you."

As I said, it was just as well I was already lying down.

The afternoon ebbed away, along with Judy's patience and any hope that I might still harbor.

I looked at her in despair.

"Judy, what am I going to do?"

"Look," she said matter-of-factly, "in two days you'll be getting out of here. You still have somewhere to live, you have enough money to feed yourself and the baby, you'll be going back to work in six months, you've got a newborn child to look after and give James some time and eventually the two of you will work something out."

"But Judy," I wailed. "He wants a *divorce*."

Although James seemed to have forgotten one big fact. There is no divorce in Ireland. James and I had been married in Ireland. Our marriage had been blessed by the fathers of the Church of Our Lady of Perpetual Succour. Although a fat lot of good it had obviously done us. So long, Succour.

I was at a total loss. I felt alone and afraid. I wanted to pull the blankets over my head and die. But I couldn't because I had a poor defenseless child to look after.

What a start in life she was getting. Less than two days old and already she'd been deserted by her father, and her mother was on the verge of cracking up.

For the millionth time I wondered how James could do this to me.

"How could James do this to me?" I asked Judy.

"You've asked me that about a million times," she said.

So I had.

I didn't know how James could do this to me. I just knew that he had.

Up to now I suppose that I'd thought that life doled out the unpleasant things to me in evenly spaced bite-size pieces. That it never gave me more than I could cope with at one time.

When I used to hear about people who had serial disasters,

like having a car accident, losing a job and catching their boyfriend in bed with their sister all in one week, I used to kind of think it was their fault. Well, not exactly their *fault*. But I thought that if people behaved like victims they would become victims, if people expected the worst to happen then it invariably did.

I could see now how wrong I was. Sometimes people don't volunteer to be victims and they become victims anyway. It's not their fault. It certainly wasn't my fault that my husband thought that he'd fallen in love with someone else. I didn't expect it to happen and I certainly didn't *want* it to happen. But it had happened.

I knew then that life was no respecter of circumstance. The force that flings disasters at us doesn't say "Well, I won't give her that lump in her breast for another year. Best to let her recover from the death of her mother first." It just goes right on ahead and does whatever it feels like, whenever it feels like it.

Now I realized that no one is immune from the serial disaster syndrome. Not that I thought that having a baby was a disaster, but it could certainly come under the heading of upheaval.

Judy and I sat on the bed in silence, both trying to think of something constructive to say. Suddenly I had the answer. Well, maybe not *the* answer, but *an* answer. Something to do for the time being.

"I know what I'll do," I said to Judy.

"Oh thank God," I could feel her thinking fervently. *"Thank God."*

And like Scarlett O'Hara in the last few lines of *Gone With the Wind*, I said plaintively, "I'll go home. I'll go home to Dublin."

Yes, I agree with you. "Dublin" doesn't have quite the same ring to it as "Tara," but what would be the point in my going home to Tara? I knew no one there.

two

Judy picked me up from the hospital a couple of days later. She had booked me and my baby on a one-way flight to Dublin. She took me home to pack some things.

I had heard nothing from James in the meantime. I was stumbling around in a grief-sodden daze.

Sometimes I simply couldn't believe it. Everything he'd said to me seemed like a dream. I couldn't really remember the details, but I could remember the feeling. That sick feeling that something was very wrong.

But sometimes the loss would make a guest appearance.

It would invade me. It would take me over. It was like a physical force. It knocked the life out of me. It took my breath away. It was savage.

It hated me.

It had to, to hurt me so much.

I can't really remember how I spent those couple of days in hospital.

I can vaguely remember being bewildered when all the other new mothers talked about how their lives had now altered forever, how it would never be just oneself ever again, the problems of having to adjust their lives to fit in with their new baby and all that.

But I couldn't see what the problem was. Already I couldn't imagine life without my baby. "It's you and me, sweetheart," I whispered to her.

The fact that we had both been abandoned by the man in

our lives probably sped up the bonding process. Nothing like a crisis to bring people together, as they say.

I spent a lot of time sitting very still, holding her.

Touching her tiny, *tiny* little doll's feet, her perfect pink miniature toes, her tightly curled up little fists, her velvety ears, gently stroking the delicate skin of her incredibly small little face, wondering what color her eyes were going to be.

She was so beautiful, so perfect, such a miracle.

I had been told to expect to feel overwhelming love for my child, God knows, no one could say that I hadn't been warned. But nothing could have prepared me for this intensity. This feeling that I would kill anyone who so much as touched one of the blond wispy hairs on her soft little head.

I could understand James leaving me—well, actually, I couldn't—but I *really* couldn't understand how he could leave this beautiful, perfect little child.

She cried a lot.

But I can't really complain because so did I.

I tried and tried to comfort her, but she rarely stopped.

After she cried for about eight hours solid on the first day and I had changed her diaper a hundred and twenty times and fed her forty-nine thousand times I became slightly hysterical and demanded that a doctor look at her.

"There *must* be something terribly wrong with her," I declared to the exhausted-looking youth who was the doctor. "She can't *possibly* be hungry, but she won't stop crying."

"Well, I've examined her and there's absolutely nothing wrong with her, so far as I can see," he patiently explained.

"But why is she crying?"

"Because she's a baby," he said. "It's what they do."

He'd studied medicine for seven years and that was the best he could come up with?

I wasn't convinced.

Maybe she was crying because she somehow sensed that her dad had abandoned her.

Or maybe—major pang of guilt—she was crying because I wasn't breast-feeding her. Maybe she deeply resented being fed from a bottle. Yes, I know, you're probably outraged that I didn't breast-feed her. You probably think that I wasn't a proper mother. But, long ago, *before* I had my baby, I had thought it would be permissible to have my body returned to me after I had loaned it out for nine months. I knew that I wouldn't be able to call my soul my own now that I was a mother. But I had kind of hoped that I might be able to call my nipples my own. And I'm ashamed to say that I was afraid that, if I breast-fed, I would be a victim of "shrunken, flat, droopy tit" syndrome.

Now that I was with my gorgeous, perfect child my breast-feeding worries seemed petty and selfish. Everything really *does* change when you give birth. I never thought I'd see the day when I'd put anyone else's needs before the attractiveness of my tits.

So if my little sweetheart didn't stop crying soon, I was going to consider breast-feeding her. If it made her happy, I'd put up with cracked nipples, leaky tits and sniggering thirteen-year-old boys trying to get a look at my jugs on the bus.

Judy, baby and I arrived home. I let us into our apartment and, even though James had told me he was moving out, I still wasn't prepared for the bare spaces in the bathroom, the empty wardrobe, the gaps in the bookshelf.

It was so awful.

I sat down slowly on our bed. The pillow still smelled like him. And I missed him so much.

"I can't believe it," I sobbed to Judy. "He's really gone."

My baby started to cry also, as if she felt the emptiness too.

And it was only about five minutes since she'd last stopped.

Poor Judy looked helpless. She didn't know which one of us to comfort.

After a while I stopped crying and slowly turned my tear-streaked face to Judy. I felt exhausted with grief.

"Come on," I said. "I'd better pack."

"Fine," she whispered, still rocking me and the baby in her arms.

I started throwing things into a baby bag. I packed everything I thought I would need. I was all set to bring a pile of disposable diapers the size of a small South American country, but Judy made me leave them behind. "They *do* sell them in Dublin too," she gently reminded me. I flung in baby bottles, a bottle warmer with a picture of a cow jumping over the moon on the side of it, pacifiers, toys, rattles, little socks the size of postage stamps, everything I could possibly think of for my poor fatherless child.

As I was now a single parent I was obviously overcompensating. "I'm sorry, darling, I've deprived you of your father because I wasn't smart or beautiful enough to hold on to him, but let me make it up to you by showering you with material goods."

Then I asked Judy to give me back a couple of diapers.

"What for?" she demanded, holding them tightly to her.

"In case we have an accident on the plane," I said, trying to grab them from her.

"Didn't they give you any sanitary pads in the hospital?" she asked, sounding shocked.

"Not if *I* have an accident, stupid. If the *baby* has one. Although strictly speaking, it wouldn't really be an accident, would it?" I said thoughtfully. "More like an occupational hazard."

She doled out three diapers. But reluctantly.

"You know, you can't keep calling her 'the baby,'" said Judy. "You're going to have to give her a name."

"I can't think about that just at the moment," I said, starting to feel panicky.

"But what have you been doing for the past nine months?" Judy sounded shocked. "You must have thought of *some* names."

"I did," I said, my lip starting to tremble. "But I thought of them with James. And it wouldn't feel right to call her one of those names."

Judy looked a bit annoyed with me. But I was on the verge of tears again, so she didn't say anything further.

I hardly brought anything for myself apart from a handful of baby books. "Why would I bother," I thought, "now that my life is over?"

And besides, nothing fitted me any longer.

I opened my wardrobe and recoiled from the disgusted looks all my little dresses gave me. There was no doubt about it. They were all talking about me.

I could almost see them elbowing each other and saying

"Look at her, the size of her. Does she honestly think that dainty little size tens like us would have any dealings with that size-fourteen body she's dragging around? Small wonder that her husband ran off with another woman."

I knew what they were thinking.

"You've let yourself go. And you always said that you wouldn't. You've let us down and you've let yourself down."

"I'm sorry," I explained cringingly. "I'll lose weight. I'll be back for you, I promise. Just as soon as I'm able."

Their skepticism was palpable.

I had a choice of wearing my maternity clothes or a pair of jeans that James had left behind in his haste to get going. I put on the jeans and caught sight of my revolting overweight body in the bedroom mirror. God, I was horrific! I looked as if I was wearing my big sister's Michelin Man suit. Or worse again, I looked like I was still pregnant.

In the few weeks before I gave birth I had been absolutely enormous.

Completely circular. The fact that the only thing that fit me was my green wool jumper, coupled with the fact that due to continuous nausea my face was always green, gave me the appearance of a watermelon who had put on a pair of boots and a bit of lipstick.

Now, although I was no longer green, I still looked like a watermelon in every other respect.

What was happening to me? Where had the real me and my real life *gone*?

With a heart that wasn't the only heavy thing about me, I went to call a taxi to take us to the airport.

When the buzzer rang, I took one last look around my living room, at the gap-toothed shelves, the shiny new unused baby intercom up on the wall (the *waste*!), the hillock of abandoned diapers on the floor.

I closed the door behind me before I could start crying again.

Firmly.

Then I realized that I was missing something. "Oh Jesus," I said, "my rings." I ran back in and got my engagement and wedding rings from my bedroom. They had been on the dressing table for the past two months because my fingers were so fat and swollen that I couldn't wear them. I jammed them onto my hand and they just about fit me.

I caught Judy giving me a funny look.

"He's still my husband, you know," I said defiantly to her. "Which means that I'm still married!"

"I didn't say anything," she said, affecting an innocent expression.

Judy and I struggled down in the elevator, juggling bags, purses, and a two-day-old child in her car seat.

And that's another thing they don't tell you about having a baby! The manuals should say something like "It is imperative that your husband does not leave you in the first few months after your child's birth, as otherwise you will have to carry everything yourself."

Judy was hoisting everything into the taxi when I saw, with horror, Denise's husband coming up the sidewalk. He must have been on his way home from work.

"Oh Christ," I said ominously.

"What?" asked Judy in alarm, her face red and sweaty from her exertions.

"Denise's husband," I muttered.

"So what?" she said loudly.

I was expecting some kind of terrible emotional scene from him. As I said, he was Italian. Or I was afraid that he would suggest some kind of alliance between me and him. Something along the lines of "my enemy's enemy is my friend." I *certainly* didn't want that.

My eyes locked with his and I felt, in my guilty and fearful state, that I knew exactly what he was thinking. "It's all your fault. If only you had been as attractive as my Denise, your husband might have stayed with you and I would still be happily married. But no, you had to go and ruin everything, you fat ugly cow."

"Fine," I thought, "two can play at that game."

I stared back at him, returning his thought messages. "Well, if you hadn't married a husband-stealing, home-wrecking floozy none of us would be in this mess."

I was probably doing the poor man a terrible injustice. He didn't say anything to me. He just looked at me in a kind of sad and accusatory way.

I hugged Judy good-bye. We were both crying. For once my baby wasn't.

"Heathrow, Terminal One," I said tearfully to the taxi driver and we swept away from the curb, leaving Mr. Andrucetti staring bleakly after us.

As I struggled down the aisle on the Aer Lingus plane, I bumped against several irate passengers with my bag of baby supplies. When I finally located my seat a man got up to help me stow my bags. As I smiled my thanks at him, I automatically wondered if he thought I was pretty.

It was so awful. That was one of the things I'd really liked about being married. For a couple of years I'd been off that horrible merry-go-round of trying to meet the right man, finding out that he was already married, or living with another man, or pathologically stingy, or read Jeffrey Archer, or could only have an orgasm if he could call you "Mother," or any one of the thousands of character flaws that weren't immediately obvious the first time you shook his hand and smiled into his eyes and got a warm buzzy feeling in the pit of your stomach, and thought to yourself, "Hey, this could be the one."

Now I was back in the situation where every man is a potential boyfriend. I was back in a world where there are eight hundred exquisitely beautiful women to every one straight single man. And that is even before we start weeding out the truly hideous ones.

I looked at the helpful man carefully. He wasn't even that attractive. He was probably gay. Or, more likely, this being an Aer Lingus flight, he was probably a priest.

And as for me, a deserted wife with a two-day-old baby, the self-esteem of an amoeba (that much?), forty pounds overweight, incipient postpartum depression, and a vagina stretched out to ten times its normal size, I was hardly a prize catch myself.

The plane took off and the houses and buildings and streets of London circled away below me. I looked down as the roads got smaller and smaller. I was leaving behind six years of my life.

Is this how a refugee feels? I wondered.

My husband was down there somewhere. My apartment

was down there somewhere. My friends were down there somewhere. My life was down there somewhere.

I had been happy there.

And then the view was obscured by cloud.

I sat back in my seat, my baby on my lap. I suppose I must have looked just like a normal mother to all the other passengers. But—and the thought struck me quite forcibly—I wasn't. I was now a deserted wife. I was a statistic.

I had been lots of things in my life. I had been Claire the dutiful daughter. I had been Claire the scourge of a daughter. I had been Claire the student. I had been Claire the harlot (briefly—as I said, if we get the time, I'll fill you in). I had been Claire the administrator. I had been Claire the wife. And now here I was being Claire the deserted wife. And the idea did not sit comfortably with me at all, I can tell you.

I had always thought (in spite of my professed liberalism) that deserted wives were women whose husbands, pausing only to blacken their eyes, left with a bottle of vodka, the Christmas Club money and the children's allowance book, leaving them behind weeping with a huge mound of unpaid utilities bills, a spurious story about walking into a door and four dysfunctional children, all under the age of six.

It was a humbling and enlightening experience to find out how wrong I had been. *I* was a deserted wife. Me, middle-class Claire.

Well, it would have been a humbling and enlightening experience if I hadn't been feeling so bitter and angry and betrayed. What was I? Some kind of Tibetan monk?

But I did realize, in some funny way, through the self-pity and the self-righteousness, that someday, when all this was over, I might be a nicer person as a result of it, that I would be stronger and wiser and more compassionate.

But maybe not just yet.

"Your father is a bastard," I whispered to my child.

The helpful gay priest jumped.

He must have heard me.

Within an hour we began the descent to Dublin Airport. We circled the green fields of north Dublin and, even though I knew that she couldn't really see anything yet, I held my baby up to the window to give her her first view of Ireland.

It looked so different from the view of London we had just left behind. As I looked at the blue of the Irish sea and the gray mist over the green fields, I had never felt worse. I felt like such a failure.

I had left Ireland six years before, full of excitement about the future. I was going to get a great job in London, meet a wonderful man and live happily ever after. And I *had* gotten a great job, I *had* met a wonderful man and I *had* lived happily ever after—well, at least for a while—but somehow it had all gone wrong and here I was back in Dublin with a humiliating sense of déjà vu.

But one major thing had changed.

Now I had a child. A perfect, beautiful, wonderful child. I wouldn't have changed that for anything.

The helpful gay priest beside me looked very embarrassed as I cried helplessly. "Tough," I thought. "Be embarrassed. You're a man. You've probably made countless women cry like this too."

I'd had more rational days.

He made a fairly lively exit once we landed. In fact, he couldn't get off the plane fast enough. No offers to help me unstow my bags. I couldn't blame him.

three

And so to the baggage pickup area!

I always find it such an ordeal.

Do you know what I mean?

The anxiety starts the minute I get to the carousel, when I suddenly become convinced that all the nice, mild-mannered people I shared a plane journey with have turned into nasty luggage thieves. That every single one of them is watching the carousel with the express purpose of stealing my bags.

I stand there with narrowed eyes and a suspicious face. One eye on the hatch where the bags come out and the other eye darting from person to person, trying to convey to them that I'm wise to their intentions. That they've picked the wrong person to mess with.

I suppose it would help matters slightly if I was one of those well-organized people who somehow manage to stand near the start of the carousel. But instead I'm always down at the far end, squinting and standing on tiptoe, trying to see what's coming out of the hatch, and when I finally see my bag emerging I'm so afraid that someone will steal it that I can't stand patiently and wait for the carousel to deliver it to me in due course. Instead I run to catch it before someone else does. Except that I usually find it impossible to breach the tightly knit cordon of other people's baggage carts. So my bag sails serenely past me and circumnavigates the carousel several times before I'm able to grab it.

It's a nightmare!

This time, to my surprise, I managed to secure myself a place quite near the hatch.

Maybe people were being nicer to me because I had a baby about my person.

I knew she'd come in useful.

So I waited at the carousel, trying to be patient, jostling with all the other people who had just gotten off the flight, buckling at the knees every so often as a fellow passenger delivered a killer blow to the back of my ankles with his cart.

I made eye contact with as many people as possible, hoping to convince them not to steal my bags. Isn't that the kind of advice criminologists give you? You know the stuff I'm talking about. That if you've been taken hostage you must befriend your captor. Make eye contact with him, so that he realizes that you're a human being and so is less likely to kill you.

Anyway. I'm sure you know what I mean.

Nothing happened for the longest time.

All eyes were trained on the little hatch for the first glimpse of our suitcases.

Nobody spoke. Nobody even dared to breathe. Then suddenly! The noise of a carousel starting up!

Great!

Except it wasn't ours.

An announcement over the loudspeaker. "Will passengers recently arrived from London on Flight E1179 proceed to carousel number four to reclaim their baggage."

This, in spite of the fact that the screen above carousel two had confidently assured us for the last twenty minutes that our baggage would shortly be making an appearance there.

So a mad scramble to carousel four. People shoving and pushing as though their lives depended on it. And this time no one seemed quite so concerned about the infant in my arms.

As a result I was at the very end of the new carousel.

And for a while I was all right.

Calm even.

I tried to look determinedly cheerful as one by one the people around me rescued their bags.

But when the only thing left on the carousel was a set of golf clubs that looked as if they had been there since the late seventies and they had passed me for the fourteenth time and my baby and I were the only human beings left in the arrivals hall and the tumbleweed had started blowing past me, it was finally time to read the writing on the wall.

"I knew they'd get me one day," I thought, feeling sick. "It was only a matter of time. I bet it was that old lady with the rosary beads. It's always the quiet ones."

I began to run up and down, my baby in my arms, frantically searching for an official. Eventually I found a little office with two fairly jovial looking porters within.

"Come in, come in!" one of them invited me as I hovered uncertainly by the door. "What can we do for you on this fine wet Irish afternoon?"

I launched into my story of my stolen bags and car seat. I was nearly in tears again. I felt so *victimized*.

"Don't worry, missus," I was assured. "They're not stolen. They're only lost. I'll find them for you. I've got a hot line to St. Anthony."

And sure enough, about five minutes later he returned with all my luggage. "Are these yours, love?" he asked.

I assured him that they were.

"And you're not going to Boston?"

"I'm not going to Boston," I agreed as evenly as I could manage.

"Are you sure?" he asked doubtfully.

"Quite sure," I promised.

"Well, someone seemed to think that you were, but never mind. Off you go now." He laughed.

I thanked them and hurried toward the "Nothing to Declare" line.

I rushed through with my cart and my baby and my retrieved luggage. My heart sank as one of the customs men stopped me.

"Easy, easy," he said. "Where's the fire? Have you anything to declare?"

"No, I haven't."

"What's that you've got there?"

"It's a baby."

"*Your* baby?"

"Yes, my baby."

My heart had nearly stopped beating. I hadn't told James

that I was leaving. But had he guessed that I would come here? Had he told the police that I had kidnapped our child? Were all the ports and airports being watched? Would they take my baby away from me? Would I be deported?

I was terrified.

"So," the customs man continued, "you have nothing to declare but your genes." He guffawed heartily.

"Oh yes, very funny," I said limply.

"A great wit, our Mr. Wilde," said the customs man conversationally. "A venerable gentleman."

"Oh absolutely," I agreed.

"You gave me a terrible fright." I smiled at him.

He assumed a sheriff-type stance and drawl.

"That's okay, ma'am." He winked. "Jest doin' mah job."

It was nice to be home.

four

I rushed out into the arrivals lounge. On the other side of the barrier I could see my mother and father waiting for me. They looked smaller and older than they'd looked the last time I saw them, six months before. I felt so guilty. They were both in their late fifties and had worried about me from the day I was born. Well, from before the day I was born, if I'm to be quite accurate, because I was three weeks overdue and they thought they'd have to send a welcome committee in to get me.

I've heard of people being late for their own funeral but I started life with the distinction of being late for my own birth.

And they worried about me when I was six weeks old and had colic.

And when I was two years old and wouldn't eat anything but canned peaches for an entire year. They worried about me when I was seven and doing really badly at school. And they worried about me when I was eight and doing really well at school and had no friends. They worried about me when I was eleven and broke my ankle. They worried about me when I went to a school dance and had to be brought home blind drunk by one of the teachers, when I was fifteen. They worried about me when I was eighteen and in my first year in college and never went to any classes. They worried about me when I was taking my finals and was never missing a class. They worried about me when I was twenty and split up with my first true love and lay in a darkened bedroom crying for two weeks. They worried about me when I gave up my job and went to London to work as a waitress when I was twenty-three.

And here I was nearly thirty, married with a baby of my own and they were still having to worry about me. I mean, it wasn't very fair, was it? Just as they'd taken a big sigh of relief and thought, "Thank God, she's managed to land herself a fairly respectable man, maybe we can let him worry about her from now on and get on with the business of worrying about her four younger sisters," I had the audacity to turn around and say, "Sorry, folks, false alarm, I'm back and this one is worse than any of the other things I've forced you to worry about."

No wonder they were looking a little bit gray and cowed.

"Oh thank God," said my mother when she saw me. "We thought you'd missed the flight."

"I'm sorry," I said, and burst into tears again. And we all hugged each other and they both cried when they saw my baby, their first grandchild.

I really would have to give her a name soon.

We negotiated the maze that is the parking lot in Dublin Airport. Proceedings were delayed slightly when my father attempted to leave by the prepaid exit, when he hadn't, and all the cars backed up behind him had to reverse to let him out. He lost his temper slightly and so did another driver, but let's not dwell on that.

When we got out on the road we drove for a while in silence. It was a very strange situation. My mother sat in the back with me and she held the baby and rocked her gently. I wished that I was still a baby and that my mother could hold me and make me feel so safe and that everything was going to be all right.

"So Unlucky Jim took off," my father said abruptly.

"Yes, Dad," I said tearfully.

My father had never really liked James. My father is the only man in a house full of women and he craves male company, someone to talk to about football and that kind of thing. James didn't play enough rugby and knew far too much about cooking for his liking. It didn't matter that my father did all the housework in our house, cooking was a different matter—

women's work, he called it. But the last thing he wanted was to see me unhappy.

"Now look, Claire," he said in a voice that I recognized as the "I'm about to make a speech concerning emotional issues, I'm not used to doing it and I'm very uncomfortable doing it, but it has to be done and I do actually mean it" voice. "We're your family and we love you and this is always your home. You and the baby can stay with us for as long as you like. And . . . er . . . both your mother and I know how unhappy you are and if we can help in any way just let us know. Ah . . . er . . . right." And with that he accelerated, mightily relieved that he'd gotten that out of the way.

"Thanks, Dad," I said, crying again. "I do know it."

I was immensely grateful. It was wonderful knowing that they loved me. It was just that it was no substitute for losing a man who was my soulmate, my best friend, my lover, my one reliable thing in an unreliable world.

We finally reached home. It looked just the same. Why shouldn't it? Life, against its better judgment, goes on. And it smelled just the same. It was so familiar, so comforting. We carried the bags and car seat up the stairs to the room that I shared with my sister Margaret all my life until I moved to London. (Margaret, was twenty-six, sporty, outgoing, living in Chicago, working as a paralegal, married to the only boyfriend she'd ever had.) The room looked really funny, because no one had stayed in it for so long. Some of Margaret's shoes were on the floor, but covered in dust. Some of her old clothes were still hanging in the wardrobe. It was like some kind of shrine to our teenage years.

I flung a few of the bags on the floor, I set up the car seat and put the baby in it, I put the bottle warmer with the picture of the cow jumping over the moon on the side on the dressing table, I sat on the bed and kicked off my shoes, I put my books on the shelves, I left my makeup bag spilling over on the bedside table. And in no time at all the place looked like a pigsty.

There, that was miles better.

"So, who's here?" I asked Mum.

"Well, just us and Dad at the moment," she said. "Helen

is at college, she should be home later. God alone knows where Anna is. I haven't seen her for days."

Anna and Helen were my two youngest sisters. They were the only ones still living at home.

My mother sat with me while I fed the baby. After I had burped the baby and put her back to sleep, my mother and I sat quietly on the bed, saying nothing. The rain stopped and the sun came out. The smell of the wet garden came in through the open window, and the sound of the breeze blowing through the branches of the trees. It was a peaceful February evening.

"Will you eat something?" she finally asked.

I shook my head.

"But you must eat, especially now that you've got the baby to look after. You have to keep strong. Can I make you some soup?"

I winced involuntarily. "No, really, Mum, I'm fine."

Perhaps I'd better explain. The ability to cook skips a generation. I could cook. Ergo, my daughter wouldn't be able to. God love her. What kind of start in life was she getting? And by the same token my mother couldn't cook.

Nightmarish memories of family dinners came flooding back to me. Was I out of my mind? What the hell had I come home for? Did I really want to *starve* to death?

The next time you have to lose a lot of weight very quickly—that two-week beach vacation? your sister's wedding? a date with the office hunk?—don't bother joining Weight Watchers, or try to subsist on Lean Cuisine, or fiddle around with powdered meals. Just come and stay in our house for a couple of weeks and insist that Mum cook for you.

Seriously, there's plenty of space; you can have Rachel's room. You'll be skin and bone at the end of the two weeks. Because no matter how hungry you are you still won't be able to bring yourself to eat a thing my mother makes.

I'm amazed that none of us was ever hospitalized for malnutrition when we were younger.

My siblings and I would be summoned for our evening meal. We would all sit down and stare silently at the plates in front of us for a few perplexed moments. Finally one of us would speak.

"Any ideas?"

"Would it be chicken?" says Margaret doubtfully, poking it tentatively with her fork.

"Oh no, I thought it was cauliflower," says Rachel, the vegetarian, rushing off to gag.

"Well, whatever it is, I'm not touching it," says Helen. "At least you know what you're getting with cornflakes," and she leaves the table to get herself a bowl.

So by the time my mother sat down at the table and told us what it was we would all have released ourselves from the dinner table on our own recognizance and would be foraging around in the kitchen cupboards trying to find something vaguely edible.

"Margaret," my mother would call, knowing that Margaret was the most dutiful of all of us, "wouldn't you even try it?"

And Margaret, being a good girl, would lift a sliver to her lips.

"Well?" my mother would ask, hardly daring to breathe.

"You wouldn't give it [whatever it was!] to the dog," Margaret would reply. Honesty was another of her virtues, alongside obedience and bravery.

So after several years of tearful evening meals and ever-increasing breakfast cereal bills, my mother, to everyone's eternal relief, decided to stop cooking altogether.

So, if any of her daughters or her husband told her that they were hungry, she'd take them silently by the hand and into the kitchen. She'd say, "Behold the upright freezer full of frozen convenience foods," and flinging wide the freezer door, with several flourishes, exhort them to survey the myriad delights within. Then she'd cross the kitchen with the would-be diner and say, "All hail the microwave. My advice to you is to befriend these two machines. You will find them invaluable in your fight against hunger in this house."

So now you realize why I was so reluctant to take her up on her offer of soup.

But the wonderful thing about my mother's not cooking or doing any housework is that it meant that she had plenty of time for the truly important things in life. She watched an average of six soap operas a day and read about four novels a week, so she was expertly placed to give her daughters advice on their broken romances.

She was no stranger to romantic tragedy.

We sat there in the darkening room, listening to the sound of my baby breathing contentedly.

"She's so beautiful," Mum said.

"Yes," I said, and started to cry quietly.

"What happened?" Mum asked.

"I don't know," I said. "I thought everything was fine. I thought he was as excited about the baby as I was. I know that the pregnancy wasn't easy. I was always sick and I got fat and we hardly ever had sex, but I thought that he understood."

And my mother was so good. She didn't give me any of that nonsense about men being . . . well . . . different from us, dear. They have . . . needs . . . dear, in the same way that animals do. She didn't insult me by assuming that James left because we hadn't had sex while I was pregnant.

"What am I going to do?" I asked her, knowing that she no more had the answer to that than I did.

"You've just got to live through it," she said. "That's all you can do. Don't try to make sense of it, you'll drive yourself crazy. The only person who can tell you why James left is James, and if he doesn't want to talk to you, you can't force him. Maybe he doesn't understand it himself. But you can't change the way he feels. If he says he doesn't love you anymore and does love this other woman, you've got to accept it. Maybe he will come back, maybe he won't, but either way, you've got to live through this."

"But it hurts so much," I said helplessly.

"I know it does," she said sadly. "And if I could make it go away, you know I would."

I looked down at my little girl, asleep, so peaceful, so innocent, so safe and happy now, and felt an unbearable anguish. I wanted her to always be happy. I wanted to hug her and hug her and never let her go. I never wanted her to feel the rejection and loneliness and shock that I was feeling now.

I wanted to protect her always from pain. But I wouldn't be able to. Life would see to that.

Just then the door opened, jolting us both out of the misery that we had sunk into. It was my youngest sister, Helen. (Helen, eighteen, had scraped into her first year of college by the skin of her small white even teeth to study something incredibly useful like anthropology, history of art and ancient Greek. Helen, of the long black hair, slanty cat eyes, constant laughter, extremely bad behavior, who was loved by most people, especially the men whose hearts she broke by the truckload.)

"You're here!" she shouted as she burst into the room. "Give me a look at my niece," she screeched. "Isn't it great! Imagine me being an auntie! Was it awful? Is it really like trying to shit a couch? Tell me, I've always wanted to know, what do they boil the water and tear the sheets up for?"

Without waiting for an answer, she thrust her face right into the car seat. The poor child started to cry in terror. Helen picked up the baby and held her under her arm like a rugby player just about to score the winning try for Ireland.

"Why's she crying?" she demanded.

What could I say?

"What's her name?" she asked.

"Claire hasn't decided on a name just yet," said Mum.

"No, I have," I said, deciding to add to the general confusion.

I looked at Mum. "I've decided I'm going to name her after your mother."

"What?" screeched Helen, in horror. "You can't call her Granny Maguire. That's no name for a baby."

"No, Helen," I said wearily. "I'm going to call her Kate."

She stared at me for a moment, wrinkling up her beautiful little nose, as understanding dawned on her.

"Oh, I *see*," she said, laughing.

And then she muttered, not quite under her breath, "Well, that's still no name for a baby."

She handed the baby back to me, rather in the manner that farmers unload sacks of potatoes from their trucks. That is, clumsily, carelessly, with scant regard to the welfare or comfort of the potatoes. Then, to my horror, she said, "Hey, is James here? Where's James?"

She obviously didn't know.

I started to cry.

"Jesus," she said, shocked.

"Why's *she* crying?" she demanded of my mother.

My mother just stared dumbly at her. She couldn't answer her.

Would you believe it? She was crying.

Helen stared in baffled disgust at three generations of Walsh women, all crying.

"What's *wrong* with all of you? What have I said? Mum, why are you crying?" she said in exasperation.

We just looked at her, huddled together on the bed, tears rolling down our respective faces, newly christened Kate roaring like a train.

"What's going *on*?" she said in frustration.

Still we sat there. Still we said nothing.

"I'm going downstairs to ask Dad," she threatened. But then she bit her lip and lingered by the door as she thought about it. "Unless he's going to start crying too."

Finally Mum managed to speak. "No, don't go anywhere, love," she said, stretching out her hand to Helen. "Come and sit down. You haven't done anything."

"Then why are you crying?" asked Helen, reluctantly returning to us weeping on the bed.

"Yes, why are *you* crying?" I asked my mother. I was just as curious as Helen. Had her husband just left her? Did her diaper need changing?

"Because I was just thinking about Granny," she sniffed. "And how she didn't live to see her first great-grandchild. And it's lovely that you've named the baby after her. She would have been glad. And honored."

I felt so guilty. At least *my* mother was still alive. Poor Mum, Granny had only died last year and we all missed her so much. I hugged Mum and baby Kate, both of them crying.

"It's such a pity," mused Helen wistfully.

"What is?" I asked her.

"Oh you know, that Granny wasn't named something nice like Tamsin or Isolda or Jet," she said.

I don't know why I didn't kill her there and then.

But for some reason it was very hard to get angry with her.

And then she turned her attention to me. "And why are you crying?" she demanded of me. "Oh, God, I know, I bet you've got that postnatal depression thing. There was a thing in the paper about a woman who had that and she threw her baby out of a twelfth-story window and then she wouldn't open the door when the police came and they had to break the door down and she hadn't taken the trash out for weeks and the place was disgusting and then she tried to kill herself and they had to put her in an electric chair. Or something." Helen spoke with relish, never one to let annoying little details like hard facts interfere with the telling of a good blood-thirsty tale.

"Or maybe they just locked her up, or something," she admitted reluctantly, trailing off.

"Anyway, is that what's wrong with you?" she demanded cheerfully of me, back on track. "Just as well we don't live on the twelfth floor, isn't it, Mum? Otherwise it'd be splatted baby all over the patio. And Michael would go crazy about the mess."

Michael was our ill-tempered, work-shy, superstitious octogenarian gardener. The wrath of Michael was a fearful thing to behold, as was Michael's gardening. My father was far too frightened of him to fire him. In fact, the whole family was terrified of Michael. Even Helen was quite subdued around him.

I remembered the afternoon the year before when my poor mother stood, freezing, in her apron (which she wore purely for the sake of appearances) in the garden, nodding desperately, smiling tightly, far too afraid to leave, as Michael explained, in great detail, with inarticulate grunts and frighteningly wide-sweeping gestures with the shears, how, for example, if the hedge was trimmed the wall would fall down. ("You see, it needs the hedge for the support, missus.") Or how if the lawn was cut all the grass would wither and die. ("The germs gets into the grass, in through the cut bits, and it all just ups and dies on you.")

My mother finally made her way back into the kitchen, where she tearfully banged utensils as she boiled the kettle for Michael's tea.

"The lazy old bastard," she sobbed to myself and Helen. "He never does anything. And he made me miss *The Flying Doctor* and *Countdown*. And the grass is up to our knees. I'm

ashamed of my life of it. We're the only house in the neighborhood with a jungle of a garden. I've a good mind to spit into
his tea!"

A tearful pause. A count of three.

"May God forgive me," she quavered. "Helen, leave those
cookies alone! They're for Michael's tea."

Michael was at the back door at this stage, conspicuously
holding his back, as if it ached from the rigors of his labor.

"Can I pour your tea?" my mother asked him
obsequiously.

But later that evening I heard my parents arguing in the
kitchen.

"Jack, you'll have to say something to him."

"Look, Mary, I'll cut the grass myself."

"No, Jack, we pay him to do it. So he should do it. Giving
me all that nonsense about grass catching germs! He must take
me for a right bloody idiot."

"All right, all right, I'll talk to him!"

But Dad never "talked" to Michael. And I happened to
know for a fact that he cut the grass himself—the day Mum
went to Limerick to see Auntie Kitty—and told my mother a
barefaced lie about it.

Helen was right. If a baby was "splatted" (is there such a
word?) all over the patio, Michael would indeed go crazy
about the mess.

But it wasn't going to happen.

Although if Kate didn't stop crying soon, I'd have to recon-
sider that.

"No, Helen," I explained to her. "I don't have postnatal
depression. Well, I don't think I do. Not yet, anyway."

Christ! That was all I needed.

But before I could tell her about James's leaving me, my
dad came into the bedroom.

We were going to have to start moving some of the furniture out into the hall if the visitors continued to arrive at
this rate.

"Hijack," we all chorused.

My father acknowledged this greeting with a smile and a
bow of his head. You see, my father's name was Jack, and in
the early seventies when hijacking was the popular news item

(since overshadowed by child abuse), an uncle from America greeted my father with the words "Hi Jack." My sisters and I nearly did ourselves an injury with mirth. It never failed to raise a smile.

Well, perhaps you needed to be there. "I've come to see my first grandchild," announced my dad. "Can I hold her?"

I handed Kate over to Dad and he held her expertly. Immediately Kate stopped crying. She lay placidly in his arms, clenching and unclenching her little starfish hands.

Just like her mother, I thought sadly—putty in men's hands.

I really would have to nip this in the bud with Kate. Get some self-respect, girl! You don't need a man for your happiness! Every other mother would be reading her little girl stories about engines that could talk and wolves that meet their comeuppance. I would read my child feminist diatribes instead, I decided.

Out with *The Little Mermaid* and in with *The Female Eunuch*.

"When are you going to give her a name?" asked Dad.

"Oh, I just have," I told him. "I'm going to call her after Granny."

"Lovely," beamed Dad.

"Hello, little Nora," he said to the pink bundle in a sing-song baby voice.

Helen, Mum and I exchanged stricken looks.

Wrong granny!

"Er, no Dad," I said awkwardly. "I've called her Kate."

"But my mother isn't called Kate." He frowned in confusion.

"I know, Dad," I faltered. (Oh Christ, why was life so fraught with pitfalls?) "But I've called her after Granny Maguire, not Granny Walsh."

"Oh, I see," he said a bit coldly.

"But I'll give her Nora for her second name," I promised cringingly.

"No way!" interrupted Helen. "Call her something nice. I know! How about Elena? Elena is Greek for Helen, you know."

"Shush, Helen," admonished Mum. "It's Claire's baby."

Really, Helen was exhausting.

However, as she had the attention span of a saucepan—

that is, absolutely none whatsoever—she soon turned her attention to other things.

"Hey, Dad, can I have a lift to Linda's?"

"Helen, I'm not a chauffeur," replied Dad, evenly and tightly.

"Dad, I didn't ask you what you do for a living. I *know* what you do for a living. I simply asked you for a lift," Helen said in a very "I'm prepared to be reasonable about this" voice.

"No, Helen, you can bloody well walk!" exclaimed Dad. "I honestly don't know what's wrong with all you young people. Laziness, that's what it is. Now, when I—"

"Dad," Helen interrupted him sharply, "*please* don't tell me again how you had to walk three miles to school in your bare feet. I really couldn't bear it. Just give me a lift." And she gave him a little cat smile from under her long black fringe.

He stared at her in exasperation for a moment and then he started to laugh. "Oh, all right then," he said, jingling his car keys. "Come on."

He handed Kate back to me.

The way a baby should be handed back.

"Night, night, Kate Nora," he said.

Dad and Helen left.

Mum, Kate Nora, and I remained on the bed, savoring the silence occasioned by Helen's departure.

"Now," I said sternly to Kate, "that was your first lesson on how to treat a man, courtesy of your Auntie Helen. I hope you took lots of notice. Treat them like slaves and, sure enough, they'll behave like slaves."

Kate stared wide-eyed up at me.

My mother just smiled inscrutably.

A smug, secret smile.

A knowing kind of a smile.

The smile of a woman whose husband has done the vacuuming for the past fifteen years.

five

And so to bed.

It felt very odd to be going to sleep in the bed in which I had spent my teenage years. And it was kind of weird to be kissed good-night by my mother when I had my own child in a bassinet beside me.

I was a mother, but I didn't need Sigmund Freud to tell me that I still felt like a child myself.

Kate stared open-eyed at the ceiling. She was probably still in shock from her encounter with Helen. I was a bit anxious about her but, to my surprise, I actually felt quite tired. I went to sleep quickly. Although I'd thought that I really wouldn't be able to sleep at all.

Ever again, I mean.

Kate gently roused me at about two A.M. by crying at about a million decibels. I wondered if she had gone to sleep at all. I fed her. Then I went back to bed.

I went back to sleep but, a few hours later, I jolted awake again, filled with horror. Horror that had nothing to do with the exuberantly flowery Laura Ashleyesque wallpaper, curtains and duvet cover that surrounded me and that I could dimly see through the darkness.

Horror that I was in Dublin and not in my apartment in London with my beloved James.

I looked at the clock and it was (yes, you guessed it) four A.M. I should have taken comfort from the fact that approximately a quarter of the Greenwich Mean Time world had just jolted awake also and were lying, staring miserably into the darkness, worrying about everything from "Will I be laid off?" to "Will I ever meet someone who really loves me?" to "Am I pregnant?"

But it was no comfort.

Because I felt as if I was in Hell.

And comparing it to someone else's Hell didn't make the pain of mine any less.

I sat up in bed in the dark.

Kate slept peacefully beside me.

We were like night watchmen, staying awake in shifts. Although the resemblance ended there, because I couldn't say— well, at least not with any sincerity—"Four o'clock and all is well."

My stomach lurched with the horror of it all. I couldn't believe that I was in my parents' house in Dublin and not in my apartment in London with my husband. I felt that I must have been out of my mind to have left London and abandoned James to another woman! Had I gone completely mad? I had to go back. I had to fight for him! I had to get him back!

I *couldn't* be without James.

He was part of me.

If my arm had fallen off I wouldn't have said, "Oh, leave it there for the moment. It'll come back if it's meant to be. No point in forcing it. It might only drive it away." After all, it was my arm, and James was much more a part of me than any old arm.

I needed him a lot more.

I loved him a lot more.

I simply couldn't be without him.

I wanted him back. I wanted my life with him back. And I was going to get him back. (And get him on his back.)

(Sorry, that was flippant and vulgar.)

I was panic-stricken: I should never have left.

I should have stood my ground and just told him that he and I would be able to work things out. That he couldn't possibly love Denise. That he loved me. That I was too much a part of him for him not to love me.

But I had admitted defeat and delivered him into Denise's cellulitey (but they were!) arms without any kind of protest.

I had to speak to him now.

He wouldn't mind my calling him at four in the morning. I mean, this was James we were talking about here. He was my best friend. I could do *anything* and James didn't mind. He understood me. He knew me.

And I would fly back to London with Kate in the morning. And my life would be fixed.

The last week would be forgotten. The break in our lives would be mended seamlessly. The scar would fade. Only if you looked very closely would you ever see it.

I know what you're thinking.

No, really, I do.

You're thinking, "She's gone mad."

Well, maybe I had. Maybe I was deranged with grief.

You're thinking, "Have some self-respect, Claire."

But I'd realized that my marriage mattered more to me than my self-respect. Self-respect doesn't keep you warm at night. Self-respect doesn't listen to you at the end of each day. Self-respect doesn't tell you that it would rather have sex with you than with Cindy Crawford.

I struggled out of bed, fighting my way through the acres of nightgown that my mother had insisted that I wear. When I fled London I had forgotten to pack a nightgown. And when my mother discovered this she tartly informed me that no one was sleeping naked under her roof. "What if there was a fire?" and "That might be how they do things in London, but you're not in London now." So I had a choice of wearing a pair of Dad's paisley pajamas or borrowing one of Mum's huge, Victorian, floorlength, high-collared, fleece-lined, flowery nighties. How the woman ever managed to get a man to impregnate her even once, never mind five times, while associating with such garments was beyond me. They could have dimmed the ardor of a fifteen-year-old Italian.

I had chosen the nightgown over Dad's pajamas because the huge quantities of fabric in the nightdress made me feel waiflike and skinny and cute. Whereas Dad's pajamas were alarmingly and depressingly snug.

So keep your smart remarks about my nightgown to yourself. There was method to my madness (well, at least to that particular aspect of it). I happened to know what I was doing. Emaciated, that's how I felt. Skinny and floaty and girllike. It took me about ten minutes to get out of bed, and when I finally managed to stand on the floor, I nearly hung myself by standing on the back hem of the nightie, thereby pulling the front collar upward tightly and violently onto my throat in a vicelike grip.

I coughed and choked a good bit and Kate started to move and fret restlessly in her cot. "Oh, don't wake up, darling," I thought frantically. "Don't cry. There's no need. Everything's going to be all right. I'm going to get your daddy back. You'll see. You hold down the fort here."

And miraculously she settled and didn't wake up. I tiptoed out of the dark room and out into the landing. The huge nightgown swirled roomily around me in a pleasing manner as I went down the unlit stairs. The phone was downstairs in the hall. The only light was from the street lamp outside the house, which shone through the panes of frosted glass in the front door.

I started to dial the number of my apartment in London. There were a couple of clicks as the phone in Dublin connected with the phone in an empty apartment in a city four hundred miles away.

I let it ring. It might have been a hundred times. It might have been a thousand times.

It rang and rang, calling out to a cold dark empty apartment. I could imagine the phone, ringing and ringing, beside the smooth, unruffled, unslept-in bed, shadows from the window thrown on it as the lights from the street streamed in through the open curtains. Open, because there was no one there to close them.

And still, I let it ring and ring. And slowly hope left me.

James wasn't answering.

Because James wasn't there.

James was in another apartment. In another bed.

With another woman.

I was crazy to think that I could have got him back just

because I wanted him back. Temporary insanity had come a-calling and I had shouted "Come on in, the door is open." Luckily, Reality had come home unexpectedly and found Temporary Insanity roaming the corridors of my mind unchecked, going into rooms, opening cupboards, reading my letters, looking in my underwear drawer, that kind of thing. Reality had run and got Sanity. And after a tussle, they both had managed to throw out Temporary Insanity and slam the door in his face. Temporary Insanity now lay on the gravel in the driveway of my mind, panting and furious, shouting, "She invited me in, you know. She *asked* me in. She *wanted* me there."

Reality and Sanity were leaning out of an upstairs window, shouting, "Go on, get going. You're not wanted around here. If you're not gone in five minutes, we'll call the Emotions Police."

I suppose any psychiatrist worth his salt would have said that I was In Denial. That the shock of James's leaving me so suddenly was too great for me to assimilate.

I sat on the floor, in the cold, dark hall. After a long time I hung up the phone.

My heart, which had been beating frantically, returned to normal. My hands stopped shaking. My head stopped fantasizing.

I wouldn't be going back to London in the morning.

My life was here now. At least for the moment.

And although I felt as weary as a person a thousand years old, I felt that I would never be able to sleep again.

How I wished that we had a neurotic mother. One who kept sleeping pills and Valium and antidepressants by the crateload in the medicine cabinet in the bathroom. As it was she acted as if we were prospective candidates for the Betty Ford Clinic if we asked for two aspirin for a sore throat/stomachache/broken leg/perforated duodenal ulcer. "Offer it up," she would say. "Think of Our Lord suffering on the cross." To which she might receive the reply, "Being nailed to a cross would be a day at the races compared to this earache."

This, of course, would reduce the chance, however slim, of extracting drugs from my mother. Blasphemy was high on her list of unforgivable things. As it was, the chances of procuring even an alcoholic drink were unpredictable. Neither of my parents drank very much. And they kept very little alcohol in the house. In my younger days, those halcyon days before I discovered what alcohol could do for me, we had a full, if eclectic, liquor cabinet.

Purest Polish vodka jostled shoulders with liter bottles of Malibu. Bottles of Hungarian Slibovitch behaved as if they had every right to stand next to a bottle of Southern Comfort. There was no cold war in our liquor cabinet.

You see, Dad was forever winning bottles of brandy or whiskey at golf. And Mum would occasionally win a bottle of sherry or some kind of girlie liqueur at bridge. People brought us presents of bottles of fancy drink when they went on vacation. Our next-door neighbor brought us back a bottle of ouzo from Cyprus.

Dad's secretary brought us the Slibovitch when she went on her vacation behind the Iron Curtain. (This was in 1979, and myself and my sisters all thought she was really daring and brave and questioned her at length on her return as to whether she had witnessed any violation of the human rights of the Hungarians.) Anna won a bottle of fluorescent yellow banana schnapps at the St. Vincent de Paul Christmas raffle. Someone else came by a stray bottle of apricot schnapps.

Bit by bit our alcohol collection grew. And, as my parents barely drank and we children hadn't started yet, our liquor cabinet overfloweth.

However, those happy days were no more.

I'm sorry to report that when I was about fifteen, I discovered the delights of alcohol. And quickly came to realize that my pocket money was not going to stretch to accommodate my newfound passion. With the result that I spent many an anxious hour looking over my shoulder as I siphoned off small amounts from the various bottles in the cupboard in the sitting room.

I decanted them into a small lemonade bottle I had procured as a receptacle for the concoction I would make. I was afraid to take too much from any one bottle, so I would choose from a wide spectrum of drinks. And put it all into the one lemonade bottle, you understand. With scant regard to what the final product tasted like. My priority was to get drunk. And if I had to drink something that tasted disgusting to do so, then I would.

I spent many a happy hour, after drinking the mixture of (let's just say) perhaps sherry, vodka, gin, brandy and Vermouth (Auntie Kitty had brought us the Vermouth from her trip to Rome), joyfully inebriated, at whatever bar I managed to bully or hoodwink my parents into letting me go to.

Great days. Glorious days.

To avoid any awkward and embarrassing scenes with my parents I would replace whatever I had taken from each bottle with a corresponding amount of water. What could be neater, I thought?

However, like those delicate plants that are overwatered and die, I managed to also overwater a lot of alcohol. A bottle of vodka, in particular.

My day of reckoning finally came.

One Saturday evening, when I was about seventeen, Mum and Dad had the Kellys and the Smiths over for drinks. Mum and Mrs. Kelly happened to be drinking vodka. Or so they thought. However, thanks to my efforts over the previous eighteen months or so, what was once Smirnoff was now more or less 100 percent purest, unadulterated water, untainted by the merest hint of alcohol.

The rest of the party had the good fortune to be drinking actual alcohol.

So, as Dad, Mr. Kelly, Mr. Smith and Mrs. Smith got louder and redder and chattier and laughed at things that weren't remotely funny, and Dad told everyone that he didn't declare all his income to the tax man and the Smiths revealed that Mr. Smith had had an affair last year and that they'd nearly split up but they were making a go of things now, Mum and Mrs. Kelly sat stiff and poker-faced, smiling tightly as the others guffawed with laughter.

Mum found nothing even remotely amusing in Mrs. Smith's spilling her Bacardi and Coke (I didn't really like Bacardi, so its alcoholic content was pretty much intact) all over the good sitting room carpet, but Dad was highly entertained by it. Mirth abounded. All except for the vodka drinkers.

The penny dropped with my mother the next day.

The bottle of vodka was sent for and subjected to several tests. (As in, "Here, smell that. What does that smell like to you?" "Nothing, Mum." "*Exactly!*")

Results from the makeshift forensics lab set up in the kitchen showed that the bottle of vodka had indeed been tampered with. Tampered with repeatedly, in fact.

There was a tearful scene between myself and my parents. Well, my mother, at least, was tearful. But with embarrassment and rage. "Oh, the shame of it," she wailed. "Inviting people over and offering them drinks and giving them watered-down stuff instead. I could die! How could you? And you took the pledge and promised not to drink until you were eighteen."

I was surly and sullen and silent. I hung my head to hide my shame and my fury at being caught.

Dad was silent and sad.

A purge ensued. The alcohol was all rounded up and incarcerated. Detained without trial in a secure cupboard that had a key. Only Mum knew where that key was kept, and as she said herself, she would rather suffer the torments of the damned than reveal its whereabouts.

Naturally it was only a matter of time before myself or one of my sisters figured out how to pick the lock.

A type of guerrilla warfare ensued, with my mother forever seeking new hiding places for the rapidly diminishing supply of alcohol. In fact, Helen swears that she heard Mum on the phone to Auntie Julia, who is an alcoholic, asking her to recommend good hiding places. But this has never been corroborated, so don't take it as gospel.

But Mum was only ever a tiny step ahead of us. No sooner had she found a new place for her cache than one of us would find it. In the same way that new antibiotics have to be constantly invented to combat new and resistant strains of bacteria, so Mum had to constantly invent new hiding places. Unfortunately for her, they never stayed new or hidden for long.

She even tried sitting down and reasoning with us. "Please

don't drink so much. Or at least please don't drink so much of my and your father's alcohol."

And the answer she usually got—uttered more in sorrow than in anger, I have to say—would be something like, "But Mum, we like to drink. We are poor. We are left with no choice. Do you think we *enjoy* behaving like common thieves?"

Now, even though Margaret, Rachel and I had left home and could afford to support whatever bad habits we chose, Helen and Anna were both still living at home and were bone-crunchingly poor. So the battle continued.

And what was once a proud and noble alcohol collection was now a tatty and raggedy and depleted few bottles traveling nomadically around the closets and cellars and under the beds, looking for a safe haven. Long gone were the full and sparkling bottles of spirits with recognizable brand names. All that remained in their stead were a sticky bottle of Drambuie, covered in dust, with about an inch left in the bottom, or half an inch of Cuban vodka (honestly, there is such a thing—obviously the right drink for the ideologically sound comrade in Cuba) and the almost full bottle of banana schnapps, which Helen and Anna have both declared that they would rather die of thirst than drink.

I continued to sit on the cold floor in the dark hall. I really felt as if I needed a drink. I would even have drunk the banana schnapps if I'd known where to find it. I felt so unbearably *lonely*. I toyed with the idea of waking my mother up and asking her to give me a drink, but I felt really guilty at that idea. She was so worried about me, if the poor woman had managed to get to sleep I couldn't in all conscience wake her.

Maybe Helen could help.

I wearily climbed the stairs to her bedroom. But when I crept into her room her bed was empty. Either she had spent the night at Linda's or else some young man had got very lucky. If she had spent the night with a man, his suicided body would probably be found in the morning with a note beside it saying something like "I have achieved everything I ever wanted to do in life. I will never be as happy as this ever again. I want to die on this note of ecstasy. PS: She is a Goddess."

Then, as if I wasn't feeling awful enough, I was suddenly gripped with a panicky fear that something terrible had happened to Kate.

That she'd been the victim of crib death. Or choked on vomit. Or suffocated. Or *something*.

I raced back to my room and I was so relieved to find that she was still breathing.

She was just lying there, a wrinkled, pink, fragrant bundle, her eyes screwed shut.

As I waited for my breathing to return to normal and for the sweat to evaporate from my forehead I wondered how other parents coped. How did they let their children out to play with other children? Didn't they panic every time they were away from their children for more than five minutes?

I was finding it hard enough now. How the hell would I cope when she had to go to school? There was no way I could be expected to just abandon her like that. The school would have to let me sit at the back of the classroom.

Now I *really* needed a drink.

Maybe Anna was home.

I dragged myself over to her room and quietly opened the door.

The fumes hit me instantaneously.

The alcohol fumes, that is.

Bingo!

"Thank God," I thought. I'd obviously come to the right place.

Anna was curled up in bed, her long black hair spread out all around her on the pillow.

"Anna," I whispered loudly to her, and shook her a bit.

No response.

"Anna!" I whispered, a good deal more loudly this time, and shook her shoulder vigorously.

I turned on her bedside lamp and shone it into her face, Gestapo style. Wake up!

She opened her eyes and stared at me.

"Claire?" she croaked disbelievingly.

She looked really quite frightened, as though she thought she might be hallucinating.

And as this was Anna, it was quite possible.

That she was hallucinating, that is.

Fond of the mood-altering substances, if you follow me.

The poor girl. As far as she knew I was four hundred miles away, in another city, in another life. But here I was manifesting myself in her bedroom in the middle of the night.

"Anna, sorry to disturb you like this but have you anything I could drink?" I asked her.

She just stared at me.

"Why are you here?" she asked in a little frightened voice.

"Because I'm looking for a bloody drink," I said exasperatedly.

"Have you a message for me?" she asked, still staring at me wide-eyed.

"Oh Christ," I thought in annoyance.

Anna loved anything to do with the occult. There was nothing she would like more than to be possessed by the devil. Or to live in a haunted house. Or to be able to foretell disasters. She was obviously hoping that I was some kind of paranormal phenomenon. Either that or she was drunker than usual.

"Yes, Anna," I said, deciding to humor her but at the same time feeling a bit foolish. "They have sent me. I've been sent to get the drink."

"In my backpack," she said faintly.

Her backpack was flung on the floor with one shoe (what had happened to the other one?), her coat and a can of Budweiser. I had difficulty opening the bag as two helium balloons were attached to the cord. Anna had obviously been to some kind of party.

I nearly cried with relief when I found a bottle of white wine in her bag.

"Thanks, Anna," I said. "I'll repay you tomorrow." And left.

She was still looking dazed and frightened. She nodded dumbly. "Okay," she managed to mumble.

I checked Kate. She was still sleeping peacefully.

I had half expected her to be sitting up with her arms folded, demanding to know where the father I had promised her was. But she was just asleep dreaming baby dreams about pink clouds and warm beds and soft people who smell nice and lots to eat and lots of sleep and lots of people who love you.

And never having to line up for the bathroom.

I took the bottle of wine downstairs to the kitchen and wearily opened it. I knew I would feel better after having a drink. Just as I was pouring myself a glass of wine, Anna appeared at the kitchen door, rubbing her eyes, looking confused and anxious, her long black hair strewn around her white face.

"Oh, Claire, it really is you. So I didn't imagine it," she said, sounding half relieved, half disappointed. "I thought I might have the DTs. And then I thought you might be a vision. But I thought if you were a vision that you would appear in something nicer than Mum's awful nightgown."

"Yes, it really is me." I smiled at her. "Sorry if I gave you a fright. But I was dying for a drink." I went over to her and put my arms around her. It really was lovely to see her.

Anna looked a lot like Helen, little white face, slanty cat eyes, cute little nose.

But the resemblance ended there. For starters I didn't want to kill Anna about twenty times a day. Anna was a lot quieter, a lot sweeter. She was very kind to everyone. She was also, unfortunately, very vague and very ethereal.

Well, I suppose I had better be perfectly frank with you. There's no getting away from the fact that Anna was a bit of . . . well . . . a bit of a hippie, I suppose.

She got jobs intermittently. Usually in vegetarian restaurants. But they never seemed to last any length of time. Well, neither did the restaurants either, for some odd reason.

She went on welfare.

She, as I should have mentioned, sold drugs. But only briefly. And in the nicest possible way.

No honestly.

She never hung around school gates trying to sell high-grade heroin to eight-year-olds.

She just sold the odd bit of hash to her friends and family. And doubtless made a loss on it.

She made jewelry and occasionally even sold some.

A precarious kind of existence, but she didn't seem too bothered by the insecure nature of it.

Dad despaired of Anna. He called her irresponsible. And, of course, the blame for Anna's instability was laid squarely, if not particularly fairly, at my door. Dad said that I had high-tailed it (his word) to London at a time when Anna was at a very impressionable age and I had given her the idea that it was perfectly acceptable to give up a good job and go off and work as a waitress. What kind of role model was I? he asked me.

Dad had desperately tried to mold Anna into a responsible, tax-paying citizen. He managed to get her a job in an office working for a construction company.

Apparently someone owed him a favor.

It must have been a very large favor.

It was a mistake to try to force Anna to work in an office. Like trying to squash a round peg into a square hole. Or wearing your shoes on the wrong feet. Unpleasant, uncomfortable and almost certainly doomed to failure.

It was a disaster.

She lost track of the time every lunch hour because she had found a swan's nest at the canal near the office and would spend ages watching the birds and cooing over the eggs. (And rolling and partaking of several joints also, if the rumormongers are to be believed.)

But the day she suggested changing the filing system for the construction workers, so that instead of organizing them by their surnames, she would do it by their astrological star signs instead, Mr. Ballard, the office manager, decided that he had enough. Although Anna protested that really she had only been joking (she said, laughing, no doubt making things worse for herself, "Honestly, how could we possibly consider filing them by their star signs? I mean, we don't even know their rising signs"), she soon found herself once more without gainful employment.

Dad was furious and mortified with embarrassment. "What goes on in her bloody head?" he thundered. "I'd nearly swear she's on drugs."

Honestly, for an intelligent man, there were times when he was alarmingly naive.

Once she had established that I wasn't a psychic phenomenon, Anna, though disappointed, decided to make the best of the situation.

"Pour me a glass of that too," she said, gesturing at the bottle of wine, so I did, and we both sat down at the kitchen table.

It was about five AM.

Anna seemed to find nothing remotely strange at the lateness or, more accurately, the earliness of the hour.

"Cheers," she said, raising her glass to me.

"Yes, cheers," I replied hollowly. I drained the glass in one gulp. Anna looked admiringly at me.

"So what are you doing here?" she asked conversationally. "I didn't know that you were coming. No one told me . . . well, I *think* no one told me," she said a bit doubtfully. "I haven't been home in about a week."

"Well, Anna, it was a bit of a sudden decision," I said, sighing as I geared up for a long tortuous explanation of my tragic circumstances.

But before I could, she interrupted me abruptly.

"Oh my God!" she said, suddenly clapping a hand to her mouth.

"What?" I demanded, feeling very alarmed. Was the corkscrew hovering in midair? Had a banshee's face appeared at the window?

"You're not pregnant anymore!" she exclaimed.

I smiled in spite of myself.

"No, Anna, I'm not. Can you figure it out?"

"You've had a baby?" she asked slowly.

"Yes," I confirmed, still smiling.

"Jesus!" she screamed. "Isn't that fabulous!" And flung her arms around me. "Is it a girl?"

"Yes," I told her.

"Is she here? Can I see her?" Anna asked, all excited.

"Yes, she's in my room. But she's asleep. And if you don't mind I'd prefer not to wake her. Not until I've finished this bottle of wine, anyway," I said morosely.

"Well, fair enough," conceded Anna, pouring me another glass of wine, one alcohophile to another. "Get that inside you. I suppose it's a long time since you've been allowed to drink alcohol. No wonder you're knocking it back."

"Well, it is a long time since I've been able to have a drink. But that's not why I'm so desperate to get drunk," I told her.

"Oh?" she asked me quizzically.

So I told her about James.

And she was so gentle, so sympathetic, so unjudgmental and, in her own flaky way, so wise, that I slowly started to feel a bit better. A little bit calmer. A little less weary. A little more hopeful.

I suppose the bottle of wine had also better get a mention on the credits. It played a small but not insignificant part in the lifting of my spirits. But it was mostly thanks to Anna.

She murmured stuff like "If it's meant to be, it's meant to be" and "We're all being taken care of, even if it doesn't feel like it at the time" and "There is a plan for all of us" and "Everything happens for a reason."

Hippie-type talk. But I found it very comforting.

And at about six o'clock, just when the birds were starting to sing, we abandoned the kitchen, leaving the table strewn with glasses, the well-and-truly empty bottle, the cork, the corkscrew and Anna's overflowing ashtray.

Dad would be getting up in an hour to make breakfast for himself and Mum. He would deal with the mess, we reasoned. He liked to do things, we agreed. He needed to feel needed.

We slowly climbed the stairs, our arms around each other, and I fell into bed, feeling sleepy and relaxed and calm. Anna spent a few minutes gazing in wonder at Kate and then insisted on getting the two helium balloons (which she had misappropriated from the party she had been to, along with the bottle of wine) and tying them onto Kate's bassinet. Then Anna kissed me good-night and tiptoed out of the room. I went straight into a deep, dreamless sleep.

Kate woke me fifteen minutes later screeching for her breakfast.

I fed her and then staggered back to bed.

Just as I was drifting back to sleep I heard Dad getting up. A few minutes later I heard him pounding up the stairs shouting to my mother, "Your daughters are drunken pups!" (They were always her daughters when they lost jobs, didn't go to mass, stayed out late and dressed indecently. They were his daughters when they passed exams, got degrees, married accountants and bought houses.) "Drinking all night and lying in bed all day! Am I supposed to clear up the mess in the kitchen?"

Dad had obviously discovered the remains of our little party.

Mum wailed plaintively, "Oh no, they've found the drink again. I thought they'd never find it out under the oil tank. Now I'll have to find a new place to hide it."

After a while this commotion died down. Just as I was hoping against hope that I might catch an hour or two of sleep, someone started ringing at the front door. Naturally, this was quite alarming because it was only seven-thirty in the morning. I heard Dad open the door and engage in conversation with a man's voice. I strained to hear what was going on. Could it possibly be James? I felt such a surge of hope that it nearly hurt.

Then there was the sound of Dad running up the stairs. He shouted to my mother, "There's a madman at the front door with a shoe. He wants to know if we own it. What'll I do?"

There was a perplexed silence from my mother.

"I'm going to be late for work with all these interruptions this morning, you know," Dad told her, as if it was her fault.

I started to cry with disappointment. It wasn't James at the front door. I knew exactly who it was.

"Dad," I called tearfully. "Daaaaaad!"

He stuck his head around the door. "Morning, love," he said. "I'll be with you in a minute. I'll make you some tea. It's just that there's a lunatic downstairs and I'd better get rid of him first."

"No, Dad," I told him. "He's not a lunatic. He's a taxi driver. Wake Anna. I bet it's her shoe."

"Oh, so she's finally bothered to come home, has she?" shouted Mum from her room.

Dad went off to Anna's room muttering "I might have known Anna would be involved in this."

Anna was duly roused. And it turned out that the man at the front door was the taxi driver who had dropped Anna home in the early hours of the morning. When he'd finished his shift he found a shoe in the back of his car. And was now traveling, in the manner of Prince Charming, to all the houses of the young women he had delivered home during the night, trying to match the shoe to the young woman. Anna was indeed his Cinderella.

Anna gave effusive thanks. The taxi driver left. Anna went back to bed. Dad went to work. I closed my eyes. Kate started to cry.

So did I.

six

Wet and windy and miserable. For the first two weeks that I was home it rained every day. Apparently it was the wettest February in living memory.

I would wake in the middle of every night to the sound of the raindrops cracking and spattering at the window, drumming and pounding on the roof.

The weather made everyone miserable. Luckily I was suicidal anyway.

In fact, the weather made me feel slightly better. It seemed like Fate's way of evening up my miserable life with everyone else's happy life, if you know what I mean.

Anna and Helen lounged moodily around the house, staring longingly out the windows, wondering if it would ever stop.

Mum talked gloomily about building an ark.

Dad tried to play golf while up to his knees in water on a flooded golf course.

I spent hours just lying on my bed, staring at nothing, Kate beside me, while the rain poured down outside, steaming up the windows, turning the garden into a quagmire.

My mother would bounce into my room each morning and fling back the curtains on another gray, sodden day, and say, "Well, what's on the agenda for today?"

I knew that she was only trying to cheer me up. And I tried to be cheerful. It was just that I was so tired all the time. She would then offer to make me my breakfast, but as soon as she left my room I would drag myself over to the window and close the curtains again.

I didn't neglect Kate. Really, I didn't.

Well, maybe I did.

To my eternal shame Mum brought her to the doctor for her check-up. Mum drove to the supermarket and bought mounds and mounds of disposable diapers and baby formula and talc and bottle sterilizer and everything else that Kate needed.

In fairness to me, I didn't abandon Kate entirely. I *did* take care of her in lots of ways. I fed her and changed her and washed her and worried about her. Sometimes I even played with her. I just couldn't seem to do anything that involved leaving the house for her.

Getting dressed was such a huge undertaking that I never managed it. On the rare occasions that I did get out of bed I put one of Dad's golfing sweaters on over Mum's nightgown and wore a pair of hiking socks. I would genuinely *intend* to get dressed for real. But later.

"As soon as I've fed Kate," I would say.

But after that I would be so exhausted that I would have to lie down for a while and read a few lines of an article in *Hello* magazine.

After lying down for a while I might have to pee. I would spend about half an hour trying to summon the energy to go to the bathroom. It was as if I were made of lead.

Once I got to the bathroom it was all I could do to stagger back to bed again.

"I'll just lie down again for five minutes," I would promise myself, "and then I really will get dressed."

But by then it would be time to feed Kate again.

And after that I would have to lie down again, just for five minutes. . . .

Somehow I just never got around to it.

If only I was left alone to sleep forever I would be all right. That's what I thought. But people kept bothering me.

I was lying in bed one afternoon (I don't know why I say "one afternoon"—it's not as though it wasn't a regular event) when a Neanderthal-looking young man carrying a hammer strolled into the room.

My initial reaction was that I had been cooped up too long and had started to hallucinate.

Then Mum burst in all breathless and anxious.

It turned out that the young man had come to install a baby intercom between my bedroom and the living room. Mum had watched him like a hawk downstairs but when she had gone to answer the phone he had escaped and made his way to my room.

Mum rushed over and forced me out of the bed as though it was the middle of the night and she was a group of secret policemen who were about to take me away and torture me. I still have her finger marks on my arms. My God, but she'd be lethal with an electric cattle prod. You see, she thought that I might give the intercom man impure thoughts if he had to work in close proximity to me while I was still in my nightgown, so it was a matter of acute urgency to get me moved as quickly as possible.

In addition to my displacement troubles with the intercom man, Helen never gave me a moment's peace. Most mornings she would stand in the bedroom doorway and look at me lying prostrate on my bed, and bellow, "Your breakfast is ready. And last one down the stairs is a big fat smelly pig!"

In an instant she would be gone, thundering back down the stairs to the kitchen, while I limply tried to tell her that I was a big fat smelly pig already. Therefore her challenge meant nothing to me.

Well, I was big and fat, that was for sure. Very watermelonesque. Well, at least I had been when I arrived in Dublin. I couldn't be certain now as I hadn't looked in a mirror or tried on any clothes since the day I left my apartment in London.

I was most certainly smelly. There was as much chance of me climbing Mount Everest as there was of me washing my hair.

I did have the occasional bath, but only because my mother organized the whole thing.

A combination of persuasion and coercion.

She would fill the bath with steaming and fragrant bubble bath so that I would smell of kiwifruit and papaya. She would put huge soft towels on the heated towel rack for me. She would offer me a loan of her lavender body lotion (ugh, no thanks). She would threaten to report me to the authorities for being an unfit mother. Kate, she told me, would be put in a foster home.

So I would have a bath every day or so.

Grudgingly.

But perhaps I wasn't a pig. I honestly couldn't remember the last time I had eaten anything. I was never hungry. The thought of eating something scared the life out of me. I knew that I wouldn't be able to. I felt frozen. As if my throat was blocked up and I wouldn't ever be able to swallow anything.

I couldn't believe that this was happening to me—I'd always had a very robust appetite. When I was pregnant, it was better than robust, more like steel-reinforced. I spent my teenage years praying desperately to be anorexic. I never lost my appetite, no matter what the occasion. Exam nerves, job interviews, wedding day jitters, food poisoning—nothing short of death made the slightest difference to my ability to eat like a racehorse. Whenever I met a thin person who would trill, "Oh, silly old me, I simply forget to eat," I would stare with ill-concealed bafflement and bitterness, feeling unglamorous and lumpy and bovine. The lucky bitches, I would think. How could *anyone* forget to eat? I had an appetite—what an untrendy and shameful thing to have.

Because when the world ends and we have shuffled off our mortal coils and we're all in Heaven and time ceases to exist and we are pure of spirit and have eternal life, which we will spend contemplating the Almighty, I will still need a Kit Kat every morning at eleven o'clock.

But I would console myself with the thought that these skinny people were probably lying through their teeth. They were really raging bulimics or taking amphetamines or having liposuction every weekend.

The days dragged on. Sometimes I would get out of bed and take Kate downstairs to watch a soap opera with Mum. I would have a cup of tea with her and then I would go back to my room.

Helen continued to plague me. Three days after the baby intercom was installed she tiptoed very elaborately into the room. "Is that on?" she mouthed, pointing at the intercom.

"What?" I asked crossly, looking up from my copy of a magazine. "No, of course it's not on. Why the hell would it be? Kate is here and so am I."

"Fine," she said, "fine, fine." With that she doubled over with mirth. She sat on the bed, shaking with laughter; tears ran down her face. I sat and stared at her with ill-concealed distaste.

"Sorry," she said, wiping her eyes and trying to assemble herself. "Ahem, right, sorry, sorry."

"What's going on?" I asked as Helen sat up straight.

"I'll show you now," she promised. "But you're not to make any noise."

She went over to the intercom and switched it on and started to say things into it in a croony, singsongy type of voice. "Anna," she crooned, "oooooohhhhhh, Aaaaaaan-nnaaaaaa."

I stared in fascination. "What on earth are you doing?" I asked.

"Shut up," she hissed as she turned the intercom off. "I'm giving Anna a psychic experience, d'you see?"

Still the rain bucketed down. The canal burst its banks. Roads were impassable. Cars were abandoned in flooded lanes. I heard about all these things from other people, as I never left the house.

I thought about James all the time. I would dream about him. Lovely dreams where we were still together. And when I woke up I would forget, for a few minutes, where I was and what had happened. I would be bathed in a gorgeous warm fuzzy happy feeling. And then I would remember. It was like being kicked in the stomach.

I had heard nothing from him. Absolutely nothing. I really had thought that after a week or so he would contact me. Just to see how I was or at least how Kate was. I couldn't believe that he had no interest at all in Kate, regardless of me.

The saddest thing of all was that he didn't even know her name was Kate.

I rang Judy when I'd been back in Dublin about five days. I asked her if James knew where I was and held my breath. Hoping and hoping that she would say that, no, he didn't know. That would at least explain why he hadn't contacted me. But she said, sadly, that James did know. Then, though it tore me apart to do so, I asked her if James was still with Denise. Once again, she said yes.

I felt, not that I was crying inside, but that I was bleeding inside. Bleeding to death.

I thanked Judy, and hung up the phone. My hands shook, my forehead sweated, I felt sick at heart.

There were times when I felt that James really would come back, sooner or later. That he had loved me so much that he just couldn't stop loving me overnight. That it was just a matter of time before he appeared on the doorstep, distraught with remorse, beside himself with guilt, wondering if it was too late to reclaim his wife and child. And, in that case, that it might be an idea to get out of bed and wash my hair and put on some makeup and wear some decent clothes in honor of his imminent arrival. But then I remembered what a contrary bastard Fate is. The more hideous I looked, the higher were the chances that James would arrive out of the blue.

So I stayed in the nightgown, the golfing sweater and the hiking socks. I wouldn't have known what lipstick was if it jumped up and bit me.

I often felt like calling him. But it always happened in the middle of the night. I would be gripped by terrible panic at the enormity of my loss. But I had no idea how to contact him. I hadn't been able to humble myself sufficiently to ask Judy for the phone number of the apartment he was sharing with Denise. I could have called him at work during the day, but the anxiety and the desire to talk to him never really came upon me in the daytime. I was really very glad about this. What good would calling him do? What could I say to him?

"Do you still not love me? Do you still love Denise?" To which he would reply, "No to the first question, yes to the second. Thank you for asking. Goodbye."

Time passed. Slowly, very slowly, my feelings started to change. The landscape of the desert changes very gradually as little breezes lift grains of sand and move them, sometimes a few feet, sometimes miles and miles, so that at the end of the day, when the sun sets, the face of the desert is completely different from the landscape it had in the morning when the sun rose on it. In the same way, tiny little changes happened in me.

But they were nearly too small for me to notice them as they were happening.

It wasn't so much that the lead weight of hopelessness had left. But something else had arrived. Ladies and gentlemen, put your hands together and give a warm welcome to Humiliation.

Yes, I started to feel humiliated.

What took you so long? I can hear you saying.

Well, sorry, chaps, but I had a major backlog of Loss and Abandonment in my in-box.

A little twinge of humiliation at first. An odd little feeling one day when I wondered how long Judy had known about James and Denise. That feeling expanded like a balloon until humiliation was nearly all I felt. I smarted with it. I was raw with it. My soul blushed with it.

Who had known that James was having an affair? I wondered.

Had all my friends known about it and talked about it among themselves and agonized about telling me?

Did they say things like "Oh, we can't tell her now, not when she's pregnant."

Did they look at me with pity?

Did they thank God that at least they could trust their husbands or boyfriends?

Did they say to themselves, "The one thing Dave/Frank/William would never do is have an affair. He mightn't do any housework/give me enough money/ever discuss a problem, but at least he wouldn't be unfaithful."

Did they look at me and sigh huge sighs of relief and say, even while feeling guilty, "I'm so glad it's her and not me."

I was so angry. I wanted to shout at the world, "You're wrong! I thought I could trust my husband! I thought he was too goddamn *lazy* to have an affair. But he did have one. And so could Dave/Frank/William."

When I thought about Denise I cringed. When I thought about herself and myself exchanging pleasantries about the weather and me complimenting her on how well she was looking and telling her how my pregnancy was going and thinking that she was so sweet and nice, when all the time she was having sex with my husband and making him fall in love with her, I wanted to travel back in time and grab myself by the scruff of the neck and drag myself, protesting, away from the conversation with Denise and admonish myself, like a mother to a naughty child, "Don't speak to that horrible woman."

And then I wanted to get Denise and beat the living daylights out of her.

Then I started to feel extremely angry at James.

The humiliation arrived gradually. It sidled its way in and one day I turned around and it was there, grinning at me. "Hi there," it said, as though we were old friends. "Remember me? And I'm sure my friend Jealousy needs no introduction."

I was with my mother one afternoon when she put a video on. Some film that was supposed to be a romance, but it was really an excuse for pornography. She was engrossed in it, and "tut-tutted" energetically. I tried to pay attention to it and feed Kate at the same time. I kept losing track of the plot. "Who's that he's having sex with now? Is that the woman from the elevator?"

"No, silly," said Mum. "It's the woman from the elevator's *daughter*."

"But I thought he was found in bed with the woman from the elevator," I said, confused.

"Yes, he was," explained Mum kindly. "But he's being unfaithful to her now, with her daughter."

"The poor woman from the elevator," I said sorrowfully.

Mum gave me a sharp glance. Oh God, no. I could feel her thinking in alarm. Was I going to start crying? I bet she was sorry that she hadn't gotten something innocuous like *The Amityville Horror* or *The Texas Chainsaw Massacre*.

I watched the two people on the screen, having sex, enjoying themselves at the cost of the woman in the elevator's happiness. I suddenly thought of James and Denise in bed.

They do this, you know, a voice in my head told me.

They go to bed together. They have sex. They lose themselves in their passion for each other. She touches him. She sleeps with his beautiful body and his delicious skin and his silky black hair. She can wake up and watch him sleeping, his spiky black eyelashes throwing little shadows on his face.

What are they like together? I found myself wondering. What way does he treat her? What's he like when he's with her?

Does he gently scrape his stubbly jaw across her face in the morning, the way he used to do to me and then laugh at my shout of outrage, his even teeth showing very white in his handsome face?

Does she go to sleep with her head on his muscular chest, her arm thrown across his stomach, his manly arm around her neck, smelling the faint scent of Tuscany from his lightly tanned skin, the way I used to?

Does he wake her in the morning by trailing his hands along her thighs, the way he used to with me, and instantly turn her on, the way he used to with me?

Does he pin her down in bed, his hands holding her arms above her head, his legs locking hers, grinning down at her, leaving her deliciously helpless as he moves slowly against her, driving her mad with desire, the way he used to with me?

Does he kiss her with an ice cube in his mouth, turning her mouth cold and her body hot with desire, the way he used to with me?

Does he gently bite the curve of her neck and shoulder and send shivers of lust through her whole body, the way he used to with me?

When she wakes up in the morning is her first thought, "Jesus, he's beautiful and he's in bed with me"? Because mine always was.

I was insane with jealousy.

Or do they do it differently? I wondered. Is she different from me in bed? Is she better? What's her body like? Has she a smaller butt, bigger tits, flatter stomach, longer legs? Is she really adventurous and does she drive him crazy with passion?

I wondered all this, even though I knew Denise and could have answered most of those questions myself. (Smaller butt? No. Bigger tits? Yes. Flatter stomach? Unlikely. Longer legs? Hard to tell. We're probably neck and neck.)

She didn't act or behave like a sex kitten. She had always seemed so nice and well . . . *ordinary*, I suppose, but now in my head she was Helen of Troy or Sharon Stone or Madonna.

I was being torn apart by jealousy. It was like having a

burning spiky ball in my chest that was sending out green poisonous rays all over my body, choking me so that I could barely breathe. My head was filled with pictures of what I imagined they were like together in bed.

I just couldn't bear the idea of his desiring her. It filled me with powerful and impotent rage. And fury. I felt like killing them both. I felt like sobbing hysterically. I felt ugly with jealousy. Disfigured with it. I felt my face was twisted and green with it.

It's such an ugly emotion. And it's so utterly pointless. And it has nowhere to go.

If you lose someone or something, you feel a loss, then after a while you fill in the hole in your life and the loss gradually gets smaller and smaller and eventually goes away. There's a point to the pain. There's a reason and a direction.

But there was nothing to be gained by feeling jealous. And I wouldn't have minded but the jealousy was caused entirely by myself. It was my own imagination that was causing me the pain.

And I was feeling the pain, not because something had happened to me but because something hadn't happened to me. Why did something that was going on between two other people and didn't involve me in any way hurt me so much?

Well, I was damned if I knew.

I just knew that it did.

seven

The time that followed is still referred to in our house as the Great Terror. Helen alludes to it even now by saying something like "Do you remember the time when you started behaving like Adolf Hitler and we all hated you and wished that you would go back to London?"

The change in me was terrible.

It was as though someone had flicked a switch.

I went from feeling sad and lonely and miserable to explosive rage and jealousy and desire for revenge on Denise and James. I fantasized about terrible disasters befalling them.

I was like a madman on a rampage. I had so much anger and hatred in me, and the person who should have been receiving the brunt of it—i.e., James—wasn't there. So my family, who were innocent bystanders, who, in fact, were trying to help me, ended up being shouted at and having their doors slammed instead of him.

When I first returned from London there had been a dignity to my suffering. I felt a bit like a Victorian heroine who had been disappointed in love and had no choice but to turn her face to the wall and die, albeit beautifully, surrounded by smelling salts, from her grief. Like Michelle Pfeiffer in *Dangerous Liaisons*.

Now I was more like Christopher Walken in *The Deer Hunter*. Psychotic. Crazed. A danger to myself and others. Walking around the house with a mad look in my eyes. Rooms full of conversation falling silent when I entered them. Mum

71

and Dad watching me fearfully. Anna and Helen leaving rooms when I arrived.

I wasn't wearing battle camouflage and didn't have a belt of bullets slung across my chest and wasn't carrying some kind of fearsome-looking automatic weapon and didn't have a grenade in my pocket. My face wasn't smeared with dirt (although on reflection it might have been; the baths went by the wayside completely during this terrible time). But I felt as powerful as if I had all those weapons, and I was treated with as much fear as if I did have them.

The Great Terror started the day I watched that video with Mum. (I won't go into the details of what happened there. I'm too ashamed of myself. And anyway the video shop agreed to drop the charges. It was totally true what the assistant said. They only stock the videos. It was no reflection on their personal opinions or morals. I was just a little bit overwrought at the time.)

The Great Terror continued for several war-torn days. Anything could trigger a tantrum in me, but especially romantic scenes on the television. My head constantly played a video of James and Denise in bed together. When I saw other loving couples on television I was pushed to overload.

Luckily I saw no loving couples in real life or I might not have been responsible for my actions. Mum and Dad certainly didn't behave like a loving couple. And Helen had a steady stream of young suitors through the house but she made cruel, teasing fun of them and their puppylike devotion. Which pleased me in a grim, cold kind of way. As for Anna—well, that's another story, to be told another day.

I cried an awful lot during this time. And swore. And threw things.

As I said, television usually upset me. I'd see a man lean over and kiss a woman and immediately the green fire of jealousy would rush through me, excruciating energy would fill me. I would think of James. And I would think of my James with another woman. For a second it would just be a thought in the abstract, as if he was still with me and I was being silly and imagining "worst possible" scenarios. And then I would remember that it *had* happened and that he *was* with another woman. The realization hurt just as much each time. The tenth time it happened it was as awful and as shocking and as sick-making as the first time.

So I might throw a book at the television, or some shoes at the wall, or Kate's bottle at the window. Or really anything handy or close by at all would be thrown at a nearby surface. Then I would swear like a fishwife and stomp from the room, slamming the door so hard that slates probably fell off the roof. It got so bad that when I thumped into the sitting room and the television was on, Anna or Helen, or whoever was there, would flick the remote control and quickly change the channel from whatever they were watching to something inoffensive like the Open University program on applied physics or a documentary about how fridges work or a game show in which all the contestants had obviously had lobotomies.

"What's on?" I would growl at them.

"Oh, err . . . just this," they would reply nervously, indicating the television with a flutter of their hands.

We would all sit there in silence, pretending to watch whatever program the remote control had found for us, me giving off palpably frightening vibes, Anna or Helen or Mum or Dad sitting stiffly, afraid to talk, afraid to suggest changing channels and waiting for a decent interval to elapse so they could leave and continue watching their program on the small television in Mum's room.

And when they would get up and start sidling to the door, I'd pounce on them. "Where are you going?" I'd demand. "You can't even bear to be in the same room as me, can you? It's bad enough that my husband has to leave me but imagine my own family treating me like this."

The poor victim would stand there awkwardly, feeling shamed into not leaving but definitely not wanting to stay.

And hating me for it.

"Well, go on then," I'd tell them viciously. "Go."

Because I was so terrifying no one, not even Helen, had the courage to tell me that I was being incredibly selfish and, in the vernacular, a right little bitch. I held the whole family at ransom with my wild tempers and unpredictable mood swings.

Kate was the only one I treated with any respect. And even that only happened occasionally.

Once when she started crying I shouted sharply at her, "Shut up, Kate!" Quite unbelievably, she stopped immediately. The silence that followed sounded almost stunned. Try as I might I haven't been able to reproduce that tone of voice since. I've practiced with all kinds of different inflections, like "Shut *up*, Kate," or "Shut up, *Kate*," or "*Shut* up, Kate," but it makes no difference. She blithely continues to bellow, no doubt thinking, "Ha! You might have frightened me once, for about a nanosecond, but you can be damn sure it won't happen again."

I had so much energy. My body wasn't big enough to contain all the energy that flowed through me. I went from having no energy to having far too much of it. I had no idea what to do with it. I felt as if I was going to explode with it. Or go crazy with it. I was torn because I didn't want to leave the house but I felt as if I could run a hundred miles. That I would go crazy if I didn't. I had the strength of ten men. During those awful couple of weeks I could have won gold medals in the Olympic games in any sport you care to mention.

I felt that I could run faster, jump higher, throw farther, lift heavier, punch harder than anyone alive.

That first night that the jealousy kicked in, I drank half a bottle of vodka.

I bullied Anna into loaning me fifteen pounds for it and Helen into going to the liquor store for it.

Anna would have willingly gone to the store for me.

And Anna would have willingly come back from the store for me.

But when, is the question.

She might have reappeared in a week with some vague story about how on the way to the store she met some people in a van who were going to Stonehenge and how she thought it might be nice to join them. Or how she had some strange out-of-body experience and lost a week.

I could have told her that there was nothing strange about it. That if she went over to her boyfriend Shane's apartment and smoked a lot of drugs that was what generally happened. And that the correct name for it was an out-of-your-head experience, not an out-of-body experience.

Not that it was an easy battle to win with Helen. "I'll drown," she grumbled, the weather still being inclement.

"You won't," I assured her grimly through gritted teeth, my tone of voice implying, "But it would be no trouble at all to arrange."

"It'll cost you," she told me, changing tack.

"How much?"

"A fiver."

"Give her another fiver," I ordered Anna.

Money changed hands.

"That's twenty that you owe me now," said Anna anxiously.

"Have I ever reneged on my debts before?" I asked Anna coldly.

"Er, no," said the poor girl, far too frightened to remind me that I still owed her for the bottle of wine that I "borrowed" from her the first night that she was home.

"And where are you going?" I asked Helen imperiously.

"Upstairs to change into my Speedos."

When Helen returned from the liquor store, a long time later, drenched wet and dripping water everywhere and complaining loudly, she handed me the liter bottle of vodka, which was in a soaking wet bag.

Change from the fifteen pounds was not asked for.

Nor was it offered.

By the time I discovered that the bottle had already been opened and about a quarter of it was missing, Helen was long gone.

As were her chances of making it alive to her nineteenth birthday.

My vengeance would be a terrible and awesome spectacle to behold, once I got my hands on her.

I was not a woman to be trifled with.

In spite of the vodka I still couldn't sleep. I roamed the house from room to room late at night when everyone else was asleep. Carrying the bottle and my glass. Looking for somewhere that I felt safe. Hoping to find a place where those horrible pictures would stop running through my head. But my jealousy and hatred kept me awake. They kept prodding at me and I couldn't settle anywhere. I couldn't find any peace.

In desperation, I thought that perhaps if I tried a different bed or a different room I might be able to sleep.

I went into Rachel's old room. (You know, the room you'll be staying in when you come on your starvation week.) I turned on the light.

The room had that same ghostly feeling that my and Margaret's room had had when I first arrived back from London, the feeling that no one had slept in there for a long time. Although clothes still hung in the wardrobe and posters were still on the wall and a plate was still under the bed. Then I came across the exercise bike and the rowing machine that Dad had bought about nine years ago in an enthusiastic but short-lived attempt to get fit.

There they were, on the floor of Rachel's room, covered in dust, looking old-fashioned and creaky and cobwebby, a far cry from the exercise bikes and rowing machines of today, with their computer programs, their video screens and their electronic calorie counters.

I looked at them affectionately, prehistoric and all that they were, and memories came rushing back in waves.

The excitement the day the van delivered them! Dad, my sisters and I were thrilled.

Mum was the only one who wasn't excited. She said that she couldn't understand what all the fuss was about, that she had no need to go courting pain and suffering. That she already had a surfeit of that in her life, what with being married to Dad and mother to the five of us.

The rest of us were beside ourselves.

We all clustered around oohing and aahing as the chrome-and-metal machines were unloaded and installed. We all held great hopes and high expectations. We thought that we would have bodies like Jamie Lee Curtis (she was very *in* then) from the briefest contact with them, and naturally demand to use them was high. Dad also said that he wanted a body like Jamie Lee Curtis, and Mum didn't speak to him for a week.

We all jostled and fought to use the machines in the beginning. Like a wartime munitions production line, they were in use around the clock, and more than one tear was shed and more than one harsh word was spoken in the pitched battles about who was next.

We especially loved the bike. Margaret, Rachel and I were obsessed with the size of our butts and thighs, and we spent the best part of our teenage years standing with our backs to full-length mirrors, almost breaking our respective necks as we tried to swivel our heads around without moving our bodies to see what our butts looked like from the back.

Asking each other anxiously, "What does my butt look like? Really big or just mediumly big?"

We wasted so much time torturing ourselves and worrying about the size of our butts.

It was so sad!

Because we were beautiful.

We had such lovely figures.

And we had no idea.

I'd now pay very large sums of money indeed to have the body that I had then. This made me think in alarm, "Jesus, will a day come when I look back at the body I have today and wish that I still had it?" Although I couldn't possibly imagine ever being that desperate.

A combination of accidents and disappointed expectations eventually caused the novelty of the madness to wear off.

Although Helen was only nine, she decided that she alone knew how the rowing machine worked. She assembled us all for a demonstration. To impress us, she set the weights far too high and then attempted to lift them without doing any warm-up exercises. She promptly pulled a muscle in her chest. And caused an almighty fuss.

The poor creatures who suffered at the hands of the Spanish Inquisition didn't screech and carry on as much as Helen did. She claimed to be paralyzed down one side; the only thing that relieved any of her symptoms was huge quantities of chocolate and around-the-clock attention.

Helen was Helen from a very early age.

According to her the pain was unbearable. She asked Dr. Blenheim to put her out of her misery. The rest of us also found her pain unbearable and agreed that she should indeed be put out of her misery.

But Dr. Blenheim said there was some kind of law against doing this. Murder or willful manslaughter or something, I believe he called it. Dad assured him that we preferred to call it a mercy killing.

And, as none of the rest of us ended up looking even remotely like Jamie Lee Curtis, in spite of all our exertions, we felt a little bit let down and disappointed and decided to get our own back on the bike by ignoring it.

After a while even Dad stopped pretending to use the machines. He muttered something vague about having read an article in *Cosmopolitan* about too much exercise's being as bad for you as none at all. I had read the article in question myself. It was actually about compulsive exercisers, truly sick people, but as far as Dad was concerned he now had a cast-iron excuse. He was perfectly justified in abandoning the bike and the rowing machine.

So the two machines were sadly discarded and left to gather dust, along with the pink leg warmers and pink-and-blue twisted sweatbands that we'd bought to look good on them.

In fact, Margaret and I had even bought Dad a pair of pink leg warmers and a sweatband. He wore them once to entertain us. I think there's still a photograph of it around somewhere.

In any event, I was very surprised when I almost tripped over the bike and the rowing machine in Rachel's room.

I hadn't seen them in years. I had thought that they would have long ago been exiled to the Siberia that is the garage along with the SpaceHopper, the pogo sticks, the roller skates, the skateboards, the game of Kerplunk!, the Trivial Pursuit, the swing ball, the squash rackets, the chopper bikes, the Teach Yourself Spanish tapes, the fiberglass canoe and the thousands of other toys and diversions that enjoyed a period of brief but fierce popularity—not to mention causing countless fights—in our family before they fell from favor and their appeal faded and they were cast into the outer darkness, to live with the lawn mower and the screwdrivers.

I was very glad to see them.

If a bit taken aback.

They were like old friends I hadn't seen in years and whom I had bumped into somewhere totally unexpectedly.

I can see now with the benefit of hindsight that what I really needed was a punching bag. So that I could have worked off some of the terrible anger I felt toward James and Denise.

But in the absence of a punching bag, and the fact that the current legislation forbade me from using Helen's head, the discovery of the bike and the rowing machine was a Godsend. I somehow realized that a little bit of physical exercise might be the one thing that would stop me from going around the bend and exploding with jealousy and resentment.

Either that or vast quantities of alcohol.

So I put down my bottle and my glass on Rachel's dressing table and climbed up on the bike, tucking the nightgown under me. Yes, I was still wearing one of Mum's nightgowns. Not the same nightgown that I started wearing the night I arrived back. Things hadn't gotten that bad. I hadn't sunk that low. But a nightgown that was definitely from the same stable.

Feeling a bit foolish (but not that foolish; after all, I had a half bottle of vodka under my belt), I started to cycle. And while the rest of the house slept I cycled and sweated. And then for a while I rowed and sweated. And then I got back on the bike again and cycled and sweated a bit more.

While James slumbered peacefully somewhere in London, his arm thrown protectively over Denis, I cycled like a madman, in a bedroom that still had posters of Don Johnson on the wall, hot, angry tears pouring down my puce face.

I couldn't help but feel sorry for myself at the poignant juxtaposition.

Every time I pictured the two of them in bed together I cycled even faster, as though if I cycled hard enough I'd get away from the pain.

When I thought of her touching his beautiful naked body I would get another spurt of furious sickening energy and I pushed my body even harder.

I was afraid that I would kill someone if I stopped cycling.

I hadn't exercised in months, had done nothing strenuous in ages (apart from give birth to a child) but I didn't get tired or even get out of breath.

The harder I pushed myself the easier it got.

I felt as if my thigh muscles were made of steel (and they definitely weren't, let me assure you). The pedals whizzed around in a blur. I felt as if my legs were lubricated, they worked so easily. It was as if someone had oiled my joints. I cycled faster and faster until eventually the tight hard knot in my chest started to unravel. A feeling of calm settled on me.

I was able to breathe almost normally.

When I eventually clambered down from the bike, the handlebars slippery from my sweat, my nightgown sticking to me, I felt nearly elated.

I went back into my room and lay down.

Kate eyed my scarlet face and my soaking nightgown but didn't seem particularly interested. I put my burning face on the cool pillow and knew that now I would be able to sleep.

I woke up very early the next morning. I even beat Kate to it. In fact, in a neat reversal of roles I woke her up with the sound of me crying.

"Now you see what it's like," I thought as I sobbed. "Is it any way to start the day?"

The specters of jealousy and anger returned.

They had stood over me as I slept, looking down at me. "Should we wake her now?" one consulted the other.

"All right," said Jealousy. "Would you like to do it?"

"Oh no, why don't you?" said Anger politely.

"It would be my pleasure," said Jealousy graciously. Then grabbed me roughly by the shoulder and shook me awake.

And I woke to the horrible picture in my head of James in bed with Denise.

The bitter rage was back, coursing through me like poison.

So after I fed Kate, I finished the rest of the vodka and then went back into Rachel's room and got back up on the exercise bike.

If there was any justice in the world I should have been as stiff as a poker after my exertions the previous night. But the one thing that I had learned over the past month was that there wasn't any.

Justice, that is.

So I wasn't as stiff as a poker.

I spent the next week or so eaten up by anger and jealousy. I hated James and Denise. I terrorized my family without even realizing that I was doing it. And when things got too much for me I climbed aboard the bike and tried to cycle away some of my terrible rage. I also drank far too much.

I owed Anna a fortune.

Helen was charging me extortionate amounts for going to the liquor store for me.

And the forces of supply and demand dictated that I had no choice but to pay her.

I was a buyer in a seller's market.

I couldn't face leaving the house yet, therefore I paid her.

Or rather, because I had no hard cash myself, Anna did.

I had every intention of paying Anna back, but in my own time. I wasn't particularly worried about the impact I was having on Anna's cash flow.

But I should have been.

I mean, she was only on welfare.

And she had a mid-weight to heavy drug habit to support. But I only cared about myself.

I was kind of half drunk most of the time. I thought that I'd numb the pain and anger by getting drunk. But it didn't really help. I just felt sort of lost and confused. And then when I sobered up, in the few minutes it would take for me to drink my next drink and for the effects to hit me, I would feel horribly depressed. Really, really bad.

It was only when I accidentally overheard a conversation among Mum, Helen and Anna that I realized how awful I was being.

I was just about to go into the kitchen when I caught the sleeve of my sweater (well, *Dad's* sweater) on a knob on the cabinet in the hall. While I extricated myself I heard Helen talking in the kitchen.

"She's such a bitch," Helen was complaining. "And we're afraid to watch anything on TV that has people kissing in it or anything, in case she goes ballistic."

Who were they talking about? I wondered. I was perfectly prepared to join in the character assassination, no matter who the unfortunate person was. That's how mean and bitter I was.

"Yes," Anna said, joining in. "I mean, yesterday when we were watching TV she threw the vase that I made for you for Christmas at the door, just because Sheila told Scott that she loved him."

"Did she?" asked Mum, sounding outraged.

I realized, with a shock, that they were talking about me.

Well, it must have been me. I was the one who had thrown that horrible vase at the door.

I stood quietly at the door and continued to eavesdrop like the horrible person that I had become.

"I really can't believe it," Mum went on, sounding shaken to the core. "And what had Scott to say about that?"

"Oh, Mum, can't you forget about *Down Drongo Way* for five minutes?" said Helen, sounding like she was going to cry with frustration. "This is serious. Claire is behaving like a monster."

"Well, maybe I am, but I learned everything I know from you, my dear," I thought acidly.

"It's like she's possessed!" continued Helen.

"Do you think she might be?" asked Anna with great excitement, obviously ready to whip out her Filofax and give them the name of a good exorcist. ("I hear he's great. All my friends use him.")

"Look, girls," said Mum gently, "she's been through an awful lot."

"Yes, I bloody well have," I silently agreed, standing frozen at the door.

"So have a bit of sympathy. Try and have a little bit of patience. You can't imagine how awful she must feel."

"No, you most certainly can't," I mutely concurred.

A silence followed.

"Good," I thought, "that's shamed them."

"She broke your Aynsley ashtray last night," mumbled Helen.

"She did what?" said Mum sharply.

"Yes, she did," confirmed Anna.

"Right," said Mum decisively. "She's gone far enough."

"Ha!" said Helen triumphantly, obviously speaking to Anna. "I told you that Mum didn't care about that crappy old vase that you made for her."

"Time I left," I thought.

I quietly went back upstairs, feeling shaken. A strange feeling had come over me. I later looked it up in my emotional reference book and identified it. There could be no doubt about it.

It was definitely Shame.

Later that evening I had a visit from my dad. I'd been expecting it.

This is what used to happen whenever I misbehaved when I was younger. Mum would discover the indiscretion or misdeed or wrongdoing or whatever. She would then send in the heavy guns by telling Dad.

He knocked quietly and then stuck his head around my bedroom door, looking distinctly sheepish.

It had been a long time since he'd had to do this. No doubt Mum was behind him, in the hall with an electric cattle prod, hissing, "Get in there and tell her. Put the fear of God in her. She won't listen to me. She's afraid of you."

"Hello, Claire, can I come in?" he asked.

"Sit down, Dad," I said, indicating the bed.

"Hello, my favorite grandchild," he said to Kate.

I didn't catch her reply.

"Well!" he said, trying to be jovial.

"Well," I agreed dryly. I was not making this easy for him.

I was feeling a horrible mixture of feelings. A combination of shame, mortification, embarrassment at my childish behavior, defensiveness at being told off, resentment at being treated like a child and a realization that it was time that I stopped behaving like a selfish bitch. I was also worried that he'd spot the two empty vodka bottles under the bed.

"You're being selfish and irresponsible," said Dad.

"I know," I mumbled.

I felt sick with guilt.

And what kind of mother was I being to Kate?

"And what kind of mother are you being to Kate?" he asked.

"A terrible one," I mumbled.

The poor child, I thought, it's bad enough that her father has abandoned her.

"The poor child," said Dad. "It's bad enough that her father has abandoned her. Drink never drowns anyone's sorrows," he went on. "It only teaches them how to swim."

You might think that this was a very profound and true thing that he'd just said.

So had I.

The first eight hundred times I heard it.

But now I recognize it for what it really is. It's the first line, the opening paragraph, in Dad's "The Evils of Drink" lecture. I heard it so many times in my teenage years that I could practically recite it myself.

And, God knows, I don't want to end up like Auntie Julia, I thought.

"And, God knows, you don't want to end up like Aunt Julia," said Dad wearily.

Poor Dad. Auntie Julia was his youngest sister and he'd had to bear the brunt of most of her alcohol-related crises.

When she would lose her job because she was drunk at work, the first thing she did was to call Dad.

When she got knocked down by a bicycle because she was wandering the road drunk late at night who did the police call?

That's right.

Dad.

It's money down the drain, I thought.

"And it's money down the drain," he said heavily.

Money I don't have.

"Money you don't have," he continued.

And it'll destroy my health.

"And it'll destroy your health," he advised.

It'll ruin my looks.

"It solves nothing," he concluded.

Wrong! He forgot to tell me that it'll ruin my looks. I'd better remind him.

"And it'll ruin my looks," I reminded him gently.

"Oh, yes," he said hurriedly. "And it'll ruin your looks."

"Dad, I'm sorry for everything," I told him. "I know I've been really mean to everyone and a worry to you all, but I'll stop. I promise."

"Good girl." He gave me a little smile.

I felt as if I was about three and a half all over again.

"I know it can't be easy for you," he said.

"It's still no excuse to behave like a bitch," I admitted.

We sat in silence for a few minutes.

The only sounds were of Kate snoring happily—maybe she was as glad as everyone else that I'd had my comeuppance—and me sniffing back tears.

"And you'll let the girls watch their shows on the TV?" Dad inquired.

"Of course," I sniveled.

"And you'll stop shouting at us all?" he asked.

"I will," I said, hanging my head.

"And you won't throw any more things?"

"I won't throw any more things."

"You're a good girl, you know." He half smiled at me. "No matter what your mother and your sisters say."

eight

After Dad had given me my pep talk the previous evening he kissed me—awkwardly, mind you—but it was still a kiss, and without being able to look me in the eyes he told me he loved me.

Then he gently shook Kate's soft pink little foot and left the room.

And I lay on my bed for a long time thinking about what he had said. And what I had overheard Mum and my sisters saying earlier.

And some kind of change came over me.

Some kind of peace entered my soul.

Life goes on.

Even my life.

I had spent the last month releasing myself on my own recognizance from life. The excessive sleeping, the drinking, the exercising, the not washing myself. They were all things I had used to keep life at bay.

But life was an irrepressible kind of a chap, and no matter how much I tried to pretend that he wasn't there he kept poking his head through any gaps in my defenses and trying to get me to play with him.

"Oh, *there* you are," he would say exuberantly, as bouncy as a rubber ball, as I lay on my bed alone.

"Oh, fuck off and leave me alone," I would reply. But after Dad's talk I decided that I had to start living again.

And I had to stop thinking just of myself.

I had to do it. And I would be able to do it.

I still loved James very much. I still wanted him back. I was still heartbroken. I still missed him like a limb. I would probably still cry myself to sleep every night for the next century.

But I was no longer utterly crippled by my loss.

I had been cracked across the ankles by the cricket bat of James's infidelity and betrayal. It had sent me crashing to the ground, leaving me lying there gasping with pain, unable to stand up.

But, contrary to first impressions, nothing was broken. Now I was clambering painfully to my feet and seeing if I could still walk.

And though I was limping badly, I discovered to my joy that I could.

I'm not saying that I didn't feel jealous. Or angry.

Because I did.

But it wasn't so bad. The feeling wasn't as big. Wasn't as powerful. Wasn't as horrible.

Put it this way. I still wouldn't have turned down the chance to punch Denise in the stomach or to blacken James's eye but I no longer entertained fantasies of sneaking into their secret love nest and pouring a huge vat of boiling oil over their sleeping bodies.

Believe me, this was progress.

So bloodied and bowed, but not *as* bowed, I decided to relaunch myself on the world with the minimum of fanfare.

As I drifted off to sleep I counted my blessings.

Well, that's not exactly true. I didn't actually *count* them. I didn't say to myself, "Well, that's five blessings that I have. Now I can go to sleep happy."

But I did think about the good things in my life:

I had a beautiful daughter.

I had a loving family. (Well, I was sure they'd be loving again just as soon as I stopped behaving like an Antichrist.)

I was still youngish.

I had somewhere to live.

I had a job to go back to in five months.

I had my health (bizarre—I never thought I'd hear myself say that this side of ninety).

And most of all, and I'd no idea where it came from, I had some hope.

I slept like a baby.

Actually, I did nothing of the sort. Did I wake every two hours, demanding to be fed or changed? No I did not. But I slept very peacefully.

And that was plenty for now.

I would love to be able to tell you that the next morning when I woke up the rain had stopped and the clouds had been chased away and the sun had come out on a brand-new blue-skied day.

However, real life isn't like that.

It was still drizzling.

But what the hell.

I woke at the usual crack-of-dawn time and fed Kate. I gently probed my feelings, the way you probe the gum around a sore tooth with your tongue. And I was delighted to discover that my mood hadn't changed from the previous evening. I was still feeling alive and hopeful.

It was absolutely thrilling.

I went back to sleep and woke again at about eleven. There was a bit of a fuss going on in the shower room. Apparently, Helen had discovered a lump in her breast and was screaming bloody murder. Mum came running up the stairs and after a consultation I heard her telling Helen angrily, "Helen, that's not a lump on your breast, that *is* your breast."

Mum thumped back down the stairs muttering to herself. "Frightening the life out of me . . . I'll kill her."

Helen got dressed and left for college.

And I had a shower.

I even washed my hair.

And then I tidied my room.

I fished the two empty vodka bottles out from under the bed. Next I rounded up all the glasses I had used over the past couple of weeks and assembled them in military formation to be brought downstairs to the dishwasher. I picked up the pieces of the glass I had broken by flinging it at the wall one particularly upset and drunken night and wrapped the shards in an old newspaper.

And most symbolic of all, I threw out every magazine in the room. I felt cleansed and purified.

I no longer wanted to read crappy magazines. I would put myself on a strict diet of *Time*, the *Economist* and the *Financial Times* from now on.

And just once in a while I would glance at the copy of *Marie Claire* that Dad bought every month, ostensibly for Helen and Anna, but which he really bought for himself. He absolutely loved it. Although he dismissed it as womanly rubbish. Frequently we would stumble upon him surreptitiously reading it. While he neglected his household chores, I might add. Often he would be found engrossed in some article, maybe about female circumcision or compulsive sexual behavior or the best methods of removing the hair from one's legs, while the carpets remained unvaccumed.

Finally, after having mulled it over for about a month, I decided that I would get dressed.

And would you believe it, when I tried on the pair of James's jeans that I had worn over on the plane from London they no longer fit me.

What I mean is they were far too *big*.

That's what living on a diet of vodka and orange juice for a month does for you. (But don't try this at home.)

So I went into Helen's room to raid her wardrobe. Because, by God, she owed me. She'd bled me dry over the past two weeks or so with her extortionate demands for "expenses" for going to the store for me. And fond as I was of Anna, I didn't want to wear one of her long shapeless dresses, all bells and mirrors and tassles.

In Helen's room, on her chair—along with a huge mound of pristine, totally untouched, very expensive textbooks—I found a lovely pair of leggings.

Very flattering. They made my legs look long and slim.

In her wardrobe I found a beautiful blue silk shirt.

And would you believe that was very flattering also. It made my skin look very clear and my eyes look very blue.

I looked at myself in the mirror and got a shock of recognition.

"Hey, I know her," I thought. "It's me. I'm back."

For the first time in months my reflection looked normal. I didn't look like a watermelon with legs because I was no longer either great with child or as fat as a fool. And I didn't look like some kind of escapee from a mental institution, all uncombed hair and voluminous nightgown and deranged face.

It was just me, the way I remembered myself.

I drenched myself in Helen's Obsession, even though I hated it, and after satisfying myself that there was nothing else of hers that I could help myself to, I went back to my room.

I even put on some makeup. Just a little bit. I didn't want Mum calling the police to report a strange woman intruder on the premises.

Then I leaned over Kate's bassinet and introduced the new me (or rather the old me) to her.

"Hello, darling," I cooed. "Say hello to Mummy."

Before I could apologize to her for looking like such a mess for the first month of her life, she started crying.

She obviously had no idea who I was. I didn't look or smell anything like the person she was used to.

I shushed her and calmed her down. I explained to her that this was actually the real me and the other woman who had been looking after her for the past month was an evil impersonation of her mother.

She seemed to find this a reasonable enough explanation.

And then I went downstairs to see Mum, who was watching television.

"Hi, Mum," I said as I came into the sitting room.

"Hello, love," she said, glancing up from the TV. Then she swiveled around, doing a double take that nearly gave her whiplash.

"Claire!" she exclaimed. "You're up! You're dressed! You look beautiful. Isn't this great!" And she got up from the couch and came over to me and gave me a huge hug. She looked so happy. I hugged her back and the two of us stood there like idiots, grinning, with tears in our eyes.

"I think I'm getting over it," I said shakily to her. "At least I think I'm starting to get over it. And I'm sorry for being such a bitch. And I'm sorry for worrying you all so much."

"You know you don't have to apologize," she said gently,

still holding me by the arms and smiling into my eyes. "We know it's been awful for you. And we just want you to be happy."

"Thanks, Mum," I whispered.

"So what are you going to do today then?" she asked cheerfully.

"Well, I think I'll watch the end of this with you," I said, indicating the television. "And then I'm going to cook dinner for all of us this evening."

"That's very nice of you, Claire," said Mum a bit doubtfully. "But we all know how to work the microwave."

"No, no," I protested, laughing. "I mean I'm going to actually cook a real dinner for you all. As in, you know, go to the supermarket and buy fresh ingredients and make something from scratch."

"Oh really," said my mother, and a faraway look came into her eyes. "It's a long time since a real dinner was cooked in that kitchen."

She said it in the manner that some wise ancient old crone from a legend might say, "Oh, it be many a long and luckless year since a tall strong young man from the McQuilty clan broke bread under the same roof as a young man from the McBrandawn clan that we didn't hear the clash of steel on steel, and the streets didn't run with the blood of brave young warriors"—or something similar.

It was on the tip of my tongue to say that a real dinner had *never* been cooked in that kitchen, at least not while it was the ancestral family home of the Walsh clan and while Mum was at the helm of the nourishment ship, but I stopped myself from saying it just in time.

"It's no big deal, Mum," I told her. "I'll just do some pasta or something."

"Pasta," she breathed, still with the faraway look in her eyes, as if recalling another life, another time, another world. "Yes." She nodded, some kind of recognition appearing in her eyes. "Yes, I remember pasta." (She was still using the sort of voice where you would expect her to say "aye" instead of "yes.")

"Jesus!" I thought in alarm. "Has she been so traumatized

in the past by her encounters with cooking that this suggestion has unhinged her totally?"

"So is it all right if I borrow the car to go down to the shopping center to buy some stuff?" I asked her, feeling a bit nervous about it.

"If you must," she said faintly, resignedly. "If you must."

She gave me the car keys and we put Kate on the back seat in her car seat. Mum stood on the step and waved me off as if I was going away forever, instead of just down the road to the supermarket.

But it was a bit of an adventure. I hadn't left the house in weeks. It was an indication that I was on the mend.

"Have a good time," she said. "And remember, if you change your mind about making the dinner, don't worry. No harm done. You won't be letting any of us down. We can have the usual. No one will mind."

Why did I get the idea that she didn't want me to cook anything? I wondered as I drove away.

I had a really lovely time in the supermarket, strolling the aisles, pushing my cart, with Kate in a sling on my front. Buying the provisions for myself and my child, playing happy families, even if it happened to be happy single parent families.

I bought another twenty tons of Pampers for Kate. Mum and Dad had been so good, buying all the baby provisions while I had been prostrate with either grief or alcohol. But it was time for me to be responsible. I would be the one who took care of Kate from now on.

I flung all kinds of frivolous and exotic food into my trolley. Galia melons? Yes, I'll have a couple of them. A box of hand-made fresh cream chocolates? Why not. A bag of highly over-priced glamorous lettuces? Go right ahead.

I was having a great time.

Hang the expense. Because I was going to pay by credit card.

And where did the credit card bills get sent to?

That's correct. My apartment in London.

So who was going to have the responsibility of paying it?

Right again.

James.

I smiled at other young and not-so-young mothers who were also doing their shopping.

I must have seemed just like one of them. A young woman with a new baby. With absolutely nothing to worry about except perhaps the possibility of not getting a full night's sleep in the next decade. There was nothing to indicate that my husband had left me.

I no longer carried my humiliation like a weapon.

And I didn't begrudge anyone else her perfect life. I didn't hate every other woman in the world whose husband hadn't left her.

How did I know that the woman I exchanged smirks with over the avocados was blissfully happy?

How did I know that the woman I gently jostled as I got my bottle of honey and mustard dressing off the shelf was completely free of all concerns?

Everyone had their own worries.

Nobody was perfectly happy.

I hadn't been singled out especially by the gods for misery to descend on me.

I was just an ordinary woman with ordinary problems, doing her shopping, among other ordinary women.

I passed the alcohol department and I caught a glimpse of rows and rows of bottles of vodka, glittering and shimmering, silver light glinting off them. Almost as though I could hear them all calling, "Hey, Claire, over here! Pick me, pick me! Can we come home with you?" I instinctively turned my trolley in that direction.

And then turned it away again.

"Remember Auntie Julia," I told myself sternly.

A little bit shaken, I cruised the frozen desserts aisle. When I was pregnant I'd eaten frozen chocolate mousse by the truckload. In fact, it used to really annoy James.

So I thought I'd get myself one for old time's sake.

And as a mark of defiance.

I held Kate up to show her the rows and rows of boxes of chocolate mousse.

"Meet the family," I said.

I took out a box and held it for her to see.

"You see that?" I told her. "Without that you probably

wouldn't be here." She looked at it with her round blue eyes and reached out her fat little arm to touch the condensation on the box. Obviously something in her blood was calling out to the chocolate mousse, something as old as mankind, recognizing something that had befriended her mother through rough times.

I went and paid, gaining a lot of pleasure from the astronomical amount that James would be charged on the credit card.

And home we went.

On the way we stopped at the bank. As soon as Anna got home I was going to give her back every penny that I owed her. At least now she could pay her dealer. And thereby continue to have an intact pair of kneecaps.

nine

I had to ring the doorbell when we arrived back home as I had left without a key. Mum answered.

"I'm home," I said to her. "We had a great time, didn't we, Katie?" Mum watched me as I carried plastic bag after plastic bag into the kitchen, circling me suspiciously while I unpacked the groceries onto the kitchen table.

"Did you get everything you needed?" she asked tremulously.

"Everything!" I confirmed enthusiastically.

"So you're still going ahead with this idea of making them their dinner?" she said, sounding on the verge of tears.

"Yes, Mum," I told her. "Why are you upset about it?"

"I really wish you wouldn't do this," she said anxiously. "You'll give them notions, you know. They'll expect cooked dinners all the time after this. And who'll be expected to do it? Not you, that's for sure. Because by then, you'll have gone off back to London."

Poor Mum, I thought. Maybe I was being insensitive, showing off my fancy cooking in her kitchen.

She paused while I cheerfully put some fresh pasta on a shelf in the fridge. "Are you listening to me?" She raised her voice, as her view of me was blocked by the fridge door.

"They're perfectly happy with the microwave stuff," she continued. "Did you ever hear the expression 'if it ain't broke, don't fix it?' And what's that?" she demanded, pouncing on a cellophane bag of fresh basil leaves and poking them suspiciously.

"That's basil, Mum," I said, swishing past her to pack some pine nuts away in the cupboard.

"And what does that do?" she asked, staring at it as if it were radioactive.

"It's an herb," I replied patiently. Poor Mum, I understood now insecure and threatened she was feeling.

"Well, it can't be much of an herb if they couldn't even put it in a jar," she declared triumphantly.

She might be feeling insecure and threatened, but she had still better watch her step, I thought grimly.

And immediately I regretted it. I was feeling, hell, almost happy. No need to be mean to anyone. No need to get cross with anyone.

"Don't worry, Mum," I told her apologetically. "I'm not making anything special. They probably won't even notice the difference between this and the frozen stuff."

"Maybe today you won't make it as nice as you usually do," she said hopefully.

"Maybe I won't," I agreed kindly.

I started opening and shutting cupboards, searching for utensils for making the pesto sauce. It soon became apparent that despite our refrigerator-freezer and our microwave, in all other respects our kitchen was the Kitchen That Time Forgot. In one of the cupboards there was an enormous heavy beige ceramic mixing bowl with about an inch of dust on it. It was probably a wedding present when Mum got married nearly thirty years ago. And it looked as if it had yet to be used. There was a charming artifact of a hand whisk that could have been from the Bronze Age or could be even older. It was in marvelous condition, considering its great age.

There was even a cookbook that was printed in 1952 with recipes that included powdered egg in the list of ingredients and faded sepia-tinted pictures of heavily decorated Victorian sandwiches.

Positively prehistoric.

It wouldn't have surprised me in the slightest if a couple of dinosaurs lumbered through the kitchen door, had a slice of bread and butter and a glass of milk while standing at the counter, put their plates and glasses in the dishwasher, nodded civilly to me and lumbered out again.

I thought with a pang of loss of my well-stocked kitchen in London. My blender, my food processor that could do everything except tell funny stories, my juice extractor—not just a citrus fruit one, mind, but a proper juicer. I could certainly have done with them now.

"Haven't you got anything at all that I could use for chopping?" I asked Mum in exasperation.

"Well," she aid doubtfully, "how about this? Would this be any good?" she said anxiously, offering me an egg mandolin, still in its box.

"Thanks, Mum, but no." I sighed. "What am I going to use to chop the basil?"

"In the past I've usually found that one of these works quite well," she said, now in a slightly sarcastic tone, obviously a little bit fed up with my pretentious antics. "It's called a knife. I'm sure that if we ring around we could find a shop in Dublin that stocks them."

Suitably humbled, I accepted the knife and started to chop the basil.

"And what exactly are you making?" asked Mum, who sat watching me looking half resentful, half fascinated, as if she couldn't believe something as outlandish as cooking was going on in her kitchen.

"A sauce to go with the pasta," I told her as I stood chopping. "It's called pesto."

She sat there silently, just looking at me as I worked.

"And what's in that?" she asked after a while, obviously hating herself for asking.

"Basil, olive oil, pine nuts, Parmesan cheese and garlic," I told her calmly and matter-of-factly.

I didn't want to panic her.

"Oh yes," she murmured, nodding sagely, knowingly, as if she encountered such ingredients every day of her life.

"First of all I chop the basil very finely," I told her, in the same manner that a surgeon uses to explain to his prospective patient how he will perform the triple bypass.

Gently, thoroughly, dispelling any mystique.

("First of all, I break your sternum.")

"Then I add the olive oil," I continued.

("Then I open up your rib cage.")

"Then I crush the pine nuts, from the bag here," I told her, rustling the bag.

("Then I borrow some veins from your leg—have a look on the chart here.")

"Finally I add the crushed garlic and the Parmesan cheese," I finished. "Simple!"

("Then we sew you back up and in a month's time you'll be walking two miles a day!")

Mum seemed to take all this information calmly in her stride. I must say, I was proud of her.

"Well, go easy on the garlic," she told me. "It's hard enough to get Anna to come home as it is. We don't want the poor little vampire to think we're picking on her."

"Anna's not a vampire." I laughed.

"How do you know?" asked Mum. "She certainly looks like one a lot of the time, all that hair and those awful long purple dresses and that desperate makeup. Would you not have a word with her and try to get her to smarten herself up a bit?"

"But the way she looks is the way she is," I told Mum as I put the chopped basil into a saucepan. "It's Anna. She wouldn't be Anna if she looked different."

"I know," sighed Mum. "But I'm sure the neighbors think we don't clothe the child at all. And those boots! I've a good mind to just throw them out on her."

"Oh no, Mum, please don't do that," I said anxiously, thinking that Anna would break her heart without the Doc Martens she had so lovingly painted with sunrises and flowers.

I must admit that I was also slightly concerned about whose shoes Anna would wear if hers were thrown out. I feared for mine.

"I'll have to see," threatened Mum darkly. "And now what are you doing?"

"I'm adding the olive oil," I told her.

"What did you buy oil for?" she demanded, obviously thinking that she had a bunch of idiots for daughters. "There's a bottle of oil that I use to fry french fries. You could have used that and saved yourself the money."

"Er . . . thanks. I'll know the next time," I told her.

There was really no point in trying to explain to her the difference between, on the one hand, extra extra virgin Tuscan cold-pressed prime olive oil and, on the other hand, vegetable oil that had been recycled about ten times and had little bits of blackened, charred french fries floating in it.

I might be unnecessarily pretentious when it comes to food, but goddammit, you can go too far in the other direction too.

"Right!" I said. "For my next trick, I will, without the aid of a safety net, grate the Parmesan cheese."

I took the hunk of cheese out of the fridge, where it was obviously terrorizing everything else in it. The packets of sliced plastic cheese were shrinking against the back wall of the fridge, frightened out of their wits by this exotic newcomer.

But grating the cheese was easier said than done.

I searched high and low but there wasn't a grater to be found.

Eventually I located a grater of sorts, though it barely belonged to the genus "grater." It wasn't even one of the round ones that at least stand by themselves, never mind an electric one. It was just a little piece of metal with ridges on it. And you would have to be a more dexterous person than I am to be able to maneuver the lump of cheese and grate it successfully on this contraption. My hands kept slipping and I would grate a goodly portion of my knuckles along with the cheese.

Mum tut-tutted as I blasphemed and then she started sniffing in alarm as the characteristic aroma of the Parmesan cheese filled the kitchen.

A commotion broke out in the hall. The sounds of voices and laughter. Mum glanced at the clock hanging on the kitchen wall.

She did this although the clock hands had stood at ten to four since the Christmas before last.

"They're home," she said.

Dad brought Helen home from college most evenings, so they arrived together. He did this in spite of the fact that he had to drive about ten miles out of his way to get her.

Helen burst through the door, looking absolutely beautiful. In fact, even more beautiful than usual, if that could be possible. There was a kind of radiance around her. Even though she was just wearing jeans and a top she looked exquisite. Her hair long and silky, her skin translucent, her eyes glowing, her perfect little mouth in a charming smile.

"Hi everyone, we're home," she announced. "Hey, what's that awful smell? Phew! Did someone get sick?"

We could hear the sounds of people talking in the hall. Dad was talking to someone with a male voice.

We obviously had company.

My heart did an involuntary little somersault. I still hadn't stopped hoping for James to arrive unexpectedly on the doorstep. However, the male voice was more likely to belong to one of Helen's friends.

Although it would be more accurate to call them Helen's slaves.

Even though I knew I was being silly to think that James might just appear out of the blue I still felt a pang of disappointment pierce me when Helen said, "Oh, I brought a friend home with me. Dad's showing him where to hang his coat up."

Then she looked at me. "Hey!" she shouted. "What are you doing wearing my clothes? Get them off this minute."

"Sorry, Helen," I stammered. "But I had nothing else. I'll buy new ones and you can borrow them all."

"You can be bloody sure of it," she said darkly.

And she left it at that.

Thank God! She must be in a good mood.

"Who's this lad that you've brought?" asked Mum.

"His name is Adam," said Helen. "And you have to be nice to him because he's going to write my essay."

Mum and I started to assemble our facial features into expressions that were both welcoming and compassionate. Another poor boy had fallen for Helen. Like a lamb to the slaughter, we were both thinking.

I went back to grating the cheese and my knuckles.

"That's Mum," said Helen's voice, obviously introducing the doomed Adam to Mum.

"And that's Claire over there," continued Helen. "You know, the one I told you about. The one with the baby."

Thank you, Helen, you little cow, I thought, for making my life sound like some kind of dreary inner-city kitchen sink drama.

I turned around, ready to smile kindly at Adam, and extended my hand, reeking of Parmesan and with its pulped knuckles.

And got a bit of a shock.

This wasn't one of Helen's usual callow youths.

This one really was a man.

A young one, I grant you.

But undeniably a man.

Over six feet tall and very sexy.

Long legs. Muscley arms. Blue eyes. Square jaw. Big smile.

If we had a testosteroneometer hanging on the kitchen wall the mercury level would have gone through the ceiling. And I was just in time to see him giving Mum the firmest handshake of her life.

He then turned his attention to me. Out of the corner of my eye I saw Mum shaking her crushed hand and surreptitiously inspecting her wedding ring to see if it had been bent out of shape.

"Er, hello," I said, feeling flustered and confused. It was a long time since I had encountered such a strong concentration of manliness.

"Nice to meet you." He smiled at me, holding my mutilated hand gently in his huge one.

My God, I thought, feeling a bit overwhelmed, you know you're getting old when you start noticing how young-looking all the gorgeous men are.

I could hear Helen's voice, but it seemed to be coming from a long way away. It was drowned out by the roaring sound of all the blood in my body rushing to my face to make me blush in a way that I haven't done since I was fifteen.

"Seriously," she was saying. "There's an awful smell of puke."

"That's not puke," Mum was saying knowledgeably. "That's the smell of the Palmerstown cheese. You know, for the presto sauce."

ten

Dinner was a bit of an odd affair because we were all slightly taken aback by Adam.

Helen has always had hordes of men (although it's more accurate to call them boys) in love with her. A day didn't pass that the phone didn't ring with some stammering youth on the other end of the line.

And the house had a steady stream of male visitors. Their invitation to tea usually coinciding with the breakdown of Helen's stereo, or Helen's desire to have her room painted, or, as in this case, Helen's needing to have an essay written and Helen's having no intention of doing it herself.

And the promised tea rarely materialized on completion of the task.

But none of them had been like Adam.

They were usually a bit more like Jim, one of Helen's earliest conquests.

Poor Jim, to give him his full title.

He was lanky and skinny and went around wearing black all the time and all year round. Even at the height of summer, he wore a long black overcoat that was miles too big for him and big black boots. He dyed his plentiful hair black and never looked me in the eye. He didn't talk much, and when he did it was usually to discuss suicide methods. Or to talk about singers from obscure bands who had killed themselves. He once said "Hello" to me and gave me a kind of sweet little smile, and I thought that I had misjudged him but I later discovered that he was blind drunk.

He always carried a decrepit copy of *Fear and Loathing in Las Vegas* or *American Psycho* in the torn lining of his black overcoat. He wanted to be in a band and kill himself when he was eighteen.

Helen absolutely hated him.

He was always calling her, and whenever he did, Mum would speak to him on the phone and lie through her teeth as to Helen's whereabouts. She would say something like "No, Helen's missing, presumed drunk" while Helen stood in the hall looking at Mum, waving her arms frantically and mouthing "Tell him I'm dead."

After Mum had hung up the phone she would shout at Helen.

"I'm not doing any more lying for you. I'm putting my immortal soul in peril. And why won't you talk to him? He's a nice lad."

"He's an asshole," Helen would reply.

"He's just shy," Mum would say in his defense.

"He's an asshole," Helen would maintain, louder this time.

On occasions like Valentine's Day or Helen's birthday, at least one bunch of black roses would be delivered from him. Handmade cards would come in the post with very graphic pictures of shattered hearts and blood, or a single red teardrop. Terribly symbolic.

There was a time when you couldn't go into our kitchen without finding Jim in there, still wearing the long black coat and talking to Mum. Mum had become his best friend. His only ally in his quest to win Helen's heart.

Most of Helen's would-be boyfriends spent far more time with Mum than they ever did with Helen.

Dad hated him. Possibly even more than Helen did.

I think he felt disappointed by Jim.

Because Dad was so starved of male company he had hoped to do a bit of male bonding with him, what with Jim being a more or less permanent fixture in the kitchen along with the oven and the refrigerator.

One evening he came home from work, and as usual found Jim sitting in the kitchen with Mum. Helen went straight to her room as soon as she heard that Jim was on the premises. Dad sat at the kitchen table attempting to talk to Jim.

He said, "Did you see the game?"

Jim just looked at Dad completely blankly.

So that was the end of that: now Dad also thought Jim was a dead loss. He said that Jim should put his money where his mouth was and stop just talking about killing himself and actually get on with it.

Mum said that Jim was really a little pet, once you got to know him. And that it was a sin to encourage someone to take his own life.

It felt as if Jim was always around. Whenever I came home from London he seemed to be drooped over the kitchen table, with a little black cloud hovering over his head. But I always said "Hello, Jim" to him. At least I was polite.

Even if he totally ignored me.

Then I discovered why he had been ignoring me.

On my second day home from London the doorbell rang and I went and answered it and found a haircut wearing a big long black coat standing on the front doorstep. I wasn't sure whether he had come to see Helen or Mum, but Mum was out so I called Helen.

"Helen, Jim's at the door."

Helen came down the stairs looking puzzled.

"Oh hello, Conor," she said to the gloomy youth on the step.

She turned to me.

"Where's Jim?" she asked.

"Well . . . here . . . isn't he?" I said, a bit startled, indicating the boy in the long black overcoat.

"That's not Jim, that's Conor. I haven't seen Jim in about a year. I suppose you'd better come in, Conor," she said ungraciously. "Oh, and by the way, that's my sister Claire. She's home from London because her husband left her."

"Nice one, Claire," she hissed angrily at me as she herded Conor into the sitting room. "I've been avoiding him for the last month."

There is no doubt but that she will burn in Hell.

At least that explained why Jim ignored me every time I said "Hello, Jim."

Because it wasn't Jim at all.

But it looked just like him.

Then every time I saw Jim, I would say "Hello, Conor."

Apparently I was still wrong.

His name was William.

But he was the absolute image of Jim and Conor.

But Adam was a different proposition entirely from Jim and his clones.

Handsome, intelligent(ish), presentable . . . you know, *normal!* He had one or two social skills, didn't look as if he would crumble into dust if he was caught in a direct ray of sunlight, and could do more than just stare glassy-eyed at Helen and dribble.

After he had shaken hands with us all he then said politely to Mum, "Can I help you to set the table?"

Mum was very taken aback. Not just at the offer of help. Which was indeed remarkable in itself.

But at the suggestion that we set the table at all.

You see, people tend to fend for themselves at mealtimes in our house and eat their dinners in front of the television watching *Neighbours* instead of at the kitchen table.

"Erm, no, that's all right thanks, Adam, I'll do it."

And looking slightly bemused, she did just that.

"You're in for a treat tonight," she said girlishly to Adam. Honestly, it was so embarrassing. A grown woman and she was behaving like a starstruck teenager. "Claire has made the dinner for us."

"Yes, I heard that Claire was a great cook." He smiled at me, throwing me into pleasurable confusion. He really shouldn't smile at me like that while I'm draining the pasta, I thought, as I nursed my scalded hand.

I wondered who had told him that I was a great cook, because I was sure that it certainly wasn't Helen.

Maybe he was just being charming. But, hey, what's wrong with that?

"All right, ladies and gentlemen, please take your seats for this evening's performance," I called out, indicating that the dinner was ready.

Adam laughed.

I was pathetically pleased.

There was a general shuffling and scraping of chairs as everyone sat down.

Adam looked totally incongruous as he sat at the table, completely dwarfing his chair, looking ridiculously square-jawed and handsome.

I placed the salad that I had prepared in the center of the table. Then I put the pasta and sauce on plates and brought them over to the diners. The arrival of the food threw Mum, Dad and Helen into a bit of a quandary. The fact that it was homemade made Dad and Helen suspicious.

Quite rightly.

God knows they had every reason to be suspicious after the ways they had suffered in the past. I suppose it was too reminiscent of all Mum's disasters.

And naturally Mum was only too happy to foment trouble. If she encouraged them to refuse point-blank to eat it, it would mean that I wouldn't cook any more dinners and the old order would be restored, thereby letting her off the hook.

When Helen's plate was put in front of her she made noises as if she was vomiting. "Uuuugggghhhh!" she said, staring in disgust at her plate. "What the *hell* is that?"

"Just pasta and sauce," I said calmly.

"*Sauce?*" she screeched. "But it's *green*."

"Yes," I confirmed, not for a second denying that the sauce was green. "It's green. Sauce can be green, you know."

Then Adam came to the rescue. He was tucking in with great gusto.

I suppose he was one of those penniless students who can go for months without getting a square meal and so would eat just about anything. But he was acting as if he was enjoying it. And that was good enough for me.

"This is absolutely delicious," he said, charmingly cutting through Helen's histrionics. "You should really try it, Helen."

Helen glared at him. "I'm not touching that. It looks revolting."

Dad, Mum and Helen stared, with held breath, their faces frozen with horror, at Adam as he swallowed a mouthful of food, obviously waiting for him to die. And when, after about five minutes, he was still alive and not rolling around on the floor like a victim of the Borgias, screaming to be put out of his misery, Dad ventured a try.

Now, I would love to be able to tell you that one by one every member of my family picked up a fork and despite their earlier prejudices were won over to my fancy cooking. But I can't do that.

Helen, with great shudders and contorted face, noisily refused to touch it, in spite of the beautiful Adam giving it his seal of approval.

She made herself some toast.

Dad ate a little bit and declared that no doubt it was lovely but that his tastes were humble. That he couldn't possibly appreciate such exotic and sophisticated food. As he said, "I'm a simple man. I never even tasted lemon meringue pie until I was thirty-five."

Mum also ate a little bit but with a martyred air. She made it very clear that to waste good food was a sin.

Even horrible food.

Therefore she ate it. Her attitude seemed to be that we were put on this earth to suffer and that this dinner was sent to her as some kind of penance. But at the same time she was hard-pressed to contain her glee at Dad and Helen refusing to eat it. Every so often she would catch my eye and it was obviously a bit of a struggle for her to maintain her poker face.

Though she would rather have died than admit it, she was thrilled.

Then Anna arrived home.

She wandered into the kitchen looking very pretty in a rather ethnic, ethereal kind of way, all trailing scarves and long crocheted see-through skirt and colorful jewelry. She had obviously met Adam previously.

"Oh hi, Adam," she said breathily, obviously delighted, flushing with pleasure.

Does he make every woman he comes into contact with blush? I wondered.

Or was it just our family?

Somehow I suspected not.

What hope could there be for a man so young who had such an intense effect on women? He could only grow up to be a complete and total bastard. Expecting women to weep, faint, scream and fall in love with him as easily as breathing. He was far too handsome for his own good. A disfigurement or two wouldn't have hurt at all.

"Hi, Anna." He smiled at her. "Nice to see you again."

"Er, yes," she muttered, blushing even more and knocking over a cup.

Conversation wasn't exactly scintillating at the dinner table. Helen, never the hostess with the mostest at the best of times (unless we include the hostess with the mostest rudeness), had picked up a magazine and read through dinner.

"Helen, put down the magazine," Dad told her sharply, obviously embarrassed.

"Shut up, Dad," said Helen in a monotone, not even looking up.

But every now and then she would look up at Adam and give him a witchy little smile. He would look at her, totally enchanted, and after holding her gaze for a little while, smile back at her.

You could have cut the sexual tension with a breadknife.

Anna, never a great conversationalist at the best of times, seemed to be completely struck dumb by Adam, such was her awe. Any time he addressed a question to her, she just simpered and giggled, hung her head and acted like some sort of village idiot.

It was quite annoying, to be honest with you. He was only a man, and a very young one at that, for God's sake. Not some sort of deity.

Mum and Dad pushed their food nervously around their plates. They didn't talk much either.

Dad made a brief stab at talking to Adam.

"Rugby?" he murmured at him, as if he was in a secret society and he was trying to find out if Adam was a member also.

"Sorry?" said Adam, looking quizzically at Dad, desperately trying to figure out what he was trying to say to him.

"Rugby?"

"Em, er, sorry, but what do you mean?"

"Rugby? Do you play it?" Dad decided to lay his cards on the table.

"No."

"Oh," Dad sighed like a deflating balloon.

"But I like watching it," said Adam gamely.

"Ah pshaw!" said Dad, practically turning his back on him, making his disappointment felt with a dismissive wave of his arm. And that, I suppose, was the end of that fledgling friendship.

For some reason I felt that it was my responsibility to talk to our visitor. Maybe it was because I had gotten used to being in civilized society, where guests were treated like guests. Where if someone invites you to dinner they don't throw you in with a crowd of strangers and completely ignore you.

"So you're in Helen's class in college?" I asked him with false brightness, desperately trying to kick-start some kind of conversation.

"Yes," he replied. "I'm in her anthropology group."

And that seemed to be the end of that topic.

"This is really delicious," he said, smiling at me. "Any chance of some more?"

"Of course," said Mum coquettishly, almost knocking over her chair in her haste to serve him. "I'll get it for you. And would you like another glass of milk?"

"Thanks very much, Mrs. Walsh," he said politely.

He was so nice. And I'm not just saying that because he was the only one who ate the dinner I made. He was so boyish in a manly kind of way. But even though he was alarmingly good-looking I felt very relaxed with him, because I knew that he must be only about eighteen or so. Although he looked and behaved with a lot more maturity.

To be honest, I nearly felt a little bit jealous of Helen, landing herself such a hunk. I remembered vaguely what it was like to be young and in love. But I told myself not to be so silly. I'd fix things with James. Or else I'd meet someone else as nice.

(Nice? I thought in alarm. Did I just say nice? That was hardly the right word to describe James at that moment.)

But Adam, the hero, saved the conversation.

Mum asked him where he lived.

This was part of a routine inquiry and was the first question in a set of two that Mum religiously asked gentlemen callers. The second question involved finding out from the young man what his father did for a living.

And thereby assessing the approximate wealth of the family just in case Helen happened to marry into it. And so that Mum would have a rough idea of how much she would be expected to spend on the "mother-of-the-bride" dress.

But Adam managed to head Mum off at the pass and avoid being asked to produce a recent copy of his father's payslip by entertaining us all with snippets of his life story. Apparently he was from America. Both his parents had recently returned to New York, so he lived in an apartment in Rathmines. Although both his parents were Irish and he had lived in Ireland since he was twelve, he still looked American.

It must be something they put in the air in America, I thought. Fluoride, or something, that made them grow so big and beefy.

Adam amused us all with stories of what it was like for him when he first moved from New York to Dublin. And how the native children welcomed him by calling him "fascist imperialist Yank" and acting as though he was personally responsible for the U.S. invasion of Grenada, and beating the crap out of him for calling tomatoes "tom-ay-toes" and for calling his mother "Mom" instead of "Mammy."

And how, when he tried to defend himself by beating up some of the native children he got called a bully because he was so much bigger than the other boys.

We all nodded sympathetically, sitting around with our elbows on the kitchen table, looking at Adam, our hearts breaking for the poor lonely twelve-year-old boy who couldn't do anything right. You could have heard a pin drop. The mood had suddenly changed from a lighthearted one to a somber one.

Even Dad looked on the verge of tears. He was obviously thinking, "He might not play rugby but that's still no way to treat the lad."

Then Adam turned the full force of his attention onto me. He twisted around in his chair and fixed me with an intense look. In a funny way, he made me feel as if I were the only person in the room.

He was so eager and enthusiastic about everything. Like a little puppy. Well, like an enormous puppy, actually.

"So, Claire, tell me about your job," he said. "Helen tells me that you've got a really important job working for a charity."

I bloomed under the warmth of his interest—like a flower in the sun—and started to tell him.

But before I could, Helen interrupted. "I didn't say it was important," she said sourly. "I just said it was a job. And anyway, she had to give it up when she had the baby."

"Oh, the baby," he said. "Can I see her?"

"Of course," I said, delighted, but wondering why Helen was being so nasty. Why she was being even nastier than usual, I mean.

"Kate's asleep at the moment but she'll be awake in about half an hour so you can see her then."

"Great," he said, looking at me.

Honestly, he was gorgeous. His eyes were a kind of navy blue. And he had the most beautiful body. I thought this purely from an objective point of view. He was my sister's boyfriend, so it was all right for me to admire his beauty just aesthetically speaking, as it were.

I felt a bit like a wise old woman admiring the handsome young men. Realizing how gorgeous they were while acknowledging that my day of dalliance with them was long gone.

For dessert I produced the chocolate mousse, which was greeted with a great deal more enthusiasm than the dinner was. The jostling and scuffling that broke out among Anna, Helen and Dad for the biggest piece was nothing short of shameful, and us with a visitor in the house.

But Adam just laughed good-naturedly.

After a while I took him to see Kate.

We tiptoed into the room.

"Can I hold her?" he asked reverently.

"Of course." I smiled, very touched by his awe.

I thought it was the sweetest thing I'd ever heard that such a big tough man wanted to see my baby, sort of like a huge burly truck driver crying at country and western songs. Incongruous and touching. I handed Kate gently to him and he took her and held her gingerly.

She didn't even wake up.

The idiot! What kind of daughter was I rearing? Being held, for the first time, by a beautiful man and she slept through it. It made such a beautiful picture. The huge young man holding the perfect little baby.

"What color are her eyes?" he asked.

"Blue," I said. "But all babies have blue eyes first. Then they usually change to another color."

He continued to stare at her with an expression of wonder on his face.

"You know, if you and I had a baby its eyes would definitely be blue," he mused, sounding almost as if he was talking to himself.

I jumped with shock. Was he flirting with me? I felt a surge of rage.

I had thought he was so innocent and nice. A sweet young man.

The *nerve* of him!

Not only was I old enough to be his mother . . . Well, very nearly. But he was here with my *sister* and was doing a very good impression of being her boyfriend.

Had he no respect?

No sense of decency?

But I was wrong. I looked at him and our eyes locked for a minute. I could see that he was really deathly embarrassed.

He definitely knew that he had made a faux pas.

The room was full of tension and embarrassment.

"Well, I'd better get back to Helen and the essay," he said hurriedly, practically flinging Kate back to me and rushing from the room without a second glance.

I sat on the bed feeling a bit funny.

Was I feeling foolish for overreacting?

Was I feeling sad at my cynicism for just jumping to the wrong conclusion?

Was I feeling . . . God forbid . . . *disappointed*?

No, I decided. Definitely not disappointed. But certainly a bit foolish. You've been away from men too long, I told myself sternly. You'd better get back into circulation. So that the next time you meet an attractive one you won't be jumping to any ridiculous conclusions.

But at the same time I must admit that I was slightly piqued by the way he'd reacted at the suggestion that we have a baby. There was no need for him to look quite so horrified.

God, but it was typical.

In time-honored tradition I had gone from being furious at the suggestion that he did like me to being furious at the suggestion that he didn't like me in about thirty seconds. Being rational was never my strong point.

I mean, I might well be an "older woman" but I wasn't exactly the Bride of Dracula. I'd have him know, plenty of men found me attractive. Well, I was sure there must be some somewhere who did. There were three billion people on this planet. Out of that lot I was sure I could have rustled up a few poor misfortunates who liked the look of me.

The nerve of the guy. Just because he happened to be extremely good-looking didn't give him any right to make me feel like a horror.

And I might not have been quite as beautiful as Helen.

In fact, I wasn't even remotely as beautiful as Helen.

But I was a kind person.

Not that anyone ever liked someone because they were a kind person.

I fed Kate and put her back to bed.

Then I went downstairs to Mum.

I passed Helen's bedroom on the way and the door was firmly shut. The pair of them were obviously well ensconced in there. Easy writing, indeed! Mum and Dad might have bought that line, but I've used it enough times myself to know what it really means.

But at the same time, if they were having sex, they were doing it very quietly. Not, of course, that I was listening at the door or anything. And not, of course, that it had anything, in the whole wide world, to do with me.

Helen could screw whomever she liked.

With great purpose I watched television with Mum.

Much later we heard Helen and Adam in the kitchen.

Then we heard her saying good-bye to him.

He stuck his head around the door and thanked us for the lovely dinner and said that he hoped to see us again soon.

Mum and I smiled our good-byes at him.

"Lovely polite lad," said Mum in a satisfied fashion.

I didn't answer her. I was thinking that he didn't look too disheveled for someone who had just been having sex. And wondering why I cared.

eleven

After Adam left, and Helen had sent him out into the wet and wild March night to make his way home to Rathmines, she closed the front door behind him and came into the television room and sat down with Mum and me.

"He seemed like a lovely lad," said Mum approvingly.

"Did he?" said Helen distantly.

"*Lovely,*" said Mum emphatically.

"Oh, don't go on like you usually do," snapped Helen irritably.

There was a little bit of an awkward pause.

Then I spoke.

"How old is Adam?" I asked Helen casually.

"Why?" she asked without looking away from the television screen. "Do you like him?"

"No," I protested, blushing hotly.

"Oh, really?" she said. "Everyone else does. The whole college does. Mum does."

Mum looked a little bit taken aback and startled and like she was about to defend herself. Before she could, though, Helen started talking again to me.

"And you looked like you *fancied* him. Giggling and smiling at him. You're worse than Anna. I was mortified."

"I was being *polite,*" I insisted.

"You weren't being polite," she told me tonelessly, still looking at the screen. "You fancied him."

"Helen, for God's sake, did you expect me to ignore him and not talk to him?" I asked her angrily.

"No," she said coldly. "But you didn't have to be so obvious about fancying him."

"Helen, I'm a married woman," I said, raising my voice at her. "Of course I didn't fancy him. And he's much younger than me."

"Hah!" she shouted back at me. "So you do fancy him. You're just afraid that he's too young. Well, don't worry, because Professor Staunton is married and she's in love with him and got drunk and was crying in the bar and saying she'd leave her husband and everything. We were all in fits laughing. And she's *ancient*. Even older than you!"

At that Helen jumped up and ran out of the room, slamming the door thunderously behind her. No doubt dislodging the last few remaining slates from the roof.

"Oh God," sighed Mum wearily. "It's like a bloody relay race around here. No sooner does one daughter stop behaving like an Antichrist than another one starts. How did you all get to be so temperamental? You're like a pack of Italians."

"What's *wrong* with her?" I asked Mum. "Why is she getting all touchy about Adam?"

"Oh, I suppose she's in love with him," said Mum vaguely. "Or at least she thinks she might be."

"What?" I asked, aghast. "Helen in love? Are you out of your mind? The only person Helen is in love with is herself."

"That's a very unkind thing to say about your sister," said Mum, looking at me thoughtfully.

"Well, I don't mean it unkindly," I explained hurriedly. "I just mean that everyone's always in love with her. It's never the other way around."

"There's a first time for everything," said Mum wisely.

We sat quietly.

Mum broke the silence.

"Anyway, she was right."

"About what?" I asked her, wondering what she was talking about.

"You *did* like him."

"I did *not* like him," I said indignantly.

Mum turned to me with raised eyebrows and a knowing look.

"Don't be ridiculous," she scoffed. "He was *gorgeous!* I liked him myself. If I was twenty years younger I'd give him a run for his money."

I said nothing. I was feeling a bit upset.

"And what's more," Mum continued, "he *liked* you. No wonder Helen's nose is out of joint."

"That's crap!" I protested loudly.

"It's not," said Mum calmly. "It was obvious that he *liked* you. Although, then again," she continued doubtfully, "I thought he *liked* me too. Maybe he's just one of those men who make every women feel beautiful."

Now I was feeling very confused indeed.

"But Mum," I tried to explain, "I'm married to James and I love him and I want to fix my marriage."

"I know that," she said. "But maybe a little fling is exactly what you need. To get your self-confidence back. And to get your feelings for James in perspective."

I stared at Mum in horror. What was she talking about? This was my *mother*, for God's sake. What on earth was she doing encouraging me to have a fling, and me a married woman? And with my younger sister's boyfriend, of all people.

"Mum!" I said. "Get a grip. You're scaring me. I mean, I'm not eighteen anymore. I no longer think that the best way to get over one man is to get under another!"

Too late, I realized what I had said. I could have bitten my tongue off.

Mum looked at me with narrowed eyes.

"I don't know where you heard a vulgar expression like that," she hissed. "But it certainly wasn't in this house. Is that the way they talk in London?"

"Sorry, Mum," I mumbled, feeling mortified and ashamed but at least back on familiar territory.

I sat on the couch beside her feeling awful.

"Well," she said after a while in a more conciliatory tone, "we'll say no more about what you just said."

"Okay," I said, feeling relieved.

Thank God! I was just about to start packing my bags for my move back to London.

"Anyway," she said, "he's twenty-four."

"How do you know?" I asked her, amazed.

"Aha." She winked at me, touching her nose. "I have my sources."

"You mean you asked him," I said. I knew my mother of old.

"I might have," she said coyly, giving nothing away.

"So you see," she continued, "he's not too young for you at all."

"Mum," I wailed in anguish. "What's this all about? Anyway, I'm nearly thirty and he's only twenty-four. So he's still far too young for me."

"Nonsense," said Mum briskly. "Look at Britt Ekland, always being photographed with that fellow who's young enough to be her grandson. Although maybe he is her grandson. And that other floozy, the one who goes around with no clothes on, what's her name?"

"Madonna?" I ventured cautiously.

"No, no, not her. You know the one. She has a tattoo on her backside."

"Oh, you mean Cher," I told her.

"Yes, that's the one," said Mum. "I mean, she must be my age if she's a day and look at the way she carries on. None of them a day over sixteen. I suppose Ike must have been the last man she was with who was older than her."

"Ike?" I asked her, my head swimming slightly.

"Yes, Ike. Her husband," said Mum impatiently.

"No Mum, I don't think Cher was married to Ike. Cher was married to Sonny. Ike was married to Tina," I told her.

"Who's Tina?" she asked me, sounding baffled.

"Tina Turner," I gently explained.

"What's she got to do with anything?" said Mum, sounding outraged, looking at me as if I'd gone completely crazy.

"Nothing at all," I tried to explain, feeling that I was fast losing any grip on this conversation. "It's just that you said that Cher and Ike . . . Oh, never mind, never mind. Just forget it."

Mum sulkily muttered to herself that she didn't have to forget anything. That I was the one who had brought Tina Turner into the conversation.

"Stop being angry, Mum," I told her in a placatory fashion. "I get your point. I see what you're saying. Adam isn't too young for me."

I glanced nervously at the door as soon as I had said this. I half expected Helen to come bursting through and shout, "I knew you fancied him, you horrible old lady." And then attempt to strangle me.

She didn't. But the fear still lingered.

"But anyway, Mum," I continued, "the age question aside, aren't you forgetting a couple of other vital points? Like the small fact that Adam is Helen's boyfriend."

"Aha!" she said, holding up her index finger and going all sagelike and wise-old-womanly on me. She practically put on a black headscarf and developed a squint, "but is he?"

"Well, why else was he here?" I asked, reasonably, I thought.

"To help her to write her essay," said Mum.

"And why would he do that if he's not her boyfriend? Or at least if he's not making a damn good attempt to be," I asked again, reasonably, I thought.

"Because he's a nice person?" said Mum. But she sounded a bit doubtful.

"Anyway," I said, "it was obvious that he really **liked** her."

"Was it?" she said, sounding genuinely surprised.

"Yes," I said, quite emphatically.

"But even if he is her boyfriend, he won't be for long," predicted Mum.

"Why do you say that?" I asked, wondering what other information she had gleaned from the beautiful Adam.

"Because of the way Helen is," said Mum. "Helen just wants to make him fall for her. Then she'll torment him for a while. And then she'll discard him," said Mum. "She was always like that. Even as a child. For months before Christmas she'd be pestering us for this doll and that bike. And the turkey wouldn't be even eaten before she had broken every single thing that Santa brought her. She wasn't happy until she had destroyed everything. Dolls' heads and legs and bicycle chains and saddles all over the place. You'd break your neck on them."

"That's not a very nice way to talk about Helen," I said, echoing what Mum had said to me earlier.

"Maybe not," said Mum with a sigh. "But it's the truth. I love her and she's a good girl, really. She just needs to grow up a little bit. Well, a big bit, I suppose."

"But you said that Helen might be in love with Adam," I said.

"I said that Helen might *think* she's in love with him. An entirely different proposition," she said. "And even if she is in love with him, although if you ask me I think she's too immature to be capable of it," continued Mum, "it would do her no harm at all to be dealt a little bit of hardship by life. She's had everything far too easy. A little bit of heartbreak goes a long way. I mean, look at how good it's been for you. It gives you humility."

"So you want me to have a fling with Helen's boyfriend to give me back my confidence and to give Helen a bit of humility," I said, finally thinking that I had grasped what Mum was saying to me.

"Good God," said Mum, annoyed. "You're making me sound like that one out of *Dynasty*. Playing God with people's lives and all that. It sounds very cold-blooded when you say it like that."

"I'm not saying that I want anything to happen, exactly," she continued. "But I really did feel that Adam was very attracted to you. And that, if he is, and if anything was to happen, and if you survive Helen's attempts on your life—by Jingo, there's an awful lot of 'ifs' there—then maybe you should just let what's going to happen happen."

"Oh, Mum," I sighed. "You've made me all confused."

"I'm sorry, sweetheart," she said. "Maybe I've got it all wrong. Maybe he doesn't **like** you at all."

I've had enough, I thought.

"Well, I'm off to bed," I said.

"Sweet dreams," said Mum, squeezing my hand. "I'll be in to kiss Kate good-night."

And off I went to my bedroom and got ready for bed. My nightgown was obviously annoyed with me. It didn't take kindly to being neglected and left at home while I wore Helen's leggings and shirt to the shopping center. I was your friend, it told me. I saw you through the rough times, it reminded me. You're fickle and nothing but a foul weather friend. The minute things pick up, and you start feeling a bit more normal, you just discard me, throw me over.

Oh shut up, I thought, or I'll never wear you again. And then you really will have something to complain about.

I had more important things on my mind than disgruntled nighties and their grievances.

As I lay down I realized that I hadn't really thought of James in about three hours.

This was an absolute miracle.

All in all, it had been a most unusual day.

twelve

The following day dawned bright cold and blustery.

I know this because I was awake at dawn.

It was a typical March day.

The rain had finally stopped.

But there's absolutely no symbolism in this fact. Let's face it, the bloody rain had to stop sometime.

After I had given Kate her bottle, I sat with her on the bed as I burped her. It was fast becoming clear to me that although I had been lucky enough to be dragged out of the mire of misery, this newfound liberation brought with it certain responsibilities.

Yesterday had been very nice. Really good fun.

But, and the thought came to me unbidden, there's more to life than having fun.

The little man in my head with the sandwich board, which normally says "The End Is Nigh," was today proclaiming "There's More to Life Than Having Fun."

He works for my Conscience Department.

I hate him.

The miserable bastard.

He's always showing up with his board and ruining things on me, especially when I'm shopping, proclaiming weighty things like, "You Have Four Pairs of Boots Already" and "How Can You Justify Spending Twelve Pounds on a Lipstick."

He would completely ruin my shopping. Either I wouldn't

buy the item in question. "I'm sorry," I would stammer as the assistant paused putting the shoes into the box and fixed me with a murderous stare. "I've changed my mind." Or else I would buy it but I'd feel so guilty about it that all the enjoyment would be gone.

Anyway, today the miserable old killjoy reminded me that I had to do a lot more with my life than hanging around a supermarket introducing Kate to boxes of frozen chocolate mousse. What kind of value system was I giving her?

Or making dinner for my family. Or getting odd little crushes on my sister's boyfriend.

I walked over to the window with Kate in my arms and we stood looking down at the garden that Michael so lovingly didn't tend. I was feeling a bit like a man who is just about to face a firing squad. It was time for me to face the music.

I had to address various horrible questions.

Involving money and custody of our child and the marital home.

And I swear to God it was so painful, my brain winced as I considered each subject.

This was the first time since I had watched James's back as he walked out of the hospital ward that I had looked at the practicalities of splitting up with him. Like, should James and I meet to consider selling our apartment? Should we divide our possessions equally between the two of us? That would be extremely amusing.

For example, would we drag our three-piece living room set out into the middle of the room and saw the couch in half, and take a piece each with all the foam and stuffing spilling out, plus a matching chair?

You know, that kind of thing.

I honestly didn't know how we were going to divide most of our possessions. Because they didn't belong to me and they didn't belong to James. They belonged to the elusive third party, "us." The person or energy, or whatever you want to call it, that was formed by the union of James and me. Which was much more than the sum of its parts.

How I wished I could find the missing "us." If only I could track it down and lure it back with offers of all these wonderful possessions. Like some awful third-rate game show host.

See that lovely television.

It's yours. Now will you stay?

Have a look at the fine remodeled kitchen.

Beautiful, isn't it? Well, it can all be yours if only you'll come back.

Though I suppose you wouldn't get anything like a remodeled kitchen on a third-rate game show.

You'd be lucky to get your bus fare home.

But I wished that it could be as easy as that to get the James and Claire "us" back.

Or if all I had to do would be to put an announcement on the evening news that said something like "Would the James and Claire 'us,' last known to be touring the [let's just say] Kerry area please contact the police in Dublin for an urgent message."

But it looked like the "us" wasn't just missing. It was dead. Killed by James.

And it died intestate.

In theory the state inherits all the possessions belonging to "us."

In practice, of course, nothing so surreal and ridiculous as that was going to happen.

Now pass me that saw, would you?

You see, I firmly believe that there was only one way to deal with unpleasant situations—and what was my current situation if not unpleasant? And that was to take a deep breath, face them fairly and squarely, look them in the eye, stare them down and show them who's boss.

I really believed very strongly in this.

And perhaps one day I might even take my own advice and actually do it.

To sum up my attitude, let me just tell you that I don't think I have ever, in my whole life, done the dishes on the actual night of a dinner party.

I always promised myself that I would. That waking up, with a hangover, to filthy plates and a kitchen that looked like a battleground was too horrible to contemplate. But you know what it's like.

The end of the evening has rolled around and the table is

strewn with half-full dishes of melting baked Alaska, which I have more or less abandoned.

Now I must say, in my defense, that up to this point I am usually a model hostess, positively dancing attendance on my guests, ferrying plates and dishes and cutlery to and from the kitchen as though I was on a conveyor belt. However, my sense of hospitality decreases in direct proportion to the number of glasses of wine that I've had, so by dessert and coffee time I am usually far too relaxed (all right then, far too drunk, if you will insist on calling a spade a spade) and no longer feel any need to clear the table. If the table had collapsed in front of me under the weight of the uncleared dishes, I would have just laughed.

If my guests wanted a clean table I'm afraid that they'd have had to do it themselves. They knew where the kitchen was. Were they waiting for an engraved invitation?

In the middle of the table there always was a completely untouched bowl of fruit.

I mean, what's the problem? Fruit is lovely.

I *always* bought fruit and no one ever ate it. Protestant dessert, Judy called it. My friends said that it was bad enough for me to insult them by offering them something like a banana or an orange for dessert. That their idea of a decent dessert—nay, their *only* idea of a dessert—was something positively bursting with saturated fats and refined sugar and double cream and alcohol and egg whites and cholesterol. The kind of dessert that your arteries contract an inch or two just from looking at. I was sure that they developed such attitudes in their deprived childhoods.

So the upshot was that I always bought fruit and my guests always never ate it. If you follow me.

And the view of the table was always obscured by about a thousand glasses, several of them overturned, with their contents, be it white wine, gin and tonic, Irish coffees or Baileys, fast spreading out and intermingling and making friends with each other on the tablecloth, forming little seas around the islands of salt, which some conscientious poor soul (usually James) had thrown down to halt the trail of devastation wreaked by the advancing hordes of spilled red wine.

And I would be on my twenty-second Sambucca and reclining on the two back legs of my chair, or sitting on James's knee telling anyone who'd listen how much I love him.

I had no shame.

My sobriety was less than judgelike, but I was at one with the universe.

Every morning after a party I staggered down to the kitchen and for a second I paused with my hand on the kitchen doorknob and had a beautiful warm fantasy that when I flung wide the door the place would be gleaming, the sun glinting off the polished surfaces, all the cups and plates and bowls and pots and pans scrubbed and put away (in the correct cupboards).

Instead, as I gingerly picked my way through the debris, I was hard-pressed to find even an unbroken glass for my much-needed couple of aspirin, never mind a clean one.

And while we're on the subject of dinner parties, I'd like the answer to a couple of questions.

Why, at dinner parties, does someone always tear all the paper off the labels on all the bottles of wine, so that when you come down in the morning the table is covered with little annoying sticky scraps of paper that stick to everything?

Why do I always use the butter dish as an ashtray?

Why does at least one person always say—usually fairly late in the evening—"I wonder what Dubonnet and Guinness would taste like?" or "What would happen if I lit my glass of Jack Daniels?"

And then proceed to find out.

Just for the record, the Guinness causes the Dubonnet to curdle in the most disgusting fashion and the Jack Daniels goes up like a Kuwaiti oil well, blistering the paint on the dining room ceiling.

To be fair to James—although why should I, the bastard—he was always very good about housework and especially about cleaning up after said dinner parties. He never got as drunk as I did, so at the very least he was in a fit condition to move most of the carnage from the dining table to the kitchen so that in the morning one room was fairly presentable. Apart from, of course, the Jack Daniels scorch marks on the ceiling. But at least I knew I could paint over them.

Again.

I had some paint left from the last dinner party.

And the inevitable couple of hungover bodies usually to be found in an unshaven and disheveled state (and that's just the women) on the living room couch. In fact, they were nearly harder to get rid of than said scorch marks on the ceiling. Or the cigarette burns on the carpet.

Lying around for half the day, groaning and demanding cups of tea and aspirin and saying that they'll vomit if they move.

Anyway, I was doing it again.

Procrastinating, that is.

Trying to make myself think about the practicalities of no longer being with James was like trying to make myself look directly at the sun on a really bright day. Hard to do either, and they both made my eyes water.

I suppose I'd better think about the custody of Kate problem. Although was it a problem? James hadn't shown the slightest bit of interest in her. And, after all, he was the (boo, hiss!) adulterer. And because of this, what with him being the wrongdoer and everything, I supposed custody would be automatically awarded to me.

But instead of feeling triumphant about it, I didn't even feel relieved.

This was no victory.

I wanted James to care about our child.

I wanted my child to have a father.

I would have much preferred for James to bring me to court and indulge in bitter verbal battles and slander me by calling me a lesbian or a woman of low morals (no grounds for slander there, I'm afraid) or whatever. Because, by trying to get custody of Kate by blackening my name, he would at least be caring about her.

I hugged Kate fiercely. I felt so guilty. Because somehow, somewhere, without my even knowing that I was doing it, I had messed up and because of that, poor Kate, innocent little bystander, had to do without her dad.

I just couldn't understand James.

Didn't he have any curiosity at all about Kate?

I couldn't make sense of it.

Was it because Kate is a girl?

If the baby had been a boy would James have tried to make a go of things with me?

Who knew? I was just trying to make sense of a senseless situation.

And what about our apartment?

We had bought it together and it was in both our names. So what did we do?

Sell it and split the proceeds?

Me buy out his share and live there with Kate?

Me sell James my share and let him live there with Denise?

No way!

Over my dead body.

You know, anytime I'd heard people saying that passionately I just thought that they were being all Mediterranean and hot-blooded. That they were just playing to the camera and overreacting. And I knew that I'd said it myself thousands of times, but I'd never really meant it until that minute. But I meant it, really meant it then.

And what about money? How on earth was I going to manage to support Kate and myself on my salary?

I felt as if I'd wandered out onto a balcony and suddenly realized, to my horror, that there was no ground at all beneath me. Just lots and lots of limitless, empty space for me to fall through.

The thought of being without money was terrifying.

I felt as though I was nothing.

That I was just this faceless woman afloat in a big hostile universe with absolutely nothing to anchor me to anything.

I hated myself for being so insecure and so dependent. I should have been a strong, sassy, independent, nineties woman. The type of woman who has strong views and who goes to the movies on her own and who cares about the environment and can change a fuse and goes for aromatherapy and has an herb garden and can speak fluent Italian and has a session in a flotation tank once a week and doesn't need a man to shore up her fragile sense of self-esteem.

But the fact is, I wasn't.

I was perfectly happy to be a homemaker while my husband went out to earn the loot.

And if my husband was prepared to share the household

chores as well as earn the lion's share of the loot, then so much the better.

I suppose I wanted to have my cake and eat it.

But then again, what were you going to do with your cake if not eat it?

Frame it?

Use it as a sachet in your underwear drawer?

How were James and I going to separate the funds from our joint bank account? I would have nearly given up all rights to the money to save all the inevitable wrangling. The only thing that was stopping me was the idea of James's spending it on Denise.

Besides, I'd seen a really nice pair of shoes yesterday in the mall and I wanted them for my own.

I can't describe the feeling of immediate familiarity that rushed between us. The moment I clapped eyes on them I felt like I already owned them. I could only suppose that we were together in a former life. That they were my shoes when I was a serving maid in medieval Britain or when I was a princess in ancient Egypt. Or perhaps they were the princess and I was the shoes. Who's to know? Either way I knew that we were meant to be together.

And I had no immediate access to funds. Therefore I had to lay claim to my money in England.

Sordid and unpleasant as it might be.

My head swam slightly at all this, kind of like the way it had swum the night before when Mum started her Cher and Ike conversation.

Little did I think, the warm April day three years ago when I married James, that our union would end in such a way. That something that started out as such good fun and so full of hope and excitement could end in heartbreak and legalese.

That I would be dealing in so many clichés.

Arguing about money and possessions.

I'd always thought that James and I would be different. That even though we might be married there was no reason that we had to act it, goddammit!

That fun and love and passion would always be the most important things to us.

I'd vowed that there would never come a day when I would

walk into a room and say to James, without even looking at him, "The tiles in the bathroom are coming loose. You'd better take a look at them." Or, again giving him but the most cursory of glances, "I hope you're not thinking of wearing that sweater to the Reynolds' dinner."

Hadn't I realized that thousands of women before me had made a pact with themselves never to lose the magic in their marriages? The same way that they fiercely promised themselves that they would never let their gray hair show, would never let their breasts droop, would never get wrinkles. But it still happened.

Their will wasn't strong enough to fight the inevitable, to reverse the waves of time.

And neither was mine.

I lay Kate back down in her bassinet while I went to take a shower. I was obviously really getting to grips with this living business, I thought to myself proudly.

"Cleanliness," I told Kate, feeling very self-righteous, feeling that I was a Good Mother, "is next to godliness. And I'll tell you what godliness is when you're a bit older."

In the shower, I couldn't stop thinking about James. Not in a maudlin or bitter way. Just remembering how great it had been. Really, even though he had hurt me in a way I never thought he would, I couldn't forget just how great it was with him.

When I first met James and we were out with other people, I would watch him across a room, talking to someone else. I would always think to myself how sexy and handsome he looked. Especially if he was looking all serious and accountantlike. That always made me smile. He looked as if he was no fun at all.

But let me tell you, I knew differently.

And it gave me such a thrill to know that when the party or whatever had ended my man would be coming home with me. I wanted it always to be like that.

I had met a man who loved me unconditionally. Even better than the unconditional love that my mother had for me, because unfortunately that unconditional love had certain conditions attached.

And he'd made me laugh in the same way that my sisters

or my girlfriends could make me laugh. But it was even better because I didn't usually wake up in the same bed as my sisters or my girlfriends.

So the opportunities for having a good laugh with James were far more plentiful and in far better places.

And *about* far better places too, I suppose.

You know, I thought if anyone was going to have an affair that it would be me. Not that I thought I *would* have had one, if you know what I mean.

But I was always the loud rowdy one who was regarded as great fun. And popular opinion held James to be the sensible reliable one. Quiet, self-contained, as steady as a rock.

That's the trouble with men who wear suits and reading glasses and who fix you with a sincere gaze and say things like "Well, in a period of low inflation, a fixed-rate mortgage is your best bet," or "I would sell the treasury stock and buy government equities," or some such similar statement.

You get hoodwinked into thinking that they're as dull as ditchwater and as safe as houses.

And I suppose that even I did a bit with James.

I felt that I could behave or misbehave in any fashion that took my fancy and he would smile tolerantly on me. He was amused by me.

No, not amused. That sounds sort of patronizing and disdainful.

But he was certainly entertained by me.

He really thought I was great.

And I, on the other hand, felt very safe and secure and protected with James.

The very fact that I knew I could make a fool of myself and James would still love me insured that I *didn't* make a fool of myself.

I didn't get drunk very often anymore.

But even in the days when I did and I would wake up the next morning with a pounding headache and cringing from the few snippets of what I could remember of the previous evening, he would be so sweet.

He would laugh kindly and get me glasses of water and lean over and kiss me on my throbbing forehead as I lay like a corpse in the bed and say soothing things like "No, sweetie, you weren't obnoxious. You were really funny," and "No, darling, you weren't overbearing. You had us all in stitches," and "Your bag will turn up. It was probably under some coats at Lisa's. I'll call her now," and "Of *course* you can look those people in the eye again. I mean, *everyone* was plastered. You weren't the drunkest by any stretch of the imagination."

And on one really awful occasion, my worst "morning after" ever, I think—the promises to never drink again were thick on the ground that morning, I can tell you—"Hurry up, angel, your hearing is at nine-thirty. You can't be late because the lawyer said your judge is a bastard."

Now look, wait a minute. Just let me explain. Please hear me out.

Yes, I was arrested one night but it wasn't because I did anything illegal. I was simply in the wrong place at the wrong time. I just happened to be somewhere that just happened to be an unlicensed drinking club. I had no idea that the people running the place were doing anything criminal.

Apart from the price they were charging for the wine.

And the suits the bouncers were wearing. The suits alone deserved ten years in solitary confinement.

I don't know how I managed to get mixed up in it. All I know for sure is that drink was taken and spirits were high.

When we saw the policemen entering the club and everyone started hiding their drinks under their tables, Judy and Laura and I thought it was great fun.

"Just like Prohibition," we laughingly agreed.

I decided that I would tell my favorite joke to some of the policemen, which is the one that goes: How many policemen does it take to break a lightbulb? The answer being, of course, none. It fell down the stairs.

And one of the policemen took great umbrage at this and told me that, if I didn't behave, he would arrest me.

"Arrest me then." I smiled up at him saucily and extended both my wrists for him to put the bracelets on. I obviously hadn't come to terms with the fact that these were real policemen and not just cartoons.

So no one was more surprised than I was when the policeman did just that.

Of course, I realized that he was only doing his duty.

I bore him no grudges. I wasn't bitter.

The bastard.

I must admit that I was very, very taken aback.

I tried to tell him that I was just a suburban, middle-class young woman. That I had even managed to get a man to marry me and that *he* was an accountant. I told him all this to let him know that I was on the same side as him. Righting wrongs and fighting injustice and all that.

And that by arresting me he was throwing everyone's stereotype of a drunk and disorderly person into disarray.

So off I went in the squad car, peering tearfully out the window at Laura and Judy.

"Call James," I mouthed at them as I was driven off.

I knew that he would know what to do.

And he did.

He bailed me out and got me a lawyer.

And I don't think I have ever, ever in my whole life been so frightened. I was convinced that I would have a confession beaten out of me and I'd be jailed for several lifetimes and I'd never see James or my friends or family again. I'd never see blue sky again, except from the exercise yard, I thought, feeling intensely sorry for myself. I'd never wear nice clothes again. I'd have to wear those horrible prison sack dresses.

And I'd have to become a lesbian. I'd have to become the girlfriend of Missus Big so that she'd protect me from all the other girls and their Coke bottles.

And I already had a degree and it was no big deal.

And I'd have to start smoking again.

I was distraught.

So when James came to the police station and bailed me out—or "sprung" me, as I preferred to call it—I couldn't believe that there were no television cameras and delirious crowds with banners outside.

Just another squad car which screeched to a halt, scraping the curb. About five drunks tumbling out.

James took me home.

He got the name of a lawyer from a friend and called him.

He woke me in the morning, when I couldn't open my eyes because of the terrible sense of foreboding.

He wiped off my lipstick and told me it might be better for my case if I didn't look like a good-time girl.

He made me wear a long skirt and a high-necked blouse for the same reason.

He sat in the courtroom holding my hand as I waited for my turn to come.

He hummed little songs to me as I sat there white-faced and nauseous with the shock and the hangover.

I found the songs that he was humming very comforting.

Until I caught a few words of one.

Something about breaking rocks and being on a chain gang.

I turned and glared at him tearfully, ready to tell him to fuck off and go home if he found my predicament that amusing.

But I caught his eye.

And I just couldn't help it.

I started to laugh.

He was right.

The whole situation was so ridiculous that there was no point in *not* laughing at it.

The pair of us sniggered like schoolchildren.

The judge gave us a filthy look.

"That's another ten years onto your sentence," snorted James, and the pair of us collapsed again.

I got off with a fifty-pound fine, which James laughingly paid. "You can pay it yourself the next time." He grinned at me.

I couldn't believe his attitude. If someone woke me at two in the morning to tell me that James had been arrested I would have been horrified. I certainly wouldn't have found the situation funny the way he had.

I would have seriously asked myself to think about what kind of man I had married.

I wouldn't have been indulgent and so completely supportive and forgiving the way James was.

In fact, he wasn't even forgiving, because he never for a second acted as if I had done something wrong.

So now the next time I got arrested I wouldn't have anyone to hold my hand in the courtroom and make me laugh.

Sometimes he was just so sweet. When I used to wake in the middle of the night to worry, he was wonderful.

"What's wrong, baby?" he used to ask.

"Nothing," I'd say, unable to put words on that horrible, nameless, free-floating anxiety.

"Can't you sleep?"

"No."

"Should I bore you to sleep?"

"Yes, please."

And I would eventually fall into a peaceful sleep, lulled by the sound of James's soothing voice explaining tax breaks for charities or the new economic regulations set by the European Union.

I turned off the shower and dried myself.

I'd better call him, I told myself.

I went back into my room and started to get dressed.

"Call him," I ordered myself sternly.

"After I've fed Kate," I replied in a vague and wishy-washy fashion.

"Call him!" I told myself again.

"Do you want the child to *starve?*" I asked, trying to sound outraged. "I'll call him when I've fed her."

"No you won't. Call him *now!*"

I was up to my old tricks again.

Procrastinating, avoiding responsibility, running away from unpleasant situations.

But I was so afraid.

I *knew* that I had to talk to James about money and the apartment and all that. I wasn't denying that for a minute. But I felt that the moment I actually spoke to him about these things they would become real.

And if they were real it meant that my marriage was over.

"Oh God," I sighed.

I looked at Kate, lying in her bassinet, soft and plump and fragrant in her little pink pajamas.

And I knew that I had to call James. I could be a yaller-bellied, lily-livered, cringing coward on my own account all I liked, but I owed it to this beautiful child of mine to sort out her future.

"Right," I said resignedly, looking at her. "You've twisted my arm. I'll call him."

I went into Mum's room to use the phone there.

I started to dial the number of James's office in London and I began to feel dizzy.

Excited and frightened at the same time.

In a few moments I'd hear his voice.

And I couldn't wait.

I was warm and shaky with anticipation.

I'd be speaking to him, to my James, my best friend. Except, of course, he wasn't anymore, was he? But sometimes I forgot. Just for a second.

It was becoming very hard for me to breathe. My breath didn't seem to be able to go down all the way.

The phone connected and started to ring.

A thrill ran through me and I thought I might throw up. The receptionist answered.

"Um, can I speak to Mr. James Webster, please," I asked, my voice wobbling. My lips felt as if I'd been given an injection to numb them.

There were a couple of clicks on the line.

I'd be speaking to him in a moment.

I held my breath.

It wasn't as if the breathing that I had been doing had been particularly successful anyway.

Another click.

And the receptionist was back.

"I'm sorry, Mr. Webster is away this week. Can anyone else help?"

The disappointment was so painful that I could hardly stammer out, "No, that's all right, thank you."

And I hung up the phone.

I stayed sitting on Mum's bed.

I didn't really know what to do now.

It had been such an ordeal to ring him. It was such a hard thing to do. And then, in spite of myself, I had been excited about talking to him. And he wasn't even there. I had gallons of adrenaline coursing through my body, making prickles of sweat break out on my forehead, making my hands wet and shaky, making me light-headed, and I just didn't know what to do with it.

And then the thought just struck me, where *was* James?

Please don't tell me that he's gone on vacation.

On vacation?

How could he go on vacation when his marriage was breaking up? Had broken up, in fact.

Maybe he's on a business trip, I thought desperately.

I half thought of calling the receptionist back and asking her where James was.

But I stopped myself. I wasn't going to throw away the tiny bit of pride I had left. Maybe he's sick, I thought. Maybe he has the flu.

I probably would have welcomed the news that he had terminal cancer. Anything, but don't let him have gone on vacation.

The thought of him having a life without me, the thought of him actually *enjoying* that life, was deeply unpleasant.

He mustn't have a care in the world, I thought, my imagination running wild. Probably off with his fancy woman in some exotic resort. Drinking Piña Coladas from Denise's shoe. His life resonating to the sound of champagne corks popping and fireworks exploding and surrounded by music and happy people, wearing party hats and decorated with streamers, dancing past him, whooping and doing the conga.

While I was freezing in this March weather, I became fully convinced that James was living it up in some very expensive Caribbean resort, where he had fourteen houseboys and a private swimming pool and the air was scented with frangipani blossoms.

I had no idea what frangipani blossoms were like. I simply knew that they regularly appeared in this type of scenario.

"Oh dear," I thought, swallowing. I certainly hadn't expected to feel like this.

Now what do I do?

Mum marched into the room with a huge bundle of freshly ironed clothes in her arms.

She stopped in surprise when she saw me.

"What's wrong with you?" she demanded, looking at my white, miserable face.

"I called James," I told her, and burst into tears.

"Oh Lord," she said, putting the pile of clothes down on a chair and coming over to sit beside me.

"What did he say?" she asked.

"Nothing," I sobbed. "He wasn't there. I bet he's gone on a vacation with that fat bitch. And I bet they flew first-class. And I bet they have a Jacuzzi in their bathroom."

Mum put her arms around me.

And eventually I stopped crying.

"Do you want a hand putting the ironing away?" I asked Mum in a snivelly and tearful voice.

That made her look *really* worried. "Are you okay?" she said anxiously.

"Yes," I said. "I'm fine."

"Are you sure?" she said, still not convinced.

"Yes," I insisted, a bit annoyed.

I was fine.

I had better get used to feeling this upset, I decided.

Because it was going to happen a lot. At least until I came to terms with the fact that it really was over with James.

All right, so I really did feel awful now.

Hurt and shocked.

But in a while those feelings wouldn't hurt so much. The pain would go away.

So I wasn't going to take to the bed for a week.

I was going to square my shoulders and get on with things.

And I'd call him on Monday.

That'd be a really good time to talk to him. He was bound to be feeling really miserable then anyway, what with being back at work and having the postvacation blues and jet lag. I was trying to cheer myself up by pretending that I would be glad to see him being miserable.

And if I didn't think too hard about it, it would work for a little while.

"Right then, Mum," I said determinedly. "Let's put these clothes away."

I went purposefully over to the pile of freshly ironed clothes on the chair. Mum looked a little bit blown away as I started to quickly sort them out.

I picked up an armful and said to Mum, "I'll put these in Anna's drawer."

"But . . ." started Mum.

"No buts," I told her soothingly.

"No, Claire . . ." she said anxiously.

"Mum," I insisted, quite touched by her concern but determined to pull myself together and be a dutiful daughter, "I'm fine now."

And I left her bedroom, making for Anna's.

Mum's door swung shut behind me. So her voice was muffled when she called out to me. "Claire! For God's sake. How am I going to explain to your father why his underpants are in Anna's drawer?"

I was on my knees in front of Anna's chest of drawers.

I paused in what I was going.

I wasn't putting Dad's underpants in Anna's drawer, was I? I was.

I realized that I had better move them. Because there was no way that Anna would realize that there was anything unusual when she changed her underwear and found herself wearing huge, baggy men's briefs.

Assuming that she did in fact change her underwear.

Or wear underwear at all, now that I came to think of it.

I was sure I'd heard her going on about clothes—especially underclothes—being a form of fascism. Vague talk of air needing to circulate and skin needing to breathe and needing to feel liberated and unrestricted just led me to suspect that underwear and the wearing thereof might not feature highly on Anna's list of priorities.

With a martyred sigh, I gathered up the bundle of underpants.

thirteen

I was meeting Laura for a drink that evening.

I'd better give you a little bit of background here.

Laura, Judy and I were in college together. And we have been friends ever since.

Judy lived in London.

And Laura lived in Dublin.

I hadn't seen Laura since I fled from London, minus a husband and with a baby, but I had spoken on the phone to her a few times. I told her I was far too depressed to see her.

And because she was a good friend, she didn't get all huffy with me, but told me not to worry and that I would feel better eventually and that she'd see me then.

I told her that I would never feel better and that I would never see her again but that it had been lovely knowing her.

I had a feeling that she had rung Mum a few times over the past month to make discreet inquiries about the state of my heart (still broken at the last checkup), my mental health (still very unstable) and my popularity (at an all-time low).

But she hadn't pestered me, and for that I was very grateful.

But now I was feeling a good deal better so I called her and suggested meeting in town for a drink. Laura sounded delighted at this idea.

"We'll get plastered," she said enthusiastically over the phone.

I'm not sure whether this was a suggestion or a prediction. Either way it was a foregone conclusion.

"I'd say we will all right," I agreed, if our encounters over the past ten years or so were anything to go by. I was feeling quite alarmed. I'd forgotten what an unbridled hedonist Laura was—she could have shown those Roman emperors a thing or two.

Mum said she would be only too delighted to look after Kate.

After dinner (microwaved frozen shepherd's pie, not too bad actually), I went upstairs to get ready for my first social outing since my husband left me. Quite an occasion. A bit like losing my virginity or making my first Communion or getting married. Something that only happens once.

I hadn't a stitch to wear.

I began to feel very sorry and very foolish indeed about the martyrish way I had left all my lovely clothes behind in London. Behaving like a condemned man on his way to the gallows, crying dramatically, saying my life was over and that I wouldn't be needing clothes where I was going.

I was left with no option but to misappropriate some of Helen's things. She would be annoyed. But she was annoyed with me anyway for the alleged flirting with her boyfriend, so what did I have to lose?

I started to riffle frantically through Helen's hangers. Honestly, she had some really lovely clothes.

I felt the sap rising, the old juices start to flow.

I loved clothes.

I was like a man who was dying of thirst in the desert, who unexpectedly stumbles across a fridge full of ice-cold 7-UP. I had spent far too long in that nightgown.

I found a little wine-colored dress in her wardrobe. That'll do nicely, I thought as I clambered feverishly into it. I went back to my room and looked at myself in the mirror, and for the second time in two days I was surprised and delighted with what I saw.

I looked tallish and slimmish and youngish.

Not a bit like a single parent.

Or a deserted wife.

Whatever they're supposed to look like.

With a pair of woolly tights and my boots I looked pleasingly girlish (ha!) and innocent (double ha!).

And, if the dress was a little bit too short for me, exposing an alarming amount of my thigh (what with Helen being a good deal smaller than me), then so much the better.

Then I piled on the makeup. I was quite excited about going out—I'd forgotten what fun it was.

Gray eyeliner and black mascara made my eyes look really blue. And with my newly washed shiny hair I was very pleased with the overall effect.

Of course, Mum wasn't.

"Are you going to wear a skirt with that top?" she asked.

"Mum, you know perfectly well that this is a dress, not a top," I told her calmly.

Nothing she could say or do would stop me from feeling good about myself.

"It might well be a dress on Helen," she acknowledged. "But it's too short to be anything but a top on you."

I ignored her.

"And did you ask Helen if you could borrow it?" she said, obviously hell-bent on destroying my good mood. "Because I'll get the flak from Helen. You won't care. You'll be in town with your rowdy friends knocking back the Malibu or whatever it is you drink. And I'll be here, being shouted at by my youngest daughter. And it's not like any of us are in Helen's good graces at the moment anyway."

"Oh shut up, Mum," I told her. "I'll leave a note for Helen explaining that I've borrowed it. And when I get my clothes from London she can borrow some of mine."

Silence from Mum.

"Is that okay?" I asked her.

"Yes." She smiled. "And you look lovely," she added grudgingly.

Just before I left my bedroom to go downstairs, a glint from the dressing table caught my eye. It was my wedding ring. I had forgotten to put it back on after my shower. It lay there winking up at me, obviously eager to get out of the house for a bit. So I went over and picked it up. But I didn't put it on. My marriage is over, I thought, and maybe I'll start to believe it if I don't wear my wedding ring anymore. I put the ring back down on the dressing table.

Of course it was furious—it just couldn't believe that I wasn't going to wear it. And then it was upset. But I didn't give in. I couldn't afford any sentiment. I decided to leave before the recriminations started. "Sorry," I said shortly, turning my back, switching off the light and walking from the room.

Dad was watching golf on the television when I went in to him to borrow his car keys. I think I gave him a bit of a fright when I finally managed to wrench his attention away from the men in the plaid pants.

"You're very glamorous," he said, looking startled. "Where are you off to?"

"Into town to meet Laura," I told him.

"Well, don't get the bloody car vandalized," he said, alarmed.

Dad came from a small town in the west of Ireland, and although he had lived in Dublin for thirty-three years, he still didn't trust Dubliners. He thought that they were all petty criminals and thugs.

And he seemed to think that the center of Dublin was like Beirut. Except that Beirut was far nicer.

"I won't get it vandalized, Dad," I told him. "I'll leave it in a parking lot."

But that didn't calm him down either.

"Well, make sure that you pick it up by midnight," he said, getting very agitated. "Because all the parking lots close then. And if you don't get it, I'll have to walk to work in the morning."

I forbore from telling him, but only just, that he wouldn't have to walk anywhere in the morning if I got the car impounded. That there was actually nothing stopping him from borrowing Mum's car or using public transport.

"Don't worry, Dad," I assured him. "Now give me the keys."

He reluctantly handed them over.

"And don't go changing the radio station. I don't want to turn it on in the morning and be deafened by pop music."

"If I change it, I'll change it back," I sighed.

"And if you adjust the seat forward make sure you move it back again. I don't want to get in in the morning and think I've put on loads of weight in the night."

"Don't worry, Dad," I told him patiently as I picked up my coat and bag. "See you later."

It is easier for a camel to pass through the eye of a needle than to borrow the car off Dad.

As I closed the sitting room door behind me I heard him calling after me, "Where are you going without a skirt?" but I kept walking.

It was awful leaving Kate. It was the first time that I had gone out without her and it was a real wrench. In fact, I nearly brought her with me but then I realized that she'd be spending enough time in noisy smoky pubs when she was older, so no call for her to start just yet.

"You *will* check on her every fifteen minutes," I said tearfully to Mum.

"Yes," she said.

"Every *fifteen* minutes," I emphasized.

"Yes," she said.

"You won't forget?" I said anxiously.

"No," she said, starting to sound a bit annoyed.

"But what if you're watching something on TV and you get distracted?" I suggested.

"I won't forget!" she said, sounding definitely annoyed. "I know how to look after a child, you know. I *have* managed to rear five of my own."

"I know," I told her, "it's just that Kate is special."

"Claire!" said Mum in exasperation, "'will you just bloody well go!"

"Fine, fine," I said, quickly checking that the baby intercom was switched on, "I'm going."

"Have a nice time," called Mum.

"I'll try," I said, bottom lip trembling.

The drive into town was nightmarish.

Did you know that if you listen hard enough *everything* sounds like a baby crying? The wind in the trees, the rain on the roof of the car, the hum of the engine.

I was convinced that I could hear Kate crying for me, al-

ways faintly, nearly out of earshot. It was unbearable, and I
very nearly turned the car around and went back home.

If it wasn't for Common Sense making a guest appearance
in my head, that's probably exactly what I would have done.

"You're being ridiculous," said Common Sense.

"You're obviously not a mother yourself," I retorted.

"No," admitted Common Sense, "I'm not. But you've got
to realize that you can't be with her every moment for the rest
of her life. What about when you go back to work and she
has to go to day care? Well, how are you going to cope then?
Just think of this as good practice."

"You're right," I sighed, calming down for a moment. Then
panic gripped me again. What if she died? What if she died
that night?

Just then, like an oasis in the desert, I spotted a pay phone.
I swung the car over, much to the annoyance of the drivers
behind me, beeping their horns and shouting things at me, the
heartless bastards.

"Mum," I said tremulously.

"Who's this?" she asked.

"It's *me*," I said, feeling as if I was going to burst into tears.

"*Claire?*" she said, sounding outraged. "What the hell do
you want?"

"Has anything happened to Kate?" I asked breathlessly.

"Claire! Stop this! Kate is absolutely fine."

"Really?" I asked, hardly daring to believe it.

"Really," she said in a nicer voice. "Look, this does get
easier, you know. The first time is the worst. Now go and enjoy
yourself and I promise that I'll call you if anything happens."

"Thanks, Mum," I said, feeling a lot better.

I got back into the car and drove into town and parked the
car (yes, in a parking lot) and went down to the pub to meet
Laura. She was already there when I arrived, and it was wonderful to see her. I hadn't seen her in months.

I told her she looked lovely, because she did. She told me
that I looked lovely. Although I'm not sure whether I did or
not.

She said that she looked like an old hag.

I said that I looked like a dog.

I said that she didn't look like an old hag.

She said that I didn't look like a dog.

Pleasantries over, I went to get us some drinks.

There were several million people in the pub. Or at least that was how it felt. But Laura and I were lucky enough to get seats.

I suppose I must be getting old. There was a time when I would have cheerfully stood, pint in hand, in the midst of all these people, being swept along like seaweed in the tide. Not minding that the person I was supposed to be talking to was now several yards away and that most of my wine was spilled on my wrist.

Laura wanted to know all about Kate. And I was only too happy to tell her.

When I was younger I'd promised myself that I would never turn into a baby-bore. You know, the kind of people who go on and on about their baby and how she smiled at them for the first time today and how beautiful she is and all that, while all around them people are twitching and going into spasms of boredom. And I was a bit alarmed to find that that's exactly what I was doing. But I couldn't help it. It was different when it was your own baby. The only thing I can say in my defense is that when you have one yourself you'll know what I mean.

Maybe Laura was bored out of her skull, but she did a very decent impression of being interested in Kate.

"I'm dying to see her," she said. Gamely, I thought.

"Why don't you come out this weekend?" I said. "We'll spend an afternoon together and you can play with her."

And then Laura wanted to know what giving birth was like. So we discussed that in gory detail for a while. Laura started to look a bit sweaty and faint.

And then, of course, we moved onto the main item on the agenda. The real business of the evening. The main feature. The star act.

James.

James Webster, the Incredible Disappearing Husband.

Laura had all the details already.

From a variety of sources—my mother, Judy and a lot of other friends. So she didn't really need to know what had happened. She was more interested in how I was now and what I was planning to do.

"I don't know, Laura," I told her. "I don't know whether I'll go back to London or whether I'll stay here. I don't know what to do about my apartment. I don't really know what to do about anything."

"You'll really have to talk to James," she told me.

"Oh, don't I know it," I said. Slightly bitterly, I must admit.

So we discussed my responsibilities for a while. And we hazarded guesses as to what my future was going to be like.

Then I got a bit distressed talking about that, so I changed the subject and asked Laura who she was currently having sex with. It was much more entertaining talking about that, let me tell you, especially as it turned out that the lucky recipient of Laura's current sexual favors was a nineteen-year-old art student.

"Nineteen!" I shrieked, at a decibel level that caused glasses to shatter in the hands of several startled drinkers in a pub about half a mile away. "Nineteen! Are you serious?"

"Yes." She laughed. "But it's a disaster really. He never has a penny so all we can afford to do is have sex."

"But couldn't you pay for the two of you to go out?" I asked.

"I could, I suppose," she said. "But I'd be too ashamed to bring him anywhere."

"Is he always covered in paint?" I asked.

"He is," she said. "But it's not just that. He seems to have only one sweater. And no socks. And the less said about his jocks, the better."

"Ugh," I said. "That sounds awful."

"Ah no, it's not really," Laura assured me. "He's crazy about me. He thinks I'm gorgeous. And my ego could do with it."

"So do you really just have sex?" I asked, intrigued. "I mean, don't you talk and that?"

"Not really," she said. "Honestly, we have nothing in common. He's from a different generation. He comes over. We have sex and a bit of a laugh. He tells me I'm the most beautiful woman he's ever met—I'm probably the *only* woman he's ever met—and he leaves in the morning—usually taking a pair of my socks with him—asks me for his bus fare and off he goes. It's great!"

Gosh, I thought, looking at Laura with frank admiration. "You're such a nineties woman," I told her. "You're so cool."

"Not really," she said. "I'm just keeping the wolf from the door. Any port in a storm, that kind of thing."

"So is he your *boyfriend*?" I asked. "I mean, would you walk down Grafton Street holding his hand?"

"Lord no!" she said, looking horrified. "What if I met someone I knew? No, no, the little angel is purely a temporary measure. Keeping the bed warm until Mr. Right gets here. Although I can't think what's taking him so long."

Although I was very happy to see Laura, I was very aware that this was actually my first social outing as a single woman in over five years.

And it was my first social outing without my wedding ring. I felt very vulnerable and naked without it. It was only when I wasn't wearing it that I realized how secure I felt when I was wearing it. You know, it makes a statement, it says something like "I'm not desperate for a man, because I already have one. No, really, I do. Just look at my wedding ring."

Laura had split up with her boyfriend, Frank, about a year or so before.

So, in spite of Laura's teenaged lover, we were, to all intents and purposes, two single women sipping wine in a crowded downtown pub on a Thursday night in March.

I wondered if men could smell desperation from us.

I wondered if there was desperation to be smelled.

Was I giving Laura my undivided attention? Or was one part of my attention scanning the crowd for attractive men? Was I keeping tabs on how many men had given me admiring glances since I arrived?

None, actually, just for the record.

Not, of course, that I was counting or anything.

I laughed at something Laura told me. But I couldn't be sure that I was really laughing. Maybe I just wanted to show the men in the pub that I was perfectly happy and well-adjusted and not feeling like a quarter of a person without a man.

My God, but I was really starting to feel depressed. I felt as if I was wearing a neon sign over my head that said "Recently

Dumped" in flashing pink and purple lights, and then "Worthless Without a Man" in orange and red lights.

All my confidence in myself had gone.

Laura noticed that I had started to droop like a dying plant and made routine inquiries. I tearfully tried to tell her how I was feeling.

"Don't worry," she told me kindly. "When Frank left me for the twenty-year-old I felt so *ashamed*. Like it was all my fault that he had run off. And I felt that I was worth less than nothing without him. But that passes."

"Does it?" I asked her, my eyes brimming with tears.

"Honestly, it does," she promised me.

"I feel like such a reject," I tried to explain to her.

"I know, I know," she said. "And you feel like everyone else knows it."

"*Exactly*," I said, feeling thankful that I wasn't the only person who'd ever felt like this.

"All right," I said, drying my eyes. "Time for more drinks."

I fought my way through the happy crowds of people and finally got to the bar. I stood there, being jostled and having elbows stuck in my face and drinks spilled down my back as I tried to attract the bartender's attention. Just as I was coming to the conclusion that I would have to lift up my dress and show him my boobs before he would notice me, someone put his hands on my waist and squeezed.

This was all I needed! Someone taking advantage of a single woman of a certain age!

Outraged, I turned around as quickly as I could in the confined space, ready to apprehend someone for sexual harassment.

And came face-to-face, as it were, with someone's chest.

It was the beautiful Adam.

Adam, who might or might not be Helen's boyfriend.

The jury was still out.

"Hello." He smiled charmingly. "I saw you from the other side of the bar. Do you need a hand?"

"Oh hello," I said, maintaining my composure but feeling delighted to meet him. What a stroke of luck that Laura chose this pub, I thought.

"Am I damn glad to see you?" I said. "I haven't even placed my order yet. The bartender hates me."

He laughed.

And I laughed. I had completely forgotten that we were supposed to be feeling awkward with each other after the little scene in my bedroom where he practically suggested that we make babies.

Adam said, "I'll order the drinks for you."

I gave him the money and told him to get two glasses of red wine and whatever he was having. I took pride in remembering where I came from—I too was once a penniless student. I remembered watching people practically lighting their cigarettes with fivers and wishing enviously that they would buy me a pint of Carlsberg, just one pint.

Adam squashed into the bar. My cheek was practically resting on his chest. I could faintly smell him. Soap. He smelled so fresh and clean.

I wryly told myself to get a grip on myself. I was starting to behave like Blanche Du Bois. Or the mad old alcoholic from *Sunset Boulevard*, whatever her name is. Or any of the myriad old hags featured in any story about Beverly Hills, face-lifted to within an inch of their lives, consumed with lust for much younger men. Sad and pathetic. And I didn't want to be like that.

Naturally, in no time at all Adam had got the drinks. Bartenders treat guys like him with respect. They have no time at all for women like me. Especially ones whose husbands have run off on them.

Like every other man in the universe, the bartender obviously knew I was a loser.

Adam handed me the two glasses of wine and then he said, "Here's your change."

"Oh, I've no free hands," I said, indicating the two glasses of wine.

"No problem," he said, and slid his hand into a pocket on the side of the dress I was wearing. Just for a second his hand rested on my hipbone. I could feel the heat of it through the fabric of the dress.

I held my breath.

I think he did too.

Then he let go of the money and it jangled into my pocket.

What did you expect me to do? Slap him for taking liberties? I mean, the boy had to give me my change and I had no free hands. He did exactly the right thing.

Although I did think that people that attractive should carry permits. They should have to take some kind of exam to prove that they can be trusted to behave responsibly out on the streets looking so gorgeous. And it wasn't just that he was so handsome. Which he undeniably was. But he was so big and manly.

He made me feel like such a feminine little woman.

It was the large nightgown syndrome all over again.

He said, "Who are you here with?"

And I said, "My friend Laura."

He said, "Can I join you?"

I said, "Of course."

Why not, I thought. He's entertaining and sweet and Laura will enjoy him.

Although he might be a bit old for her.

He steered me through the packed pub. I must say, people treated me with a lot more respect with him around.

I don't think I had more than one drop of alcohol spilled on me on my journey back from the bar as opposed to an entire brewery-full on the outward journey.

Very unfair, of course, but there we are.

We passed a crowd of people who seemed to know Adam.

"Adam, where are you going?" demanded one of the girls. Blond. Pink pouty mouth. Very young. Very pretty.

"I've met an old friend," he told her. "I'm going to have a drink with her."

I quickly scanned the crowd to make sure that Helen wasn't there. Thankfully, I couldn't see her.

However, I did notice an older woman in among them, looking very anxious as Adam bypassed their little group. Could this be the poor lovesick Professor Staunton?

I was aware of several hostile looks. All from girls. It was almost funny. Fuck them, I thought cheerfully. If only they knew, they have nothing to fear from me. My husband dumped me, I wanted to tell them, and he was only average good-looking.

I brought Adam over and introduced him to Laura.

She blushed.

So he did have this effect on every woman he met, I observed. And not just on the women in my family.

Somehow Adam found a spare seat.

He was that kind of guy.

"You're a terrible fibber." I smiled at him.

"Why?" he asked, opening his blue eyes very wide and looking all innocent and little-boyish.

"Telling that poor girl that I'm an old friend," I told him.

"Well, you are," he said. "You're old."

"As in 'older than me' kind of 'old,'" he told me hastily as he noticed my eyes starting to narrow. "And I only know that because I asked Helen what age you were. I thought you were much younger."

I just looked at him, thinking, I've got to hand it to him.

"And," he continued, "even though we've only met once before I feel like you're a friend."

Yes, I thought, he's *definitely* redeemed himself.

It was at this stage, Laura later told me, that she took off her underpants and lifted her skirt but that neither of us noticed. I don't believe her for a second, but I do believe I understand the point she was making.

Laura asked Adam how he knew me and he said, "I'm in college with Helen."

Laura gave me a look that said a lot. Something like, "Oh God no, a bloody student. We'll have to pretend to be interested in whatever boring subject he's studying."

"It's okay." He smiled at Laura. "You don't have to ask me what I'm studying."

"Oh," she said, a bit embarrassed. "In that case I won't."

There was a little bit of a pause.

"Well," said Laura, "I'm actually curious now."

"That wasn't my intention." Adam laughed. "But seeing as you've asked, I'm in first year doing English, psychology and anthropology."

"First year?" asked Laura with a raise of her eyebrows, obviously alluding to his—what shall we say—less than boyish demeanor.

"Yes," said Adam. "I'm a mature student. Or so they tell

me. I don't feel a bit mature. Only when I compare myself with my classmates, I suppose."

"Are they awful?" I asked, willing him to say yes.

"Not awful," he said. "Just young. I suppose somebody has to be. I mean, they're all seventeen or eighteen and they're all just out of school and they're only going to college to put off being responsible for another couple of years. Not because they have any great interest in learning. Or love of their subjects."

Laura and I had the grace to look extremely shamefaced as he said this. Laura and Judy and I had been prime examples of the lazy, self-indulgent types he was describing.

"How awful for you," I murmured.

Laura and I smirked at each other.

"And how come you're going to college now?" I asked him.

"Well, I never wanted to go before. I never really knew what I wanted to do when I left school. So I did all the wrong things," he said intriguingly.

"And recently I've got my life back together. It was in a bit of a mess," he continued, even more intriguingly. "And now I'm ready for college. I really love it."

"Really?" I said, impressed by his maturity and his single-mindedness.

"Yes," he said.

Then he continued hesitantly, "I think I'm lucky to have waited until now. Because now I can really appreciate it. I think everyone should have to go and work for a couple of years before deciding whether they want to study some more."

"Is that what you did?" I asked him. "Did you work?"

"Sort of," he said abruptly, obviously not wanting to say anymore.

Curiouser and curiouser.

So squeaky-clean Adam has a Past.

Well, that's how he was making it sound.

I bet he's just trying to be all mysterious and create a myth around himself, I thought uncharitably. He's probably worked in the civil service for the past six years. Probably in the least glamorous department, like the livestock licensing one, if there is such a thing.

Laura asked Adam the second question that one always asks students. (The first being, What are you studying?) "What do you want to do when you get your degree?" she asked.

I waited with bated breath.

Please God, oh please God, don't let him say he wants to be a writer or a journalist, I begged.

It would be just too much of a cliché.

I was starting to like and respect him, and this would ruin it entirely.

I put my hands together in prayer and sent my eyes heavenward.

"I'd like to do something with the psychology," he said. (Phew! I thought.) "I'm interested in the way people's minds work. I might like to be some kind of counselor. Or I might like to get involved in advertising. And use the psychology that way," he explained. "Anyway, it's a long way away."

"And what about English?" I asked him nervously. "Don't you enjoy that?"

"Of course," he said. "It's my favorite. But I can't see myself getting a job out of it. Unless I want to try to become a writer or a journalist. And everybody wants to do that."

Thank God! I thought.

I'm glad that he likes it. I just couldn't bear to hear another person going on about how he wants to write a book. So we chatted pleasantly. Laura went to the bar to get more drinks.

Adam turned to me and smiled.

"This is great," he said. "It's so nice to have a bit of intelligent conversation."

I glowed.

Adam moved a little bit closer to me.

So I may not have the body of a seventeen-year-old but I can still entertain a man, I thought smugly.

"Adam, we're leaving now. Are you coming?"

The pretty blond girl appeared at Adam's side.

"No, Melissa, not yet. But I'll see you tomorrow. Okay?" said Adam.

It was obviously far from okay. Melissa looked outraged.

"But . . . I thought . . . aren't you coming to the party?" she asked, sounding as if she couldn't believe her ears.

"No, I don't think so," said Adam, a bit more firmly this time.

"Fine!" said Melissa, letting Adam know that it was far from fine. "Here's your bag." And she let a huge sports bag fall with a thud onto the floor.

She cast venomous looks at both Laura and me.

Puzzled but venomous.

She really couldn't understand what Adam was doing with two old bags like us when he could have had his pick of all the nubile seventeen-year-olds in the place.

Quite frankly, neither could I.

Melissa flounced away and Adam sighed.

"I couldn't stand it," he explained wearily. "Another student party. Cans of warm Heineken. And not being able to get into the bathroom because someone's having sex in there. And you leave your jacket on the bed and someone pukes on it. I'm too old."

I suddenly felt genuinely sorry for him.

I thought he was being sincere when he told me he was enjoying a bit of intelligent conversation.

It couldn't be easy to be surrounded by giggly excitable eighteen-year-olds like Helen and Melissa when you're a lot more grown-up than that. And it also couldn't be easy, I realized, to have so many young girls in love with you. Not if you were a kind person, like Adam seemed to be, and didn't want to hurt or upset them. Sometimes, not that I'd know or anything, but being beautiful isn't all fun and games. You have to use your power wisely and responsibly.

For the next ten minutes or so a steady stream of young girls came over to say good-bye to Adam. Well, that was their pretext. Melissa had obviously reported back and they were really coming to see how hideous and old Laura and I were. I have to admit, if the tables were turned, I'd be one of the first over to criticize and ridicule the shoes, clothes, makeup and hair of the offending women.

As it happened, Laura looked beautiful, red curls, alabaster skin and nothing like her thirty years. I don't think I looked too awful either. But I'm sure that didn't stop anyone from saying how ancient we looked. And what did it matter?

Someone stuck a can under my nose and rattled it a bit.

"Would you like to make a contribution to children in need?" asked a harassed-looking man in a wet overcoat.

"Certainly," I said, and shoved a pound into the can.

"Yourself?" he said, looking at Laura. He hadn't even asked Adam to contribute. He obviously recognized a penniless student when he saw one.

"Oh, I make my contributions directly," Laura explained to the man.

"Do you?" I asked, puzzled. I hadn't known that Laura was involved in any children's charities.

"Well, I have sex with a child on a regular basis," she declared. "If that isn't contributing directly, I don't know what is."

The man looked horrified and moved on to the next table at high speed.

Adam roared with laughter.

"I've never met a pedophile before," he said to her.

"I'm only joking. I'm not really a child molester at all," she told Adam. "The child in question is nineteen."

We finished our drinks and put on our coats and got ready to leave.

The pub was starting to empty. Everyone at the tables around us seemed in high spirits, except the bartenders, who were practically begging people to leave. "I've worked thirteen nights in a row," I heard one bartender telling a particularly rowdy table of revelers. "I'm exhausted." In fairness, he did look exhausted, but I think he was wasting his time trying to appeal to their humanitarian side.

"You're bringing tears to my eyes," said a rather drunk young man with grave irony.

"Finish that beer, or I'm taking it," threatened another bartender, at another nearby table.

So the customer drank nearly a whole pint in one gulp, to the encouraging comments of his friends—"Good man," "Waste not, want not," and various other shouts.

Even Laura called over, "Swalley that down."

We passed the customer about five minutes later, just outside the pub, as he was being assisted by a couple of his equally drunk friends while vomiting copiously.

When we got to the door of the pub, we found that the rain had started again.

"I'm only parked up the road," said Laura. "I'll run."

We hugged each other.

"I'll be out on Sunday to see Kate," she said. "Lovely meeting you, Adam." And off she ran into the wet night, almost colliding with the vomiting man.

"Sorry," she called to him, her voice floating back to us on the damp night air.

Adam and I stood at the door for a moment or two. I wasn't sure what to say to him, and he said nothing at all.

"Can I give you a lift home?" I asked.

I felt a bit awkward about asking him.

As though I was the rich older woman who was desperate for love and sex and buying the penniless handsome young man.

"That would be really great," he said. "I think I've missed the last bus."

He flushed a smile at me.

I relaxed.

I was doing him a favor. Not trying to take advantage of him.

We walked briskly along the wet streets until we reached the parking lot, and believe me, there was nothing even remotely romantic about the walk in the rain. Utter misery is what it was. My boots are suede. I'll have to spend the rest of my life standing with them over a steaming kettle to restore them to their former glory.

We got into the car. He threw his soaking bag on the back seat. He sat in the passenger seat and, I swear to God, he practically filled the whole front of the car.

Off we went.

He started fiddling with the radio station.

"Oh don't!" I told him. "Dad'll kill me."

I told him the conversation that I'd had with Dad before I left and he laughed heartily.

"You're a good driver," he said after a while.

Naturally, as soon as he said that I got all flustered and stalled the car, and then nearly drove into a pole. He gave me directions to his apartment in Rathmines and we drove along in the rain.

Neither of us spoke.

The only sound was the swishing of the car wheels on the road and the squeaking of the windshield wipers.

But it was a nice silence.

I pulled up outside his house and smiled good-bye at him. It really had been a lovely evening.

"Thanks for the lift," he said.

"You're welcome." I smiled.

"Er, em . . . would you like, I mean . . . can I offer you a cup of tea?" he asked awkwardly.

"When . . . like . . . now, do you mean?" I asked just as awkwardly.

"No, I was thinking of sometime around next December." He smiled at me.

My refusal was automatic—it was in my mouth before I even knew it. I had several excuses: It was late, I was soaked, this was my first night to leave Kate with someone else, Helen would machete me.

"Yes," I said, totally surprising myself. "Why not?"

I parked the car and in we went.

I was filled with trepidation. My fear was well-founded. I had been to enough students' apartments to expect the worst. All kinds of odd arrangements. You know, six or seven people sleeping in the front room, a couple of people living in the kitchen, having to go through a bedroom to get to the bathroom, having to go through the bathroom to get to the living room.

Bedrooms divided by a tartan rug hanging from the ceiling, to give a pretense of privacy. Wardrobes in the hall. Chests of drawers in the kitchen. Saucepans and buckets in the bathroom. The fridge on the landing. The coffee table in the front room consisting of four blue milk crates and a slab of chipboard.

You know, that kind of thing.

A kitchen that looked like if it were struck by a bolt of lightning, the process of evolution would begin all over again, curtains askew and crooked, broken blinds hanging from the windows, crushed cans of beer underfoot, the cistern being used to make home brew.

Oh yes, believe me, I've paid my dues at the student apartments of this world.

So I was greatly relieved when Adam opened the front door and let me into an apartment that looked normal—in fact, I'd go so far as to say downright pleasant.

"Come into the kitchen," he said, taking off his wet jacket.

We went into the kitchen and Adam put on the kettle and a heater. I was suspicious.

"The other people who live here," I asked him, "are they students also?"

"No," he said, taking my coat off me and hanging it up near the heater. "They both work." Well, that explained a lot.

"Are you soaked?" he asked nicely. "Would you like me to get you a sweater?"

"No, I'm fine," I said gamely. "My coat protected me from the worst of the precipitation."

He smiled.

"Well, I'll get you a towel to dry your hair," he said, and left for a moment.

He was back almost immediately with a big blue towel in his hand, and I'm glad to be able to put your mind at rest here and tell you that, no, he didn't dry my hair for me.

No, he gave me the towel and I gave my hair a few half-hearted scrubs. I didn't want to end up with it sticking up all over the place and drying at funny angles.

Quite frankly, I'd rather have caught pneumonia.

I took off my boots and put them in front of the heater. Adam gave me a cup of tea and we sat at the table in the pleasant warm kitchen. He even found a packet of biscuits.

"They're Jenny's," he explained. "I'll tell her in the morning that I had a special visitor last night. She'll understand."

He made it seem so easy to be charming. It never came across as smarmy or insincere.

"So how long is it since you've had Kate?" he asked, putting the sugar in front of me.

"Over a month now," I said.

"Look, I hope you don't mind," he said awkwardly. "But Helen has told me the situation with you and your husband."

"And?" I said, minding.

"Well, nothing really," he said hurriedly. "I mean, I know it's none of my business or anything, but I'm sure it's not easy for you. I went through something a bit similar myself and I know how awful it is."

"Really?" I said, intrigued.

"Well, yes," he said. "But I'm not trying to pry into your life or anything."

Never mind that, I was thinking, tell me! You can pry into my life if I can pry into yours.

"And," he continued, "I know you've got lots of friends in Dublin, but if you ever want to talk to me you can."

"You're not using me as some kind of experiment for your psychology course?" I asked suspiciously.

"Not at all." He laughed. "It's just that I liked you from the moment I met you. And I like you more after tonight. And I'd like it if we were friends."

"Why?" I asked, even more suspiciously.

Well, I was perfectly entitled to ask, wasn't I? I mean, I just didn't get it. I was just perfectly ordinary. Why had Adam decided that I was special and worth being friends with?

I wasn't putting myself down here. I had lots of good qualities, I knew that. I wasn't just being Queen of the Low Self-Esteem. But lots of people have good qualities. There wasn't anything particularly *unusual* about me. Now Adam, on the other hand, must have met millions of women, funny, beautiful, clever, entertaining, rich, waiflike, cute, sexy, interesting women.

Why had he singled me out?

"Because you're nice," he said.

Nice! I ask you.

Who wants to be picked by a beautiful man like Adam just because she's nice?

"And you're very funny. And clever. And interesting," he said.

That's more like it, I thought.

Any chance of sexy or beautiful?

I'd even have settled for attractive.

But nothing doing.

Sexy, beautiful and attractive were not on offer.

But what the hell. It was nice talking to him. I was enjoying myself.

I wasn't attracted to him.

Although I probably would have been if circumstances had been different.

He wasn't attracted to me.

We were just two adults who happened to like each other's company.

I was a married woman.

On Monday I would be ringing James.

Adam was spoken for. If not by my sister Helen, then by some other woman, I didn't doubt.

So no big deal.

"What are you doing tomorrow?" he asked.

"Well, I don't know," I told him. "I haven't really got into any routine since I came back from London. I suppose I'll just take care of Kate."

"Well, that's why I was asking you how long it is since you've had Kate. I was wondering if you'd like to come to the gym with me?"

"Me?" I said in horror. "Why?"

"Not because I think you need to," he said anxiously. "But because I think you might like to."

Me, with my saggy, out-of-shape body, go to the gym with this Adonis? Was he joking? But on the other hand, my body would stay saggy and out of shape if I didn't do anything about it. And I used to enjoy going to the gym before I had Kate.

Maybe this was the best suggestion I'd heard in a long time.

"Well . . ." I said cautiously, "I'm very out of shape."

"You've got to start somewhere," he said quickly.

"And who would watch Kate?"

"Wouldn't your mother do it? It would only be for a couple of hours."

"Maybe," I said doubtfully. This was all moving a bit too fast for me.

Goddammit, I only went out to have a drink with Laura. Now I was signing up for some fitness program with a person I'd only met yesterday.

And yesterday evening, at that.

"Look, come tomorrow. I bet you'll enjoy it. What have you got to lose?" he said.

I thought about it.

Nothing, apart from my life if Helen found out.

"Okay, I'll come."

I arranged to meet him the following day in town at three o'clock, though I could hardly believe I was doing it. I finished my tea. He saw me to my car.

He closed my car door for me and stood at the gate—in the rain, I might add—as I drove away.

I was starting to feel guilty before I even got to the end of the road.

Guilt at neglecting Kate.

Guilt at associating with my youngest sister's boyfriend, blameless and all as it was.

Guilt at the idea of wasting time in the gym when I should be talking to a lawyer and sorting out my finances and all that.

As soon as I got home I ran up the stairs to Kate. It was such a relief to see that she was alive and well. I felt so guilty that I was convinced that something terrible had to happen. I held her so tightly I thought I would squeeze the life out of her.

"I missed you, darling," I told her as she struggled for breath. "On Monday I'm going to call Daddy and I'll try and work things out for us. Everything's going to be fine, I promise."

I had had such a nice evening. I simply couldn't understand why I felt so depressed.

fourteen

I had planned to call Mr. Hasdell, the lawyer whose name Laura had given me, as soon as he got to his desk at nine o'clock the following morning.

But I just couldn't bring myself to do it.

I fed Kate.

I played with Kate.

I worried about what to wear to the gym.

I worried about what would happen if Helen found out that I was going to the gym with Adam.

I worried in case I was neglecting Kate.

I worried in case Mum refused to watch Kate on the grounds that it would make her an accomplice to my meeting Adam.

I worried about everything other than the important thing.

I knew that I had to call my bank. I had practically no money. But I was far more concerned about how my butt was going to look in the leotard and leggings that I had found in Rachel's room.

My child was growing up without a father, but instead of getting on the phone and calling a family lawyer and trying to work something out, I stood in front of a mirror holding my stomach in, checking my profile and finally, as though the years had rolled away and I was still fifteen, twisting my head around, trying to see what my butt looked like in the mirror.

Mum was highly suspicious when I asked her would she look after Kate for me in the afternoon.

"Again?" she asked.

"Yes, but only for a couple of hours," I muttered.

"Why?" she demanded. "What are you up to?"

"Nothing, Mum. I just wanted to go to the gym and start getting back into shape," I told her. I didn't want to lie to her. But I wasn't too comfortable telling the truth either.

"Oh, the gym," she said, sounding quite pleased. "Well, that's good. Just mind that you don't, you know, pull any . . . you know . . . do yourself any damage. It's not so long since you gave birth, don't forget."

"Thanks, Mum," I said, amused at her delicacy. "But I think my insides are in fine condition. Raring to go, to be quite honest with you."

I shouldn't have said that.

It made her suspicious again.

I know that she had encouraged me to have a fling with Adam, but I felt so guilty about meeting him that I didn't want anyone to know. So off I drove into town, feeling sick with guilt and the fear of being caught and the fear of something happening to Kate. About halfway there, I decided that I wasn't cut out for this life of deceit and intrigue and child neglect and that I would turn around and go home.

But the traffic was so bad that, by the time I got to turn the car, I was feeling guilty about just leaving Adam standing there. So I decided that I would go in, meet him, tell him that I couldn't meet him—if you follow me—and go right back home again.

And then I couldn't find a parking space. I practically had to get a bus from where I parked the car to where I had to meet Adam.

So I was very late meeting him.

I was running along the road when I saw him standing outside the shop where we had arranged to meet. He was looking up and down the street with an anxious expression on his face, totally oblivious to all the admiring stares he was getting from passing women.

Every time I saw him I got a shock.

I'd forgotten how handsome he is. This tall beautiful man with the long muscley legs is waiting for *me*, I thought, feeling a bit overwhelmed.

Why?

"Claire!" he said, looking delighted to see me. "I thought you weren't coming."

"I'm not," I mumbled.

"So have you just sent a hologram of yourself along or what?" he asked, smiling.

"No, I mean, Adam . . . look, I'm not sure if this is a good idea," I stuttered. "Like, you know . . ." I trailed off miserably.

"What isn't a good idea?" he asked gently as he steered me out of the path of oncoming pedestrians.

"Meeting you and that . . . you know, I'm married and all that," I said, not meeting his eyes.

Then I looked up at him and I couldn't believe how hurt he looked.

"I know you're married," he said quietly as he looked down into my eyes. "I wouldn't dare make any assumptions. I don't want to make any moves on you—I want to be your friend."

I was mortified. Absolutely mortified. What on earth made me say that to him? All right, so I was feeling guilty about meeting him. But wasn't that my problem? Why should I attribute any improper motives to him just because I had some myself?

Oh God! Or did I have some improper motives myself?

"Look, you'd better go home," said Adam.

He wasn't being cold and angry, but it was as if he didn't want me to touch him or anything.

"No!" I said.

Jesus, would I ever make up my mind!

"No," I said, not quite so frantically. "I'm sorry. I shouldn't have said what I said. I was being silly and overreacting."

We were attracting all kinds of curious and interested looks from the shoppers as they passed in and out of the doorway.

"Great," I overheard one young woman saying gleefully to her companion. "There's nothing I love more than seeing other people arguing."

Her voice floated back to me from up the street. "It makes me feel like I'm not the only person in the world who's miserable."

Oh don't worry, I thought, you're not. Adam stared at me and sighed in exasperation.

"What do you want?"

"Nothing," I said. "Can we forget that this happened and just go to the gym like we had planned?"

"All right," he said. But not in a very friendly way.

"Ah, be nice to her. Give her a kiss," called out a scruffy old man who had several opened bottles of Guinness sticking out of his torn overcoat pocket and who had been watching the proceedings with great interest. "She's sorry. Aren't you, love?"

"Come on," I mumbled to Adam.

I didn't want a crowd to start forming.

"Give her a smack," shouted the old man, who seemed to have suddenly turned a bit nasty. "It's the only language they understand!"

We hurried up the road; the old man's cries got a bit fainter.

"Jesus," I said in relief as we rounded a corner and we couldn't hear him anymore. Adam smiled briefly, but things still felt tense and uncomfortable.

We got to the gym and he tersely signed me in. I went off to the women's changing rooms and eventually sidled out, as self-conscious as a virgin bride in my leotard and leggings, hugging the wall for fear that anyone would catch a twenty-twenty, full-on, four-square view of my butt.

But I needn't have bothered. He barely glanced at me.

"The bikes are over there " he said, pointing. "And the free weights are in this room here. The rest of the machines are over that way."

And he left me to get on with things.

"That's lovely," I thought resentfully. "I could be pulling muscles left, right and center and he doesn't give a damn." I stood for a moment waiting for him to come back and show me how to do things.

To be perfectly honest, I suppose that I had entertained all kinds of thoughts, albeit guilty ones, about him bending over me as I lay flat on my back on the bench press, to adjust the weight or something. And for us to suddenly realize that we were close enough to kiss.

That kind of romantic stuff.

But Adam ignored me completely, so I reluctantly decided that I might as well get a grip on my runaway imagination and do a bit of exercise.

I did my warm-ups and my stretches.

And before I knew it, I realized that I was enjoying myself.

"I'm not actually happy," I assured myself. "It's the artificial high that people get from exercise. Pheromones or something. No, it's endorphins, isn't it?"

Good God, I was turning into Helen.

I stole a glance at Adam.

(Whoops! That was very Romantic Novelish. People are always "stealing" glances in them.)

All right then, I stole nothing.

Not guilty of any kind of larceny.

Although I did know a guy in a pub who would have taken a couple of boxes of glances off my hands for a decent price. No questions asked.

But I did look at Adam when he didn't know that I was.

He pushed and lifted vast quantities of weights.

He looked wonderful.

Very grim and serious-looking and handsome.

A man who took his body seriously.

And with good reason.

Although he was just wearing sweatpants and a T-shirt he was pretty spectacular-looking.

Beautiful strong arms, with a glistening of sweat on them.

And a really lovely butt.

I'm sorry. I shouldn't have said that.

But he did.

After about an hour or so I decided that I had had enough.

"Okay." He smiled. "Go and have a shower and I'll meet you in the café."

He was already sitting in the café when I emerged, having spent far too long doing my makeup.

His hair was all wet and shiny and he had what looked like about twenty cartons of milk in front of him.

"Finally," he said when he saw me. "Well, did you enjoy that?"

"It was great," I told him.

"Glad you came?" he asked with a deadpan expression.

"Yes," I said, looking him in the eye.

"Good," he said, and started to laugh.

So did I.

Thank God! I was so relieved that he didn't seem to be annoyed with me anymore.

I got myself a cup of coffee and joined him. We were the only two people in the café. It was a Friday evening, and I suppose most sensible people had better things to do. Going to the pub and getting drunk, I'd bet.

Suddenly things were very nice with Adam again. The tension was gone. We didn't talk about anything unpleasant or sensible. I didn't ask him if Helen was his girlfriend and he returned the favor by not asking me anything about James. I didn't ask him about his lectures and he very decently reciprocated by not asking me about my job.

He asked me what my favorite animal was.

And I asked him what his earliest memory was.

We talked about going to discos when we were fifteen.

And we discussed what one ability we would choose if we could choose anything.

"I'd like to be able to fly," he said.

"Well, why don't you learn?" I asked him.

"No, I wish *I* could fly," he said, laughing. "You know, without a plane or anything. And what about you, what would you like?"

"Sometimes I wish I could see into the future," I told him. "Not everything and not years ahead or anything. Maybe a couple of hours ahead."

"That'd be great," said Adam. "Think of all the money you could win on the horses."

I laughed.

"Or I wish I could be invisible. That would be great fun. I bet you can find out much more about a person when they don't think that you're there."

"You're right," he said.

There was a little pause.

"I'd love to be able to travel through time," he said after a while.

"Oh, that's a good one," I said, excited. "Imagine going

into the future. Or imagine going back to really exciting times, like ancient Egypt. Though knowing my luck I'd end up as some poor old gladiator."

"I'm not sure if there were any gladiators in ancient Egypt," he said. But in a nice way.

I suppose he's used to correcting Helen.

"Anyway," he continued, "I'm sure you'd be a princess. Maybe not Cleopatra. Your coloring is too fair," he said, lightly touching my hair. "But you'd definitely be a princess."

"Um, would I?" I mumbled.

Witty and gracious, that's me.

Sparkling and Repartee are my middle names.

"When would you like to travel back to?" I asked him, anxious for the conversation to return to a less intimate footing and for my breathing to return to normal.

"Well," he said, "sometimes I wish I could travel back in my own life. You know, go back to a time when I was really happy. Or go back and change things. Fix things that I did wrong. Or do things that I should have done and didn't."

I was absolutely intrigued. *What* had gone on in his life that sounded so traumatic? But before I could probe I suddenly noticed the time.

It was ten past seven.

"Jesus!" I said, jumping up in alarm. "Look at the time. I thought it was about five o'clock."

I picked up my bag and made for the door.

"I have to go. Thanks for bringing me. Bye."

"Wait," he said. "I'll walk you to your car."

"No, there's no need," I told him.

And off I ran.

I was in a total panic.

Where had the time gone?

How could I have neglected Kate like this? God would punish me. Something was bound to have happened to her.

I drove home at high speed, the roads clear of rush hour traffic because it was so late. Mum was tight-lipped and suspicious when I arrived. "What kind of time do you call this?" she demanded.

"Sorry," I gasped. "I lost track of the time."

"I've fed Kate," she told me.

(Thank God! That must mean that she's still alive!)

"Thanks, Mum."

"Five times."

"Thanks, Mum."

"And I've changed her."

"Thanks, Mum."

"Three times."

"Thanks, Mum."

"I hope you're grateful."

"Oh, I am, Mum."

"She's not my child, you know."

"I know, Mum."

"My childbearing days are over."

"I know, Mum."

Then she was really suspicious.

Why was I being so nice?

Hurriedly, I raised my voice at her.

"She's your flesh and blood too, you know," I told her.

But it was a poor effort.

I just couldn't concentrate on getting annoyed by her. I'd think to myself, "My God, but she's being particularly irritating," but just as I was getting myself worked up into a nice bit of a lather of annoyance my thoughts would slide Adamward, and I'd suddenly feel happy.

Well, happyish.

My head didn't know where it was. All manner of unusual behavior going on.

A large battalion of my thoughts was marching determinedly on its way to Annoyance but it was distracted and took a wrong turn at Adam and found, to its surprise, that it had ended up in the entirely different destination of Dreamy Contentment.

Which caused no end of confusion and consternation amongst the ranks, I can tell you.

I rushed upstairs to see Kate.

She was in her bassinet, fed, changed and asleep.

The little angel.

She snuffled contentedly in her sleep, moving her fat pink little legs. With a shock I realized how lucky I was. This beautiful miniature human being was my child. I gave birth to her. She was my daughter.

For the first time I realized—*really* realized—that my marriage was not a failure.

James and I might not be together but we had created this wonderful little person.

This living miracle.

I was not becursed.

I was not benighted.

I was very, very lucky.

fifteen

I spent Friday night watching television with Mum. I felt that I had done enough gallivanting over the past couple of days. And I was totally exhausted. Taking care of a young baby is a grueling task. Although how would I know, I hear you asking.

All right, all right, I admit that I'd had a lot of help from my parents, but I still felt exhausted.

How I was going to cope with returning to work was beyond me.

How do people do it? It made me feel so inadequate.

Especially when I thought of women in, was it China? You know, when they're out digging up the fields with their bare hands and they say, "Oh excuse me for a moment," as if they were going to the ladies' room at a posh reception and they lift their skirt and out pops a newborn baby into a plowed furrow or onto a bag of seeds or whatever.

"Aaah, that feels better," they might say.

And on they go, tilling and plowing and uprooting mighty oaks with one hand, their newborn child attached to their breast.

And they're pregnant again by nightfall.

And the newborn child has been given a suit of clothes and set to work driving a tractor.

As I watched television with Mum, my thoughts kept straying to Adam. And in true adolescent fashion I would get a little tingle every time I thought of him.

I'd had such a lovely time with him. If I hadn't loved James, I might have been attracted to Adam.

That's not to say that I was *un*attracted to him.

I mean, he was very attractive.

Hypothetically speaking, it is possible to be in love with one man—in my case, James—and have a crush on another—in this case, Adam.

It wasn't as if a crush does any harm.

It didn't mean that I'm a fickle person.

It was good for me.

Because I didn't have to act on that crush.

And, even if, God forbid, I *did* act on it, well it wasn't the end of the world, now was it?

Yes, if Helen found out about it, it could well have been the end of the world.

But that was assuming that Adam was attracted to me.

But I thought he was.

Was that very conceited?

Maybe he used that trick with all the women.

You know, coming on all sincere and vulnerable and adoring, so the women would think he was the nicest man they ever met, that he was really different.

And before they knew it they'd be in Adam's bed with their underwear flung to one of the four corners of the room and Adam would be clambering off them, saying, "When I told you that I'd respect you in the morning, I lied."

And then he'd call them exactly seventy-two hours later to say, "Oh, by the way, the condom burst. You did say you were ovulating, didn't you?"

Yes, I thought angrily, I bet he's a bastard. How dare he! Making me feel beautiful and special. The barefaced arrogance of him!

Well, if he thinks I'm going to have sex with him now, then I'm afraid that I've got some very bad news for him.

Adam, darling, I've changed my mind!

It took me a couple of seconds to realize that I had talked myself through an entire affair with Adam, from falling for him to being dumped by him to being furious with him.

Whoops, I thought. It's that bad penny, Temporary Insanity, back again.

"What's wrong with you?" said Mum, tearing her attention away from Inspector Morse. "You're looking very angry."

"Nothing, Mum," I told her, my head reeling slightly. "Just thinking."

"You *can* think too much," she told me.

For once I agreed with her.

But before she could expound on the evils of a university education and the dangers of opening your mind, the phone rang.

"I'll answer it," I yelped, and ran from the room, cutting her off mid-sentence.

"What's the use of being an intellectual?" she shouted after me. "I bet James Joyce couldn't change a spark plug."

"Hello," I said as I picked up the phone.

"Helen?" asked a man's voice.

"No. Helen's not here," I said. "She's missing, presumed drunk."

The voice laughed.

"Adam?" I asked, wobbling slightly.

The shock of hearing his voice briefly destabilized me.

I could hardly believe that he had spent the afternoon with me and here he was calling for Helen, my *sister*.

What kind of sicko was he, playing the two of us off against each other?

I *knew* it.

He *was* a bastard, just like all the others.

"Claire," he said. "Yes, it's me."

What do you want? I thought coldly. "Yes?" I said icily.

"Well, I'll tell Helen that you called."

"No wait," he said. "I called to talk to you."

"That's funny," I continued with great hauteur. "Because my name is Claire, not Helen."

"I know that," he continued in a reasonable tone. "But I thought it might be a bit weird if I called to speak to you and Helen answered and I didn't acknowledge her."

I paused.

"I mean," he continued gently, "Helen is my friend too. If it wasn't for Helen I would never have met you."

Still I said nothing.

"Are you annoyed?" he asked. "Have I done something wrong?"

Now I felt foolish. Hysterical and female.

"No," I said in much sweeter tones. "Of course I'm not annoyed."

"All right then," he said. "If you're sure."

"I'm sure."

"I hope you don't mind my calling you," he said. "But you ran off in such a hurry today that I didn't get a chance to ask you if maybe . . . I mean . . . that's if you don't mind . . . if I could see you again. You know, if you've got time."

Relief and happiness rushed through me.

As they say, there's one born every minute.

"Yes," I told him breathlessly. "I'd love to."

"I had such a nice time," he said.

I glowed with happiness and pride.

"So did I," I told him.

"What are you doing tomorrow?" he asked.

Tomorrow, I thought.

Golly, but he didn't let the grass grow under his feet.

"I'm going into town to buy some clothes," I said.

This was news to me.

The first I had heard of it.

"So you can meet me for coffee if you like," I told him. "But I'll have to bring Kate."

"That's great," he said, sounding all excited. "Kate's beautiful. Please bring her."

"Okay then," I said, a little taken aback at his enthusiasm, and we made an arrangement to meet in town the following day.

I went back into Mum.

"Who was that?" she asked, looking at my flushed, happy face.

I opened my mouth to tell her and I'm afraid to tell you that I stalled at the final hurdle.

I just couldn't tell her.

I really didn't know why.

Or maybe I did.

Maybe because it was no longer innocent.

Maybe it never was.

sixteen

The following day brought it home to me good and proper, not that I had failed to notice already, how my life had been altered forever by my having given birth to Kate.

Especially one of the most important areas of my life.

I speak, of course, of the shopping area of my life.

My old shopping life, like the morning dew in the midday sun, gone forever.

No more running into a clothes shop, picking thirty or so garments up off the racks and then spending a leisurely six hours or more in the changing room admiring myself.

No sir!

You'd be amazed the difference having a child strapped to your front makes. Ease of movement greatly hampered. Not to mention the terrible fear I had that someone was going to bump into Kate and hurt her.

Or worse still, wake her.

It hadn't been too bad that day in the supermarket where civilized serene mothers glided through the roomy aisles. I trusted them not to jostle and bump Kate.

But this was Saturday afternoon, in clothes shops, for God's sake!

These girl shoppers were surely mercenaries who had been given the afternoon off from causing bloodshed and mayhem somewhere like the former Yugoslavia.

Vicious, I'm telling you.

Crazed.

*   *   *

I couldn't relax and just look for something to wear.

I stood at the door of one shop, a little bit dazed, swerving and ducking the passing shoppers as I wondered if I was a jeans and sweatshirt girl, or if I was an ankle-length skirt and cropped sweater kind of woman.

I mean, what was I now?

It was so long since I'd bought regular clothes.

Ones that weren't jeans, I mean.

Or ones that didn't have expanding adjustable Velcro waists. Or acres and acres of fabric. In fact, it was only a week since I'd started wearing normal underwear again.

Let me explain.

Maybe you don't know it, but you don't return to normal living—and, more important, normal clothes—the moment you give birth.

It's a long time before certain bodily processes stop. I don't want to sound unnecessarily gory here but can I just say that I could have given Lady Macbeth a run for her money.

Don't talk to *me* about blood being everywhere, missus!

And because of that I'd had to wear these funny mesh paper-type underpants.

They were horrible and they were huge.

Armpit huggers.

But I'm happy to announce that the previous week normal underwear had been restored. That's right, I repeat, normal underwear had been restored.

What about the rest of my clothes?

I was no longer a pregnant woman.

I was just a woman.

So what was I going to wear?

I had so little to define me now.

I wouldn't be going back to work for ages, so I didn't have to buy clothes for that.

So I didn't even have that to give me form.

I was just shopping for me.

Whoever she was.

I picked up a couple of little dresses from a rack and

pushed through the hordes of people to get to the changing room, practically bent double over Kate to protect her.

A further shock awaited me at the changing room.

Where on earth was I going to put Kate?

She wasn't exactly like a gym bag that you just fling on the floor.

A quick U-turn and back the way I came, easing my way through the throng, with my head lowered and thrust forward so that I looked a bit like a bull. I bought a lot of things anyway, even though I hadn't tried them on. I *had* to buy something.

After all, I had a reputation to uphold.

There was a time when my name was legendary among Women Who Shop. A time when there was no such thing as choosing between the black pair and the green pair. No such thing as standing, agonizing, my index finger pressed to my face, my brow furrowed in girlish consternation.

No siree, I bought both of them.

And quite apart from upholding my reputation, I hadn't a stitch to wear. And I had a man to impress.

I paid for everything with the credit card.

Or, I suppose I should say that James did.

I was quite amazed that alarm bells didn't go off when the assistant passed the bags over the counter to me and vanloads of policemen and German Shepherd dogs didn't rush into the shop and drag me off.

Because I was sure that I had spent miles over the limit.

After my halfhearted, yet nonetheless prolific purchasing, I went off to meet Adam, who was, after all, my real reason for coming into town.

If I'm perfectly honest, the shopping was just a ruse.

A cunning ploy.

I fought my way up the street, arms protectively around Kate.

Wave after wave of shoppers came toward me.

Touch my child and I'll kill you, I thought fiercely, looking angrily at passersby.

Who, in their innocence, looked very startled and afraid.

Apart from the anxiety about Kate's getting hurt, I became aware of another funny feeling in my stomach.

Indigestion?

With a curious little shock I realized that the funny feeling was butterflies.

Butterflies that were dancing jigs in my intestines. They had obviously pushed back the tables and chairs in my stomach and were going for it in a big way. Linking arms and swinging each other around and high-kicking and whooping and changing partners and generally having a wild old time for themselves.

Oh dear, I thought, realization dawning, so it's official.

I have a crush on Adam.

Or should I say I HAVE A CRUSH ON ADAM!!!!!

Should celestial trumpets have blown? Should I have suddenly seen the world with pink fuzzy edging? Should I have walked, or indeed run, the rest of the way to meet him in slow motion? And be swung slowly into his arms, twirling around and around, both of us smiling like joyful idiots?

But no, being me, I had to go straight into worry mode. I reluctantly dragged my feet the rest of the way to meet him, my head working at high speed.

Why did I have to like him?

What kind of person was I?

I was in love with James and it was only six weeks—well, nearly seven, actually—since we split up, so shouldn't I still have been faithful to him?

I felt so disloyal.

Although why the hell should I?

James was having his fun, so why shouldn't I?

But it wasn't that simple.

I was never any good at having sex with people without getting emotionally involved.

Although then again, who said anything about having sex?

Oh God!

I was so distraught.

I couldn't understand all the different ways I was feeling.

I was so confused.

I *did* have a crush on Adam. But I felt so guilty about it because that must make me a very shallow person when I was supposed to be in love with James. But was I in love with James? I was afraid to think about that one. It was too huge to contemplate.

And then I felt angry with James. Why couldn't I flirt with Adam and have a bit of fun?

But then I felt guilty again because Adam was a person, a nice person, and he deserved better than to be treated by me as some sort of ego balm.

A bit like getting my hair done.

Or getting my legs waxed.

And then I felt angry again, because I didn't think of Adam that way. I got a real thrill from talking to him and being with him. Although I'd only known him a few days.

Which brought me neatly back to the question of how could I like someone I'd only known a few days when I was still in love with James.

Oh, fuck it, I thought frantically.

I squared my shoulders and got ready for Adam.

I saw him standing outside the coffee shop where I was to meet him.

My stomach gave a little lurch.

He looked so good.

"Hello." He grinned. "You're only fifteen minutes late. You're obviously getting the hang of this."

"Shut up." I smiled. "Sorry."

It was wonderful to be with him.

"Hello, angel," he said, looking at Kate in her little pouch.

Although I preferred to think that he was just using this as an excuse to look at my tits.

Kate said nothing.

And in we went for coffee, fighting our way through the hordes of agitated and excited people.

It was Saturday afternoon and madness was abroad. It was as though people were afflicted with some kind of lunacy. Shopping syndrome, or something. I'm sure there's a fancy medical name for it.

I suppose it must be something akin to the Mistral that

descends every so often on villages in, is it Italy? All the men
hit their wives and the dogs howl and the hens won't lay and
the women shout and cry (well, fair enough—their husbands
are hitting them, after all) and refuse to do any housework.
As though the entire village was afflicted with PMS.

The Mistral madness seemed to be child's play compared
to the goings-on this particular Saturday afternoon.

I once read somewhere that shopping has a huge effect on
one's adrenaline levels. Sending blood pressure levels soaring
and causing one to hyperventilate and making one's eyes bulge
and all kinds of other effects. It made perfect sense to me—all
that excitement!

Apparently this in turn affects one's blood sugar levels.
Which is why everyone needs strong sweet tea or coffee after—
or indeed even during—their shopping orgy.

A bit like a postcoital cigarette, I suppose.

As a result of excessive shopping, Dublin was full of hyper-
ventilating, bulgy-eyed, red-faced (that's from the high blood
pressure) maniacs with hundreds of shopping bags affixed
around their persons and wallets full of credit cards that were
positively humming and zinging after all their activity.

So if it's a cup of coffee that you're after, as Adam, Kate
and I were, don't hold your breath while you're waiting for a
seat. We stood in the middle of the crowded café as pitiful
hollow-eyed souls roamed past carrying trays of coffee and
doughnuts. They had obviously been there several weeks
and still hadn't secured a chair for themselves. But Adam,
being Adam, found the only table that had been vacated in
the last three weeks or so. That was one of the many advan-
tages of having a tall man around. And after he made sure
that Kate and I were sitting comfortably, he went off to
get coffee.

What a hero!

He was back in record time with a tray overflowing with
pastries.

"I didn't know what kind you liked," he explained. "So I
got you one of each."

"Oh Adam," I said. "You shouldn't have! You're a penniless student."

I was so touched I could have cried. He had probably just spent his entire summer term grant on buns for me. "And I'll never eat them all," I lied.

"Well, don't worry about it," he said, smiling and looking really gorgeous. "I'm sure I'll eat whatever you don't."

Then he sat down and turned all his attention to me. "How are you?" he asked. And he managed to make it sound as if he really was interested.

"Fine," I said, smiling shyly and feeling all silly and girlie. What is it?

The moment you realize that you like someone you turn into a complete half-wit.

Well, at least I do.

"Can I hold Kate for a while for you?" he asked.

"If you like," I said, taking her out of the sling and tenderly passing her over to his gentle arms.

The lucky bitch!

What a pity that she can't talk yet, I thought regretfully. Otherwise I could debrief her fully on exactly what it felt like to be held in Adam's arms.

We sat there chatting idly while the tides of humanity, with their fluctuating blood sugar levels, swirled and washed and ebbed and flowed around us. Adam, Kate and I were an oasis of calm in the chaos of Dublin.

As though the three of us were in our own little world.

We didn't really talk that much. We just sat in relaxed silence, drinking coffee, eating buns, my shopping strewn all around us.

Adam was busy playing with Kate, admiring her, and examining her tiny little fingers and touching her cute little face.

He had such a look of intense wonder, almost of yearning, on his face that I got slightly alarmed.

Never mind Laura, I thought, is Adam a child molester!

"Do you reckon," he said thoughtfully, talking to me but still looking at Kate, "that if people didn't know better, they'd think that I was Kate's dad? You know, that we're just a typical nuclear family, as they say in my anthropology tutorials, out shopping on a Saturday afternoon."

He looked up and smiled at me.

And although I had been thinking almost exactly the same thing myself, I felt a little bit, I don't know, funny, yes funny and sad, about Adam's saying that.

Disloyal, that's the way I felt.

I was glad that Adam seemed to be so fond of Kate.

But Adam wasn't Kate's father.

James was Kate's father.

And James wasn't here.

It was all so funny and mixed-up and strange and sad.

Why couldn't Adam be her father?

Or why couldn't her father care?

"Would you like to have children?" I asked Adam. "I don't mean now, but, you know, someday?"

He stopped what he was doing and sat very still for a minute. Then he turned and looked at me.

There was such an odd expression on his face. He looked very sad. Lost almost. But before he answered me we were interrupted by girls' voices.

"Hey look, it's Adam," "Great, where?" "Adam, how are you?" "Oh hi, Adam, where were you last night?"

Three beautiful young women, obviously classmates of Adam's, had arrived at the table and were clustering around him.

The way women did around Adam.

They were like beautiful exotic birds. Very colorful and very noisy. They oohed and aahed loudly at Kate and then lost interest in her completely when they discovered that she wasn't Adam's child.

Although why should she be? I wondered.

Adam introduced us all.

"Meet Kate," he said, picking up her little pink hand and waving it at the girls.

It looked so gorgeous, my little girl and this beautiful man, that I thought my heart would break.

Why can't James be here to do this? I wondered.

Even when I was happy, the sadness was only a moment away.

"And this is Claire," he continued.

"Hi." I smiled gamely at the girls with their young translucent skin and their outrageous clothes, trying not to feel like an old hag.

"And these are . . ."

And he said three names that might have been Alethia, Koo and Freddie. Or could have been Alexia, Sooz and Charlie.

Or then again might have been Atlanta, Jools and Micki.

Odd names. Cool names.

And, I was prepared to take my oath, made-up names.

The three of them kind of looked the same.

They all had short hair.

And I do mean very short hair.

Sooz/Koo/Jools was nearly totally bald.

And Atlanta/Alexia/Alethia looked like a very unugly duckling, with her little cap of blond fluffy hair.

She looked a bit like Kate, to be honest.

Which means that Adam, the suspected pedophile, is probably mad about her, I thought sourly.

I was feeling a bit jealous.

All four of them talked away about some party that had been on the previous evening. I really wished that they would leave, so I could have Adam all to myself and Kate again, but I tried to be grown-up and adult about these three gorgeous young women clamoring for Adam's attention.

My face hurt from trying to look as if I was good fun too, that I didn't mind being ignored as they chattered and laughed charmingly and effortlessly. It looked as if the three of them were settling in for a long stay.

My heart sank to my (new) boots as all three pulled over chairs and gathered around our tiny little table, each of them practically sitting on Adam's knee.

They hadn't even bought a cup of tea among them. .

But, really, I wasn't being judgmental.

I knew what it was like to be a poor student.

They had to save their money for beer and drugs.

Of course I understood.

But when Freddie/Charlie/Micki started to eat one of the pastries, one of *my* pastries, I nearly burst into tears. I wanted to stamp my foot and shout hysterically, like a child throwing a tantrum, "That's mine. Adam bought it for *me*!"

I swallowed hard.

I was totally out of place here. It was silly to think that someone like me could have any place in someone like Adam's life. He was young and handsome and had a full and happy life.

And I felt tired and old and silly and foolish.

As Adam continued to talk animatedly to the girls, I stood up and put Kate's sling back on. Then I leaned over and took Kate rather brusquely from Adam's arms (Give me back my child!), interrupting a lively conversation about someone named Olivia Burke, who apparently had given Malcolm Travis a blow job at the party last night in full view of the guests.

Even through my self-pity and misery I was pleased to hear that Adam wasn't being in any way judgmental about Olivia Burke's behavior. His censure was reserved for Malcolm because apparently Malcolm had a steady girlfriend named Alison. And Olivia didn't know about her.

"That guy is so low," Adam said. "He's being disrespectful to the two women at once by behaving that way."

Right on, brother!

Kate started to cry when I took her from Adam's arms. I didn't blame her.

Adam turned and looked at me with a surprised look on his face.

"You're not going, are you?" he asked.

"Yes, I think so," I said, trying to sound casual. "Kate's tired and she'll need a change soon."

I turned to the gorgeous girls.

"Bye." I nodded. "Nice meeting you."

At least I could never be accused of being rude, I thought self-righteously.

"Bye," they chorused. "Bye-bye, Kate."

Then I felt ashamed.

They were nice girls. I was the one with the problem.

Jealous and insecure.

Childish and overly sensitive and spoiled.

Off I struggled, loaded down with a baby, bags and huge quantities of feeling sorry for myself, trying to look dignified and unconcerned as I battled through the unyielding crowds toward the door. I could feel Adam's eyes on me, but I refused to meet his look.

He caught up with me before I had gone two yards.

If I was to be perfectly honest—not always an easy thing to be—I'd have to say that was exactly what I had wanted him to do.

"Claire," he said in surprised tones, "where are you going?"

"Home," I mumbled.

I was hoping desperately that he hadn't realized how jealous I was.

"Look, I'm sorry," he said, looking into my eyes. "Were they really getting on your nerves?"

"No," I protested. "No, they were nice."

"You don't have to be polite," he said, looking at me with a concerned expression. "I know they must have seemed like silly little girls to a woman like you."

"No Adam, honestly, they were fine," I insisted.

I felt *really* awful.

I didn't enjoy being with Alexandria, Zoo and Gerri or whatever their bloody names were because I was *jealous* of them, not because I was terribly mature and disdainful.

"Honestly, they're lovely girls," he said. "I just wanted to be with you and Kate but I didn't know how to keep them from sitting down with us without seeming rude," he explained.

"It's really fine," I insisted. "Look, I'd better go," I said as yet another person with a tray bumped into me and tisked at me for standing in the middle of an aisle.

"Are you sure?" he asked, standing very close to me.

"I am," I promised him.

"Really?" he asked, his face moving nearer to mine.

"Really," I promised him.

But I didn't move.

I wanted to stay there, close to him.

Just for a moment.

I wanted him to kiss me.

But there was very little chance of that happening with several thousand people milling around us. Not to mention the fact that Kate would probably suffocate in her sling if Adam pulled me manfully into his arms.

"Can I walk you to your car?" he asked.

"No, really Adam, there's no need."

"I'll see you soon," he said gently.

"Yes." I gave him a little smile.

A nice smile.

A real one.

And he put his hands on my shoulders and pulled me to him (but with the utmost regard for Kate's comfort) and gave me the lightest little kiss on my forehead.

I closed my eyes, surrendering to the moment.

And I caught my breath because I could hardly believe that this was happening.

His mouth felt warm and firm.

He smelled of soap and warm smooth skin.

Through the din of voices that surrounded us in the café I heard someone say, "Look, it's those two again."

A voice said, "Which two?"

"You know, the two who were having the fight outside Switzer's yesterday."

The voices belonged to the girls who had taken great comfort in witnessing the little exchange between Adam and me yesterday.

My God, was it really only yesterday?

They continued to loudly discuss us.

"Oh yes, them. Well, it looks as if they've made it up."

I opened my eyes and looked at Adam. We both started to laugh.

"In that case I really am going," I told him.

I passed the girls on the way out.

"I'm sure she didn't have a baby yesterday," one of them said.

"Would you say it's his?" the other wanted to know.

I carried on.

My forehead didn't stop tingling until I was a hundred yards from home.

Yes, yes, I know.

A kiss on the forehead hardly qualifies as raunchy sex. I couldn't name you even one Swedish film that was made about a kiss on the forehead. But it was so yearning and so tender and in its own chaste way so erotic that it was lots better than raunchy sex.

Well, as good as, I suppose.

seventeen

Laura came out on Sunday afternoon and we lounged around drinking tea and playing with Kate.

Playing with Kate involved, for the most part, feeding her, burping her and changing her.

Laura wore a filthy paint-stained T-shirt, which I presumed belonged to her teenage lover. She looked young and contented and happy.

And well she might.

She had had sex four times the previous night, stories of which she attempted to regale me with except we kept being interrupted by Mum or Dad.

"Any word from James?" she inquired, having given up on the idea of spending the afternoon talking dirty after Dad had left the room for about the twentieth time.

He'd come in, nodded at Laura and started lifting cushions off the couch and moving armchairs, muttering something about not having read the *Independent*, if Helen had taken it he'd kill her. And how he was the one who paid for the papers so why was he always the one who didn't get to read them.

Then he was back about three minutes later to see if the fire was lighting properly and had a big discussion, mostly with himself, about the merits of anthracite coal ("There's great heat in it, even if it does cost more.")

Laura and I just sat there, curled up on the couch, Kate on Laura's lap, all of us, even Kate, looking bored as we waited for him to finish his tirade and leave.

He was no sooner gone than Mum paid a visit.

"Any word from James?" Laura asked again as the sitting room door closed yet another time.

"He's away," I said shortly. "But I'll call him tomorrow." I didn't want to talk about James, not then anyway. I was sick of hashing it and rehashing it and trying to make sense of it and worrying about what to do.

As they say in New York, "Get over it, and if you can't get over it, get over talking about it."

Sound advice.

Laura was in the house for a good hour before she broached the subject of Adam. I was amazed that it took her so long. "So what's the story with yourself and young Lochinvar?" she inquired ultra casually as she rubbed Kate's back with circular motions.

"Who?" I asked. Deliberately obtuse.

"The gorgeous Adam," she said in slight exasperation.

"What about him?" I asked.

"Well, for one thing he's crazy about you, and for another thing he's absolutely beautiful-looking. If he was five or six years younger, I might even be interested myself."

"Laura, he's not crazy about me," I protested. Of course I only said this so that Laura would insist that Adam was indeed crazy about me so that I could get that warm feeling of delight in my stomach again.

"He is crazy about you," she told me. "And what's more, you know it."

"But so what?" I said. "Even if he is crazy about me—and we have no proof that he is—what am I supposed to do about it?"

"Sleep with him," she said.

She hadn't an ounce of shame, that one.

"Laura! For God's sake, I'm married," I yelled at her.

"Oh yes?" she said smugly. "So where's your husband?"

I was silent.

"Claire," she said kindly, after we sat saying nothing for five tense minutes, "all I'm saying is that he's a lovely man and he seems to really like you and you've had a rough time and even if things do eventually work out with James, maybe you should have a little bit of fun in the meantime."

"What is it around here?" I asked. "Everyone's encouraging me to have a relationship with Adam. Even my own mother!"

"Your mother told you to sleep with Adam?" screeched Laura in astonishment.

Well, not exactly in those words, I suppose," I said. "But that's what she meant."

"So what's stopping you?" asked Laura in delight. "You've got your mother's blessing. What a brilliant omen."

I thought for a few moments.

"Yes," I sighed. "I suppose I should."

'What!" barked Laura. "Are you serious?"

"For God's sake," I raised my voice at her. "Isn't that just what you've been encouraging me to do?"

I *knew* this would happen. I just *knew* it.

People are always encouraging each other to do things that they know the other person won't do. And then get the shock of their lives when the person actually does it.

I'm culpable myself.

For years and years I encouraged Dad to get himself a pair of jeans. "Honestly, Dad, they'd be gorgeous on you," I often said.

And Dad would say, "Ah, go away. I'm far too old."

"No, Dad, you're not."

The day that Dad actually turned up wearing a pair of board-stiff navy blue Wranglers, with a twelve-inch turn-up on the hem, smiling shyly and proudly, the shock nearly killed me.

"Yes, I know," Laura said, seeming a little bit distressed. "But it just seems so out of character for you. I mean, you're always so loyal."

"Laura, I'm hardly being disloyal to James if I have sex with Adam, am I?" I asked her nicely. I could see how shocked she was.

Although I had a veneer of good-time-girlness, I had pretty much always been Claire the Constant. My veneer of debauchery was paper-thin—practically transparent, in fact. I always wanted to be boring and settled down with a man, but because that was considered to be the most insulting thing you can say about someone—that is, that all she wants is to be settled down with a man—I'd done my level best to hide it.

Few people knew my shameful secret.

"Claire, do you like this Adam?" she asked in concern.

I was amused to note that Adam had gone from being "the gorgeous Adam" to "this Adam" in a matter of minutes.

"Of course I like him," I told her, laughing at her horror. "He's delicious—or hadn't you noticed?"

"Handsome, I grant you," she said cautiously. "But what do you know about him?"

"I know that he's nice and he makes me feel smart and beautiful and desirable."

"Claire, don't forget that you're very vulnerable right now. You *are* on the rebound."

"No kidding?" I said. I thought I sounded **very** clever.

"Anyway," I said with great curiosity, "what are you doing, encouraging me to have a fling with him and then when I say I will you go all judgmental on me?"

"Sorry, Claire," she said humbly. "I really am. It's just that I thought it might be an ego boost for you to know that he liked you. But I didn't think for a second that you'd actually do anything about it. You're such a one-man woman that this has come as a little bit of a shock."

"Laura, I'm a no-man woman at the moment," I reminded her.

"I know, but you love James so much that . . . I don't know . . . I just didn't think that you'd even consider anyone else."

"Things change, people change," I said. "I don't know how I feel about James anymore. All I really know is that being with Adam is lovely."

Laura suddenly pulled herself together.

"Well, if that's the case, you couldn't have picked a bigger hunk to have a fling with. He's so good-looking. And so nice. Smart too," she added as an afterthought.

This was good coming from Laura, who is usually more concerned with the organ between his legs than the organ between his ears.

"And you'd better get into training." She grinned. "Didn't they give you exercises to do to tone yourself up? Pelvic floor exercises or whatever they're called. You don't want sex with Adam to be like throwing a sausage up O'Connell Street."

"Thank you, Laura," I said dryly. "You make me sound like such a catch."

After Laura left I just couldn't settle down.

There was no one around.

Anna had done another of her disappearing acts.

Helen apparently was at Linda's, although I was glad about that. I was feeling so guilty about Adam that I don't think I could have looked her in the eye. I was pretty sure that Adam wasn't her boyfriend, but it might be a good time to find out for sure.

On the other hand, I didn't necessarily want to find out that he was in fact her man. What would that tell me about him? That he was some sort of weirdo who got great enjoyment from wrecking homes and pitting sister against sister and tearing families asunder.

If Adam was Helen's man then I would back off immediately and have nothing further to do with him. That part was easy.

But what if Adam wasn't Helen's man but Helen wanted him?

Well, if Adam wanted her also, then the same principle applied. I would back off immediately and have nothing further to do with him.

But what if Helen wanted Adam and Adam didn't want Helen and if, delicious thought, Adam wanted me? Then what?

That was a tough one.

I did love Helen.

God knows why, but I did.

And I didn't want to do anything to upset her.

No, really, I didn't.

The best thing I could do was talk to Adam about all this. Just ask him straight out what the story was between himself and Helen.

"My God, Claire." Mum scowled at me as I changed the television channel yet again. "What's wrong with you? Can't you sit still? You're like someone with a feather in her underwear."

"Sorry, Mum."

Just then the phone rang.

"Jesus, Claire, my foot!" yelped Dad, like a dog with his tail caught in a door, as I raced to answer it and crushed several of his metatarsals in the process.

"Hello," I gasped into the phone.

"Hello, is your daddy there?" slurred a voice on the other end.

"Dad," I called. "Daaad!" Auntie Julia for you."

Dammit, I thought. That meant Dad would be on the phone for hours; Auntie Julia was impossible to get off the phone when she was drunk. She usually called to apologize for doing something like cheating at a card game. A game that had taken place as recently as about forty-five years ago.

Why was I so bothered about the phone's being free anyway? I wondered, nimbly sidestepping Dad as he grumpily hobbled past me on his way to the phone.

Had anybody said that he'd call me?

Was I expecting any calls?

No and once again, no.

I sat down in the hall to eavesdrop unashamedly on Dad's conversation with Auntie Julia. It usually made for interesting, if slightly bizarre, listening.

"Now, Julia, listen to me," Dad said agitatedly. Oh dear, I thought, it must have been a very important card game for Dad to be getting so upset.

"Dampen a tea towel and throw it over it immediately!" he roared into the phone.

Oh good, I thought, as I realized that Auntie Julia was only in the process of attempting to burn her house down and wasn't calling up for a long, remorseful conversation.

"No, under the tap, Julia, under the tap!" Dad yelled.

How on earth had she been proposing to dampen the tea towel? Best not to think about it.

"Now, Julia, I'm going to hang up the phone here and you're to do the same," said Dad slowly and carefully, as if he were talking to a four-year-old child.

"And you're to dial 999 and ask for the fire department," he continued. "And then you're to call me back and tell me that you've done it and that they're on their way."

He slammed down the phone and leaned against the wall.

"Christ," he said, looking exhausted.

"What's she done now?" asked Mum, who had appeared in the hall.

"Somehow she's set the oven on fire and it's gotten out of control," sighed Dad. 'God, will it ever end?"

The phone rang.

"That'll be her calling back," said Dad, as Mum reached for the phone.

"Hello," said Mum.

Then her face changed.

"Yes, she's here. Who's calling please?"

"It's Adam, for you," she said, handing me the phone with an expressionless face.

"Oh," I said, taking the receiver from her, exhaling with relief.

This was what I had been waiting for all evening, without even realizing it.

"Hello," I said, delighted but trying to hide it in front of Mum and Dad.

"Claire," he said in his lovely voice. "How are you?"

"Fine," I said, a bit awkwardly. Mum and Dad were still standing in the hall, both of them looking at me.

"Get lost," I hissed at them, waving my free arm.

"We've a bloody emergency on our hands," Dad barked. "Get off that phone!"

"In a minute," I told him.

"One minute," he said threateningly.

But then the pair of them left.

"Sorry about that," I told Adam as Mum and Dad returned reluctantly to the sitting room. "A minor family crisis."

"Is everyone okay?" he inquired anxiously.

"Fine," I said.

I was the one who felt anxious now. Was he worried because he was concerned about Helen? About his *girlfriend* Helen?

"Claire," he continued, "I hope you don't mind my calling. I mean, I don't want you to feel as if I'm plaguing you. Just tell me and I'll stop."

Plague me all you like, I thought.

"No, Adam, of course I don't mind you calling me. I like talking to you."

"Great," he said. I could hear the smile in his voice.

I sat on the floor and started to settle in for a comfortable hour or so of conversation.

And as I did so I heard the rattle of someone's key in the front door.

"Oh God," I said as I heard Helen bellow, "I'm home. Feed me! Or I'll report you for neglect."

"What is it?" asked Adam.

"Helen's here," I said.

"Oh is she? Well say hello from me."

"No, I won't," I blurted out.

"Why?" he asked, sounding shocked.

Helen passed me in the hall. She winked and gave me an enchanting smile.

"Hi, Claire, your boots are lovely," she said, and continued on. Sometimes—in fact, usually when I least expect it—she can be so sweet and so charming that I could kill her.

"Why won't you tell Helen I said hello?" asked Adam again.

Now's the time to get this thing sorted out once and for all, I decided. If Adam is messing me and my little sister around, then this is my chance to put an end to it.

I was managing to get nicely worked up. The bloody arrogance of him. Just because he's really handsome he thinks he can waltz in here and ride roughshod over all of us, I thought, mixing my metaphors and quickly working myself up into a self-righteous fury.

"Look, Adam," I said sharply as soon as I could hear Helen, Mum and Dad arguing in the living room and I knew that it was safe to speak. "I don't really know how to say this. In fact, I don't even know what I should say."

"For God's sake, what?" he interjected forcefully.

Go on, you tell him, I encouraged myself.

You have every right to know.

But I was already starting to lose my nerve.

"Look, maybe it's none of my business, but are you Helen's boyfriend?" I finally managed.

A silence followed.

Oh God, I thought. He *is* going out with Helen. And he was just being nice to me because I'm Helen's reject older sister. And now he knows that I like him. Damn, damn, damn. I should have kept my fool mouth shut. I've ruined everything because I have no patience.

"Claire," he eventually said, sounding stunned, "what on earth are you talking about?"

"You know," I said. I felt highly foolish, but even more relieved.

"No," he said, sounding a bit cold. "I don't know."

"Oh," I said, *really* embarrassed now.

"So you think I'm Helen's boyfriend?" he said stonily.

"Well, I thought you might be . . ." I said, mortified.

"And just what exactly did you think I was doing by asking if I could see you?" he continued, sounding almost contemptuous. "Well?" he prompted as I remained silent.

"Either you think I'm extremely thick or extremely cynical," he said. "And I'm not sure which one I'm more offended by."

I still said nothing.

Mostly because I didn't know what to say.

I felt terrible. Adam had been nothing but decent and respectful to me. I had no proof that he was having anything at all to do with Helen, and now I had hurt him by doubting his motives.

"Claire," he said, sounding exhausted. "Claire, Claire, Claire, listen to me. I am not now, nor have I ever in the past been, your sister Helen's boyfriend. And I don't want to be either.

"She's a lovely girl," he added hastily. "But she's not for me."

"Look, Adam," I stammered. "I'm really sorry, but I didn't know . . ."

"I'm sorry too," he said. "I keep forgetting what you've just been through. You've been badly hurt. Who could blame you for thinking that we're all a crowd of two-timing bastards?"

My hero, I thought, melting.

"Claire," he continued, "I don't know what kind of impression you've formed of me, but it's obviously not the one I was hoping for."

"No . . . Adam . . ." I protested weakly. I had so much to say and I didn't know where to start.

"Just give me a minute," he said. "Just listen to me. Will you?"

He sounded so earnest and boyish, how could I resist? "Of course," I said.

"I have lots of women friends but I don't do the romance thing a lot. Hardly ever, in fact. Well, hardly ever compared with the other people in my year in college, but maybe they're just especially prolific."

"That's fine," I said, anxious for him to shut up now. You don't have to explain anything to me, I wanted to tell him.

I had established that he wasn't Helen's boyfriend and that was plenty for now. Mortified by my earlier histrionics and accusations, I just wanted to forget the whole thing now. The poor guy! He only knew me a few days and already we'd had several mini-fights.

What on earth made him think that I was worth the bother?

But before I got to think about this, Dad reappeared in the hall with a face like thunder.

"Claire!" he yelled. "Off the phone, *now!*"

"You've got to go?" Adam asked.

"Yes," I said. "I'm sorry."

I didn't want to end the conversation until I knew that everything was all right. That Adam wasn't annoyed with me for thinking that he was some kind of home-wrecking Lothario. I also wouldn't have minded some kind of indication that, apart from not wanting to do the romance thing, as he so delicately put it, with Helen, he might want to do the romance thing with me.

As Mum would say, I wanted jam on it.

"Oh, I nearly forgot why I actually rang you," he said.

"Why's that?" I asked. Tell me that you really like me. Go on, go on, I urged him silently.

"There's a good film on at eleven o'clock. I'm sure you'd like it. You should watch it if you're not too tired."

"Oh," I said, the wind having been surgically removed from my sails. "Well thanks."

"See you soon," he said.

No wait, I wanted to shout, don't go just yet. Talk to me for one more minute. Give me your number so that I can call you. Can I see you tomorrow? Never mind tomorrow, can I see you tonight?

"Claire," Dad rumbled threateningly from the living room.

"Okay, bye," I said, hanging up.

Feeling, among other things, completely exhausted.

There was a disorderly surge from the living room the moment the phone was hung up.

Dad and Helen scuffled at the door.

Dad wanted to get straight on to Auntie Julia to see if the inferno was under control.

While Helen had other plans for the phone.

"I have to call Anthony," she shouted. "I need a lift to Belfast on Tuesday."

"Well, Julia's fire is more important," insisted Dad.

"Let her house burn down," said Helen, "That'd teach her."

Charitable to the end, that was Helen.

I walked away from the battle by the phone.

I went upstairs and moved Kate's bassinet into Mum's room and settled down to watch the recommended film on the little television there. It was the least I could do after I had been so mean to Adam. I'll be able to discuss it with him the next time I see him, I thought.

If there is a next time.

eighteen

Time had slowed to a standstill while I had been the Alcoholic Mother from Hell (and the Alcoholic Daughter from Hell and the Alcoholic Sister from Hell, if I'm to be strictly accurate). But now that I had started living again it had started to trot briskly, and before I knew it, it had broken into a sprint.

The days had started to fly past the way they do in films when the director wants to convey time passing quickly—i.e., the pages of a calendar turning over very speedily in a high wind. And tearing off and blowing away. With brown leaves blowing with the pages to indicate autumnal days and then a few flurries of snow to indicate winter's arrival.

The weekend was over before I knew it, and suddenly it was Monday morning.

James would be back from the Caribbean. Or Mustique. Or from a small, privately owned island just off the coast of Heaven. Or wherever he'd gone to, the faithless bastard.

So I was going to have to call him.

But I felt quite calm about it. What must be done must be done. Of course it was very easy for me to be calm about James when I was worried sick about Adam—it was kind of difficult to be in a mess about the two of them at the one time. Transference of affection, etc., and a big hand for Dr. Freud. But before I got to call James I had another treat in store for me on Monday morning.

My six-week, postnatal checkup with the doctor. The fun just never seemed to stop in my life.

This was a kind of symbolic, watershed type of event. It was a form of recognition that the birth had been a success. Sort of like the launch party they have after the release of a new film. Except at the party after the release of a new film, members of the cast and crew don't have to go around putting their feet in stirrups and have strange men examine their private parts.

Not unless they really want to, of course.

Kate also had an appointment, at the Baby Clinic, so off the pair of us went in the car.

My parents had taken Kate to the clinic a couple of times already, so it was old hat to her. But I wasn't really prepared for the cacophony of crying that greeted us on arrival. There seemed to be several thousand bawling babies with harassed and distraught mothers in the waiting room.

In fact, some of the mothers were crying louder than their children. "If only he'd stop crying," one women was saying tearfully to no one in particular. "Just for five minutes."

"My God," I thought in horror. I suddenly realized how lucky I was.

Kate had her checkup before me, so I carried her in her car seat into the examination room. The nurse was a glamorous red-haired young woman from Galway. Why are nurses always good-looking and sexy?

I'm sure there's some old legend that explains it.

Long, long ago there was a tribe of women who were excessively beautiful. The men were maddened by lust for them and they made all the other women feel inadequate and horrible. All kinds of riots and outbreaks of violence occurred. Homes broke up as previously happily married men fell in love with these babes. Women from the non-good-looking tribes killed themselves because they could never compete with these sirens.

Something had to be done.

So God decreed that all the good-looking women had to become nurses and wear truly awful lace-up shoes and revolting A-line dresses that make their butts look huge, so that their attractiveness would be toned down considerably. And to this very day good-looking women have to become nurses so that their beauty is diluted by the hideous uniforms. Although how this little fable of mine squares with supermodels and their revealing and flattering clothes, I'm at a loss to explain.

Anyway, never mind.

The nurse closed the door firmly behind us, but the noise of the roaring children in the waiting room was still perfectly audible, interspersed now and again with wails of "Just five minutes, that's all I ask."

"Doesn't the noise drive you mad?" I asked her curiously.

"Not at all," she said as she examined Kate. "I don't even hear it anymore."

Kate was so good, she didn't even cry.

I was very proud of her.

I felt like opening the door and saying, in schoolmarm fashion, to all the children out there, "Look, this is how you're supposed to behave. Observe this model child in here and imitate."

I watched the nurse as she inspected Kate and her vital signs.

"She's putting on weight just fine," said the nurse.

"Thank you." I beamed proudly.

"She's a perfectly healthy baby." The nurse smiled.

"Thank you," I said again.

I opened the door to leave and a fresh wave of screeching sent me reeling. We fought our way back through the throng of red-faced and yelling children. From what I could gather, a bunch of them were getting their shots and this was contributing to the general upset.

I picked my way carefully through the deafening crowd, carrying Kate. As I thankfully closed the door on the racket behind me, the last thing I heard was that poor woman wailing "Even three minutes. I'd settle for three."

Then we had to wait for a while until it was my turn to see the doctor. I read a copy of *Woman's Own* that dated from sometime around the turn of the century ("Crinolines are definitely *out* this autumn"). Kate had a little sleep.

Eventually I was called and in we went.

The doctor was a nice old codger. Gray suit, gray hair, vague kindly manner.

"Hello, ah yes, Claire, yes Claire and baby er Catherine,"

he said, reading from the notes on his desk. "Come in and sit down."

After a moment he looked up at the chair in front of him and when I wasn't there his glance darted anxiously around the room, wondering where I had gone.

I had placed Kate's car seat on the floor and I was over at the examining couch with my underwear off and my feet in the stirrups with a speed that left his head spinning.

Old habits die hard.

The next time I'd have to go to the doctor, no matter what my complaint, from an earache to a sprained wrist, I'd be hard-pressed to stop myself from whipping off my underwear and clambering up onto the couch.

The doctor did whatever it was he did, involving that old friend of mine, the lubricated glove.

I'm sorry if I'm being revolting.

There was a time when I would have felt faint at even the thought of having a Pap smear. But after being pregnant and giving birth, I think I could have a hysterectomy under just local anesthetic and still be sitting up and cheerfully discussing last night's TV with the surgeon.

Hell, why bother with the anesthetic?

"You've healed beautifully," he told me, making it sound like a great achievement.

"Thank you," I said, glowing, smiling up at him from between my legs.

I felt as though I was five years old and had got all my math homework right at school.

"Yes, no complications there at all," he continued. "Has all the bleeding stopped yet?"

(Sorry about this, I won't go on about it for long.)

"Yes, it stopped about a week ago," I told him.

"And the stitches have healed perfectly," he said, continuing to peer and poke.

"Thank you." I smiled again.

"Right, you can get down now," he told me.

"So is everything else all right?" he asked as I got dressed.

"Fine," I said. "Fine."

"Um, when can I have sex again?" I suddenly blurted out. (Now *why* did I ask that?)

"Well, your six weeks are up, so anytime you like," he said genially. "You could start right now." He threw back his head and guffawed loudly. Then he stopped abruptly as—I assume—visions of the medical council hearings and motions to have him fired began to swim before him.

There's a very fine line between an acceptable bedside manner and a lewd suggestion. Perhaps Dr. Keating hadn't quite grasped the difference yet.

"Ahem," he said, calming himself down. "Yes, anytime you like."

"Will it hurt?" I asked anxiously.

"It may feel a little bit uncomfortable at first, but it shouldn't feel *painful* as such. Ask your husband to be particularly gentle with you."

"My *husband?*" I asked the doctor, in surprise.

I hadn't even been thinking of my husband.

"Yes, your husband," he said, sounding equally surprised. "You are a married woman, aren't you, Mrs., ah, Mrs. Webster," he said, consulting my notes.

"Yes, of course I am," I said, blushing. "But I was, er, you know, just making general inquiries. I wasn't actually planning on having intercourse with anyone." I thought if I said the word *intercourse* instead of the word *sex* it might help to neutralize this embarrassing and awkward atmosphere that seemed to have suddenly developed.

"Oh," he said baldly.

Silence and Dr. Keating's bewilderment hung heavy in the air.

Time to leave, I thought.

Come on, Kate.

"How did it go?" asked Mum as she answered the door to us.

"Fine," I said. "Fine. Kate's putting on weight nicely, the nurse says."

"And how are you?" she asked.

"Couldn't be better, apparently," I said. "I'm in tip-top condition. I've a vagina to be proud of."

Mum gave me a look of distaste.

"There's no need to be vulgar," she tisked at me.

"I wasn't being vulgar," I protested.

"Come and have a cup of tea with me before *Neighbours* comes on," said Mum.

"Er, did anyone call for me while I was out?" I inquired of her, oh-so-casually, as I traipsed behind her into the kitchen.

"No."

"Oh."

"Why, who were you expecting to call?" she asked, looking at me closely.

"No one," I said, setting Kate's car seat down on the kitchen table.

"Well, why did you ask, in that case?" she said in a tone of voice which reminded me that, however much she might act like one, my mother was no fool.

"And take the child off the table!" she said, whacking my arm with a tea towel. "People have to eat off that."

"She's perfectly clean!" I protested, outraged.

How dare she.

So Adam hasn't called, I mused as I drank my tea. I wondered if he was still annoyed with me. Maybe he was never going to call me again. Not that I'd have blamed him, with me behaving all neurotic and argumentative.

And I didn't have his number, so I couldn't call him.

So that was probably the end of that.

The fling that never was.

The passionate affair that was never consummated.

The soulmates who were divided by circumstances.

The lovers who loved from afar.

Although then again it wasn't even lunchtime yet.

Give the guy a chance.

But he didn't call.

I hung around all afternoon feeling bored and dissatisfied.

I didn't want to do anything.

I couldn't be bothered reading.

And Kate was whining and crying and I didn't feel very patient with her.

I halfheartedly watched the afternoon soaps with Mum, because I couldn't come up with a good reason for why I shouldn't.

I think I would have preferred to sit through several third-rate Antipodean dramas, with the same actors reappearing in each successive program, than get into another conversation with Mum on how my university education had made me a snob.

And she knew that something was wrong.

"You're very gloomy-looking," she said.

(Although her actual words were "Claire, you're like a tree over a blessed well.")

"Why the hell wouldn't I be?" I snapped back.

"Sorry," she said. "God knows it's not easy for you."

Well, she was quite right, it was not. But she was obviously referring to my situation with James. And not my lack of one with Adam.

"No, I'm sorry," I told her, feeling rotten for biting her head off.

It was six o'clock and Dad's key was in the door before I realized with horror that I hadn't called James.

Dammit, dammit, dammit.

I really had meant to do it but because of all the things going on—the big event of going to the doctor and the major event of Adam's not calling—I had just totally forgotten.

I resolved to do it first thing in the morning.

The debacle that was dinnertime took my mind off things for a while.

Helen came home with Dad and was demanding McDonald's.

"No, Helen," shouted Dad. "We only eat McDonald's on holidays."

"Well that's stupid," she shouted back. "Other families, *normal* families, eat there on ordinary days."

Oh, but she could be very cruel.

So the upshot was that Helen got her way as usual and Dad drove off like a Grand Prix driver with a long and complicated order to McDonald's.

Helen roared after him, "No pickles on the Quarter Pounder!"

But he was already gone.

I shamelessly latched onto Helen for most of the evening,

hoping that she might say something about Adam. Of course, I could have taken the bull by the horns and just asked her for his number, seeing as she wasn't going out with him or anything. But I still couldn't bring myself to do it. Although I had established that he had no interest in her, I wasn't at all sure how Helen felt about him.

After dinner, which by the way, poor Dad had got all wrong—pickles on Mum's apple pie, cheeseburgers instead of Quarter Pounders with cheese (which, of course, gave rise to the accusation of "Cheapskate"), Coke instead of diet Coke—Dad ordered Helen to go to her room and study.

Poor Dad.

He must have been doing some kind of assertiveness training.

Amazingly enough, Helen went with only the most cursory of protests.

She called Dad a bastard and made references to the regime in the house being similar to the one in Nazi Germany. But she actually went to her room.

That was nothing short of miraculous.

I gave her a few minutes, then I took Kate and we went up and knocked on her door. There was a major scuffling. She seemed to be stuffing something down the side of the bed.

"Oh Jesus, Claire, don't do that! I thought you were Dad," she exclaimed, her eyes big and wide in her white face.

She retrieved a magazine called *True Crimes* or something similar from the gap between her bed and the wall.

"Do you *ever* study?" I asked her with curiosity.

"Noooooh," she said scornfully.

"What'll you do if you fail?" I asked her as I sat on the bed.

"Here, give me her," said Helen, taking Kate from my arms.

"I won't fail," she continued.

"How do you know?"

"I just know," she assured me.

Oh God, to have had her confidence.

"So how's college?" I asked her, willing her to talk about Adam.

"Fine," she said, looking surprised by my interest.

She said nothing at all about Adam.

And really, I couldn't, just couldn't, ask.

Then I heard the phone ring.

The first time it had rung all day. I was off that bed and down those stairs like greased lightning. Thank God I hadn't asked Helen for Adam's number, I congratulated myself in relief. I would have given the game away entirely and now there was no need!

"Hello," I said, trying to sound pleasant and unneurotic and apologetic all at the same time.

Sorry, Adam, I'll never be mean to you again.

"Yes, hello, can I speak to Jack Walsh?" said a voice.

My first thought was why on earth did Adam want to talk to Dad.

But then I realized that it wasn't Adam at all on the phone. The bastard!

How dare he!

Getting me to practically break my neck coming down those stairs only for him not to be him at all.

"Yes, hold on Mr. Brennan. I'll get him for you," I said.

And I trudged miserably back up the stairs.

A lot slower than I had come down.

I went back into Helen.

I was suitably humbled.

I still had every need of her.

She was playing with Kate and didn't see fit to comment on my death-defying flight down the stairs. That was one of the great things about being with someone as selfish as Helen. She so rarely took notice of anything that wasn't happening to her.

Just then Anna arrived, all flowing hair and traipsy skirt and vague expression on her face.

I was delighted to see her. We hadn't crossed paths since sometime the previous week. She tramped across Helen's pink and fluffy bedroom in the boots that were breaking Mum's heart and sat down beside us on the bed.

Out of her bag (embroidered, covered in mirrors and beads) she took about a hundred bars of chocolate and proceeded to efficiently eat her way through them.

I've never seen anything quite like it.

I could only assume that it was drug-related in some way. "Anna, do you have the . . . um . . . the munchies?" I asked, feeling like an old fuddy-duddy.

"Um," she said through a mouth that was crammed to capacity with chocolate.

"Gerumph!" She gesticulated angrily as Helen started ripping papers off the bars and practically inhaling them whole.

"Get your own, Helen," she finally managed, as her mouth was momentarily empty.

"Just give me this Mars and a Milky Way and I won't take any more," said Helen.

Lying, of course.

Anna agreed.

Poor Anna.

I spent the rest of the evening thrown on Helen's bed, eating chocolate, half listening to the good-natured bickering between Helen and Anna, waiting for Adam to call.

But, guess what, he didn't.

It doesn't matter, I told myself, he didn't say he would call me. He's bound to call tomorrow. He'll definitely call in the next few days, I tried to comfort myself. It's obvious that he really likes you.

But underneath all my bravado I knew he wouldn't call.

I don't know how I knew, I just did.

Obviously my ability to sense approaching disaster had improved slightly since James left me.

The practice must have helped.

nineteen

The next morning the house was like Grand Central Station.

Helen was going to Belfast for two days on a college trip and obviously believed that her preparations should not only be a last-minute affair but should also be a family event.

Instead of being woken by Kate, I woke to the sound of stealthy rustling at the foot of my bed. Someone was in my room and up to no good. I sat up sleepily.

"Who's that?" I yawned.

It was Helen.

I might have known.

She was making for the door with an armful of my new clothes.

"Oh, Claire!" she said, jumping guiltily as she dropped one of my new boots on the floor. "I thought you were asleep."

"So I see," I said dryly. "Now put them back."

"Bitch," muttered Helen, throwing a big pile of my clothes onto the floor. They had obviously been Belfast-bound.

I'm sorry, boys, I told them. I'll take you another time.

I heard her go down to the kitchen and shortly afterward there was the inevitable outbreak of raised voices. What was it about her?

Kate was awake in her bassinet, just lying there looking at the ceiling.

"Why didn't you cry, darling?" I teased her gently. "Why didn't you wake me and tell me that nasty Auntie Helen was stealing my clothes?"

I picked her up and took her into bed with me, holding her soft warm tiny little body in my arms.

We lay in bed for a while, drifting in and out of sleep, half listening to the sounds of an argument in the kitchen. I really should get up, I thought. Maybe Helen will mention Adam before she leaves.

I just held Kate tighter. My precious beautiful child.

But then she started demanding to be fed so I got out of bed and quickly got dressed, tripping over the pile of clothes on the floor in the process. The two of us went downstairs.

Where a little dispute seemed to be in process.

Anna, Mum and Helen were sitting around the table surrounded by breakfast debris, Pop-Tarts and teapots and cereal boxes all over the place.

Mum and Helen were arguing loudly.

Anna was smiling beatifically and doing something peculiar with a daisy and a paper clip.

"I know nothing about any green scarf and gloves," Mum told Helen hotly.

"But I left them on top of the fridge," Helen protested. "So what did you do with them?"

"Well, if you'd put them in their proper place you'd know where to find them," Mum answered her.

"The top of the fridge *is* the proper place," Helen replied. "It's where I always leave my things."

"Morning," I said pleasantly.

They all completely ignored me.

For no obvious reason the back door was swinging open and blasts of Siberianesque morning air blew through the kitchen.

This was ridiculous. I had a small child on the premises.

I walked briskly over and, holding Kate with one hand, managed to shut the door and lock it securely with the other.

"You shouldn't have done that," said Anna darkly.

I looked at her in surprise.

I would have thought that it was far too early in the morning, even for Anna, to be all mystical and ethereal.

"Why?" I asked gently, fondly, prepared to humor her. "Is

the Goddess of the Morn going to punish me for barring her entrance to our kitchen?"

"No," said Anna, looking at me as though I had gone crazy. Just then there was a muffled and frantic commotion outside the back door.

Someone or something was very annoyed to find the back door locked.

Lovely language for the Goddess of the Morn, let me tell you. Anna sighed and clumped over and opened the door. Dad stood on the step, almost totally obscured by the huge pile of washing which he held in his arms.

"Who locked the bloody door?" he roared through his armful of jeans and blouses.

"I might have known you'd have something to do with it," he hissed at poor Anna, as she stood with her hand on the doorknob.

"No, Dad, it was me," I told him hastily. Anna's bottom lip had started to quiver and she looked on the verge of tears.

"No, no, because we were *cold*," I explained, as Dad fixed me with a wounded look. "Not because I *wanted* to lock you out."

My God, what a crowd of neurotics!

I was so normal compared to the rest of my family.

"Right," declared Dad, throwing all the clothes onto the table, mindless of the half-eaten slices of toast and the bowls of abandoned cornflakes that were already on it. "Which of these clothes do you want?"

"Oh, Helen, why are you so difficult?" sighed Mum. "You have a roomful of clothes up there but the one thing you want has to be in the washing machine or on the line."

Helen smiled like a little cat. Smirking, she selected a few garments from the mound on the table and handed them to Dad.

"What am I to do with them now?" he asked in surprise.

"But they have to be ironed," said Helen, sounding equally surprised.

"Ironed?" said Dad. "By me?"

"Are you going to send me to Belfast with wrinkled clothes?" asked Helen, outraged.

"Right, right, right," shouted Dad, putting his arms up to defend himself from her passionate appeal.

The poor man, he never stood a chance.

Things settled down. Toast started to be eaten, coffee and tea started to be gulped, conversation—and I use the term oh so loosely—started to be made.

"Guess who I'm staying with in Belfast?" Helen asked in an innocent singsong type of voice. She sounded far too casual and blasé.

I knew that tone, and I sensed trouble.

"Who?" asked Anna.

"A Protestant," said Helen in hushed tones.

Mum continued sipping her tea.

"Mum, didn't you hear me?" Helen said petulantly. "I said I was staying with a Protestant."

Mum looked up calmly.

"So?"

"But don't we hate all Protestants?"

"No, Helen, we don't hate anyone," Mum told her, as if she was speaking to a four-year-old child.

"Not even Protestants?"

Helen was determined to have herself an argument, one way or the other.

"No, not even Protestants."

"But what if I fall under their influence and get all funny and start doing flower arranging?"

Somewhere along the line Helen had picked up some kind of vague and fussy generalization of what Protestants were like.

A funny mixture of Beelzebub and Miss Marple.

They had horns, of course, and cloven hoofs and breathed fire and made their own jam.

"Well, so what if you do," said Mum pleasantly.

"And what if I don't go to mass anymore?" gasped Helen in assumed horrified tones.

"But you don't go anyway," said Anna, sounding bewildered.

A rather tense and nasty silence followed.

Luckily, Kate, obviously sensing an awkward mood, smoothed things over by starting to cry like a banshee. I felt that she had a great future ahead of her as an ambassador, or working for the United Nations. There was a big rush to prepare her bottle; Anna and Helen practically tripped over themselves to help.

Dad busied himself by getting out the ironing board and making a great production of the ironing, pressing the steam button on the iron until the kitchen resembled a sauna.

Mum sat as though she was made of stone.

But after a while even she became roused to activity. She started to clear the table and grimly threw some cold chewy toast into the trash. Which was a pity because I kind of liked cold chewy toast. But I wasn't fool enough to cross my mother shortly after she had been notified of one of her daughters' nonattendance at mass.

Even when the daughter in question wasn't me.

Things again returned to normal. (Normal being, of course, an entirely subjective concept.)

"What'll it be like in Belfast. What if I get killed?" Helen mused. "I mean, anything could happen to me. I could get shot or blown up. This could be the last time you'll ever see me."

We all stared at her, struck dumb by emotion. Even Kate was silent.

Surely, *surely* we could never be that lucky.

"Or maybe I'll be kidnapped," she said dreamily.

My heart twisted with pity for the imaginary kidnapper. Anyone who kidnapped Helen would be convinced that he had been set up. That she was some kind of awesome secret weapon sent from the other side to destroy him from within.

Nothing frightened her.

She could be chained in some filthy basement with a lean young white-faced fanatic, all wiry muscles and burning eyes, laden with weaponry, and she could start a conversation with him about where she bought her sweater.

Or about anything really.

"I suppose you'll have to torture me a bit," she would say offhandedly. "What'll you do? I suppose you could cut off my ear and send it in the mail for the ransom money. I wouldn't mind that too much. I mean, what do I need my ear for anyway? Because I hear with the inside of my ear. Not the outside. Although it would be a bit of a problem if I wanted to wear glasses. If I only had one ear they'd be all lopsided. But I could always get contact lenses. Yes! I could make Dad buy me some of those colored contact lenses. What about brown ones? Do you think I'd look nice with brown eyes?"

And the poor terrorist would be exhausted and horrified by her.

"Shut up, bitch," he might say.

Although, this being Northern Ireland, "Shot op, botch," would be more like it.

And she might shut up for a moment or two before she'd be off again.

"These are lovely handcuffs. I have handcuffs too but they're only crappy old plastic ones. I suppose this must be one of the perks of the job, being allowed to borrow the good handcuffs. You know, to tie your girlfriend up and that. Although it must be a problem when you've got a prisoner. But I wouldn't mind. You could take them tonight and I promise I won't try to escape . . ."

And on and on until the terrorists cracked.

Grown men sobbing uncontrollably, "She's horrible, horrible! I'll do whatever you want, but just make her stop."

Helen would arrive back safely to her home, not only with the ransom money returned untouched, but with a sympathy note for her family from the terrorists.

Anyway she eventually left. Some poor idiot named Anthony had the dubious pleasure of her company on the three-hour drive to Belfast. Off she went, sitting in the front seat wearing a pious expression and clutching a bottle of holy water.

She didn't mention Adam before she left.

The cow.

Maybe he was going to Belfast also.

Maybe he was already there.

Maybe all the phone lines in Rathmines were down and that was why he hadn't called me.

Maybe he had been knocked off his bike and was in the hospital with a selection of injuries.

The important thing was that he hadn't called me.

And he wasn't going to.

So now what was I going to do?

What I really found peculiar was the way I'd barely given James a thought over the last days. My head had been full of Adam, Adam, Adam.

In the same way that the stewards on the *Titanic* were more concerned about the unemptied ashtrays on the bar than the enormous hole in the side of the ship which was letting in zillions of gallons of water, I too was worrying about the unimportant and ignoring the vital.

Sometimes it's easier that way.

Because although there was little I could do about the huge hole, it was still within my power to empty an ashtray.

A nice analogy.

But the practical consequences of my feeling that way were that I spent Tuesday mooning around the house.

Not *mooning* in the drunken football team party sense of the word.

Mooning in the feeling miserable and looking tragic sense of the word.

Did I call James?

I'm sorry, but I didn't.

I was having a bad case of the Self-Pitys.

I was stricken by a particularly virulent form of the Poor-Mes.

No excuse, I realized.

God knows, I wasn't trying to justify myself.

But I was, I was . . . I was *depressed*, goddammit.

twenty

The next day I wasn't much better.

Jesus! Did you ever meet anyone as self-pitying as me? It was ridiculous and it had to stop.

So I dragged myself out of the bed and tended to Kate. Then I tended to myself. Oh, don't worry, we're not going to have a repeat performance of the getting-drunk-and-not-washing-myself senario.

Oh no, things weren't that bad.

I got through the day.

To be fair, I didn't achieve anything really impressive.

I didn't find a cure for cancer.

I didn't invent run-proof stockings.

And I'm ashamed to tell you that I didn't even call James.

I know, I know! I'm sorry. I know that I should have. I knew that I was avoiding my responsibilities.

But I felt so empty and lonely.

Sad and alone and all the other emotions coming under the genus "Loss," subspecies "rejection."

Anyway I *did* get up on Thursday.

Not only that, but I called James.

And I wasn't even nervous.

I had Adam to thank for that, because I approached calling James with the attitude of "Huh! Don't think that you're anything special. Because you're not. You're not the only man who can make me feel sad and lonely and rejected. Oh no! There's *millions* of others who can do exactly what you did. So there!''

Perhaps not an ideal attitude from a self-esteem point of view, but whatever . . . at least when I dialed the number in London, my hands didn't shake and my voice didn't quaver.

How interesting, I thought.

James no longer had the power to reduce me to a quaking wreck. Well, at least dialing his office number no longer had the power to reduce me to a quaking wreck.

Let's not get carried away here.

In a confident and steady voice I asked the receptionist in his office in London if I could speak to him. I felt as if London was a million miles away. As remote as another planet. You'd never have thought that I saw it every evening on the news. The receptionist sounded very far away, very foreign.

Mirroring the way I felt. My life with James had become very far away, very foreign. Or maybe it was because the receptionist was Greek.

Either way, I was perfectly calm as I waited to speak to him.

I mean, what was the big deal?

What did I have to lose?

Nothing.

As someone once said—a miserable, sardonic, misanthropic someone—freedom's just another word for nothing left to lose.

Up until I heard that I'd thought freedom was being able to go swimming when you had your period.

How misinformed I was.

Of course, you believe anything when you're about twelve.

Did you know that you can't get pregnant if you do it standing up? Honestly, it's true.

And did you know that you *can* have a baby if you suck the man's thing? But the twelve-year-old me knew that would never happen to me because I'd never do anything as disgusting as suck the man's thing. And I didn't believe for one moment that anyone, anywhere, would do something so revolting and alien.

I could weep for the innocent child, the idealistic twelve-year-old, that I once was.

Oh, sorry, sorry, you want to know what happened with James.

Oh, didn't I say?

He wasn't in.

At a meeting, or something.

And, no, I didn't leave my name.

And, yes, you're right if you suspect that I was a bit relieved at not having to talk to him.

But I was in an unimpeachable position.

I'd called him, hadn't I?

I defy anyone to say that I hadn't.

Was it my fault that he was unavailable?

No, indeed it was not.

But it meant that I could stop feeling guilty for a couple of hours.

So spirits were high around Thursday lunchtime.

Happily, I picked Kate out of her bassinet and twirled her around. What a beautiful picture we must make, I thought. The beautiful child being lovingly held by her devoted mother. Kate just looked frightened and started to cry, but never mind.

I meant well. My heart was in the right place, even if Kate's center of gravity wasn't.

"Come on, darling," I said. "Let's put on our best outfits and go into town and see the people."

And so Kate and I went into town. I couldn't, in all conscience, buy any more clothes for me, but I could buy clothes for Kate.

Every day I was finding out more good things about Kate. She continued to enhance every aspect of my life.

I bought her the tiniest, most beautiful denim dress. Even the smallest one was too big for her, but she'd grow into it. It was *gorgeous*.

And I got her the sweetest little jumper, light blue, patterned with dark blue polka dots and—get this—a matching little jacket with zip front and a hood.

So that she'd fit in if she ever met any cool street kids.

And the socks!

I could go on for hours about the socks I got her. So tiny

and fluffy and snuggly and warm and soft, to cover her tiny, tiny, tiny little pink feet. Sometimes I got such a rush of love for her that I wanted to squeeze her so hard I actually feared for her safety.

Then we wandered around a bookshop for a while. My adrenaline started pumping any time I was within about a hundred yards of a bookshop. I loved books nearly as much as I loved clothes. And that's saying something.

The feel of them and the smell of them. A bookshop was like an Aladdin's cave for me. Entire worlds and lives can be found just behind that glossy cover. All you had to do was look.

So the entire world and life that I chose to enter belonged to someone called Samantha, who apparently "had it all." A palazzo in Florence, a penthouse in New York, a mews house next door to Buckingham Palace, more priceless jewels than you could shake a stick at, a publishing house or two, a Lear jet, a hot boyfriend, some count or duke or something, and the absolutely essential dark secret and hidden tragic past.

My money was riding on her having been a lesbian prostitute before her luck changed.

I could have bought an "improving book," I suppose.

Something by one of that Brontë crew. Or maybe even a bit of Joseph Conrad. He was always good for a laugh.

But I wanted something that wasn't very taxing. So, just to be on the safe side, I bought complete trash.

After I came out of the bookshop, clutching my child and my gold-embossed best-seller, I just happened to be passing the café that I had gone to with Adam the previous Saturday and I just happened to have an hour or two to kill so I just happened to sit there and—guess what?—Adam just happened to walk in only an hour and a half after I arrived.

What a coincidence!

Well, I suppose I had better come clean.

I had kind of, I suppose, nursed a little hope that maybe, just maybe, if I were to go into town that maybe, just maybe, I might run into Adam.

So I suppose that, when he finally walked in, I couldn't call it either a spiritual or a metaphysical event.

I could even be said to have engineered our meeting.

Although, dammit, that's not fair.

God helps those who help themselves.

God can't drive a parked car.

If I had stayed at home in bed with the chocolate and the *Marie Claire* would I have met him?

The answer has got to be no.

I was sitting there, with half an eye on Samantha's takeover bid and the other eye on the door. Although I was hoping that he'd come in and even half expecting him to appear, I wasn't prepared for how I felt when he actually did arrive.

He was so, he was so . . . so *gorgeous.*

So tall and strong-looking. But at the same time so boyishly cute.

"Easy, easy," I told myself. "Take deep breaths."

I resisted the urge to dump Kate on the table and run over and fling myself on him.

I reminded myself that I had used up my neuroses quota on him and that it might be a good idea to behave like a normal well-balanced woman.

Hell, after a bit of practice I might even become one.

So I sat there, poised and perched, trying to exude calmness and well-balancedness and unneuroticness.

Finally he saw me.

I held my breath.

I waited for him to rear and neigh like a startled horse and then make for the door like the hounds of hell were after him. I expected him to run like a hare through the café, knocking over tables and chairs, spilling pots of tea and cups of coffee over innocent bystanders, his hair standing on end, his eyes wide and staring, and shout at anyone who'd care to listen, stabbing his finger wildly at me and Kate. "She's crazy, that one, you know. Pure mental. Have nothing to do with her."

But he didn't do anything of the sort.

He smiled at me.

I have to admit that it was a bit of a wary smile.

But it was a smile.

"Claire!" he said, and came over to the table.

"And Kate," he continued.

Correct on both counts.

Not much got past him.

He kissed Kate.

He didn't kiss me.

But I could live with it.

I was just so glad to see him, gladder still that he wanted to speak to me. I really wasn't that concerned with which one of us he kissed.

"Why don't you sit down and join us?" I said politely.

Poised. Polished. The hostess with the mostest, that was me.

Impeccably mannered. Emotions—if indeed I had any at all, that is—firmly, strictly even, bound and strapped into place.

"All right," he said.

Wary. Cautious. Watching me carefully. Maybe waiting for me to accuse him of having the hots for my mother.

"I'll just go and get a cup of coffee," he said.

"Fine," I said, giving a magnanimous smile, well-balancedness and relaxedness exuding (I hoped) from my every pore.

Off he went.

And I waited.

And waited.

Oh dear, I thought sadly, he must have made a break for it. He mustn't want anything to do with me at all. I seemed to be developing quite a knack for this.

He was probably wedged in the tiny window in the men's room, struggling to get out among the smelly trash and cabbage leaves and empty brandy bottles that are found outside the back exits of restaurants and cafés.

I put my book in my bag—do you know, I was so glad to see him that I totally forgot to hide the cover of the trashy novel?—and rearranged Kate in the sling.

At least I tried, I thought.

And I was glad.

I hadn't got what I wanted, but at least I'd taken responsibility for my life. I'd tried to fix something, I'd tried to make something happen.

I hadn't behaved like a passive victim, just letting life happen to me.

I had taken control.

It hadn't worked, but so what.

The important thing was to try.

And the next time I met a nice man I wouldn't go all slushy and schoolgirlie on him, thinking of him as a boyfriend and suspecting every other woman of coveting him.

I had just organized myself to go when he jauntily came around the corner with a tray with coffee and pastries on it.

The bastard!

I'd just been all grown up and mature and wise for absolutely bloody nothing. I was feeling so *good* about myself, feeling saddened but enriched by the mistakes I had made. Then he had to come back and destroy it totally on me.

There went my rosy, introspective, pensive glow.

The selfish bastard!

I had a good mind to tell him to get lost and leave me alone. I had just come to terms, not even five minutes before, with losing him, so now what was I expected to do with him?

Enjoy his company?

Are you out of your mind?

"Sorry I was so long," he was saying. "The cashier had a fit and . . . hey! . . . where are you going?!"

He looked really surprised.

And then he looked upset.

"Sorry," I mumbled, feeling mortified.

If he ever had reason to think that I was hysterical and neurotic before now, this could only convince him that I was a complete tantrum-throwing little bitch.

"Why are you going?" he asked, sounding both angry and hurt. "I'm sorry I took so long. But I thought you'd wait."

"I thought you'd gone," I muttered.

"But why?" he asked in total exasperation. "Why would I leave?"

"I don't know," I said, feeling queasy with embarrassment.

Oh, you've messed it up really well this time, I told myself.

"Look!" he said, and he banged his tray down on the table and sent coffee spattering everywhere.

I jumped with fright.

"Sit down," he said angrily. He put his hands on my shoulders and pushed me back down into my chair in no uncertain terms.

"Jesus!" I thought in shock. "Take it easy."

"Oh sorry, Kate," he interjected apologetically. Her little face must have registered surprise at this abrupt change in altitude.

"Now!" he said, back in angry mode again. "What the hell is going on?"

"What do you mean?" I asked in a little voice.

He was obviously trying to keep a lot of anger in check and it was frightening.

"Why are you treating me like this?" he demanded angrily, his face very close to mine.

I couldn't believe that this was happening.

Where had nice pleasant understanding Adam gone?

Who was this furious man in his place?

"Like what?" I asked, mesmerized. I was scared of him, but like a rabbit caught in the headlights of an oncoming car, I couldn't tear myself away from the angry blue of his eyes.

"Like I'm some kind of low-life."

"I'm not," I protested in surprise.

I wasn't, was I?

"Yes, you bloody well are," he barked at me, his fingers digging into my shoulders. "You have, practically from the first time we met.

"I met you, I really liked you, I wanted to see you, what's wrong with that?" he said furiously.

"Nothing," I whispered.

"So why do you behave as if I'm some kind of Casanova bastard type, why did you think I was messing with your little sister, why did you think I'd walk away and leave you sitting here, just tell me, *why*?"

People from other tables were starting to glance interestedly at us, but Adam didn't notice and I didn't really think it would be terribly sensible to point this out, at least not while he was in his present mood.

"Don't you see how insulting it is?" he flung at me.

"No," I said, almost afraid to look at him.

"Well, it is!"

I didn't know what to say. I just sat there looking at him, his blue eyes boring into mine.

I suddenly became aware of just how close I was to him.

Our faces were inches apart.

I could see the individual hairs of his stubble, the lightly tanned skin stretched tightly over his beautiful cheekbones, the evenness of his white teeth, the sexiness of his mouth . . .

He suddenly went very still.

All the anger and violence seemed to lift from him.

We sat there like statues, his hands on my shoulders. We stared at each other.

I was so aware of him, his strength, his vulnerability. There was tension between us, vibrating slightly in the stillness.

Then he pulled away from me. Exhausted and utterly, utterly weary, he sat with his arms hanging limply by his side.

"Adam," I ventured tentatively.

He didn't even look up at me.

He sat there with his head bent.

Giving me a view of his beautiful dark hair.

"Adam," I said again, and gingerly touched his arm.

He stiffened slightly but he didn't pull away.

"It's not you, it's me," I said awkwardly.

There was a pause.

"What do you mean?" he asked.

Well, at least I thought that's what he'd said. It was kind of hard to hear him because his voice was all muffled because he was practically resting his head on his chest and talking into his sweater.

"It's my problem," I said. I found it very hard to say.

He said something else.

"Er, sorry Adam, but I didn't quite catch that," I told him apologetically.

He lifted his head and looked up at me.

He looked bad-tempered but beautiful.

"I said, what's your problem?" he repeated, rather nastily.

Another thrill of fear ran through me.

I had to make this all right.

But it was very hard to talk to him when he was being so intimidating.

"It's because I'm insecure and suspicious," I said.

He said nothing, just sat there looking moodily at me.

"You haven't done anything wrong," I continued falteringly.

He gave a grim little nod at that.

Of course, he might just have been readjusting his head's position on his neck.

But it was enough to encourage me to continue.

"I thought you'd left here because you didn't want to speak to me," I told him.

"I see," he said without any noticeable emotion.

I felt like giving him a little smack.

React, for God's sake!

Tell me I'm being ridiculous, tell me that you'd always want to see me.

He didn't.

Maybe he didn't appreciate being manipulated into complimenting me.

Fair enough.

Maybe it was time I stopped manipulating him.

Or anyone else, for that matter.

But sometimes it was as instinctive as breathing.

Not that I was proud of it or anything, mind.

I tried to explain to him.

"I thought that you wouldn't want to speak to me after I'd been so unreasonable on the phone on Sunday night."

"You were unreasonable," he agreed.

"But I'm frightened," I said sadly.

"Of what?" he asked, not sounding quite as fierce.

"Of, of, of . . . everything really," I said. And to my horror my eyes filled up with tears.

I didn't do it on purpose, I *swear* I didn't.

I was as shocked by my unexpected ocular moistness as he was.

"Sorry," I sniffed. "I'm not doing this so that you'll be nice to me."

"Good," he said. "Because it won't work."

The heartless fucker, I thought briefly, but then banished the unworthy thought from my mind.

"I only respond to crying women if they're under the age of two," he continued, half smiling, as he touched Kate's face.

"Oh," I said. I made a valiant attempt at a laugh, even though I was still crying.

"So what are you so frightened of that you have to be mean to me?" he asked. This time he almost sounded gentle.

"Oh, the usual," I said, trying to pull myself together.

"Like what?" he persisted.

"Caring for people and then losing them, making a fool of myself, being hurt, scaring people away, being too forward, being too aloof . . ." I rattled off. "Do you want me to go on? I could do this for hours."

"No, that's all right," he said. "But we're all scared of those things."

"Are we?" I asked, surprised.

"Of course," he assured me. "Why do you think you're so special? You haven't got a monopoly on feeling like that, you know. And anyway, how am I making you feel frightened?"

"Because I thought you were playing me off against Helen," I said.

"But I *told* you I wasn't," he said in exasperation. "And I *told* you that I could understand why you felt like that, even though I didn't like it."

"Anyway, why are you so touchy about it?" I asked him.

"Well, I just am," he said. He looked sad and thoughtful. I knew that he wasn't just thinking about me and Helen.

What had happened to him?

What kind of grief was he carrying?

I had to get to the bottom of this.

But first I had to sort out our current difficulties.

I plowed valiantly on.

"And after I spoke to you on Sunday night, I felt that I had seemed hysterical and like I was overreacting and like I had scared you away and that you wouldn't call me anymore," I blurted out, and then watched him carefully from under my lashes to see how he reacted to this.

"Well . . ." he said slowly.

Oh, speed it up to God's sake, I thought frantically. My nerves can't stand it.

"I wasn't going to call you," he continued.

"Oh," I said.

So I had been right.

Ten for ten on my instincts.

Minus several billion for my sense of well-being. I felt as if I'd been kicked in the stomach by a horse.

Actually that's not true, because I'd never been kicked in the stomach by a horse. Do you think that I'd be sitting here now talking to you if I'd been the lucky recipient of a kick in the stomach by a horse? The answer has got to be no.

But I felt the way I felt when I was about ten and I fell off a wall and landed belly-flop on my stomach on a lawn that had been baked hard by the summer sun and was as hard as concrete. There was that horrible feeling of shock and nausea as all the breath in my body was abruptly forced out.

That was the way I felt now.

"Not because I didn't want to call you," he continued, unaware of how much pain I was in. "But because I thought it would be best for you."

"How do you mean?" I squeaked, feeling infinitely better.

"Because you've been through too much lately. I didn't want to upset you in any way or add to your troubles."

The angel!

"You weren't upsetting me," I told him.

"But I obviously was," he said.

"But you weren't doing it on purpose," I protested.

"I know," he said. "Which is why I lost my temper earlier—sorry about that, by the way—but just being in contact with you seemed to cause you to be annoyed or upset or whatever."

Relief washed over me in waves.

"I'm sorry I was difficult," I told him. "But . . ."

And here I took a deep breath.

I was taking a bit of a risk.

Putting my feelings on the line.

"I'd rather see you than not see you," I finally managed to tell him.

"Really?" he said, sounding hopeful and excited and boyish.

"Yes."

"Are you sure?"

"I'm sure."

"Do you trust me?"

"Oh, Adam," I said, half laughing, half crying. "I said I wanted to see you. No one mentioned anything about trust."

"Okay," he said, laughing also (no sign of any tears). "But will you trust me when I say that I want to see you and not Helen?"

"Yes," I said solemnly. "I will."

"And if the cashier has a fight with someone over his change and has a fit and runs off so that I have to wait hours to pay for my coffee, you won't think that I've made a break out the back way?"

"No," I agreed. "I won't."

"So we're friends?" he asked oh-so-appealingly.

"Yes." I nodded in agreement. "We're friends."

Although my brain was saying to me, "Excuse me, excuse me, *friends*, did you say *friends*? I don't think mere friends behave in the way you want to with Adam. Laura is your friend and you don't rip the clothes off her back anytime you see her and correct me if I'm wrong but isn't that precisely what you want to do with Adam?"

"Shut up," I muttered at it.

"Sorry?" said Adam, looking at me in alarm, obviously thinking, "Oh God no, here she goes again."

"Nothing." I smiled at him. "Nothing at all."

"Well," he said. "Seeing as we've sorted out all this misunderstanding, when can I see you?"

"Oh, I don't really know," I said, going all shy and girlie on him.

"Are you doing anything on Sunday night?" he asked.

"I don't think so," I said, pretending to consider. Although my social diary stretched ahead of me as empty and as formless as the Gobi Desert.

"Well, can I cook you dinner?" he asked.

"Yes, that would be lovely," I said.

"Good," he said. "Jenny and Andy have gone away for the weekend so we'll have the place to ourselves."

"Oh," I said.

I was a woman of the world.

I knew very well that to go to a man's house, a man's house where all the other residents were absent, and submit to having a dinner cooked for oneself meant that it was more than pork chops and Black Forest gâteau that was being offered.

Great, I thought.

I couldn't believe my luck.

"Right, Adam, that sounds lovely."

And so we agreed on a time for Sunday night. He walked Kate and me to the car and home we drove.

twenty-one

The preparations for Sunday.

Ingredients:

One neglected, rejected, dejected twenty-nine-year-old woman, who had recently given birth

A generous helping of guilt

A pinch of anticipation

A packet of insecurity about the shape of her body

A sprig of excitement (wild, if possible)

A spoonful of condensed deep despair

A minor stretch marks panic

Two black lace-topped stockings

One interesting pair of black underwear

One black bra, of the miraculous rather than just the plain wondrous variety

One bottle of red wine

One dress

One pair of shoes

Decoration:

Whore-red lipstick

Several layers of dark mascara

Directions:

Put the stockings, panties, and bra to one side, for use later. Take the woman.

Add the guilt, anticipation, insecurity, excitement, despair and panic.

Mix thoroughly.

Leave to stew for a couple of days.

In a medium-size bathroom, prepare the woman by shaving her legs, coloring her hair and painting her toenails.

About an hour before commencing, baste generously in expensive body lotion, turning frequently.

Add the stockings, the pair of interesting black undies and the miraculous black bra. Have a couple of practice runs at looking seductive by letting her hair fall over her face and looking up through her eyelashes.

Check that she can still gasp and arch her back and say sentences like, "Oh baby, that was wonderful" and "Oh God, don't stop" while keeping a straight face.

Commandeer a sister, preferably Anna, to look after the aforementioned child.

Add a generous helping of whore-red lipstick, several layers of black mascara, a short purple (it is, after all, the color of passion) dress, sexy black shoes with suede ankle straps and one bottle of red wine.

Always take care not to start swigging from the bottle of red before arriving at your destination.

As an optional extra, condoms in the purse are always a nice touch.

If it's not possible to procure them—for example, they may be out of season—you will have to make do with large amounts of self-restraint. Not always ideal, but it does work.

Serve on a bed with a good-looking man.

I followed the instructions to the letter. I was lucky enough to be able to procure condoms—courtesy of Laura—what a woman!

I was feeling pretty good.

I didn't even get upset when I discovered that thanks to my hair color (it's hair *enhancer*, darling; we don't need to color our hair, we just *enhance* its natural lights), all right then, thanks to my hair *enhancer*, my ears and my hair were now color-coordinated.

But I suppose if I had to have colored ears, I could have done a lot worse than a rich, glossy, shiny chestnut color. None of your Ebony Shadow or Plum Sugar for my ears. No sir!

At about seven-thirty on Sunday evening, I was prepared. About to go forth to sin, I kissed Kate good-night.

As I was furtively making for the front door, my coat buttoned up practically to the eyebrows in case Mum should spot me looking so floozylike, the phone rang.

"Claire, it's for you," shouted Helen.

Oh God!

But it was only Laura.

Calling to wish me luck and wanting to know if I had practiced putting on a condom with my teeth, as per her instructions.

"No, I didn't!" I told her.

I was dying to get off the phone and out of the house because I was terrified of being caught.

"Why not?" she demanded. "You can't just expect him to be happy with boring old sex. You have to be a bit inventive."

"But you only gave me two!" I said, all alarm. "I didn't want to waste them. And anyway, what was I supposed to practice on?"

"Well, let's just hope that you perform adequately with the first one. Or else you won't get a chance to use the second one," she said darkly.

"Oh stop it, Laura, I'm nervous enough!"

"Good." She laughed. "It's much better when you're nervous."

I promised to call her the next day and tell her all the gory details.

"Or, if I get in early enough tonight, I'll ring you and tell you everything," I promised eagerly.

"If you get in early enough tonight to tell me everything, there won't be anything to tell,'" she told me.

"Oh," I said.

She had a point.

"Look, I'm going," I said in annoyance, and I hung up on her while she was in the middle of explaining some sort of complicated sexual activity that she said she had seen done in a show in Bangkok. Whatever it was it could only be done by a woman who was a damn sight more supple than me. I did know how to have sex, you know. I had given birth to a child. How did she think this actually came about?

While we're on the subject of sexual shenanigans I've got a confession to make.

Wait for it.

Here it comes.

I enjoy the missionary position.

There! I've said it.

I'm made to feel so *ashamed* of myself for feeling that way.

As if I'm terribly boring and repressed.

But I'm not. Honestly.

I'm not saying that it's the only position that I like.

But, really, I have no objection to it whatsoever.

Naturally, of course, this isn't the time to discuss favorite sexual positions.

But I'll just tell you very quickly that I think cunnilingus is the most boring thing God ever created. I'd rather spend a day filing than endure a five-minute stint of it.

And when they're finished with their few minutes of slurping they act like you should be so *grateful* for it. Beaming up at you like they deserve a medal. And then act like they're entitled to a year's supply of no-questions-asked blow jobs.

Of course, some women swear by it, but . . . sorry, sorry.

I finally left and drove over to his house.

twenty-two

I parked the car just outside his house and feeling a heavy mixture of excitement and sordid shame walked up to the front door. Then I remembered that I had left the bottle of wine in the car and I quickly ran back to get it.

I was going nowhere without it.

Dutch courage.

Well, Chilean courage, but whatever.

Adam opened the door almost immediately.

If I didn't know any better I'd swear he had been hiding in the hall, lurking behind the curtain, waiting for me to arrive.

Well, actually, maybe he had been.

He was doing a good job of seeming to be as excited and affected by all of this as I was.

He looked a bit anxious.

Cold feet?

Change of heart?

Pregame nerves?

But then he rallied strongly.

"Hello." He smiled. "You look lovely."

"Hello," I said. I smiled at him in spite of my nerves.

How wonderful, I thought with a thrill.

I felt so dangerously decadent.

On an assignation with a beautiful man.

Have I ever wanted any man as much as I want Adam? I wondered.

Probably, I thought, sighing.

Just being realistic for a moment.

But right then it felt as if I'd never wanted anyone else, ever.

How long will it take for us to be in bed together? I wondered.

How long can I hold off if he doesn't make a move?

What if he doesn't make a move? I thought with horror.

Or what if it's a total disaster?

Maybe he'll think I'm completely hideous, with my post-childbirth body.

Maybe I'll think he's completely hideous, because he doesn't look exactly like James.

Oh God!

I should have stayed at home.

Before I could bolt for the door, stammering that it had all been a terrible mistake, he put his arm (and what an arm!) around my shoulders and guided me toward the kitchen.

"Take off your coat," he said. "And have a drink."

"But . . . oh, all right. Make mine a pint of red wine," I said as I sat down at the kitchen table.

He laughed.

"Feeling nervous, darling?" he asked silkily as he poured me a glass.

Jesus! I thought in alarm, don't ask me things silkily. I was frightened enough. If he started behaving like some kind of arch seducer, I was out of there. All I needed now was for him to change his jeans and sweatshirt for a silk paisley dressing gown and parade around with an onyx cigarette holder.

"I'm not nervous," I blurted out. "I'm fucking terrified."

"Of what?" he asked with mock surprise. "My cooking isn't that bad."

Oh, so that's the way you want to play it, I thought.

Faux casual, is it?

Fine then.

I gave him a poised smile.

And flung my entire glass of wine down my throat before I realized what I had done.

"Relax," he said anxiously, coming over to sit beside me at the table and hold my hand. "I'm not going to bite."

Oh, aren't you? I thought. Well then I'm definitely going home.

"We're just going to have something to eat and a little chat," he said kindly. "Nothing to worry about."

"All right then," I said, making a valiant effort to relax. "What are we having anyway?"

"Homemade Stilton and Muscat Grape Soup, Boeuf Bourguignonne, with Potatoes Dauphinois and my own recipe for Zabaglione for dessert."

"Really?" I asked, astonished. I hadn't put Adam down as a fancy cook—more your spuds and chops type of fellow, quantity rather than quality.

"No." He grinned at me. "Are you joking? You're getting Spaghetti Bolognaese and you're lucky I was even able to manage that."

"I see." I laughed.

"And if you're very good"—at this point he paused and gave me a meaningful look—"and I mean *very*, then you can have some chocolate mousse."

"Oh," I said, all excited, a combination of the meaningful look and the news of the chocolate mousse. "That's great. I love chocolate mousse."

"I know," he said. "Why do you think I got it?

"And," he continued in a teasing tone. "If you're very, *very* good you can eat it off my stomach."

I burst out laughing.

He was such an angel. I couldn't suppress a shiver of lust at the thought of his flat muscley stomach, although this was probably precisely the kind of reaction he was banking on. I hurriedly poured myself another glass of wine, but this time I forced myself to sip it.

He served the dinner and it was obvious that this was not something he did on a regular basis. He seemed all out of place standing at the stove. Rushing from the sink to the stove and back to the sink again, while the pasta boiled over and the salad visibly wilted. Although it did give me a beautiful view of his butt.

Cooking, unlike most other things, did not come naturally to him, which made it all the more touching that he had gone to such bother for me.

He looked so uncertain as he carefully carried the plates over to the table and reverently placed mine in front of me.

"Have some more wine," he said, pouring me another glass. That made a change from his acting like the local branch of Alcoholics Anonymous not ten minutes earlier.

"Are you trying to get me drunk to take advantage of me?" I asked him, trying to sound annoyed.

"I'm trying to get you drunk so that you won't notice if the food tastes horrible." He laughed.

"I'm sure it's lovely," I assured him.

I'm sorry to relate that I couldn't eat more than a few mouthfuls. Not because it was horrible or anything. It's just that I was so nervous and the air was so fraught with tension and anticipation that I felt like saying to him, "Look Adam, darling, we both know why I'm here, so let's just cut to the chase."

He couldn't eat anything either.

But that might have been because of the food and not his nerves.

We sat facing each other at Adam's kitchen table, sliding spaghetti backward and forward on our plates, the salad totally untouched in its bowl, looking all mournful and abandoned.

Conversation was desultory.

Every now and again I'd look up at him and catch him watching me, and the look on his face made me feel hot and awkward. It eliminated any last chance of my eating anything at all. Not to mention that I was afraid that if I ate anything my stomach would be all bulgy and sticky-outy.

And what kind of stomach was that to have on a first night with a man?

Or that I would swing a forkful of food mouthward and the spaghetti would rebound onto my face with a whiplash-like effect and spatter me with red sauce.

The way I react to food when I'm around a man is a sure barometer of the way I feel about him. If I can't eat it means that I'm mad about him. When I can manage orange juice and some toast in the morning it's the End of the Beginning. And by the time I get around to finishing the food left on his plate it's as good as over.

Either that or I marry him.

Well, that had been the pattern so far, anyway.

"Is that all you're going to eat?" he eventually asked, looking at the mound of food on my plate.

He looked disappointed.

"Adam," I said awkwardly, "I'm sorry. I'm sure that it's lovely and everything but I just can't eat. I don't know why. I really am sorry." I looked at him appealingly.

"Never mind," he said, taking the plates away.

"Will you never cook for me again?" I asked sadly.

"Of course I will," he said. "And for God's sake please don't look so miserable."

"It's only because I'm nervous," I told him. "It's not because the food was horrible."

"Nervous?" He came over to my side of the table and sat down beside me. "You've nothing to be nervous about."

"Don't I?" I asked, looking him full in the eye.

I was quite shameless.

I'd be the first to admit it.

But, goddamit, I'd wasted enough time this evening already.

"No," he murmured. "You've got nothing to be nervous about."

And, very gently, he put his arm around my shoulder and his hand on the back of my head.

I closed my eyes.

I can't believe I'm doing this, I thought wildly, but I'm not going to stop.

I inhaled the scent of his skin as his face came nearer.

I waited for his kiss.

And when it came it was beautiful. Sweet and gentle and firm.

The kind of kiss where the person doing it is very good at it but you don't feel like he became such a good kisser by practicing on thousands of others.

He stopped kissing me and I looked up at him in alarm.

What was the meaning of this?

"Was that all right?" he asked quietly.

"All right?" I gasped. "It was better than all right."

He laughed slightly.

"No, I mean, is it all right to kiss you? You know, I don't want to overstep any boundaries."

"It's all right," I told him.

"I know you've been hurt," he said.

"But you're my friend," I told him. "It's okay."

"I want to be more than your friend," he said.

"That's okay too," I told him.

"Really?" he said, looking at me for confirmation.

"Honestly," I told him.

Oh Jesus! I hadn't left myself much room for maneuver here.

Not that I wanted to.

He kissed me again and it was just as nice as the first time.

He drew away from me and I pulled him back.

He looked at me almost wonderingly and said, "God, you're so beautiful."

"No, I'm not," I said, feeling a bit embarrassed.

"Oh, you are," he said. "You really are."

"No," I said. "Helen's beautiful."

"Look," he said, smiling. "At the risk of going all Californian on you, you're a beautiful person."

"I am?"

"You are."

A little pause.

"*And* you're a babe."

"Thanks." I laughed. "What a pity that you're so hideous."

Then he laughed. There was absolutely no vanity at all about the man, although perhaps when you're that handsome there's no need for it.

He kissed me again.

And, honestly, it was wonderful.

I felt so taken care of when I was with him and in his arms. But I also felt that I was taking care of him. That he needed me as much as I needed him.

"Do you realize that we know each other less than two weeks?" he asked me.

Oh no, I thought, does this means that he won't go to bed with me yet? Is he going to impose some kind of time limit on it? That we can't have sex until we've known each other for three months or something?

"Yes," I agreed cautiously. "Ten days, actually."

"But it feels like much longer," he said. "Much, much longer."

Thank God!

"I'm so glad I met you," he continued. "You're so special."

"Im not," I protested. "I'm very ordinary."

"You're special to me."

"But why?"

"Oh, I don't know," he said. He leaned back in his chair and looked at me. "Because you're interesting and have opinions on things and you're very funny. But mostly because you're so nice . . . Like, basically, you're a decent person."

"I'm not always," I told him. "I mean, you should have seen me a couple of weeks ago."

And then I got annoyed with myself.

Here I was, with a lovely man telling me lovely things about myself, and I was trying to convince him that none of them were true.

It was usually the other way around. I would tell them lovely things about myself and they'd spend the rest of the time trying to convince me that none of it was true.

He leaned over and kissed me again.

It was just blissful. I wanted to surrender to it. To be with him, without any guilt or worry or awkwardness. Being with him felt so *right* . . . .

You're on the rebound, I sternly warned myself.

So what? I asked myself back. I mean, it's not as if I'm going to marry the guy. Can't I have some fun?

Well, yes, I suppose I could have some fun.

But at the same time, I can't be going around sleeping with any man who asks me to.

But, then again, this isn't just any man.

This is a nice, sweet man who cares for me—well, at least he *seems* to care for me, and I care for him.

With a little shock, I realized that I did, in fact, care for him.

I mean, I'm not saying I loved him or anything, because that would be untrue. But there was something about him that touched me.

And I didn't want to hurt him.

But was I going to?

Did sleeping with him imply a commitment?

He did know that I was married.

He was fully aware of my feelings for James.

And maybe he didn't want a commitment.

Maybe he wanted to be with me because he knew that I was really with someone else and it would let him off the hook?

Oh Lord!

Traumaville!

Decision time.

I stood up and held him by the hand.

He looked at me questioningly.

"Are you okay?" he asked. "Can I get you anything?"

"Yes," I murmured.

"What?" he asked.

"Laid."

But I only said it under my breath. I didn't want him to think I was *terribly* vulgar.

Because I wasn't really.

Not all the time, anyway.

I started moving toward the kitchen door, still holding his hand.

I felt so liberated and wanton.

"Where are we going?" he asked, feigning innocence.

"Down the road for a drink," I told him.

I looked at him, and disappointment was written all over his face.

"I'm joking, you idiot." I smiled at him. "We're going upstairs." So we walked up the stairs, me leading the way, still holding his hand. With each step I took, I became more and more convinced that this was the right thing to do. We got to the top of the stairs and he pulled me into his arms and kissed me.

It was gorgeous. He felt so big and strong. I could feel the smooth skin of his back through his sweatshirt. He turned me around and steered me toward a door.

"My room," he said. "Unless you brought me up here to give you a tour of the house."

"That can wait until later," I said, barely able to speak with excitement and nerves.

His room was nice, so tidy that I knew, instantly—not that

I had ever been in any real doubt—that he had meticulously planned to get me into bed. Men's rooms are only ever clean the first time you sleep with them. Once you've had sex with them the place goes right to hell. It's as though the instant the relationship is consummated the man shouts, "Right, fellas, you can come out now!"

And out from under the bed appear armies of dirty underpants and sweaty socks and cups and plates and car magazines and hideous sweaters and pint glasses and sexist calendars and Stephen King books and damp towels and jars of Ben-Gay, all elbowing and clamoring and complaining loudly about the amount of time that they had to spend in hiding, and stretching and dusting themselves down and then draping themselves artistically on the bedroom carpet, delighted to be back where they belong.

"What took you so long?" a sock might shout cheerfully at the successful seducer. "Put up a bit of a fight, did she?"

"We thought we were stuck in there forever," a filthy pair of trousers might good-naturedly joke. "You must be losing your touch."

Adam eased my passage over the pristine floor to the bed by kissing me, so that I didn't have to march over and sit down on it, looking expectant and awkward.

No, he just kind of kissed me and sort of steered me across the room and, well, you know, we just arrived at the bed and as it was there, we thought it might be a good idea to lie on it, otherwise we would only have to go around it.

After a while he started to undo the buttons on my dress. And I put my hands under his sweatshirt onto the bare skin of his stomach and chest.

Very gently and very slowly, he unbuttoned my dress all the way down and started to take my clothes off.

It felt nice but weird. Weird but nice.

It had been a long, long time since I went to bed with someone for the first time, if you follow me. It was funny that he wasn't James. Not horrible, or unpleasant. Just, as I say, a bit funny.

I felt a bit awkward about my body, and about Adam seeing it. I wasn't exactly uninhibited at the best of times. I wasn't a great one for dancing around with no clothes on. It was all right when I was with James. I had no problems with him. Eventually, that is. But even with him, I'd been very coy for ages.

Adam kept telling me that I was beautiful. He was so glad that I was there and stroking me and caressing me and holding me and kissing me. After a while I completely relaxed. Call me old-fashioned, if you want, but for me there is no bigger turn-on than being told that I'm beautiful and being made to feel beautiful.

You can keep your fancy tongue work and elaborate hip swerves. Five minutes of flattery works a whole lot better for me.

After a good deal more of kissing and getting to know each other, if that's what you'd like to call it, it became obvious that the evening was heading in a definite direction.

Adam pulled himself away from me.

"God!" he said. "You're a witch, you're driving me wild, you're gorgeous."

I sat up a little bit and looked down at him as his hands roamed over my stomach.

I was so thankful that I hadn't eaten anything.

He was lovely. Such a beautiful body. And such a gorgeous face.

And such a nice guy.

What had I done to deserve this?

My eyes traveled down his chest, admiring his taut stomach, but I averted my gaze when my eyes moved down a little bit lower. How do I describe the state of play below Adam's waist without being overly explicit or overly coy?

It's very difficult to discuss having sex without being so crude that I sound like a pornographic book or without being so discreet that I sound like a repressed, uptight Victorian novelist who suffers regularly from vaginismus and still calls her husband Mr. Clements after twenty-seven years of marriage.

How about if I just say that mighty oaks from little acorns grow?

Isn't that good? Discreet yet symbolic?

Offensive to no one but at the same time leaving you in no doubt whatsoever that Adam had a hard-on that could cut diamonds?

Whoops!

Vulgar, vulgar, vulgar!

Although while we're on the subject I might as well tell you that it was big enough to make me fear for the safety of the light fixtures if he made any sudden movements.

Which, naturally, I wholeheartedly hoped he would.

No, I'm only joking. It wasn't that big at all.

It was of medium size.

Neither alarmingly big nor depressingly small.

Just right, really.

Of course, there are some unscrupulous women who tell whatever man they're with that he has the biggest penis they've ever seen.

You know, quite simply as a matter of course.

They shrink back against the mattress and stare round-eyed with mock horror at the man in question and squeal, "Oh my! You're not coming anywhere near me with that monster of a thing. What are you trying to do? Screw me or batter the door down?"

Sneaky tactics.

Because of course the man in question is delighted. Believing himself to be in possession of a weaponlike member, he feels invincible and all man. And gives them a seeing-to that they won't forget in a hurry. But you wouldn't catch me doing that.

Well, only very rarely.

And I also can't describe what was going on below Adam's waist because I can't think of a word that I feel comfortable with to describe his, well, you know, his . . .

Well, how can I tell you what I can't describe if I haven't got a word to describe it!

I mean, the correct word is, of course, penis.

But that sounds so clinical.

I don't think I'd like someone to say to me, "Oh, that's a beautiful vagina you've got there."

It's not exactly evocative or romantic, now is it?

Hardly the language of hearts and flowers.

And by the same token I think *penis* is far too reminiscent of biology lessons at school where a scarlet-faced substitute teacher hurriedly and scantily explains the human reproductive system to a room full of sniggering adolescents.

It's not a human-enough description.

But what else can I call it?

I know there are hundreds of words, but not one of them seems appropriate.

How about *knob*?

That one's currently very fashionable.

Weeeell, I don't know.

It sounds a bit functional to me.

Although then again, why shouldn't it?

Cock?

No, I don't like that one either.

For some reason I find it reminiscent of aging rock stars with London accents and horrible stone-washed jeans and long gray hair.

And worse again are the situations where the man has christened his member with a name. I mean, did you ever! Sidelong smirk from man, followed by wheedling noises.

"I think George is waking up."

Meaningful and wheedley smile.

"I think George wants to come out and play."

Wheedley eye contact and hopeful expression.

"George want to play hide-and-seek."

Glazed and sickly grin.

Ugh!

Well, George can just go right off and find someone else to play with. That kind of carrying on is enough to make me want to embrace celibacy.

Well, in the absence of a moniker that I like I'm going to resort to the language of romance novels and call it his Throbbing Manhood. Adam, thankfully, hadn't introduced me to his Throbbing Manhood by name, and I didn't know if I was ready to make friends with his Throbbing Manhood just yet.

I'd kind of gotten used to James's Throbbing Manhood. Not that it was an especially hard act (if you'll pardon the pun) to follow, but it suited me.

I had nothing *against* Adam's Throbbing Manhood (apart from my thigh, of course), but I felt nervous about becoming acquainted with it.

As if he sensed this, Adam caught me by the arm (no, Adam, not my *arm*, for God's sake; it hasn't got an erogenous atom in it) and said urgently, "We don't have to do anything, Claire. We can just lie here if you want to." Now, if I'd had a penny for every time I've been promised a "just lying there" scenario by a man, I'd be a very rich woman indeed. I couldn't count the number of times that I'd been promised this when I've had to spend the night with a man because I'd missed the last bus and didn't have money for a taxi.

"You can stay in my place. It's only around the corner," he'd say.

"I'll sleep on the couch," I'd say quickly.

"Well, you might as well stay in the bed with me. It's much more comfortable."

"Ah no, the couch is fine."

"Look, I'm not going to touch you. Is that what's worrying you?"

"Well, er, yes."

"No need to worry. I won't lay a finger on you."

And then those fateful words. *"We can just lie there."*

And of course not getting a wink of sleep because I had to spend the night doing some all-star wrestling with the man.

Or squashed with my face right up into the wall in a vain attempt to get away from the man, finding it damn near impossible to breathe because of the erect penis pressed into my back.

Being afraid that if I breathed out and thereby moved my lower spine—entirely involuntarily, mind you—even a tenth of a millimeter onto his hot member, this would be taken as a sign of encouragement and acquiescence.

And then, of course, if I didn't deliver the goods, as it were, there was the highly probable chance that the gentleman in question would bad-mouth me the length and breadth of Ireland, calling me a prick tease and a frigid lesbian and all manner of other terrible and totally undeserved names. Saying things like, "Oh, she was coming on to me all night. She was fooling no one with that line about not having money for a taxi."

To this very day I think I still have a faint, penis-shaped indentation on my back.

But I believed Adam.

I knew that he meant it.

I trusted him.

I knew that if he said we could just lie there, that he meant it.

But was that what I wanted?

Quite frankly, no.

Yes, I was nervous.

But, dammit, I wanted to have sex with him.

If he went all respectful on me, I'd scream.

"I don't want to stop," I whispered to him.

I suppose there was no need for me to whisper.

I didn't want to overdo the nervous little-girl act.

All right, then, time to be proactive.

"Em," I said embarrassedly, "I left my bag downstairs."

"What do you need your bag for? Your makeup is perfect." He smiled at me.

"Not for my makeup, silly."

"What for then?"

But he was teasing.

"Claire, would you relax?" he said in exasperation, rolling me over onto my back. "I presume you're referring to condoms?"

"Er, yes," I said, feeling a bit mortified.

"Well, no need to worry, I've some here."

"Oh."

I wasn't sure what else I could say.

His openness had taken the wind out of my sails nicely. He was quite right, of course. What was there to be embarrassed about? All I had to worry about now was whether I'd be any good.

He kissed me again.

And things became a lot more serious.

That kiss certainly put a stop to any lighthearted banter. I looked at him and his eyes were really dark, almost black, with desire.

"Claire," he whispered (now *he's* at it), "I haven't, you know, been with someone in a long time."

Haven't you? I thought in surprise.

I would have thought that for someone as charming and

handsome as Adam every day of his life would be a sexfest. But, then again, he did seem to be very choosy. More than once I'd witnessed him fighting off gorgeous women. And he's chosen me, I thought, my heart melting. He could have just about anyone and he's chosen me. There had to be a catch.

Any minute now, he'd offer to show me his knife collection or whip out a chainsaw and hack me to ribbons.

"It's okay," I whispered back to him. "It's ages since I've had sex either."

"Oh," he said.

Then he said in a louder voice, "Why are we whispering?"

"I don't know." I giggled.

There then followed the condom ritual. You know, rustling around in a drawer for it, the crinkling of the wrapping being undone, saying, "Is that the right way? Or does it go the other way?" Finally success in getting it on only to witness the erection disappear.

Except Adam's didn't.

Disappear, that is.

Thank God.

Now at this point I'm afraid that I'm going to have to become a little bit vague. I'm sorry to disappoint you but I won't be giving you any detailed technical descriptions of my sexual encounters with Adam. (Yes, I hope you noted the plural "encounters".) Of course, I *could* give you a description that would read more like a textbook belonging to a first-year anatomy student. And I *could* make the whole thing sound like a letter to the letters page in a pornographic magazine, all gasps and arching backs and outlandish gymnastics. But that really wouldn't convey how lovely the whole thing was (well, the whole three things, actually) and how *happy* I felt.

Could we just say that a good time was had by all?

I would be just too embarrassed to tell you that he kissed me everywhere, and I mean *everywhere*. And that when he wasn't doing that he was covering me with delicious, shivery tiny little bites.

And there's no way that I can bring myself to tell you about the moment when he was eventually inside me. And how I was so afraid that it might hurt and how gentle he was with me. It didn't hurt and it was beautiful.

And if you think I'm going to relate how he frantically whispered things to me while he was on top of me, gorgeous things like how beautiful I was and how delicious my skin tasted and how turned on he was, then you've got another think coming.

You'll just have to use your own imagination to figure out that I wrapped my legs around his back to pull him deeper inside me and I thought I would die if he stopped and would die if he didn't.

And you really don't need me to tell you that when he, er . . . when it was finished, we were both panting and gasping and slippery with sweat and that he looked down at me and grinned and gave a little laugh and said admiringly, "Jesus, you're some woman."

I'll have to resort to using a euphemism to describe the scenario.

How about, "One day my prince will come."

Well, I'm happy to report that he already had.

And, so, for the record, had I.

And there's just one other thing.

Before I had Kate I had heard rumors, nothing more than vague unsubstantiated reports, that after having a child sex is usually, well, a lot better. Because of the various commotions, upheavals and traumas in one's, um, birth canal, including the dreaded stitches, certain changes have come about. These changes resulting in, um, greater sensitivity and a greater awareness of one's erogenous zones, if you see what I mean.

And generally, all around, more exciting an enjoyable sex.

And I'm happy to be able to report that it was actually true. Sex with Adam was different, very different from the way I remembered it with James. Once I got over the initial uncomfortable feeling, it was really wonderful—actually better—than I remembered it being with James. So this is one side effect of giving birth that doesn't get the good press that it deserves.

Although of course, there's a good chance that I'm talking a load of nonsense.

And that the alleged better sex had nothing to do with anything other than the fact that Adam had a larger TM than James. (I never bought into that "size isn't everything" crap.)

*   *   *

Later, when it was all over, over for the third time, that is, we just lay in bed chatting and laughing.

"D'you remember the day in the gym?" asked Adam.

"Mmmmmmm," I said, barely able to speak, I was so relaxed and contented.

"That was awful," he said.

"Why?" I asked.

"Because I liked you so much."

"Really?" I asked, surprised and delighted.

"Yes, really."

"No, did you *really*?" I asked, like a true neurotic.

"Yes!" he insisted. "I couldn't even look at you in case I jumped you."

"But you were all serious and grim and just doing your weights," I reminded him. "You completely ignored me."

"Yes," he said dryly, "and I nearly pulled every muscle in my body. I couldn't concentrate on anything except you. You looked so cute in your gym clothes."

"Oh," I said, thrilled, snuggling up closer to him.

At about half past one I said, "I'd better go home."

"Oh no," he said, wrapping his arms and legs tightly around me. "I won't let you. I'm going to keep you chained in here. You're going to be my sex slave."

"Adam," I said, sighing, "you say the nicest things."

After a little while longer, I said, reluctantly, "I'd really better go."

"If you really have to," he said.

"You know I do."

"Would you stay if it wasn't for Kate?"

"Yes."

He sat up in bed and watched me as I got dressed.

I looked up from doing up the buttons on my dress to find him smiling at me, but smiling in a sad kind of way.

"Is something wrong?" I asked.

"You're always running away from me," he said.

"Adam, I'm not," I said indignantly. "I *have* to go."

"Sorry," he said, giving me a real smile this time.

He hopped out of bed and said, "I'll come down to the door with you."

"Not without any clothes, you won't," I said. "What if passersby see?"

There was no doubt.

I was my mother's daughter.

He kissed me lingeringly at the front door.

And it was quite an achievement that I left at all.

"Stay," he murmured against my hair.

"I can't," I told him sternly, although I felt like going straight back up the stairs and getting back into bed with him.

"I'll call you tomorrow," he said.

"Bye."

Another kiss.

Further persuasion.

Stalwart resistance from me.

Reluctant letting go.

I finally made it to the car.

No mean achievement.

I drove home.

The streets were dark and empty.

I felt very happy.

I didn't even feel guilty about leaving Kate for so long.

Well, not *very* guilty.

twenty-three

I parked the car and I put my key in the front door. There was a light on in the front room. That's funny, I thought, everyone's usually fast asleep by this hour. Please God, don't let it be Helen. Please don't let her have realized where I was and what I was up to. I was sure that my recent activities were written all over my face.

Maybe it was Anna who was up. Sacrificing a goat in the kitchen, or something like that. You know, dancing around the garden wrapped in blood-soaked sheets, chanting at the moon, biting the heads off live bats, that kind of thing.

I walked into the hall. The front room door opened and Mum appeared, with Dad standing behind her. They were both in their nightclothes. Mum was wearing her pink quilted dressing gown and had a few orange curlers stuck in the front of her hair.

They both looked white and shocked, as if something terrible had happened.

Which indeed it had, I suppose, if you want to regard my little indiscretion with Adam in that way.

"Claire!" said Mum. "Thank God you're home!"

"What?" I said, frightened. "What's happened?"

"Claire, come in and sit down," said Dad, taking charge.

My stomach lurched.

Something terrible *had* happened.

"Is it Kate?" I pleaded with Mum, clutching her arm. "Has something happened to her?"

A thousand horrible scenarios ran through my head.

She had been the victim of crib death.

She had been kidnapped.

She had choked.

Helen had dropped her.

Anna had put a spell on her.

It was all my fault.

I had left her.

I had left her while I went off to have sex with Adam.

How could I?

"No, no," said Mum soothingly. "It's not Kate."

"Well who then?" I asked, the horrible scenarios starting all over again.

Had something happened to any of my sisters?

Had Margaret been killed by a gangster in Chicago?

Had Rachel disappeared in Prague?

Had Anna got a job?

Had Helen apologized for something?

"It's James," blurted out Mum.

"James," I said dazedly, slowly sitting down on the couch. "Oh my God, James."

James.

I hadn't even thought of him when I was convinced that something awful had happened to someone that I loved. While I'd been in bed with Adam, something had happened to my husband. What kind of woman was I?

"What about James?" I asked them.

They both sat there, looking at me with caring compassionate faces.

"Oh, just tell me," I shouted. "Please tell me!"

I was prepared for the very worst: James had had an accident or something while I had been writhing in the throes of passion with another man. Of course, I realized that my life was over.

I had no other option but to embrace celibacy. Maybe I would enter a convent. It was the least I could do. This was my punishment for sleeping with someone I didn't love. I never, ever wanted to see Adam again for as long as I lived. It was all his fault.

If I hadn't gone to bed with him, James would have been all right.

"He's here," said Mum gently.

"Here!" I screeched. "What do you mean—here?"

I looked around the room frantically, as if I expected him to suddenly appear from behind a curtain or from under the couch with a smooth smile, wearing a dinner jacket and smoking a cigar to say something like "My wife, I presume."

"Do you mean he's on the premises?" I asked hysterically. My head was spinning like a top.

"No," said Mum, sounding a bit annoyed. "Do you think we'd let him stay here after all that's happened? No, he called. He's in Dublin all right, but he's staying in a hotel."

"Oh," I said. I thought I might faint.

"Does he want to see me?"

"Of course he does," said Dad. "But you don't have to if you don't want to."

"Jack," said Mum to him. "Of course she has to see him. How else are they going to work anything out? She has the child to think of, you know."

"Mary, all I'm saying is that if she can't face it then we're not going to put her under pressure. We'll help her in every way that we can."

"Jack!" said Mum sharply. "She's a grown woman and—"

"But Mary—" interrupted Dad.

"Stop it!" I said loudly.

I knew that I had better nip this in the bud. This one could run and run, as they say. They both looked at me in surprise. Almost as if they had forgotten that I was there.

"I want to see him," I said, a bit more quietly. "You're right, Mum, I *am* a grown woman. I'm the only person who can sort this out. And I do have Kate to think of. She's the most important person in all of this."

"And thanks, Dad." I nodded at him. "It's nice to know that I can rely on you to round up a lynch mob if I need one."

"A lynch mob?" he spluttered. "Well, I don't know about that. But if you think you might need one, I could ask a couple of the chaps at the golf club. See what they say."

"Oh Daddy," I said wearily. "I'm kidding."

"He said that he'd call in the morning," said Mum.

"What time?" I asked.

"Ten o'clock," said Mum.

"Okay," I said.

If James said that he would ring at ten o'clock in the morning, James would ring at ten o'clock in the morning. Not at eighteen seconds past ten, you understand, or at half a minute before ten.

But at ten.

He might have left me for another woman, but in some departments he was the most reliable man you could hope to meet.

"And what time is it now?" I asked.

"Twenty past three," said Dad.

"I suppose I'd better go to bed then," I said. "Big day tomorrow and all that."

Although I knew that I wouldn't sleep a wink.

"We'll all go to bed," said Mum. "Anyway, where were you until this hour?"

"Having sex with Adam," I told them.

Dad gave a loud bark of nervous laughter.

Mum looked stricken.

And well you might, I thought. You were the one who put the idea in my head in the first place.

"No, I'm being serious now," said Mum. "What were you up to?"

"I *am* being serious." I smiled. "Good night."

Mum looked appalled. She didn't know whether to believe me or not, but she obviously suspected the worst. She stood there opening and closing her mouth like a goldfish as I shut the door behind me.

I don't think she even noticed Dad pulling at her dressing gown and hissing at her, "Which one of them is Adam?"

twenty-four

I went to bed and I was right.

I didn't sleep a wink.

Why was James here?

Was this going to be a reconciliation attempt?

Or was it just to tidy up loose ends?

Could I bear it if he just wanted to tidy up the loose ends?

Did I want a reconciliation attempt?

Was he still with Denise?

A thought struck me—Jesus, what if he had brought Denise with him?

I sat bolt upright in bed. Fury surged through me.

The rotten bastard. He wouldn't do that, would he?

I forced myself to calm down. I had no proof that he had done anything of the sort and there was no point getting angry over things that might not have happened.

I had to keep Kate in the forefront of my mind. She was the most important person in all of this. I wanted things to be civil with James so that he would be in Kate's life. Even if he never wanted to see me again, I still wanted him to be there for her.

So I couldn't exactly go for him with a machete when I saw him.

I couldn't really believe it.

I'd be seeing him tomorrow.

And what if the unthinkable happened and he wanted to try again with me?

Then what?

I didn't know.

And what about Adam?

The man whose bed I'd just left.

I can't think about that now, I thought.

My head was so crowded, it was standing room only. In fact, a few hardy thoughts were standing outside my head, with their drinks, in the pouring rain, where at least there was a bit of space.

But there was no room at all for Adam.

Forget it, I told myself, you can't possibly think about it now. Wait till all this is over, one way or the other, and then think about him.

And then I started to wonder. Why?

You know, why had James left me? Why had James gone off with Denise when I had thought our relationship was so good? I hadn't tortured myself with these thoughts in a while.

But tomorrow I was going to at least try to get some answers to these questions.

If I could understand what had gone wrong, or what I had done wrong, maybe it wouldn't be so hard to live with.

I wished there was some kind of switch on my brain. That I could turn it off in the same way that I could turn off the television. Just click it off and immediately empty my mind of all these images and worrying thoughts. And simply leave a blank screen. Or if I could just remove my head and put it on my bedside table and forget about it until morning. And then attach it again when I needed it.

Morning finally rolled around and I was still no better off in the sleep department.

I jumped out of bed and was vaguely aware of a slight stiffness in my inner thighs. "Why's that?" I wondered. And then I remembered. "Oh, er, yes, that's right." I flushed a bit as I remembered what I had been up to the previous evening. "Adam. Sex. But I can't think about it now."

Honestly, damn James!

I was being denied the pleasure of lolling around in bed, dreamily recalling every detail of my Night of Lust with Adam.

Instead I had to get up and run around and Prepare for

His Arrival. As though he was the Pope or a visiting head of state.

After I fed Kate her bottle, I bathed her and dressed her in her sweetest outfit. A fluffy pink one with little gray elephants all over it.

I covered her in talcum powder and held her close and inhaled her beautiful milky baby smell.

"You look gorgeous," I assured her. "Any man's fancy. And if he doesn't realize it then he's an even bigger fool than I already think he is."

I wanted her to look divine. I wanted her to look like the most beautiful baby on the planet. I wanted James to ache for her.

To hold her, to kiss her, to feed her, to smell her.

I wanted him to see just how much he had forsaken.

And I wanted to make him want us back.

The whole house seemed to be up at the crack of dawn. Anna and Helen knew that James had called. Helen came into my room at about seven-thirty and ran over to Kate's bassinet and said, "Oh good, you've made her look gorgeous. That'll show him. Let's just hope that she doesn't puke on him or do a poo in her diaper when he's holding her."

She picked up Kate and admired the outfit.

"Do you think we could put a pink ribbon in her hair, to match?" she asked.

"Helen, if she had more hair, I'd consider it," I told her.

But when Helen suggested that we put some makeup on her, I decided that that was going too far.

"Right, we have to make you look beautiful too," said Helen.

I wasn't too sure if I liked her tone.

It sounded a bit doubtful or defeatist, somehow.

Then Dad arrived.

"I'm off to work now," he said. "But remember what I said. You don't have to go back with him just for Kate's sake."

"Who says he's going to ask her to go back with him?" asked Helen loudly.

There really had been no need for her to say that. But she had a point.

Then Mum arrived.

"How are you bearing up?" she asked kindly.

"Fine," I said.

"All right," she said. "You go off and have a shower. Helen and I will keep an eye on Kate."

"Oh, all right." I was a little bit taken aback at all the organizing and activity. It was nearly like the morning that I got married.

In came Anna.

I thought I might go downstairs and open the front door and start inviting strangers in off the street.

Anna smiled sweetly at me and held something out to me. "Claire, take this crystal and put it in a pocket or something. It'll bring you luck."

"She's going to need more than one of your crappy old crystals," said Helen bluntly.

"Stop that, Helen," said Mum sharply.

"What!" said Helen, outraged.

"Do you have to be so mean?" said Mum.

"I wasn't being mean," Helen defended herself hotly. "But if she looks nice and acts like she's fine he'll want her. You don't need a crystal to do that."

I looked at Helen almost in shock.

She might be one of the most irritating idiotic people I've ever met, but when it comes to the psychology of men, I had to hand it to her, she was a master.

But I took the crystal anyway.

Because you never know.

I had to get away from my family for a little while. I couldn't think straight. I had to calm myself before I could talk to James.

I'd call Laura, I decided. She'd tell me what to do.

"Laura," I said in a trembly voice when she answered.

"Oh, Claire," she burst out. "I was just about to call you. Guess what!"

That's my line, I was thinking.

"What?" I asked.

"That little bastard Adrian has just dumped me."

Adrian, being, of course, her nineteen-year-old art student.

"What?" I said again.

"Yes," she said tearfully. "Can you believe it?"

"But I thought you didn't care about him," I said in surprise.

"So did I," she sobbed. "And wait until you hear! Guess why he dumped me."

"Why," I asked, wondering what was the reason. Had she finally run out of socks?

"Because he's met someone else," declared Laura. "And guess what age she is."

"Thirteen," I hazarded.

"No!" she shouted. "Thirty-bloody-seven!"

"Good God!" I said.

I was shocked.

"Yes," she said, barely able to speak because she was crying so much. "He says that I'm immature."

"The little pup."

"That he needs someone more centered."

"How dare he!"

"And I was just doing him a favor by going out with him. And he's just left me here," she sobbed. "Without a sock to my name."

"Jesus, that's grim," I said, shaking my head in a resigned way.

"Look," she said in a tragic way, "I have to go. I'll be late for work. I'll talk to you later."

And she hung up.

How about that? She probably thought I was calling to spill the beans about my night of passion with Adam. Little did she know of the great drama that had occurred in the meantime.

I sat looking at the phone for a few seconds.

Who would I call?

No one, I decided.

I'd try to deal with this on my own.

If I couldn't deal with my own life, I couldn't in all fairness expect anyone else to be able to.

I took a shower, washed my hair and went back into my room, where some pointless argument seemed to be in process among Anna, Helen (of course) and Mum. All three of them were shouting at the same time. Kate was lying in her bassinet being completely ignored.

"I did *not* make a face at you," Anna denied as emphatically as she could, which wasn't very much.

"You bloody well did," Helen said.

"It wasn't a face," Mum said, trying to pour oil on water that was very troubled indeed. "It was more of a look."

The babel of voices stopped abruptly as soon as I came into the room and all three of them turned their faces expectantly toward me. It seemed that they had decided to abandon their internecine differences and unite with me against the common enemy, James. They ran around, got me clothes and dressed me up.

"You have to look beautiful," said Anna.

"Yes," agreed Helen. "But you have to look as if you didn't try at all. Like you just flung on any old thing."

"But he's only calling me at ten o'clock," I reminded them. "He didn't say anything about coming over."

"Yes," said Mum. "But he didn't come all the way to Dublin just to call you. He could have done that from London."

Good point.

"Okay girls," I said to Anna and Helen. "In that case make me beautiful."

"We said we'd loan you clothes and do your makeup," said Helen. "We never said that we could do miracles." But she was smiling as she said it.

We finally agreed that I would wear the leggings and blue silk shirt that I had worn the day Adam came to tea.

Adam, I thought longingly for a moment.

But then I pushed him firmly to the back of my mind.

Not now, I thought grimly.

"You look nice and skinny," said Helen, standing back and looking at me. "Now for your makeup."

Honestly, she was organizing the whole thing like a military campaign.

Anna's eyes lit up at the mention of doing my makeup. She approached with a plastic bag that seemed to be full of crayons and pencils.

"Get away," Helen told her irritably, elbowing her aside. "*I'm* doing her makeup. You probably want to do face-painting and paint stars and suns and all that new age crap on her."

Anna *did* look a little bit sheepish.

"No," Helen explained, a bit more kindly. "She has to look as if she's not wearing any makeup at all. Just naturally beautiful."

"Yes," I said, all excited. "Make me look like that."

Why was Helen being so nice to me, I wondered?

Did she suspect that I was in competition with her for Adam? If I was back with James it would mean that she could have a clear shot at Adam.

Or maybe I was just being totally cynical.

I mean, she was my sister, after all.

And anyway, she probably didn't suspect a thing.

I must say, I did look beautiful by the time Helen was finished with me: Fresh-faced, clear-skinned, bright-eyed, casually dressed.

"Smile," she ordered me.

I did.

They all nodded approvingly.

"Good," said Mum. "Do that a lot."

"What time is it now?" I asked.

"Nearly half past nine," said Mum.

"Half an hour to go," I said, feeling nauseous.

I sat on the bed.

Mum, Anna, Helen and Kate were already on it.

"Move over," I said. I was sitting on Anna's foot.

"Ouch," said Helen, as Anna moved and kind of elbowed her in the face.

We were all huddled on the bed, sort of lying on top of each other.

It was like a vigil, they were going to stay there for me until he called. I felt as if we were a raft full of survivors from a shipwreck. All squashed and uncomfortable and crowded, but there was no suggestion that we leave each other.

"Right," said Mum. "We'll play a game."

"All right," we all said in unison.

Except for Kate, of course.

Mum had great games. Word games that we used to play to pass the time on long car journeys when we were young.

For some reason the game that we were actually playing when he called was one thought up by (who else) Helen. Obviously done with more than a nod to my recent condition. It was one in which you have to think of all the different words to describe being pregnant.

I didn't think it was really what Mum had had in mind when she'd encouraged us to make up our own versions of the games that she had taught us.

"Up the pole," shouted Anna.

"On the bubble," screeched Helen.

"Expecting," muttered Mum, torn between disapproval and the desire to win.

"Your turn, Claire," said Anna.

"No," I said. "Shuusssh, is that the phone?"

The room fell silent.

It was.

"Should I answer it?" asked Mum.

"No. Thanks Mum, but I'll do it," I said.

And I left them.

twenty-five

"Hello," I said, for lack of anything better to say

"Claire," said James's voice.

So, it was him.

We finally got to speak to each other.

"James," I replied.

And then I wasn't quite sure what to say.

I wasn't too current on the etiquette of addressing runaway husbands. Especially since I was pretty sure that he wasn't in the process of trying to wheedle his way back into my affections.

We need a book. A book that tells us how to address returning runaway husbands.

You know, the type of book that tells us the correct knife to use to shell a scallop and the proper way to address, say, a bishop, for example (just for the record, "That's a lovely ring you're wearing, Your Grace" is usually regarded as polite enough for a first meeting).

So this book would gently instruct us about the correct number of times the word *bastard* could be used in any one sentence, and when it is regarded as impolite not to use physical violence, etc.

For example, if your boyfriend/husband/fella has simply disappeared for a couple of days after a particularly important football match and has just returned to the family home looking green, unshaven and disheveled, it would be appropriate to say:

"Where the fuck have you been for the past three days, you drunken, selfish, lowser?"

But as the person out there hadn't written the book yet I had to rely on my own instinct.

"How are you?" he asked.

As if you cared, I thought.

"Very well," I said politely.

A pause.

"Oh! . . . And how are you?" I asked hurriedly.

Honestly, where were my manners?

Is it any wonder that he'd left me?

"Well," he replied thoughtfully. "Yes, quite well."

Pompous fucker, I thought.

"Claire," he continued smoothly. "I'm in Dublin."

"I know," I said ungraciously. "My mother mentioned that you'd called last night."

"Yes, I don't doubt that she did," he said with faint irony.

You could never say that James was a fool.

A bastard, I grant you. But never a fool.

"Where are you staying?" I asked.

He named some downtown bed and breakfast. On a street that could only be described as On the Front Line. Not James's usual style at all. He was more likely to be found in a plush corporate type of place. All Bureau de Changes and little shops in the hotel lobby. From James's address I deduced that he was not in Dublin on business. Because if he were, he would be on expenses and staying somewhere a damn slight nicer and more expensive. And if he wasn't in Dublin on business, then just why was he here?

"So what can I do for you?" I asked in a slightly nasty tone. He wasn't the only one around here who could say things with irony.

My tone of voice was intended to convey that I would not, as the saying goes, piss on him if he was on fire.

"What you can do for me, Claire," he said, "is see me. Will you do that?"

"Of course," I said obediently.

How *else* can I break every bone in your body? I thought.

"You will?" he asked, sounding surprised. As though he had been anticipating some kind of battle.

"But certainly." I gave a little laugh. "What are you sounding so shocked about?"

Because when I've finished breaking every bone in your body, I'm going to cut off your penis and stick it in your mouth and I certainly can't do *that* over the phone either, now, can I? I thought.

"Well, um . . . nothing, nothing. That's . . . um . . . that's great," he said.

He still sounded surprised.

He'd obviously expected me to refuse to see him. That would account for the coaxing tone and the surprise at my calm agreement to meet him. But what would I gain from refusing to see him? I wanted the answers to a couple of questions.

Like, Why did you stop loving me?

And, How much money are you going to give me for Kate?

How else were we going to sort out our respective legal positions and our relationship to Kate if we didn't meet to talk about it?

Perhaps he expected to find that I'd gone to pieces totally.

But, well . . . hey! . . . I wasn't in pieces now, was I?

I wasn't better or anything like it, but no matter what way I looked at it I couldn't deny that I'd greatly improved.

How odd!

When did that happen?

You know that bit at the end of a relationship when all your friends gather around and say lots of annoying things like "Plenty more fish in the sea" and "He would never have made you happy"? Well, when they get to the part about "It'll mend with time," try to fight your initial instinct to give them a black eye.

Don't knock it, because it really does work: I was living proof. The only problem with time mending things is that it takes longer. So, effective and all as it is, it's precious little use to those of us in a hurry.

I suppose the sex with Adam hadn't hurt my recovery either. But I had to drag my thoughts back to the present. James was talking again.

"Where should we meet?" he asked.

"Why don't you come out to the house here?" I suggested.

I didn't want this to be an away game. I wanted this meeting to be on my turf, if not on my terms.

"You can get a taxi. Or if you prefer you could take a bus and ask the conductor to let you off at the traffic circle at the end of—"

"Claire!" he interrupted, laughing at how silly I was being. "I've been out to your house plenty of times. I *know* how to get there."

"Of course you do," I said smoothly.

I *knew* that.

But I couldn't resist the chance to treat him like a total stranger. To let him know that he no longer belonged.

"Will we say eleven-thirty?" I said with authority.

"Er, fine," he said.

"Lovely," I said acidly. "See you then."

And I hung up without waiting for his reply.

twenty-six

Now, I would be lying to both myself and you if I didn't admit that it would have given me a great deal of satisfaction if James had returned to me on his knees, a broken man. I would have been delighted if he had crawled up the driveway on all fours, sobbing and begging for me to take him back. I wanted him to be unshaven, filthy and wearing torn clothes. I wanted his hair to be all long and matted and for him to be looking deranged and obviously demented with grief at the terrible realization that he had lost the only woman he had ever loved. And indeed could ever love.

So vivid was this mental image of mine that when eleven-thirty rolled around and he appeared at the gate, I was hugely disappointed to find that he was in fact walking fully upright. Prehistoric man must have felt the same sense of disbelief when one of his fellows hopped down out of one of the trees and started to parade around on just two legs.

I stood at the window and watched him as he walked up the short drive. Mind you, I stood well back. I didn't think that it would enhance my dignity for him to see me with my nose pressed up against the window.

I had been wondering what he would look like. And now I would see.

That gave me a violent twist of pain.

He was no longer mine, so he would look different. My subtle but definite mark on him would be gone. And what did he look like?

Was he different?

Had Denise made him fat?

Was he badly dressed?

Had Denise sent him out in the same little jackets and sweatpants she dressed her three little boys in? All purples and turquoises. Very nasty.

Would he look like a cruel and heartless bastard, coming to take my home and my child away from me?

But he just looked so *normal*.

Walking along with his hands in his pockets. He could have been anyone going anywhere. Although he looked different from the way that I'd remembered him.

Thinner, I thought.

And I was sure that something else was different too . . . what was it? . . . I wasn't sure . . . had he . . . had he *always* been that short?

And he wasn't dressed the way I'd expected him to be.

Every time I'd thought of seeing him, I'd imagined him dressed in the same Grim Reaper suit that he wore that day at the hospital. Today he was wearing jeans, a blue shirt and some kind of jacket.

Very casual. Very laid-back.

Obviously not treating this occasion with the great weight that it deserved.

It felt wrong.

Incongruous.

Like a hangman turning up to do a day's work wearing a Hawaiian shirt and a baseball cap on back-to-front, grinning from ear to ear as he told knock-knock jokes.

He rang the bell. I took a deep breath and walked to answer the door.

My heart was thumping.

I swung back the door and there he stood.

The same. He looked so heartbreakingly the same.

His hair was still dark brown, his face was still pale, his eyes were still green, his jaw was still lean. He gave me a funny twisted half smile, and after an awkward pause, he said expressionlessly, "Claire, how are you?"

"Fine." I smiled slightly—politely—at him. "Why don't you come in?"

He came into the hall and I almost keeled over as a wave of nausea hit me.

It was one thing to banter calmly with him over the phone. But it was a hell of a lot harder to deal with him in the flesh.

However, unpleasant and all as it was, I had to behave like an adult. The days of running crying to my bedroom were long gone. And he wasn't looking too happy himself.

I knew he didn't love me anymore but he was only human. Well, I presumed he was only human. And couldn't help being affected by this momentous occasion. But I knew James. He'd recover his aplomb in no time at all.

That was what I had to do.

I graciously said to him, "Can I take your jacket?" as though he was just someone who had come to try and sell me a central heating system.

"Yes, I suppose so," he said reluctantly, and shrugged out of it and warily handed it over to me, taking what seemed like excessive care to make sure that our hands didn't touch. He looked longingly at the jacket, as though he was never going to see it again and wanted to memorize its every detail. What was he afraid of?

I wasn't going to steal the bloody jacket. It wasn't nice enough.

"I'll put this away," I said, and for the first time our eyes met properly.

He did a quick scan of my face and said levelly, "You're looking well, Claire."

He said it with the enthusiasm an undertaker usually reserves for someone who, against all the odds, survives a terrible car crash. "Yes." He nodded, a tiny bit surprised. "You *are* looking well."

"Well, why wouldn't I?" I gave him a knowing little smile, conveying—at least I hoped I conveyed—dignity and irony in equal amounts. Letting him know that although he no longer loved me, that although he had hurt and humiliated me, I was a reasonable human being and would get over it. Almost making a joke of the whole sorry mess and practically inviting him, the perpetrator, to join in and laugh along with me.

I couldn't believe that I had managed that.

I felt pretty pleased with myself.

Because, although I did not feel calm and civilized, as God is my witness, I was going to do a damn good job at acting it.

However, he didn't seem to find it as gently amusing as I managed to pretend I did.

He gave me a wintry look.

More undertakerish vibes.

The miserable fucker.

Since I was prepared to try to be nice and civil about all this, surely, *surely*, he could too. After all, what had he got to lose?

Maybe he had prepared a beautiful speech about how I would get over him, how he wasn't good enough for me, how we were never really suited, how I was better off without him. Maybe he was disappointed that he wasn't going to get to say it.

He'd probably stood in front of the mirror in his bedroom at the hotel and practiced flinging his arms around me in a beseeching manner while he told me in a voice choked with emotion that, although he still loved me, he was no longer *in love* with me.

We stood in the hall for a few seconds, James looking as if his entire family had just been wiped out in a machete attack. I'm sure I didn't look much better. The tension was terrible.

"Come on into the dining room," I told him, taking charge. Otherwise we could have stood there all day, white-faced, miserable and paralyzed by nerves. "We won't be disturbed there and we can have the table in case we need to spread out documents or whatever."

He nodded grimly and walked down the hall in front of me.

How dare he! What was he looking so bloody uptight about? Surely I was the one who should be afforded that right?

Kate was waiting in the dining room.

She lay in her crib and looked beautiful.

I picked her up and stood holding her, her face against mine.

"This is Kate," I said simply.

He stared at the two of us, opening and closing his mouth. He looked a bit like a goldfish. A pale, serious goldfish.

"She . . . she's gotten so big, she's grown so much," he finally managed.

"Babies do." I nodded at him sagely.

The subtext being, of course, "If you had stuck around, you bastard, you'd have been there for when she was doing that growing." But I didn't say it.

I didn't need to.

He knew it.

It was written all over his sheepish, shamed face.

"And she's called Kate?" he asked.

The surge of anger was so intense that I thought I would surely kill him.

He hadn't even found out her name, and there were plenty of people he could have asked.

"After Kate Bush?" he asked. Referring to a singer whom, while I certainly liked her, I wouldn't have ever considered calling my firstborn child after.

"Yes," I managed bitterly. "After Kate Bush."

I wasn't going to bother giving him the real reason. What the hell did he care?

"Hey!" he said, the idea obviously just having occurred to him. "Can I hold her?" In different circumstances he could have been described as speaking with enthusiasm.

My anger and bitterness had obviously gone right over his neatly combed head.

I *wanted* to shout at him, "Of course you can hold her, she's waited two months for you to hold her. You're her bloody *father!*" But I managed not to.

I felt like a traitor, like a third-world mother who is forced by economic circumstances to sell her child to the rich gringo. But I passed her from my arms to his.

And the look on his face.

It was as if he had suddenly become mentally retarded.

All smiles and shining eyes and reverential expression.

Of course he held her all wrong.

Crossways, instead of lengthways.

Horizontal, instead of vertical.

People who know nothing about babies hold them like that. I know because I did it for the first day or so of Kate's life until one of the other mothers, who was sick of hearing Kate roaring, wearily set me right. ("Up, not across!")

But you wouldn't catch me being sympathetic to James for making the same mistake.

Kate started to cry.

Well, of course the poor child did! Being held like a rolled-up carpet by a strange man. Wouldn't you cry? James looked frightened.

"What's wrong with her?" he asked. "How do I make her stop?" The reverential expression disappeared and was replaced by naked fear.

I had known all that mister-nice-guy stuff was too good to be true.

"Here," he said, thrusting her at me. He looked at both of us with an expression of distaste. There was obviously no room for crying women in James's world.

He hadn't always been like that, you know.

Well, he'd married me. And I wasn't famous for blinking back the tears. Better out than in was always my motto. But looking at him now, at his fastidious expression, I marveled—and it wasn't for the first time—at what a bastard he had become.

"Oh golly." I smiled acidly. "She doesn't seem to like you."

I laughed as if it was a joke and took her back from James's yielding arms.

He couldn't get rid of her fast enough. I cooed and shushed her. She stopped crying. For a moment I felt bitter satisfaction that Kate had sided with me against him.

And then I felt sad and ashamed. James was Kate's father. I should do everything in my power to make them like each other.

I'd find another man to love. But Kate had only the one father. "Sorry." I smiled apologetically at him. "It's just that you're new to her. Give her a chance. She's scared."

"You're right. It'll probably just take a bit of time," he said, cheering up a bit.

"That's all," I reassured him. But at the same time thinking, horror-struck, when exactly does he propose spending this alleged "bit of time" with her?

If he had come to Dublin to try to take Kate back to London, then he had to die. It was really quite simple.

He hadn't done the doting father bit up until now, so what did he want?

"Coffee."

"What?" I asked him sharply.

"Is there any chance of a cup of coffee?" he asked.

He was looking at me as if I was a bit peculiar.

How many times had he asked me before I heard?

"Sure," I told him.

I put Kate back in her crib and went into the kitchen to make him his coffee. I should have offered before. But in all the excitement it never crossed my mind. It was a bit of a relief to get into the kitchen. I sighed long and deep and hard when I closed the door behind me.

My hands shook so much I could hardly fill the kettle. Being with him was so hard. Having to pretend that I was fine was exhausting. And constantly keeping a lid on murderous anger was a demanding business—but I had to do it. I was going to salvage as much as I could for Kate out of this.

I brought the coffee back into the dining room.

And, no, I didn't offer cookies.

I'm sorry, but I just wasn't a big enough person.

He was leaning over the crib, attempting to talk to Kate.

He was having some kind of muttered, uptight discussion with her.

As if she were a business colleague and not a two-month-old baby.

He was not behaving the way nice, normal, warm people do in the presence of young babies. You know, as if they've left their brains out, overnight, in the rain. All singsong noises and doting rhetorical questions. Asking stupid things like "Who's the most beautiful girl in the whole world?" And the correct answer not, as you might expect, Cindy Crawford, but in fact Kate Webster.

Instead he sounded as if he was discussing tax reforms with her.

But he didn't seem to notice anything amiss.

I put the coffee down on the dining room table and the

moment the china touched the mahogany I realized that I had automatically made James's coffee the way that James liked it.

I was furious!

Couldn't I even *pretend* to have forgotten?

Couldn't I have given him a milk and two sugars instead of a black, no sugar and half cold water?

And then, when he gagged on it, nursing his burned and oversugared mouth, couldn't I have airily said something like "Oh sorry, I forgot, *you're* the one who doesn't like sugar?"

But no.

I'd missed a precious chance to let him know that he didn't matter at all to me anymore.

"Oh thanks, Claire," he said, sipping from the mug. "You remembered the way I like it." And he smiled with satisfaction.

I could have happily gone to the kitchen and doused myself in kerosene and set myself alight, so angry was I.

"You're welcome," I said from between gritted teeth.

There was a little silence.

Then James started to speak.

He seemed to have suddenly clicked into Relaxed Mode. The apparent nerves at the front door had evaporated.

I only wish mine had.

"You know, I can't believe that I'm actually here," he mused easily, leaning back in his chair, nursing the traitorous coffee between his cupped hands.

He sounded as if he had no trouble at all in believing it.

"I can't believe you let me in."

Well, actually you're not the only bloody one, I felt like telling him, but didn't.

"Why's that?" I asked with icy politeness.

"Oh," he said, shaking his head with a wry little smile, as though he couldn't quite credit his runaway imagination. "I thought that perhaps your mother and sisters might have done something really nasty when I arrived. You know, poured boiling oil down on top of me. Something like that."

And he sat there and, looking straight into my eyes, he smiled smugly, accepting the ease with which he had been readmitted to the Lion's Den as nothing less than his due, confident that, although I was from a mad family and a nation of savages, he was really quite safe.

I resisted the urge to lunge across the table at him and rip out his larynx with my teeth, hissing, "Boiling oil would be too good for you."

Instead I gave a cold little smile and said "Oh don't be ridiculous, James. We're perfectly civilized around here, no matter what you might like to think. Why would we hurt you? And after all"—tinkly little laugh like shards of ice banging off the side of a glass—"we need you to be in good health so that you can afford Kate's child support payments."

There was a resonant silence.

"What are you talking about, 'child support payments'?" he asked slowly, as though he had never before in his life heard of such a thing.

"James, you must know what child support payments are," I told him, faint with shock.

I just stared at him.

What the hell was going on?

He was a boring, accountant-type person.

He and child support agreements should be best buddies.

In fact, I was amazed that he hadn't arrived with a huge itemized agreement for me to sign. You know, detailing all kinds of things, such as the cost of keeping Kate in shoes for the rest of her life, projected economies of scale, sinking funds, amortization and suchlike.

After all, this was the man who could, and probably frequently did, calculate a waitress's tip to within fourteen decimal places.

Not that he was cheap, you understand.

But he was very, *very* organized.

Forever scribbling on the backs of envelopes or on napkins and coming up with immensely detailed calculations which, oddly enough, nearly always turned out to be correct. In five minutes he could tell you to the nearest penny how much it would cost you to decorate your bathroom, taking everything into account, including paint, fittings, labor, coffee for the workmen, workdays (your own, that is) lost from sleepless nights when the workmen disappeared for three weeks, leaving the bathtub in the hall etc. . . . Honestly, he thinks of everything!

"Child support payments," he said again thoughtfully. He didn't sound happy.

"Yes James," I said with steely resolve, although my stomach was lurching around like a ferry in rough seas. If James was going to be difficult about money, I'd die.

No, let me take that back. I wouldn't.

I'd kill him.

"Right, right, I see," he said, sounding a bit stunned. "Yes, we obviously *do* have a lot to talk about."

"Yes, we certainly do," I confirmed, trying to sound jovial. "And you're here now so we're in the happy position of being able to do so." I gave him a bright smile.

It was so reluctant that I think I damaged muscles in my face.

But I had to keep this as amiable and friendly as possible.

"So," I continued briskly, determined to sound as if I knew what I was talking about, "I know we're both unfamiliar with this sort of thing, but don't you think we should try to sort out the basic issues ourselves and let the lawyers dot the *t*'s and cross the *i*'s?" (I permitted myself a little smile at this. Which he completely ignored.) "Or would you prefer to do the whole lot, lock stock and barrel through our lawyers?"

"Aha!" He suddenly seemed to brighten up. He raised his index finger like Monsieur Poirot demonstrating the fatal flaw in the argument. "That would be fine if we had lawyers. But we haven't, have we?" He looked at me in a kindly but pitying sort of fashion as if I was a bit of a half-wit.

"But . . . well, actually I have," I told him.

"Have you?" he asked. "Have you indeed? Well, well, well." He sounded quite astonished. And not that pleased.

"Um . . . yes, of course I have," I said.

"My, my, weren't you the busy one?" he said a bit nastily. "You certainly didn't waste much time."

"James, what are you talking about? It's been two months," I protested. And to think that I had felt guilty about all the procrastination and time wasting.

I was confused.

Had I done something wrong? Was there some sort of pro-

tocol? Some sort of time limit that I had to observe before
dealing with the wreckage of my broken marriage?

Like not being allowed to go dancing in a red dress until
my husband had been dead for six years, or whatever it was
that Scarlett O'Hara so scandalized the Atlanta community
with?

"Yes," he said. "I suppose it has been two months."

He sighed.

For a moment the wild thought crossed my mind that he
might be sad. And then I realized that, yes, he probably was
sad. Wouldn't any man be sad when he suddenly realized that
he now had two families to support?

He was probably envisioning lawyers' fees and estate
agents' costs stretching as far as the eye can see into the future
as we sorted out the severing of our marriage. And of course
keeping those three little brats of Denise's in pink nylon shell
suits wouldn't come cheap either. Although, by rights, it
should.

So I put any sympathy that I might have entertained to one
side and said, "James, did you bring the deeds to the apartment with you?"

"Er, no," he said, looking a tiny bit bewildered.

"Why not?" I asked, slightly exasperated.

"I don't know," he said, looking at his shoes.

There was a perplexed pause.

"I suppose I just didn't think of it. I left London in such
a hurry."

"Do you have *any* of our documents with you?" I asked,
fighting the urge to smack him. "You know, bank statements,
our pension details, that kind of thing?"

"No," he said shortly. His face had gone very pale. He
must have been furious at being caught unprepared.

This kind of inefficiency was really very unlike him. He
was acting totally out of character. Although he hadn't exactly
been acting *in* character for quite a while. Maybe he was having a nervous breakdown? Or maybe he was so in love with
fatso Denise that he'd turned into a bimbo. His eyesight had
obviously failed him when he ran off with her. What's to say
that his brain hadn't gone the same way?

"Do we need all those documents?" he asked.

"Well, not right away, I suppose," I said. "But if we want to work things out while you're here, it would be a lot handier to have them."

"I suppose I could get some of them faxed over," he said slowly. "If that's what you really want."

"Well, it's not exactly a question of what I want," I said, feeling a bit confused. "It's so that we can try to figure out who owns what."

"God, how sordid!" he said with great distaste. "You mean, things like 'I own that towel, you own that saucepan' kind of thing."

"Well, yes, I suppose I do," I said.

What was wrong with him? Hadn't he given this any thought whatsoever?

"James," I asked him as he sat on the chair looking totally shell-shocked. "What did you think was going to happen? That the divorce fairies would come along and magically sort it all out for us while we slept?"

He managed a pale little smile at that.

"You're right," he said wearily. "You're right, you're right, you're right!"

"I am," I reassured him. "And if it makes you feel any better, you can have all the saucepans."

"Thanks," he said quietly.

"And don't worry," I told him, all fake bonhomie and back-slapping jocularity, "one day I'm sure we'll look back and laugh at all of this."

Naturally enough, I was sure of nothing of the sort. I was dimly aware that there was something deeply, deeply wrong with my having to comfort him, with my having to make light of things and encourage him to be strong.

James suddenly got to his feet. He just stood there for a few moments looking lost. He was obviously planning how to get the mortgage documents and all that stuff sent over from London, I thought. He must be mortified that he'd been so inefficient.

"I'd better go," he said.

"Right," I said. "Fine. Why don't you go back to your hotel [hotel! what a joke!] and organize the deeds of the apartment to be sent over? And then we can meet up later."

"Fine," he said, still being very quiet.

I couldn't wait for him to leave.

This was too much.

It was finally happening.

It really was really, really over.

We'd dealt with it like civilized human beings. Too civilized, in my opinion. The whole thing had a dreamlike quality, and it was horrible.

"I'll call you this afternoon," he said.

He said good-bye to Kate, and although he looked as if he was explaining her child support entitlements to her, at least he seemed to be making an effort to bond with her.

Finally I managed to get him to leave.

He looked as exhausted as I felt.

twenty-seven

I barely managed to close the door behind him before I started to cry.

As though they instinctively knew that he had left—hey, what am I talking about, because they had been lying on the floor in the bedroom above the dining room with their ears pressed to a glass trying to hear everything that was being said—Anna, Helen and Mum magically emerged from the woodwork, wearing their Concerned Expressions.

I was distraught.

As though she sensed my grief, Kate started to bawl.

Or maybe it was just because she was hungry.

Either way it was a bit of a cacophony.

"The bastard," I managed to say between sobs, tears stinging my face. "How can it be so easy for him? He's like a fucking machine, with no feelings at all."

"Wasn't he upset, even slightly?" asked Mum anxiously.

"The one thing, the *only* thing, the fucker is worried about is how *sordid* it's going to be when we have to split up our possessions."

"But that's not so bad," said Helen soothingly. "Maybe then he'll just leave everything to you. And you'll get everything."

Nice try, Helen.

Not quite what I needed to hear though.

"So there was no mention of a reconciliation?" asked Mum, her face white, her eyes worried.

"None!" I burst out, prompting a fresh bout of wailing from Kate, who was being held by a miserable-looking Anna.

"Reconciliation!" screeched Helen. "But you wouldn't take him back, would you? Not after the way he's treated you."

"But that's not the point," I sobbed. "At least I wanted the choice. I wanted the chance to tell him to fuck off and that I wouldn't touch him with a ten-foot pole. And the bastard didn't even have the decency to do that."

The three of them nodded in sympathy.

"And he was so smug!" I burst out. "I remembered how he likes his bloody coffee!"

There was a sharp intake of breath from all three of them. They stood shaking their heads sadly at my foolishness. "That's bad," said Anna. "Now he'll know that you still care."

"But I *don't*," I protested violently. "I hate his guts, his uptight, unfaithful, accountant's guts!

"And the bloody nerve of him!" I continued, tears pouring down my blotchy face.

"What?" asked the three, moving forward slightly to hear yet another of James's misdeeds.

"*He* was upset about the dividing of our things and I, I, *me!* was the one who ended up trying to make him feel better about it. Imagine it! *Me* comforting *him*. After all that's happened."

"Men," said Anna, shaking her head in weary disbelief. "Can't live with them, can't live with them."

"Can't live with them," continued Mum, "can't shoot them."

There was a pause. Then Helen spoke.

"Says who?"

"So what's the outcome?" asked Mum.

"None yet," I said. "He's calling this afternoon."

"What are you going to do until then?" Mum asked, her anxious glance straying inadvertently in the direction of the liquor cabinet, even though it had stood empty for many's the long year, but old habits die hard. It might have been more appropriate if her glance had strayed inadvertently out into the garden and under the oil tank, but never mind.

"Nothing," I said. "I'm so tired."

"Why don't you go to bed?" she said hastily. "It's been an ordeal for you. We'll take care of Kate."

Helen looked as if she was about to protest. She opened her mouth mutinously. But then she shut it again.

Nothing short of miraculous, I must say.

"Okay," I said. I dragged myself up the stairs and got into bed still wearing the lovely clothes that I had been decked out in that morning. There was no trace of the smiling, well-made-up, attractive woman I had been then. Only a red-faced, puffy-eyed, blotchy-skinned wreck.

Mid-afternoon, Mum woke me by gently shaking me by the shoulder, whispering "James is on the phone for you. Will you talk to him?"

"Yes," I said. I stumbled from the bed, clothes all crumpled, half-blinded from sleep in my eyes, drooling like a lunatic.

"Hello," I mumbled.

"Claire," he said crisply, all authority and efficiency. "I've tried to get our deeds faxed over to me but there's no fax shop in this bloody city."

Instantly I felt guilty. He made me feel as if it was all my fault. As though I had personally gone around and shut every fax shop in Dublin just to spite him.

"Oh sorry, James," I stuttered. "If you'd mentioned it I would have suggested that they could have been faxed to Dad's office."

"Well, never mind." He sighed, sounding irritable and exasperated and conveying that, if he wanted something done, he was better off doing it himself and not involving me or any members of my immediate family. "Anyway it's too late now. They're being mailed and should arrive in the morning."

You'll be lucky, I thought, thinking of the relaxed attitude of the Irish postal system, compared to the English one. But I said nothing. Doubtless when the time came and the documents didn't, I would somehow be made to feel that that was my fault also.

"But I do think that we should meet this evening anyway," he continued efficiently, ever the professional. Time is money, isn't that right, James! But in fairness he did have a point. We had to meet anyway. We had so much to talk about. It made sense. I obviously wanted everything sorted out as quickly as possible so that I could get on with my new life.

I didn't have any other motive, did I?

I wasn't pathetic enough to think that, if he saw enough of me, he might realize that he still loved me?

Maybe I just enjoyed his company.

Maybe hell!

But I had to admit that I was fascinated by the fact that he no longer loved me. You know, in the same sort of way that people always look at the blood on the road and the mangled vehicles being towed away after a car crash. I know that it's horrible but at the same time I'm so drawn to it. I know that I'll be upset afterward but I still can't stop myself.

Or maybe I just wanted the chance to beat the shit out of him. Who knows?

"Well, what should we do?" he asked. "I would come out to your house but I'm not sure I'm particularly welcome."

I could hardly believe my ears.

How dare he!

He had no right to feel welcome, but at the same time, I had treated him with the utmost good manners.

Which is more than the way he could be said to have treated me.

Hadn't I made him coffee?

Hadn't I not set the dogs on him?

Not that we had any dogs, but that wasn't the point.

Worse still, I could have set Helen on him.

Just what had he been expecting?

The roads from Dublin Airport to be lined with cheering natives, waving Union Jacks? Brass bands and red carpets? A national holiday to be declared? Me greeting him at my front door, wearing a sexy negligee, smiling and saying huskily "Welcome back, darling"?

Frankly, I was baffled.

I wasn't sure what I should say.

Sorry sir, but we're fresh out of fatted calves.

He sounded as if he was sulking. As if he wanted me to say something like, "Oh, don't be so silly, James. Of course you're welcome." But James didn't sulk. He was far too grown up for that. And no man in his right mind could have expected me to welcome him back with open arms.

But what was I going to say?

"I'm sorry you feel that way, James," I managed to say humbly. "If my family or I have behaved in any kind of inhospitable fashion, then I can only offer my apologies."

Of course, I didn't mean a word of it.

If my family *had* offended him in any way—if, for example, Helen had attracted his attention when he left the house by making horrible faces or gestures at him from an upstairs window or mooning him or something even worse—then I would personally offer rewards.

But I had to humor James.

Although I was gagging on my polite words, I always had Kate in the forefront of my mind. Nothing would have given me greater pleasure than to tell James just how unwelcome he was, but that would be cutting off my nose to spite my face. I didn't want Kate to grow up without a father, so telling James that he wasn't *un*welcome (I'm afraid that that was as far as I was prepared to go) was the price I had to pay.

"Well, should I come over then?" he asked grudgingly.

What was *wrong* with him?

He was behaving like a manipulative child.

"Oh, James," I said kindly, "I wouldn't want you to come over here if you're not feeling particularly welcome. We both want to be relaxed. Perhaps we should meet in town instead."

There was a long pause while James digested this.

"Fine," he said coldly. "We could go for dinner."

"That sounds nice," I said, thinking, that *does* sound nice.

"Well, I've got to eat something," he said ungraciously. "So you might as well come along."

"You always were a silver-tongued devil," I said, forcing a smile into my voice. But I felt suddenly so sad.

We arranged to meet at a downtown restaurant at seven-thirty.

And the preparations were, if anything, even more elaborate than the ones that morning.

I wanted, naturally, to look beautiful.

But I decided that I wanted to look sexy also.

James had always loved my legs and loved it when I wore high heels, even if they made me nearly as tall as he was.

So I wore my highest pair, with my shortest dress, black, of course and the sheerest pair of stockings I could find.

As luck would have it, hadn't I shaved my legs only the previous evening? When I was preparing to have sex with Adam, actually. But let's not talk about that right now.

I put on piles of makeup.

"More mascara," urged Helen from the sidelines. "More foundation."

The subtle approach had been, shall we say, less than successful this morning. So now we were going for overkill.

As I applied the stinging stuff that I put on my lips to keep my lipstick in place, it struck me how terrible this all was. So awful. I used to apply my makeup with that kind of care when I was going out with James first. And now here I was dolling myself up, trying my damnedest to look beautiful for the Grand Finale of our relationship.

It was all such a waste.

Failed relationships can be described as so much wasted makeup.

Forget the laughs, forget the fights, forget the sex, forget the jealousy. But take off your hat and observe a moment's silence for the legions of unknown tubes of foundation, mascara, eyeliner, blusher and lipstick who died that it might all have been possible. But who died in vain.

I looked at myself in the mirror and, I had to admit it, I looked good. Tall and slim and nearly elegant. Not a watermelon in sight.

"Jesus," said Helen, shaking her head in undisguised admiration. "Look at you. And it's such a short time since you were a fat old bitch."

Praise indeed.

"Put your hair up," suggested Helen.

"I can't, it's too short," I protested.

"No, it's not," she said, and came over to me and swept it up onto the top of my head.

Goddammit, she was right. It must have grown a bit while I completely neglected it over the previous two months.

"Oh," I said, delighted. "I haven't had long hair since I was sixteen."

Helen busied herself with slides and clips while I grinned like a lunatic at my reflection in the mirror. "James will be sickened," I said. "He'll be so sorry that he can't have a beautiful babe like me. I'll have him on his knees begging me to take him back as soon as I walk in the door."

My beautiful fantasy of a drooling and contrite James was interrupted by Helen saying loudly, "What have you done to your ears?"

"What's wrong with them?"

"They're kind of purple."

"Oh, that's just the hair color. I suppose we'd better take my hair back down to cover them," I said sorrowfully. I had very quickly grown attached to this sophisticated look.

"No, no, we'll think of something," said Helen with a bit of a gleam in her eye. "Stay there." And off she went.

She arrived back with Anna, who whistled when she saw me, and a couple of cloths and a bottle of turpentine.

"You do that ear," instructed Helen. "And I'll do this one."

I went to meet James with ears that were red, raw and almost bleeding, instead of a rich, glossy, chestnut color.

But my hair remained up.

twenty-eight

I have to say that walking into that restaurant was one of the most gratifying experiences I'd ever had. James looked up from whatever he was reading and he literally, *literally*, did a double take.

"Er, Claire," he said, all of a fluster, "um, you're looking wonderful."

I smiled in what I hoped was a mysterious, enigmatic, sophisticated way. "Thank you," I purred.

That'll teach you to leave me, you bastard, I thought as I swung into my seat, giving him an eyeful of my thighs in my sheer, shimmering stockings and my short tight black dress.

He couldn't take his eyes off me.

It was wonderful.

I had got a few funny looks as I had walked from where I had parked the car to the restaurant. I suppose I was a bit overdressed for a bright Monday evening in April, but who cared.

The waiter, a youth in an ill-fitting dinner suit—an alleged Italian, but with a Dublin accent—came rushing over and spent an unnecessary amount of time patting my napkin onto my crotch.

"Um, thank you," I said when I felt that it had gone on far too long.

"You're welcome," he drawled, as Italian as bacon and cabbage. He winked at me over James's head.

Honestly!

And then I got really paranoid.

Maybe he thought I was a hooker.

Did I look like a prostitute?

I *knew* my dress was too short.

Oh what the hell, I decided.

James smiled at me. A beautiful, warm, admiring, approving smile. And for a moment I saw the man I'd married.

Then he noticed the young waiter bending down so he could get a better look at my legs under the table and the smile vanished, leaving me feeling bereft.

"Claire." He frowned like a Victorian patriarch. "Cover yourself. Look at the way the waiter is looking at you!"

I reddened.

I felt foolish and embarrassed now in my short dress, instead of sexy and sassy. Fuck James for making me feel like this! Behaving like a bloody Amish person.

He hadn't always been like that, you know. I could remember a time when the shorter my dress was, the better he liked it. Well, times, as they say, had changed.

I put my head down and spitefully looked for the most expensive thing on the menu.

"I suppose we should talk about money," I said after the waiter had gone away.

"It's all right," he said. "I'll pay. I'll put it on the card."

"No, James," I said, wondering if he was being deliberately obtuse. "I mean, we have to talk about *our* money. You know, yours and mine, our financial situation."

I spoke slowly and deliberately, as if I was talking to a child.

"Oh, I see." He nodded.

"So, do we have any?" I asked anxiously.

"Money? Of course we do," he said, annoyed. I'd hit him where it hurt. Casting aspersions on his ability to provide for his wife and family. Or should I say his wife and families.

"Why wouldn't we have any money?" he asked.

"Well, because of my not working and only getting maternity pay and with you paying the mortgage and then the rent on another apartment and . . ."

"What do you mean, paying the rent on another apartment?" he said in loud and annoyed tones.

"You know, the apartment that you and . . . and . . . Denise live in," I said. It nearly killed me to say her name.

"But I've moved back into our apartment," he said, looking at me in a slightly baffled way. "Didn't you know?"

Several things occurred to me at once.

Could I fatally wound him with a fork?

Would a woman judge be more lenient?

What would prison food be like?

How would Kate turn out if her mother murdered her father?

James's voice swam toward me through a haze of murderous rage.

"Claire," he was saying anxiously. "Are you feeling okay?"

I realized that I was gripping my butter knife so hard that my hand hurt. And, although I couldn't see my face, I knew it had gone bright red with fury.

"You mean to tell me," I finally managed to hiss at him, "that you've moved that woman into *my* home."

I thought that I would choke or vomit or do *something* antisocial.

"No, no, Claire," he said. Sounding hurried, anxious, afraid that—heaven forbid—I might cause a bit of a scene. "I've moved back into our apartment. But Deni . . . er . . . she hasn't."

"Oh."

I was totally flabbergasted. I didn't know what to say. Because I didn't know how I felt.

"I'm not . . . er . . . you know . . . with her anymore. I haven't been for some time."

"Oh."

In a way that was almost worse.

I still wanted to strangle him.

To think that he threw away our marriage, our relationship, for something that hadn't survived even two months of living together. The *waste*. The sense of pointless loss was almost unbearable. Then I burst out, "Why didn't anyone tell me?"

What had happened to the highly efficient bush telegraph system that my friends and I operated?

James spoke to me soothingly.

"Maybe nobody knows yet. I haven't made much of a fuss

about it. And I haven't seen much of anyone over the past month," he explained, obviously keen to keep me calm.

He *must* be having a nervous breakdown, I thought. He'd become a spooky, shadowy, Howard Hughes–type reclusive figure.

"I've been away on business," he continued.

"Oh."

All right, then he wasn't having a nervous breakdown. He *hadn't* become a spooky, shadowy, Howard Hughes–type reclusive figure.

I might have known. James was far too practical to bother with nervous breakdowns. If they couldn't be justified in financial terms he wasn't interested.

At least that meant that he hadn't been away on vacation with fatso Denise that time I called him.

What a waste of all that angst and misery.

And then the curiosity started burning a hole in me.

What had happened with James and Denise?

I knew I shouldn't ask questions, but I just couldn't help myself.

"So did she kick you out?" I asked. I tried to say it lightly but it just sounded bitter. "Gone back to Mario or Sergio or whatever his name is."

"Actually, no, Claire," said James, looking at me carefully. "I left her."

"Gosh." Bitterness seeped out through my pores. "You're making quite a habit of it. Leaving women, that is," I added viciously, just in case he hadn't understood.

"Yes, Claire, I know what you meant." His tone of voice implied that somehow he felt he was *above* all this. But that he was a decent guy who was prepared to indulge me.

I carried on regardless. "And, anyway, I thought a gentleman would never say that he'd left a woman. I thought it was mannerly to say that she had left you even if she hadn't."

Even I was amazed at how illogical I was being. I was aware of the edge of hysteria in my voice. But I was powerless to stop. I had no control over my runaway emotions.

"I'm not telling the whole world that I left her," he said tightly, "I'm telling you. You asked me, remember?"

"Well, why aren't you telling the whole world that you left

her? I *want* you to tell the whole world that you left her," I said, a dangerous wobble in my voice. "Why should everyone know that you just dumped me—and Kate—and then think that she kicked you out? Why should she be spared the humiliation?"

"Fine, then, Claire," he said, sighing loudly at my unreasonable and irrational demands. "If it makes you happy I *will* tell everyone what happened with Denise."

"Good," I said, my bottom lip trembling like jelly.

This was awful! Where had the recovered poised Claire gone? I had tried so hard to stay completely in control with James, not to let him see how much he had hurt me, how devastated I was. But all the pain was so close to the surface. I was on the verge of cracking.

It was all so *embarrassing*. I was very upset and he was in control. The contrast was mortifying.

"I'm going to the ladies room," I said. Maybe I could get a grip of myself there.

"No, Claire, wait," said James as I started to stand up. He tried to grab my hand across the table.

I shook his hand away angrily. "Don't touch me," I said tearfully.

Next I'd be saying something like "You lost the right to touch me when you left me."

"You lost the right to touch me when you left me," I found myself saying.

I knew it, I just knew it! The person who had the job of writing my life's dialogue used to work on a very low budget soap opera.

But I meant it.

I wanted to hurt him badly. I wanted him to feel the same loss that I had felt. To want someone so much that it aches. And to realize that you can't have them. And most of all I wanted him to feel that it was his *fault*.

Who made it happen?

You did.

"Claire, please sit down," he said, letting go of my hand slowly. He was doing a good impression of looking pale and upset. For a moment I felt guilty. God, I couldn't win.

"Relax, James," I said coldly. "I'm not going to make a scene."

He had the grace to look ashamed.

"That's not what I'm worried about," he said.

"Oh really," I sneered at him.

"Yes, really," he said, sounding a bit more patient. "Look Claire, we've *got* to talk."

"There's nothing left to say," I responded automatically.

Whoops! There I went again. More bloody clichés! Honestly, I could have died. It was so embarrassing.

And I wouldn't mind but it wasn't even true. There was lots to say.

Whoa, whoa, steady, easy, hold on, hold on, I told myself. "Isn't calm and civilized discussion the game plan?" the reasonable part of my brain sweetly asked the argumentative part. "Well, isn't it?"

"I suppose so," the argumentative part grudgingly conceded. Like a surly teenager.

"Can we at least try to be in control?" asked the reasonable part.

"I must stop," I told myself, taking a deep breath. "I will stop."

"Claire," he said, trying to sound gentle—as he pawed for my hand again. "I know I've treated you badly."

"Badly!" I exploded before I could stop myself. "Ha! Badly! That's one way of putting it."

Well, so much for being reasonable and in control! In spite of my pathetic efforts to keep a lid on my emotions the gloves were well and truly off now. All pretense of being calm and grown-up and civilized had gone by the board. Well, all pretense of my being calm and grown-up and civilized had. He still maintained a huge amount of equilibrium.

Equilibrium was one of the things he did best.

"Appallingly, then," he conceded.

He didn't sound very contrite. He sounded as if he was humoring me.

The unfeeling bastard! How could he be so self-contained? It wasn't human.

"How could you have been so irresponsible?" I burst out. I knew that would hurt him more than anything. He could take accusations of unkindness, cruelty, hardheartedness on the chin. But to call him irresponsible was a low blow.

"How could you just have abandoned us? I *needed* you."

I ended on a high impassioned note.

A silence followed.

He sat very still—ominously still—for a moment and some kind of emotion, although not one I was familiar with, flickered across his face.

When he spoke again it became clear that a change had come over him. Something had snapped. The patience well had run dry. He had gone to fetch a packet of tolerance and the cupboard was bare.

No more Mr. Nice Guy. Not that he had been much in evidence anyway.

When he spoke it wasn't in his normal voice. But in a nasty singsong flippant tone. "Yeah," he said with a long pause between each word. "You. Certainly. Did."

"Wha . . . at?" I asked, a bit taken aback.

I was still immersed in feelings of loss and abandonment, but I managed to grasp that something had happened to James. And that this something was not to my advantage. It was immediately obvious that things weren't right when he agreed with me so readily. It was even more immediately obvious that things were very wrong indeed when he agreed with me so readily in such a peculiar tone of voice.

"Oh," he went on, still in the peculiar tone, "I'm just saying how right you are. That's what you want, isn't it? In fact, I'll say it again, will I? You *needed* me."

What had happened? Events had taken a sudden and unexpected turn. I felt as though I had wandered into someone else's discussion. Or as if James had, all on his own, decided to change channels. I was still knee-deep in the old conversation, the one about James leaving me, and felt pretty wretched about it. But he had flicked over to a new conversation about something totally different. I struggled to catch up with him.

"James, what's going on here?" I asked in confusion.

"What do you mean?" he replied unpleasantly.

"I mean, why are you being so weird all of a sudden?" I said nervously.

"Weird," he said in a thoughtful, weighty tone, and looked

around the room as if he was appealing to an invisible audience. "She says I'm being weird."

This from the man who was chatting to people who weren't there.

"Well, you are," I said. In fact, he was getting weirder by the second. "All I said was that I needed you and—"

"I heard what you said," he interrupted angrily, the singsong flippant tone abruptly gone.

He leaned across the table and fixed me with a furious face. "Here goes," I thought.

Relief mingled with my fear. At least now I'd know what the hell was up with him.

"You said that you needed me." He made some kind of annoyed sound and threw his eyes heavenward. "What an understatement!"

He paused—for impact?—and stared at me, his face hard and angry.

I didn't dare speak. I was enthralled. What was coming next?

"I *know* you needed me," he threw at me. "You needed me all the bloody time, for some bloody thing or other. How could I *not* know?"

I could only stare at him.

He didn't often get angry. So, on the special occasions when he did it was usually quite a treat. A bit spectacular. But not today. I didn't know where this anger of his came from but the message he seemed anxious to convey was that I was the one at fault.

That wasn't part of the script.

I was the one in the right. He was the bastard. That's the way it was.

"You needed me for *everything*," he almost shouted.

I think I should point out to you at this juncture that James never shouted. He'd never even almost shouted.

"You demanded constant attention," he went on. "And constant reinforcement. And you never gave a damn about me and how I felt and what I might need."

I stared openmouthed at him.

I couldn't believe what I was hearing.

Why was he attacking me?

He was the one who'd left me, right?

So if there was any accusing to be done, I was the correct person for the job.

"James . . ." I said faintly.

He ignored me and continued ranting and jabbing his finger at me.

"You were impossible. I was exhausted from you. I don't know how I stayed with you as long as I did. And I don't know how *anyone* could live with you."

Now lookit here! That was too much. Anger surged through me.

Talk about a kangaroo court.

I was being done a terrible injustice.

And I wasn't letting him get away with it.

I was *livid*.

"Oh, I see," I said, absolutely furious. "So now it's all my fault. I made you have an affair. I made you leave me. Well, that's funny, because I don't actually recall holding a gun to your head. It must have slipped my mind."

It's true what they say. Sarcasm really is the lowest form of wit. But I couldn't help myself. He was criticizing me. And I was burning, *scalded* with a sense of injustice.

"No, Claire," he said. He actually spoke through gritted teeth. Which I'd never seen anyone do before. I thought it was just a figure of speech. "Of course you didn't make me do anything."

"So then what are you saying?" I demanded.

I had a funny cold feeling in the pit of my stomach. I knew it was fear.

"I'm saying that living with you was a bit like living with a demanding child. You always wanted to go out. As though life was one big long party. And it was, for you. You were always laughing and enjoying yourself. So I had to be the grown-up one. I had to worry about money and bills. You were so *selfish*. I had to be the one who reminded you at one in the morning, at a dinner party, that we both had to be at work the next day. And then I had to put up with you calling me a boring bastard."

I was dumbfounded at this torrent from James. Apart from its unexpectedness, I felt that it was so unfair.

"James, that's the way it worked for us," I protested. "I was the funny one, you were the serious one. Everyone knew that. I was the light relief, the silly one who made you laugh and unwind. You were the strong one. That's the way we both wanted it. That's the way it was. And that's why it was so good."

"But it wasn't," he said. "I was so bloody tired of being strong."

"And I didn't ever call you a boring bastard," I exclaimed suddenly. I knew that something he had said there was wrong.

"It doesn't matter," he said irritably. "You made me feel like one."

"Yes, but you said that I—" I started to protest.

"Oh, for God's sake, Claire," he burst out angrily. "There you go again. Trying to score points. Can't you just let it be? Can't you, for once, just once, accept blame?"

"Yes, but . . ." I said weakly.

I wasn't even sure what I should accept blame for.

Never mind. I didn't have time to think about it. James drew another breath and was off again. And I had to give what he was saying all my attention.

"You just made messes." He sighed. "And I had to clean them up."

"That's not true!" I shouted.

"Well, believe me, that's how it felt," he said unkindly. "You just don't want to admit that it's true. There was always a drama. Or a trauma. And I was always the one who had to deal with it."

I was silent. Totally dumbfounded.

"And you know, Claire," he continued solemnly, "you just don't magically wake up one morning and know how to be an adult. You don't know overnight how to pay bills. You work at it. You work at being responsible."

"I know how to pay bills," I protested. "I'm not a total moron, you know."

"So how come it was me who had to take care of that end of things?" he asked primly.

"James"—my head whirled as I searched for ways to defend myself—"I did try to help."

I distinctly remembered a time when I had sat with James

as he self-importantly flicked through check stubs and ATM receipts and tap-tap-tapped with a calculator. I offered to help him that day. And he told me with a suggestive twinkle in his eye that he would stick to what he was good at and that I should stick to what I was good at. And then, if I remember correctly, and I'm sure I do, we had sex on the desk. In fact, the bank statements and the Visa bills for July 1991 still bear certain rather interesting imprints. But I couldn't find the nerve to remind him of that.

"I really did offer to help," I protested again. "But you wouldn't let me. You said that you'd be much better at it because you had a head for figures."

"And you just accepted that?" he asked nastily, shaking his head slightly as if he could hardly believe how crass and stupid I'd been.

"Well . . . yes, I suppose," I said, feeling foolish.

He was right. I had let him worry about threatening letters and disconnection notices and all that. But I'd really thought he wanted to do it. Not that there were ever any threatening letters or disconnection notices or the like. James was far too organized to allow that to happen. I thought he liked being in control. That it would be less haphazard if only one of us was involved. How wrong I was.

I wished I could turn the clock back. If only I'd paid more attention to things like the date we paid our mortgage.

"I'm sorry," I said awkwardly. "I thought you wanted to do it. I would have done it if I'd known you didn't want to."

"Why would I want to do it?" he asked nastily. "What person in their right mind would enjoy being entirely responsible for the bills of a household?"

"You're right, of course," I admitted.

"Well," said James, sounding a bit warmer, "I suppose it wasn't really your fault. You were always a bit thoughtless."

I swallowed back a retort. Now was not the time to antagonize him.

But I wasn't *thoughtless*. I know I wasn't.

James had other ideas, however.

"If only you hadn't been thoughtless when it really mattered," he mused. "Because the problems in our marriage weren't just about you not pulling your weight. It was about the way you made me feel."

"What do you mean?" I asked. I braced myself for another round of accusations. Accusations that I didn't want to hear. But ones that I had to listen to if I wanted to make sense of why he left me.

"Well, it was always about you, wasn't it?" he said.

"How? In what way?" I asked, bewildered.

"I'd come home from work, after having had a terrible day. And you wouldn't talk to me about it. You'd just go on about your day, telling me stories and expecting me to laugh at them."

"But I would ask," I protested. "And you always told me it was too boring to explain. I only told you funny stories because I knew you'd had a horrible day and I wanted to cheer you up."

"Don't try to justify yourself," he said forcefully. "It was so obvious that you never wanted to hear anything unpleasant. All you wanted were good times. You had no interest at all in hearing about anything unpleasant."

"James . . ." I said feebly.

What could I say?

His mind was so made up.

And I swear to you, this was all news to me. I had never suspected that he had felt this way. And I had no idea that I had behaved in such an insufferable way. James wouldn't by any chance be interested in absolving himself of all guilt in this sorry fiasco, would he? James wouldn't, by some freak chance, be manipulating me in any way?

I had to find out.

"James," I said in a little voice, "I'm sorry to ask this, but you wouldn't be trying to avoid the blame for leaving me? You know, by blaming me and making it all my fault."

"Oh, for God's sake," snorted James. "That's exactly the kind of childish, selfish response I should have expected from you."

"Sorry," I whispered. "I shouldn't even have asked."

Another silence.

"Why didn't you tell me?" I burst out. "We were so close. It was so beautiful."

"We weren't so close and it wasn't so beautiful," he said bluntly.

"It was. We were," I protested.

He's taken enough away from me, I thought. He's not going to take my memories.

"Claire, if it was that beautiful, why did I leave you?" he asked quietly.

And, really, what could I say? He was so right.

But, hold on. He was off again. More accusations. His grievance was an unstoppable force.

"Claire, you were absolutely impossible. I had to keep so much from you. I had to carry so much worry on my own because I felt that you couldn't cope."

"Why didn't you try me?" I asked sadly.

He didn't even bother to answer.

"You were such a bloody handful. I'd come home from work, exhausted, and you'd have decided on the spur of the moment to have a dinner party for eight people and I'd have to run around like a crazy person, buying beer and uncorking wine and whipping cream."

"James, that only happened once. And it was for six people, not eight. And it was for your friends who came down from Aberdeen. It was supposed to be a surprise for you. I was the one who whipped the cream."

"Look, I'm not going to get into specifics," he said testily. "Doubtless you can try to justify anything I say to you, but you were still in the wrong."

"I *can* try to justify anything I did because I feel that the things I did were right," I thought confusedly to myself. But I didn't say anything.

"I thought you liked me being spontaneous," I said timidly. "I thought you even encouraged it."

"Well, that's the way you would see it," he said sneeringly. "I suppose that's the way you want to see it," he said a bit more kindly.

A smiling waiter approached our table with a lively gait. But froze in his tracks and then made a sharp right turn to another table when he noticed the glower that James gave him.

"So you thought you'd help me to grow up. You thought that if you left me that it might shock me into it," I said, realization dawning gradually and unevenly. "What a pity you had to use such extreme measures."

"Oh, that wasn't why I left you," he said. "It wasn't done to make you grow up. Frankly, I didn't think that was possible. But I wanted to be with someone who cared about me. Someone who would take care of me. And Denise did."

I swallowed back the hurt.

"I *cared* for you. I *loved* you." I had to make him believe me. "You never gave me the chance to help you. You never gave me the opportunity to be strong. I *am* strong now. I *could* have taken care of you."

He looked at me. He was wearing his fatherly, indulgent face.

"Maybe you could have," he said, quite kindly. "Maybe you could have."

"And now we'll never know," I thought out loud, my heart almost breaking with a sense of loss, missed opportunities, of being misunderstood.

There was a bit of an odd pause. Then he spoke.

"Um, uh, I suppose not," he said hurriedly.

So now what?

I felt sick, sad, sorry.

Sad for both of us.

Sad for James, who had carried so much worry on his own.

Sad for me for being so misunderstood.

Or was it sad for me for being so misunderstanding?

Sad for Kate, the innocent victim.

"You must have thought I'd go to pieces completely without you," I asked him. I felt hot, angry with shame and mortification.

"Yes, I suppose I did," he admitted. "Well, you can hardly blame me, can you?"

"No," I said, hanging my head.

"But I didn't, did I?" I said. Tears poured down my face. "I coped without you. And I'll manage fine in the future without you."

"I can see that." He nodded and looked with mild amusement at my wet, tear-streaked face. "Oh, you silly thing, come here." He kind of pulled me awkwardly across the table, pushing the flower vase and the salt and pepper shakers aside, and patted my head onto his shoulder in a supposedly comforting manner.

I left my head there for a moment. I felt a bit uncomfortable and foolish. I sat up straight again. It would hardly do my cause any good if I continued to behave like a child needing comfort.

But that didn't seem to please him either.

"What's wrong?" he asked, sounding a bit annoyed.

"What do you mean?" I asked, wondering what I'd done now.

"Why are you pulling away from me? I may have left you for another woman, but do I have rabies or what?" He gave a small smirk at his little joke. Which I weakly tried to return.

"Um, no," I said, totally confused. What did he *want* from me? I couldn't please him whatever way I behaved.

I was exhausted.

Things were much more straightforward when he was a faithless, philandering bastard. I knew where I was then. I'd understood that situation. But he must be right. I must have enjoyed being irresponsible. Otherwise why couldn't I accept blame for my part in the marriage breakup?

But it was hard to accept that it was all my fault. He was the one who left me. He was the one who broke my heart.

Nothing that I had expected to happen had happened. I'd thought that he might ask if I would come back to him. Either that or for him to continue behaving like a total bastard. I certainly hadn't expected to end up apologizing for causing this situation all by myself.

Things had been black and white. He had been the darkness and I was the light. He was the wrongdoer and I was the victim.

Now it was all mixed up.

I was the wrongdoer and he was the victim.

It didn't feel right.

That was hard for me, but I was prepared to give it a chance.

"Look, James," I said, swallowing back tears, "this is all a bit of a shock. I need to think about what you've said. I'm going now. I'll talk to you tomorrow."

And with that I hopped up and made for the door, leaving

James, sitting at the table, mouthing silently like an agitated goldfish.

"Good for you, love," said one of the waiters to me as I swept past. "He's not your type, at all at all."

I drove home at high speed, jumping red lights and risking the life and limb of pedestrians and other motorists alike.

twenty-nine

I put my key in the door and, with a marvelous display of their psychic abilities, the kitchen door opened and Anna, Helen and Mum rushed out into the hall to greet me. Either that or they heard me parking the car.

"How did you get on?" asked Mum.

Obviously they were all at a very loose end at the moment. My real-life soap opera wouldn't have been afforded so much interest if they'd had anything better to do.

"What happened?" shouted Helen.

"Oh, marvelous news," I yelled tearfully as I started up the stairs to see Kate.

"Oh good." Mum beamed.

"Well, you know the way James left me and went off and lived with someone else and didn't even know Kate's name. Well, it's all okay now. Because it was my fault. I was asking for it. Apparently I was begging for it. Down on my knees begging for it!"

I swung into my room, leaving three astonished faces at the bottom of the stairs, their mouths three ohs of surprise.

Kate started bawling when she saw me. And just for the hell of it, I decided to join in. I was not finding this blame-acceptance thing easy, as you may have gathered.

But I took my frustration with the situation out on Helen, Anna and Mum, when I should have voiced it to James. And that wasn't fair to the girls and Mum. A little voice reminded me that I had tried to tell James about it and he'd said it was further proof of my childishness. Well, he was probably right. He usually was.

What a pain in the ass, I thought rebelliously.

And now I had to stop being resentful and rebellious. I was no longer a twenty-nine-year-old adolescent. If I was going to be a sensitive, considerate, caring adult then I might as well start now.

I could begin by being responsive to Kate's needs.

"What can I get you, my darling?" I asked. I wondered if that would be *mature* enough for James. I must stop!

He was right, I was wrong.

I tried to calm the crying child in my arms.

"Clean diaper, perchance? Or can I interest you in a bottle? And we have a wonderful selection of attention and affection. All are available. You only have to ask."

But no, I was even doing that wrong. According to James, people shouldn't even have to ask me for what they wanted. If I was really selfless I should know.

Just to be on the safe side I gave her all of the above. I changed her diaper, fed her and told her she was more beautiful than Claudia Schiffer.

Mum, Anna and Helen materialized in the room. They crept in cautiously, wondering how crazy I had gone.

"Oh, hi," I said when I saw the first tentative head appearing around the door. "Come in, come in. Sorry about that little display in the hall. I was upset. I had no right to take it out on you three."

"Oh, that's fine then," said Helen. The three of them marched in and took up residence on the bed while I tended to Kate and told them the story of my evening.

"So, in a funny way, knowing how difficult I was makes the fact that he left me a bit easier," I told them. "You know, at least it makes sense."

"Claire," said Mum slowly, "I'm sure that you couldn't have been as bad as he makes out."

"I know, I don't understand that either," I admitted. "But when I told him that, he said that was exactly the way he would have expected me to react."

There really wasn't anything anyone else could say.

James had me boxed in good and neatly.

That night was terrible. As bad as the early days when James had first left me. When the others finally left, having given up trying to reassure me that I couldn't be that bad, I couldn't sleep. I lay flat on my back, staring into the darkness. Questions buzzed around in my head.

This had all come as a terrible shock. I'd never known that I was so selfish and immature. No one else ever complained before. Granted, I was high-spirited. And maybe a bit noisy and lively. But I honestly thought I was considerate of other people's feelings.

The thought crossed my mind that maybe, just maybe, James was perhaps exaggerating how bad I had been. Was even making it up. I dismissed that idea again almost as quickly. That was just me trying to escape the blame. Why would James do something like that if it wasn't true? As he'd said himself—and his words kept going around and around in my head—"If I had been happy, why would I have left?"

I admit that I absolutely hated being wrong. I was really bad at graciously admitting that I was in error. I felt burning, raw, exposed, mortified. I had been so smug. I'd thought that I had right on my side. It was very humbling to find that I hadn't.

Even when I was a little girl and didn't get all my spelling words right at school, I found it very hard to bow my head and swallow and say, "You are right and I am wrong."

Well, practice makes perfect.

I finally slept.

thirty

Dad woke me the following morning by thrusting a huge manila envelope under my nose. "Here," he said ill-temperedly. "Take this. I'm late for work."

"Thanks, Dad," I said sleepily, dragging myself up in the bed as I pushed my hair out of my eyes.

I looked at the letter. It had a London postmark. With a little cold thrill, I realized it was the deed to the apartment and all the other documents that James had asked to be sent over.

I toyed with the idea of ringing the Vatican to report a miracle. Surely nothing had ever arrived from London to Dublin that quickly ever before?

I toyed with the idea of calling James instead.

It might be better if I called James.

Though I'd probably get a better reception at the Vatican.

I found the number of the LiffeySide in the phone book. Some woman answered. I asked to speak to James.

She told me to hold on a moment while she went to get him. While I was waiting I could hear noises in the background that sounded like machine gun fire. Now, granted, it might only have been the washing machine, but if you knew the LiffeySide and the street it was on, you'd be more inclined to put your money on it being machine gun fire.

"Hello," said James. He sounded all officious and important.

"James, it's me," I told him.

"Claire," he said attempting to sound friendly. "I was just about to call you."

"Were you?" I asked politely, wondering why that was. Had he just remembered some other awful way I used to treat him? Had he omitted some important criticism about my behavior in public that he had meant to tell me last night?

Now, now, I warned myself. Be selfless and adult about this.

"Would you believe it?" he asked disbelievingly. "Not one newspaper shop in this city opens before nine o'clock. I've been trying to get the *FT* since I got up, not a chance."

"Well, well, would you believe that?" I said, feeling a surge of irritation. But I tried to hide it. I had to bear in mind that although the *Financial Times* wasn't important to me, it was important to another human being, namely James, so, as an altruistic, caring, empathetic person, I *should* care.

"Was that why were you just about to ring me?" I asked. "To tell me that?"

"No, no, no. Why was it? Oh yes," he said, remembering. "I wanted to see if you were feeling all right after last night. I realize that I may have been a little bit . . . well . . . *hard* on you. I can see now that you had no idea that you were behaving so selfishly and thoughtlessly. The truth may have come as a bit of a shock to you."

"Well, a bit," I admitted. The confusion started up again. I felt like a suspect being interrogated by two policemen, one nice one and one nasty one. Just when I'd gotten used to one of them being nasty to me, the other starts by being extra nice and making me want to cry and hug him. Except there was only one James. But the effect was the same. Now that he was being nice to me I wanted to, yes, you guessed it, cry and hug him.

"You weren't deliberately awful," he went on. "You just weren't aware."

"No," I sniffed. "I wasn't."

I was so *glad* that he was being nice to me at last. I could have cried with relief.

"Must try harder," he said with a little laugh. "Isn't that right?"

"Um, yes, I suppose so. Good news, James," I said, getting to the point of my phone call.

"What's that?" he asked. He sounded pleased and indulgent.

"The documents have arrived!" I said triumphantly. "I could hardly believe it. It must be a first for the Irish postal system."

"So?" he asked sharply.

Oh God, I thought, I've annoyed him again. I see what he means. I seem to do it without even realizing it.

"So, it's good . . ." I said limply. "We needn't waste any more time. We can start sorting things out immediately."

"Oh." He sounded a bit dazed. A bit stupid.

"Oh," he said again. "Right. Fine."

"Why don't you come over here?" I suggested. "No boiling oil, I promise you."

I forced myself to laugh in a gently humoring way.

As though the very suggestion that he might suffer any kind of injury at my hands or at the hands of my family was ludicrous.

"Fine," he said shortly. "I'll be with you in an hour."

And he hung up! Just like that.

A brief thought flickered across my brain.

Was James schizophrenic?

Or was there any history of madness in his family?

I was as sure as hell finding it difficult to keep up with all these mood changes.

Something had to be causing it.

Maybe I'd find out when he arrived. Meanwhile I was going to have a sneak preview of the deeds just to see if I actually had any rights at all.

Precisely one hour later, the doorbell rang. It was James.

He greeted me with a little smile and an inquiry after Kate's health.

"Well, why don't you ask her yourself?" I asked him.

"Oh, um, fine then," he said.

We went into the dining room, where Kate was. James hesitantly tickled her. I went to the kitchen to make coffee.

I reappeared with the coffee and turned to James with a smile. "Right then," I said pleasantly. "Shall we start?"

I gestured to the documents, which were spread out on the table.

We both sat down.

"I thought it would be best if we started with the deed to the apartment first," I said.

"Okay," he said faintly.

"Now, if you look at this clause here," I said, pointing to one that referred to selling the apartment before the mortgage was paid off, "you'll see that . . ."

I launched into explanations and suggestions, peppered with the odd bit of legalese. I was proud of myself. I sounded as if I knew exactly what I was talking about. Absently, I hoped that I was impressing him. Even though we had split up it was important to me that he started to think of me as a capable woman and not some spoiled, dizzy, bimbo.

After a while I noticed that he wasn't paying any attention to what I was saying.

He just sat back in his chair and looked at my face, not at the document that I was so painstakingly explaining to him.

I stopped mid–disclaimer clause and said, "James, what's wrong? Why aren't you paying attention?"

He ruffled my hair affectionately—which came as quite a surprise, let me tell you—and said with a little smile, "You can stop now, Claire. I'm convinced."

"Convinced about what?" I asked him.

What the hell was he talking about now?

"I'm convinced that you've changed. You don't have to keep up this act."

"What act?" I asked blankly.

"You know," he said, smiling into my eyes. "This pretense that we're going to sell the apartment and settle on child support for Kate. You can stop now."

I didn't say anything. What on earth could I say?

"It's not an act," I squeaked.

"Claire," he said, smiling indulgently, "stop it! I must admit you really had me going at one stage. I nearly believed that you were serious. Did you really have to go through the charade of getting the deed sent over? Wasn't that a bit over the top?"

"James," I said faintly.

He seemed to take this as some kind of capitulation. He put his arms around me and pulled me to him. I sat there with my head poised stiffly on his shoulder.

"Look, I know you've been very difficult. Bloody difficult," he said. I could hear the rueful smile in his voice. "But I can see that you're making an effort. I can see how hard you're trying to convince me that you're responsible and grown-up and considerate now."

"I am?" I asked.

"Yes," he said kindly. He pulled away from me and looked into my eyes. "You are."

"So, we can get rid of these for a start." He rustled the papers on the table and pushed them all into an untidy pile.

"Why?" I asked.

"Because we won't be selling the apartment." He smiled.

He looked a bit more carefully at my white, shocked face.

"Oh God." He slapped his hand dramatically to his forehead. "You haven't realized, have you?"

"No," I said.

He grabbed me forcefully by the shoulders and put his face close to mine. "I love you," he said with a little laugh. "You little silly girl, hadn't you realized?"

"No," I said, feeling as if I might burst into tears.

Isn't it odd how relief can sometimes feel very much like dread?

How happiness can feel like disappointment?

"Why did you think I came to Dublin?" He shook me gently by the shoulders and gave me that same indulgent smile.

"I don't know," I faltered. "Maybe to clean up loose ends."

"I suppose you thought I'd never forgive you for the way you behaved?"

Actually, no, I wasn't thinking anything of the sort, I thought.

"But I *have* forgiven you," he told me nicely. "I'm prepared to make a go of things in the future. I'm sure things will be very different because you've grown up so much."

I nodded mutely.

Why wasn't I happy?

He still loved me.

He had never stopped loving me.

I had driven him away.

But I was different now and things could be fixed.

Wasn't that what I wanted?

Well, wasn't it?

He looked at my silent, shocked face and chucked me under the chin.

"You're not still put out about that business with Denise, are you?" he asked, as if that was a totally ludicrous idea.

"Well, actually, I am," I said in a little voice. I felt that I had no right to complain about anything now that he was being so nice to me.

"But it was nothing," he protested laughingly. "It was just a reaction to the way you made me feel. I'm sure that you won't make that mistake again." He smiled as if it were funny.

But it wasn't.

"Um, right, James," I said. I felt as if my head was going to explode. I had to get away from him for a while.

"James," I said faintly, "this has come as a terrible—"

"Surprise!" he interjected. "I know, I know."

"I need to be on my own to think about things a bit."

"What's there to think about?" he asked lightly.

"James," I said, "you hurt me an awful lot. Hurt me and humiliated me. I can't just bounce out of that feeling to please you."

"Oh dear," he sighed. "We're back to 'poor Claire' all over again. I thought you'd changed. What about the ways you hurt and humiliated me?"

"But I never meant to . . ."

"Well, I never set out to hurt you either," he replied. A slightly impatient tone in his voice. "It just happened."

"But you said you *loved* Denise," I said, remembering the part that hurt most of all.

"I *thought* I loved her," he said carefully, as if he was explaining something to a very young child. "But it turned out that I didn't."

There was a pause.

Then he spoke.

"Fine, all right!" he said belligerently. "You want me to admit that I made a mistake. Fine, I'll do it. Just to show you how committed I am to making this marriage work."

He paused and said in a singsong voice, sounding like a little boy, the type of little boy you'd like to kill, " 'I Made a Mistake.' Will that do you?"

"Um, thank you," I said politely.

Would he please just *go*.

"Of course, if you're going to hang on to grudges and grievances then there's no point in my being here, is there?" he asked. "If that's the case I'll just go straight to the airport and go back to London and I'll never refer to this again."

"No, don't do that." I felt panicky at the thought of his leaving me again. I also felt panicky about the thought of his staying.

This was too much to cope with.

The fucker left me out of the blue.

He arrived back and told me it was all my fault that he left me.

But that he still loved me and wanted to try again.

Was that the behavior of a logical person?

"Claire," he said, back to the gentle nice guy James, "I can see how overwhelmed you are by all of this. It's perfectly understandable. You thought you were all alone. And now you find that you have your old happy life back. It must be hard to take in all at once."

"That's right," I mumbled.

"So I'll leave you by yourself for a couple of hours."

"Thanks." I sagged with relief.

"I'll see about plane tickets. What day would you like to fly back to London?"

"Oh, I don't know." Panic gripped me again. I didn't want to go back to London. At least I didn't want to go back with James.

"No time like the present, eh?" He winked. "How long will it take you to pack?"

"Oh James, I don't know," I said, feeling horrorstruck. "A long time, probably, what with all Kate's stuff and that."

"Oh yes, Kate," he said, as if he'd just remembered her. "I'd better book her on the plane too."

"Well, don't do anything just yet," I said. "Give me a little bit of time to think things through."

"Well," he said, frowning, "I'm missing work by being

here. So I'd like to get back as soon as possible, now that we've
got things worked out."

"I'll talk to you later about it," I said, guiding him toward
the front door.

"Well, don't take too long about it," he said, "after all . . ."

"Time is money, I know, I know," I wearily finished off
the sentence for him.

I closed the door behind him and stood for a moment,
leaning against the door, feeling quite weak.

"Is he gone?" hissed a voice.

It was Mum, sticking her head out of her bedroom and
looking down at me in the hall.

"Yes," I said.

"What's wrong?" she asked, taking in my shocked
appearance.

"Nothing," I said faintly.

"Good," she said.

"James told me he still loves me," I said blankly.

"What!" she screeched.

"I hope you told him where to stick it," shouted a voice
from behind Mum.

"Claire, Claire," said Mum, running down the stairs, "come
in. Sit down. Tell me all about it. This is great news."

She guided me to the kitchen.

"Where's Kate?" she asked.

"In the dining room," I said, sitting down weakly at the
kitchen table.

"I'll get her," said Mum, and off she ran.

She was back in a moment, her face all eager and agog.

"So what did he say?" she demanded impatiently.

"He said that he still loves me and wants me back," I said
expressionlessly.

"Well, isn't that great?" exclaimed Mum.

"I suppose," I said doubtfully.

"And what was the situation with this Denise one?" she
asked, looking at me carefully.

"Apparently, he never loved her," I said quietly. "He only
turned to her when he felt that he wasn't getting any attention
and care and love from me."

"And it's all over with her?" asked Mum.

"Yes," I said.

"Do you believe him?" she asked.

"Funnily enough, I do," I said.

"Well, that's fine then," said Mum.

"Is it?" I asked.

Mum was silent for a few moments. She was thinking about something.

When she spoke it was in a funny solemn tone of voice.

"Claire," she said, "don't make the mistake of letting pride get in the way of forgiveness. You still love him. He still loves you. Don't throw it all away just because your feelings are hurt."

I remained silent. And she continued speaking. A misty faraway look in her eyes.

"Lots of marriages go through hiccups," she said. "And people get over them. They learn to forgive. And after a while they even learn to forget. And the marriage is usually stronger afterwards, if you work at it and stay together."

Oh no! I thought. I recognize this scenario. This is the one where the mother reveals to the daughter that the mother had an affair many years ago with someone like her husband's best friend. Or, more likely, that the daughter's father had an affair with someone. ("What? You mean Dad had an affair?") And the mother had been all set to leave him and take the children with her. ("You were only a babe in arms.") But the mother didn't leave. She forgave him. The father was distraught with contrition. And now their marriage was stronger than ever.

But if she had been about to tell me something like that she seemed to change her mind. The misty look cleared from her eyes.

She returned to the present.

"It'll take time for all the hurt to go away," she said. "You can't expect it to just disappear instantly. But, given time, it really will go."

"I don't know, Mum," I mumbled. "This feels all wrong."

"In what way?" she asked.

"I don't know . . ." I sighed. "There's no feeling of . . . of . . . of *triumph*. Of victory. And I still feel angry with him."

"It's fine to still feel angry with him," she said. "And you have plenty of right to feel angry with him. But talk it over with him. Maybe you could both go for marriage counseling. But don't let the anger blind you to everything else. After all, this is the father of your child we're talking about. If you can't swallow the anger on your behalf, think about Kate. Do it for her. Are you going to deprive your child of her father just because you're angry?"

She ended on a very impassioned note.

And before I could respond she was off again.

More impassioned invective.

"And as for wanting to feel triumph or victory at getting him back. That's so empty. So hollow. It really *is* childish to want to be a winner in this. There are no winners or losers in a situation like this. If you get your marriage back in working order then you will be a winner. You *will* be victorious!"

She should get a job writing speeches for revolutionaries. This was stirring stuff!

"All right," I said a bit doubtfully, "if you're sure."

"Oh I am," she said confidently. "Your marriage was very good for a while. Fair enough, you encountered problems. And they weren't dealt with very well. But you've probably both learned from this."

"I suppose," I said.

"And it just goes to show that you can't have been as bad as he makes out if he wants you back." She grinned.

But I didn't find it funny.

I was still finding it hard to believe that I had been that difficult at all.

Who was it that said, "Be careful what you wish for. You might get it."

And some saint or other said, "There are more tears caused by answered prayers than unanswered ones."

I could see what they meant.

I had been so hurt. I had loved him so much. And I had wanted James and my marriage and my old life back. And now that I had it, I wasn't so sure what all the fuss was about in the first place.

Why?

I was being given my marriage back, but first of all I had to accept that I was immature and difficult and selfish. And that I had been a burden to James. And I was finding that very, very difficult. I mean, I knew it must be true. There was no other reason for him to have left me. But if I wasn't even sure what I was doing wrong, then how the hell could I possibly avoid repeating it?

I still felt great humiliation and hurt about his sleeping with that fat cow. But he wouldn't let me tell him. I felt as if I couldn't whine about it because it made me look selfish and immature. I couldn't win.

I knew I loved him. But I couldn't really remember what it was that I loved about him. He seemed so . . . so . . . so *pompous*. Was he always like that? So sort of humorless and wintry.

And what was the future going to be like?

Would I be afraid to make flippant remarks and tell him funny stories?

Would I be afraid to lean on him and feel taken care of, the way I used to, in case he felt alone and uncared for?

Our roles had been reversed.

And I didn't know how we should behave toward each other.

Everything would have to be relearned. It was very frightening.

What was wrong with the way it had been?

Well, plenty, obviously, if you listened to James.

But I had liked it like that. And I wasn't sure that it could work any differently.

However, there was only one way to find out. And that was to go back with him and try again.

I had to do it, if only for Kate.

It was worth trying. Because it had been so good.

But right now it was terrible.

I still felt so raw and angry and humiliated. I wanted to give him a smack every time he said how childish I was.

Fine then. Deep breath. Squaring of shoulders.

I would go back to London with him.

Kate was entitled to her daddy.

And I was going to get a chance to put things right.

Funny. You want something so badly it hurts. And then you get it, but it needs so much restoration and renovation and knocking down of walls and rewiring of electricity and new plumbing put in that you think, fuck it, I don't want it anymore. I'll settle for something a lot smaller, with no garden, but at least it's *finished*.

Mum was still sitting looking at me. Her expression was one of anxiety.

"It's okay, Mum. I *am* going to go back to him. I will try again."

There really didn't seem to be anything else to say.

I stood up and sighed. "I'd better call James and tell him that I'm coming back."

I went to the phone. I felt as if I was about to face a firing squad. I called the LiffeySide.

"James," I said when he answered, "I've been thinking about what we talked about and I've made a decision."

"Which is?" he demanded brusquely.

"I'll come back. I'll try again."

"Good," he said. I could hear the faint smile in his voice. "Good. We'll try harder this time, eh?"

"And no more Denise?" I asked.

"No more anyone, if things work out," he said.

I didn't like the veiled threat in that.

"James," I said nervously, "you know, I'm not finding this easy. I still feel betrayed and hurt. And that won't go away immediately."

"No," he agreed in his ultrareasonable tone. "Maybe not immediately. But you must work on getting rid of those feelings, mustn't you? There's no future in this if you can't forgive me."

"I know," I said, almost sorry that I had mentioned it.

Then I took a deep breath.

"You were wrong too, weren't you?"

"I've already admitted that," he said coldly. "Are we going to have to go through this every day for the rest of our lives?"

"Well, no . . . but . . ." I said.

"But nothing," he said. "It's in the past now. We have to forget it and look to the future."

That's a lot easier for you than it is for me, I thought. But I didn't say it. There was no point. It was getting me nowhere.

"Well, when should I reserve the tickets for going back to London?" he said, breaking my resentful silence.

"Oh James, I don't know. I'll need a couple of days to get everything sorted out," I said.

The thought of leaving was horrifying.

"Claire, I can't wait a couple of days more," he said irritably, "I've got a lot of work to do at the moment."

"Well, aren't you lucky that I agreed to come back to you in just two days?" I asked bitterly. "What if I'd put up a fight and it had taken you a whole week to convince me?"

"Now, Claire," he said smoothly, "there's no good in thinking like that. I have convinced you. That's the main thing."

A pause.

"I *have* convinced you, haven't I?" he asked. And if I hadn't known better, I'd almost have said that he sounded uncertain.

"Yes, James," I said dully, "you've convinced me."

"It'll be fine," he said, "you'll see."

"Yes," I said, feeling far from sure, but I didn't have the energy or the inclination to disagree with him.

"James, you might as well go back to London right away," I suggested. "I'll come early next week with Kate."

"Why will it take you a whole week?" He sounded annoyed.

"Well . . . I've got people to say good-bye to . . . and things . . ." I faltered.

"I'd prefer if you came sooner," he said sternly.

"No, James, really, I'm sorry, but . . . I need time to adjust," I said weakly.

"Just so long as you don't change your mind," he said with what sounded like a forced guffaw.

"I won't," I said wearily, knowing that I couldn't. "I won't."

"Good!" he said. "Well then, I suppose I'll head back to London immediately. If I go to the airport now I'll be able to pick up a flight. I wonder if I can get a refund on tonight's accommodation?"

"What a pity I didn't make up my mind and tell you sooner," I said. "It's probably too late now to get your money back for tonight."

"Never mind," he said kindly, "it couldn't be helped."

What an asshole!

I was being totally sarcastic!

"I'll call you tonight when I get home," he promised.

"You do that," I said quietly.

"Give my love to Kate," he said.

"I will."

"And see you soon."

"Yes, see you soon."

thirty-one

"So when are you leaving?" asked Mum.

"You're *leaving*?" screeched Helen.

"Yes," I mumbled, aware of how weak and pathetic I must look in her eyes.

"I think you're crazy," she exclaimed.

"But Helen, you don't understand . . ." I struggled to explain to her. "It wasn't his fault. He had a really hard time with me. I was so demanding and childish. And he couldn't cope. So he looked elsewhere out of desperation."

"And you believe that?" she asked, sneering in disgust. "You're crazy. It's bad enough that he was sleeping with someone else, but for him to blame it all on you, well, that's just totally *crazy*. Have you no self-respect?"

"Helen, it's more important that self-respect," I insisted, desperately trying to convince her. Maybe if I convinced her, I might even convince myself.

"He's the father of my child. And we were happy together. Very happy"—because we had been—"and if we work at it, we can be again."

"So how come you look so miserable?" she demanded. "Shouldn't you be happy? The man you love is taking you back. Even though he was unfaithful to you."

"Helen, that's enough," said Mum in a warning tone. "You can't understand. You've never been married. You've never had a child."

"Well, I certainly never want to, if it turns me into a total basket case like her," she stormed, looking at me with contempt.

"You're *crazy!*"

And she thumped out of the room.

Silence followed.

"She has a point," Mum eventually said.

"What do you mean?" I asked listlessly.

"Well, you don't seem very, well . . . *happy* exactly. You're not having second thoughts, are you?"

"No," I sighed. "I'm not. I owe it to all of us to try again. But I feel it's all wrong. I feel manipulated. I feel kind of steamrollered by him. As though he wasn't going to take no for an answer. I sort of feel as though I'm lucky to get him back. Yes, that's how he makes me feel. *Lucky!*"

"But aren't you lucky to get a second chance? Not every woman does," said Mum.

"No, not that sort of lucky," I said, desperate to make her understand, to understand myself. "He makes me feel I'm lucky even though I don't deserve it. As though he's being nice to me even though he doesn't have to be. But because he's a good person. Out of the goodness of his heart. Or something. I don't really know. But it does feel wrong."

"But he is being nice to you," she said, seizing on the one important thing to her.

"Yes, but . . ."

"But what?"

"But . . . but . . . he's being nice to me, but like you'd be nice to a naughty child who was very bold but that you've now decided to forgive. And although I'm lot of things, I'm not a naughty child."

"You're probably just paranoid," she said, trying to be helpful.

Thanks, Mum!

"It can't have been easy for him, coming back, eating humble pie, admitting that he was wrong."

"But that's just it! He didn't eat humble pie. He barely admitted that he was wrong."

"Claire, your nose is probably out of joint. He didn't arrive back in floods of tears with a whole shop's load of red roses, he didn't beg you to take him back," she suggested.

"It would have been nice," I admitted.

"But flowers count for nothing. And love does," she said.

"Yes," I agreed despondently.

"I feel like he has me trapped now," I burst out, finally, realizing exactly how I felt. "I've got to be perfect all the time or else he'll leave me again. I can't say a word against him because it'll just prove that I'm only thinking of me. I feel I should be so grateful to be back with him that I can never dare complain about anything ever again. That he can misbehave any way he likes and I have to keep my mouth shut."

"Well, now, you don't have to put up with any more nonsense from him," blustered Mum. "Any suggestion of another woman and come back here immediately."

"Thanks, Mum."

"But in the meantime, be glad you have another chance. And give it a go. Try your best. And I bet you'll be pleasantly surprised."

"I'll try," I promised.

After all, what had I left to lose?

"One other thing," she said a bit awkwardly.

"What's that?"

"I'm not sure that I should tell you."

"What! What aren't you sure that you shouldn't tell me? Tell me, for God's sake," I demanded.

"Well," she said, looking sheepish, "that Adam called."

Adam!

My heart gave a lurch. Or it might have been my stomach. Sure as anything *something* lurched.

"When?" I demanded breathlessly. I felt excited, dizzy, happy. You know, the way James should have been making me feel.

"A few times," she admitted, looking very sheepish indeed. "Yesterday morning. Yesterday afternoon when you were asleep. Last night when you were out."

"Why didn't you tell me?"

"I didn't think you needed any distractions while you were sorting things out with James," she said humbly.

"You should have let me be the judge of that," I said, annoyed.

A thought struck me.

"You didn't tell him where I was last night, did you?" I asked quickly.

"Yes," she said, sounding defensive, "I said you were out with your husband. Why shouldn't I? It was the truth, wasn't it?"

"Yes, but . . ." I trailed off.

What did it matter now? I was going back to London. I was going back to James. No more Adam.

But I had to see him. I had to say good-bye. I had to thank him for being so nice to me. For making me feel so beautiful and desirable and interesting and special.

"Did he leave a number?" I asked hopefully.

"Er, no," she said, looking away shamefacedly.

"Maybe he'll call again," I said, a bit frantically.

"Maybe," she agreed doubtfully.

What *had* she told him?

"And if he does, I want to talk to him, do you hear?" I told her.

"No need to bite my bloody head off," she muttered.

True to his word, James called me later on Tuesday evening to say that he had arrived back safely. Had I set a date yet for my return?

"No, not yet," I said weakly, "but soon, I promise."

"Just make sure it is," he said with a suggestive leer in his voice. Which actually made a spasm of dread—fear, almost— run through me. The thought of sleeping with him, having sex with him again, was not a pleasant one.

As soon, as I—gratefully—hung up on James, the phone rang again.

It was Adam!

Beautiful, tall, kind, funny, sweet Adam.

"Hello, Claire," he said in his gorgeous voice.

"Hi, Adam." I felt so happy to hear him. I felt all girlie and giggly and tingly and simpery.

"I hear congratulations are in order," he said in a cold, hard voice.

It was a bucket of cold water on my warm delight at hearing from him.

"Wh . . . what do you mean?" I asked. I was some hard-hearted bitch who had seduced him for the fun of it. Who had no real interest in him. Now that my husband was back I had no further use for him.

"Helen just told me that you're going back to London. Going back to James," he said accusingly.

"Well, that's right," I said apologetically. "I feel as though I must. You know, for Kate's sake."

"And what about for your sake?" he asked.

I wanted to burst into tears. I felt like telling him that I was thoroughly miserable at the thought of going back to that judgmental, sanctimonious pig.

As you can see, James was growing worse in my eyes with every second that passed. Adam was growing more desirable and attractive. I *ached* to be with him.

But I couldn't tell him that. I had to make a go of things with James. Wishing that I could be with someone else was not exactly productive.

"I'll be okay," I told him.

"It certainly looks that way," he said bitterly.

I felt too ashamed to say anything.

"And what about my sake?" he demanded. "What about me? Didn't Sunday night mean anything to you?"

"Of course it did," I said.

"Well, it can't have meant very much if less than two days later you're going back to another man," he said bluntly.

"Adam, it's not like that . . ." I tried desperately to explain. "I've got to . . . I've got to give it another chance."

"Why? He was horrible to you," Adam pointed out.

"Yes, but . . . you see, it wasn't really his fault."

Adam gave a bark of humorless laughter.

"So whose fault was it, then? Don't tell me. No, please don't tell me. He said it was *your* fault," he said.

"Well, yes, but you see—"

"I just don't believe it," he interrupted angrily. "You're an intelligent woman—a *very* intelligent woman—and you let this idiot put you down.

"What did he tell you?" continued Adam, in full flight. "Let me see. He needed sex while you were pregnant but you couldn't oblige? Hmmm? Was that it?"

"No," I said in a little voice.

"Or that you were far too focused on the impending baby

and he felt ignored and crowded out and had to go elsewhere for affection?"

"No, not that either," I told him, thankful that he hadn't come across the right reason yet.

"It's pretty obvious that you're not going to tell me exactly *why* it's your fault," he stormed, "but you can be damn sure that it's *not* your fault. Why are you letting him manipulate you like this?"

And well you might ask, I thought. Good point. Why *was* I letting him manipulate me like this? Oh, yes, I remember.

"Because it was so good once that it's worth trying again," I told Adam. But it sounded insincere and feeble, even to me.

"And Adam," I continued tremulously, "I really had a lovely time with you. You made me feel beautiful and special and worthwhile again."

"Anytime," he said sarcastically.

"Oh, please don't be angry with me," I said sadly. "I'm really sorry. I really am. I've got no choice. I've got to do this."

"You do have a choice," he said.

"I don't," I replied. "Apart from anything else, what about Kate?"

"So you're going to go back to some awful relationship with a man who doesn't respect you or care for you just because of Kate," he said.

"He does care about me," I protested.

"He has a funny way of showing it," said Adam.

"Look, is there any chance we can be friends?" I asked Adam, trying desperately to salvage something from all this unpleasantness.

"No."

"Why not?" I asked frantically.

"Because I can't believe I'm talking to the same woman I was with on Sunday night. I thought that one was intelligent and had self-respect and knew what she wanted."

"I *am* intelligent. I *do* have self-respect," I said almost in tears. I had to convince him. I didn't want to lose him. I knew that there could be no romance with Adam. Not now. But I still thought he was wonderful and I wanted so badly to be his friend.

"Anyway," he sighed, "I can't be friends with you. Because

I want so much more from you. And I bet you couldn't be friends with me either. We're too attracted to each other."

"Well, if we can't be friends, then we can't be anything," I said. It was killing me, but I had to say it. I couldn't go back to James while I still carried a torch for Adam. A clean, honest break was less painful in the long run.

But I was hoping to call his bluff. Because I wasn't prepared for what he said next.

"Then we can't be anything," he said stiffly.

Panic swept over me.

At the tone of his voice. At the realization that he was so disappointed in me. At the thought of never seeing him again.

"Can I have your phone number?" I blurted out.

I couldn't *bear* the idea of just ending things with him now. I was clinging on, hoping that he might be nice to me.

Hoping that if he said he was still my friend, it would prove I was doing the right thing.

"No," he said in a voice that brooked no argument.

"Why not?" I asked, brooking an argument anyway. Whatever that means.

"Because what would you need it for?" he asked.

"To call you," I said.

"What would you want to call me for?" he asked.

"To talk to you," I said, almost crying. "I don't want to lose you."

"Claire," he sighed, "don't be stupid. You've made your decision. You're going to London to live with another man. You can't have us both. There's no *point* in you calling me to talk to me. We're not going to be friends. End of story."

"There's really nothing else I can say, is there?" I said sadly, realizing that I wasn't going to get what I wanted. He was not going to give me his blessing.

Why on earth should he?

"No," he said.

"I've let you down, haven't I?" I asked.

"You've let yourself down," he said coldly.

"I've disappointed you, haven't I?" I said, unable to stop myself from rubbing salt into the wounds.

"Yes, you've . . . disappointed me," he said after a little hesitation.

"Well, um . . . take care," I said, feeling foolish. Wanting to say so much. But being unable to say anything except platitudes.

"I will," he said.

"I'm sorry," I said, feeling wretched.

"Not as sorry as I am," he said.

And he hung up.

I stayed standing by the phone for a while. Feeling like my heart was breaking. And feeling terrible fear. Had I made a terrible mistake?

Was I standing at a turning point in my life? Was I really important to Adam?

But did it matter? Because I had decided on the direction I was going in.

But was it the right one?

How could I know?

My head was spinning. I felt frightened and out of control.

Two possible lives were being offered to me. The one with James. And maybe one with Adam.

Was I throwing the wrong one away? Had I misunderstood my destiny? Was the break-up with James meant to happen so that I could meet Adam and be a lot happier? Had I been given pain so that I would grow strong?

Had I misunderstood all the signs?

Had I gotten everything wrong?

But it was too late. I had made my decision. And I was going to go through with it. I'd make myself crazy if I kept changing my mind.

My future was with James. Adam no longer existed in my life.

I was probably just a good lay for Adam. Well, I liked to think that I was a *good* one. But maybe it was just about sex.

But, then again, maybe it wasn't.

What should I do then?

I had to get over him. I would get over him.

Of course I would.

I had only known him about three weeks.

It's just that, well, you know . . . he had an effect on me. He touched me in an unexpected way. He made me feel like taking care of him. He made me feel special and wonderful in a way that James no longer did.

Hey! Maybe this was all just down to my rampaging ego. James no longer made me feel good about myself. So I latched on to the next available man who did make me feel good.

But, in all honesty, I really didn't think that was it.

Adam was special.

Adam and I were special.

Although not anymore.

Adam despised me now. For my stupidity in buying James's crappy explanation. And for the speed with which I left his bed and went off with someone else. Even if that someone else was my husband.

It really hurt that Adam thought so little of me. Although I didn't blame him. I didn't have a lot of respect for myself either.

thirty-two

After the conversation with Adam on Tuesday, I worked hard at forgetting him. Every time I thought of him, I blanked it out. I tried to think of nice things, like the buzz of London. And the comfort of getting back to my own apartment. And how nice it would be to see all my friends again. And how interesting it would be to think about getting back to work. And how pleasant it would be to be back in a city where every second shop sells shoes.

And things would work out with James. I should be so happy. I had been granted everything that I'd absolutely *ached* for in the first month or so after he had left.

My life was going to be made all better. As though James's little indiscretion had never really happened. Hopefully I could just edit out these three months or so and carry on as planned. Kate was going to have her daddy. I was going to have my husband. We would restart our old life. And, if I had to take care to be quieter and less giddy and more serious and solicitous of James's happiness and peace of mind, then that was a small price to pay.

I was sure that if I worked at it, it wouldn't be as awful as it sounded. I'd learn my new personality. It'd be good for me. And the dread that I was feeling would pass.

And, of course, some of the sadness that I was feeling was the wrench of leaving my family. Bad and all as they were, I'd kind of grown used to them over the past weeks. Their anarchic version of family life seemed infinitely more desirable than the calm, ordered existence that lay ahead of me with James.

I'd miss them. I'd miss Mum, I'd miss Dad, I'd miss Anna. Hell, I might even miss Helen.

But maybe not.

I was finding this difficult. I still got terrible surges of anger and feeling mistreated by James. It was hard to resist the urge to pick up the phone and tell him what a selfish bastard he was. That he had no right to make me feel as if everything that had happened was all my fault. That I wasn't a bad person. That I wasn't even a selfish person. Or an immature one. But then I envisioned how he would respond to my rage. He'd be all rational explanations and condemnations. And I would feel even worse. More frustrated. As if I'd let myself down even more.

The one thing that made me able to contain all this rage was the realization that somewhere, somehow—entirely inadvertently, mind you—I had been wrong. The words that he said that night in the Italian restaurant kept echoing in my head: "If I'd been happy, why would I have left you?"

So I had no choice. I had to accept that it was my fault. He wouldn't have left me, he wouldn't have taken the terrible step of having an affair, of thinking that he was in love with someone else, if it hadn't been my fault.

James was not a womanizer. James was not a frivolous person. James thought long and hard—too bloody long and hard, if you asked me—about everything. He didn't do foolish and disruptive things just for the fun of it. He must have had no choice. He must have been at the end of his tether.

Things would be okay. Eventually things would get back to normal with James. It would just take a bit of time.

I was doing the right thing.

I finally decided that I would return to London the following Tuesday.

That would give me enough time to pack. But more importantly, to prepare myself to let go of my resentment against James, to be positive about my attitude to him.

On Friday afternoon, after two frantic days of packing clothes into a suitcase and then later finding them hanging in the back of Helen's closet, removing them from the wardrobe, repacking them into the suitcase and then a few hours later rediscovering them under Helen's bed, repacking them, etc., I decided to call James at work to tell him what time my flight was getting in on Tuesday. It was very odd. He had called me at least once a day since Tuesday, making inquiries as to when I would be getting back. He seemed almost . . . *anxious* to see me. As though he was afraid that I wouldn't return. Of course, the nasty cynical part of me decided that he hadn't had either sex or his washing done since he moved out of the place with Denise and it was no wonder that he was awaiting my return with some anticipation.

But at the same time, it was unusual to feel wanted or needed by him. After the dismissive and patronizing way he had treated me while he was in Dublin, when he had given me the impression that he was doing me a favor by taking me back.

Now, although he was doing a good job of hiding it, he seemed insecure and uncertain of me.

But he needn't have worried.

I was going back.

I might not want to. But I was coming back.

I called and got his office. Some man answered and said "No, I'm afraid Mr. Webster isn't in the office just now."

Now we all know what happens here. This is the part in the book when the disembodied voice continues and says, "No, Mr. Webster has gone to the abortion clinic with his girl-friend Denise" or "No, Mr. Webster has taken the afternooon off to go home and sleep with his girlfriend Denise silly" or something similar. And where I whisper "Thank you. No, there's no message" and hang up with shaking hands and cancel the tickets back to London.

However, nothing of the sort happened. The disembodied voice asked, "Who's calling please?"

I had to think about that one for a minute.

Who *was* calling? Then I remembered.

"Oh, er, it's his wife," I said.

"Claire!" exclaimed the man, being ultrajovial. Probably to hide his awkwardness. "How are you? George here. Great to hear from you."

George was James's partner. And his friend as well. And,

I suppose, in his macho, beer-drinking way, he was a friend of mine also.

George was a nice man. If you took certain characteristics of George as given then you would probably get along very well with him. For example, I wouldn't malign the man by saying that he played rugby. But there was no getting around the fact that he did watch it.

But he was kind. I liked him, and his wife, Aisling, was a good laugh. We had all got drunk together on many an occasion.

"Hello, George," I said, feeling a bit embarrassed.

This was the first time that I had spoken to him since the breakup and I found that I didn't know what to say. Should I refer to it or not?

Should I pretend that nothing at all had happened? That everything was fine?

Or maybe I should just brazen it out. Deal with it head-on, as it were, by trying to turn it into some kind of joke, with rueful, self-deprecating remarks? Perhaps say "Hi, this is Claire. But you can call me Denise if it's easier to remember."

I realized that I was going to find myself in this kind of situation very often for the first couple of weeks after I returned to London.

God, it was going to be humiliating.

But George rescued me by launching straight into it.

"So, you're coming back to him." George laughed. "Well, thank God for that. We might get a decent day's work out of him now."

"Oh," I said politely.

"Yes," continued George with great joviality and bonhomie. Which made me suspect that he had had a long and liquid lunch. Well, let's be fair. It was Friday, after all. "How can I put it, Claire? Let's just say that it hasn't been easy. I mean, you know what he's like. Finds it hard to talk about his feelings—well, don't we all, I suppose—and too proud for his own good. But a blind man can see how much he loves you. And it's been obvious just from looking at him that he's been devastated without you. Devastated! What! Don't talk to me about it! All I can say is it's a blessing that you took him back. We'd have had to fire him otherwise." Big bellow of Three Beers at Lunchtime laughter from George.

What on earth was George saying?

He wasn't . . . he couldn't be . . . surely he wasn't *laughing* at me, was he?

Hot angry ashamed tears filled my eyes.

Had I become a public laughingstock?

Was everyone having a good laugh at my expense?

Yes, yes, okay, to be honest, I admit that in different circumstances I'd have been the first one to laugh at a deserted wife welcoming her errant husband back into the fold with such grateful haste. And I would be a fool if I thought that people wouldn't privately snigger at how pathetic I was being by taking James back so blithely.

But I couldn't believe that George was being so openly mocking. I was well aware that James hadn't been devastated without me. And George was aware that I was aware. Well, he *must* have been. I knew that they were both men, but surely they must occasionally have discussed something other than football and cars.

But George was usually so nice. I didn't understand why he was joking about what had happened between James and me. Why was he being so cruel?

I felt so hurt. But I couldn't cry. I had to stand up for myself. Nip this in the bud. Because if I didn't everyone would think they had the right to make fun of me.

"Really?" I said with thick sarcasm to George.

Trying to convey in one word that, although James might have treated me with a total lack of respect, it didn't make me some kind of public target. James could treat me badly—well, he couldn't, but you know what I mean—but it didn't give anyone else the right to make fun of me.

The nerve of George! And to think that I had always liked him.

But George didn't respond to my "Really?"

Well, he certainly didn't seem to take any offense.

Because he continued good-naturedly. "I'm no expert on relationships, but I'm so glad that the two of you have sorted this whole sorry mess out. All I can say to you is fair play for forgiving him. It must have been awful for you. But I suppose when you saw the state of him—a bit like the living dead, wasn't he?—you realized just how sorry he was."

My head felt as if it was growing tighter with confusion.

What was going on?

Was George making fun of me?

I wasn't so sure that he was. He *sounded* sincere.

But if he wasn't mocking me, then what the hell was he talking about?

What did he mean "living dead"? Were we talking about the same James? The same sanctimonious, judgmental James who came to see me in Dublin?

But before I could gather together my confused thoughts, George was off again.

He was in the mood to talk. Friday afternoon boredom and three beers at lunchtime had obviously loosened his tongue.

"Now, Claire," he said, mock stern, "I hope you were a sensible girl and didn't forgive him straightaway. I hope you held out for at least a couple of serious pieces of jewelry and a holiday in the Maldives."

"Are you joking?" I thought in bewilderment. "I was lucky that he took me back at all. I nearly had to promise *him* the jewelry and the holiday."

"Um . . ." I said.

But George kept talking.

"He loves you so much and he thought he had no hope at all, do you know? He thought that you wouldn't have anything further to do with him. And, in a way, who could blame you?"

"George!" I interjected forcefully. I had to establish just what was going on! "What are you talking about?"

"About James," he said in surprise.

"You're saying that he was *sorry* that he and I split up?" I asked.

"Well, 'sorry' is one way of putting it," said George with a little laugh. "Devastated would be a better word in my opinion."

"But how do you know?" I asked faintly, wondering where George was getting his information from. Because it was obvious that he had been sorely misled.

"James told me," he said. "We do talk now and again, you

know. It's not just women who have the monopoly on frank and open discussions!"

"Yes, but . . . I mean, are you *sure*?"

"Of course I am," said George indignantly. "He was tortured by the thought of being without you. Tortured! He kept saying to me, 'George, I love her so much. How can I get her back?' and I just said to him, 'James, tell her the truth. Tell her you're sorry.' He was driving me crazy!"

"Is that right?" I stammered.

That was all I could manage to say. My head was spinning. This was nothing like what had actually happened.

So what was going on?

"And Claire," said George in a sympathetic tone, "I know it must have been very hard for you. But I'm sure it was very hard for James also. Because you know how he hates to be wrong. Let's face it, he very rarely is. So for him to admit that he'd made a terrible mistake, and then to apologize for it, must have been damn near impossible for him. Although, having said that, I'm sure you feel that if you hear the word *sorry* ever again you'll puke. You must be *sick* of hearing it!"

Another bellow of laughter from George.

By now I was sure that George wasn't making fun of me. That this wasn't some kind of elaborate and cruel trick. George sounded very serious. But I couldn't understand why his version of events was so different from the one James had presented to me.

I wasn't sick of hearing the word *sorry*. I would have dearly loved to hear the word *sorry*. But I didn't think I would have recognized *sorry*—certainly not from James's lips—if it jumped up and bit me.

But I had to pay attention because George was off again.

"The weird thing was that James always thought that you'd be the one to have an affair and not him."

"Why's that?" I asked. Although I kind of knew what he meant. I was always perceived as the rowdy one and James as the Goody-Two-Shoes.

"Because you've always been the party animal," said George. "The lively, charismatic one. And James never thought he was good enough for you," continued George. "Never! Always afraid that he was too serious and boring for you. Us accountants don't have an easy time with the women, you know. They think we're not exciting enough, would you believe?"

"I never knew that James thought he was too serious and boring for me," I said faintly.

"Come on now," said George disbelievingly. "Wouldn't you agree that of the two of you, you're usually the life and soul of things?"

"Yes," I tentatively agreed, desperate to keep George talking.

"And James!" George laughed. "Well you couldn't find a better bloke but at the same time he wouldn't exactly be surrounded by people and keeping them all in stitches, now, would he?"

"No, I suppose not," I said. "But if I was to quiet down a bit, then maybe he wouldn't feel so boring."

"But what would be the point of that?" exclaimed George. "Then you wouldn't be you."

"I *know*," I thought frantically. "But that's what James wants me to do."

"Well, maybe James didn't enjoy living with someone as noisy and lively as me," I suggested to George. "Maybe I got on his nerves."

What I was doing was unforgivable. I was now blatantly fishing for information from George. I was encouraging him to shop his mate.

"Don't be so silly." George laughed. "Of course you didn't get on his nerves. He *did* find it difficult sometimes. But that was only his ego and his insecurity playing up. It can't always be easy living with someone who's a lot more popular than oneself."

"Oh," I said faintly. "I see."

And, do you know something? I think I did. I think I had started to understand.

Should I tell George that?

But I had to think about everything I had just heard. I couldn't listen to any more or my head would burst.

I started to ease my way out of the conversation with George.

"How come you're such an expert on relationships all of a

sudden?" I asked him teasingly. "You've gone all sensitive and new-mannish on me."

"Oh, er," he said, sounding both embarrassed and pleased, "Aisling bought me a book about it."

"I see." I laughed. "Well, thanks a lot, George, you've been a great help."

"Good," he said. "I'm glad. Everything will work out, you'll see."

"Oh no, I won't," I thought.

"James was threatened [self-conscious usage of relationship jargon from George] by your vitality. Instead of realizing that your liveliness complemented [more self-consciousness] his calmness," said George, who sounded like he was quoting from a psychology textbook.

"But you can grow from this crisis and"—slightly embarrassed pause—"redefine the parameters of your relationship."

"Wow, George," I said, desperate to get him off the phone. I wasn't sure how much longer I could sustain this conversation. "You certainly have got in touch with your emotions."

"Yes," he said shyly. "I'm even exploring my feminine side."

This would be hilarious if I wasn't feeling so confused and frightened.

"George," I said, "it's a pleasure to talk to such a sensitive man. You have a great understanding of the dynamics of James and me. It's not every man who would be so in touch."

"Thank you, Claire," he said proudly. I could almost hear him beaming. "I feel as though I've learned an awful lot. And I'm no longer afraid to cry."

"Good, good," I said heartily, terrified that he might offer to give me a demonstration there and then.

How could I get him off the phone without sounding as if I wasn't interested in his emotional growth? I thought desperately.

I found myself asking him another question.

"And do you care for and nurture your inner child?" I asked in a gentle voice.

"Er, what?" he asked, confused.

I had lost him. Aisling hadn't given him the sequel yet. "I haven't any children, Claire. You know that."

"I know," I said kindly. No point in pushing him too far and undoing all the good work that Aisling had done.

"George . . ." I interrupted, abruptly cutting short his lyrical descriptions of how it had all worked out for James because James had followed his advice and how happy James and I were going to be and—

"George," I repeated a bit louder. I managed to get his attention.

"So, George, let me see if I've got this right," I said to him. "James loves me. James always loved me. James felt insecure and afraid that he might be too boring for me. Have I got that right?"

"But you know all this," said George, sounding confused.

"Just checking," I said lightly.

George was still prattling on. Maybe I was imagining things, but could he have been talking about something called the male period?

But I could barely listen to him. I had far more important things to worry about.

Namely, why had James told George that he loved me frantically and was afraid of losing me and why had he told me that I was damn near impossible to live with but he would take me back as almost an act of charity?

Even a blind man could see that there was a slight discrepancy between the two stories.

He was either lying to George or lying to me.

And some little tickle of instinct somewhere told me that he had been lying to me.

I had to talk to him. I had to find out.

"George," I said, interrupting him again. "I need to speak to James. Will you ask him to call me? It's important."

"Yes," he said, "will do. He should be back in about half an hour."

"Thanks," I said. "Bye now."

And I hung up.

I sat trying to make sense of what George had inadvertently told me. So James had always loved me. And James felt threatened by my being, well . . . me, I suppose, for want of a better description.

Is that why he needed to have an affair with another

woman? And why did he have to tell me that it was all my fault? And why did he have to tell me that I'd have to change totally if our marriage was to have a future?

I wasn't sure what the hell was going on. But I did know one thing. Something was.

thirty-three

Just to make sure, I called Judy.

"Claire!" she answered, sounding delighted. "Are you back?"

"No, Judy, not yet," I said miserably.

Before she could say anything I went on talking.

"Look, Judy," I blurted out, "I need to talk to you about something."

"Talk away," she said. "Are you okay? You sound a bit agitated."

"I am, Judy," I said. "I'm agitated and confused and I don't know what's going on."

"What do you mean?" she asked gently.

"Well, you know that James and I have made up," I started.

"Yes," she said.

"Well, did you know that it was my fault that James had the affair?"

"What on earth are you talking about?" she said, sounding horrified.

"He told me that it was all my fault. That I was immature and selfish and demanding and inconsiderate and that he'd only take me back if I changed radically."

"He's talking about *him* taking *you* back?" said Judy in disbelief. "Claire, Claire, slow down a minute. There's something very wrong here."

Well, if Judy thought there was something wrong then I wasn't imagining it.

But I wasn't sure whether to be relieved or not.

"Now, Claire, can we start again please?" she asked. "James said that he was forced to have an affair because you were so difficult to live with. Have I got that right?"

"Yes," I said, feeling distressed. I admit that it sounded very spurious the way that Judy said it. James made it sound a lot more *reasonable*, somehow.

"And now he's saying that *he'll* take *you* back if you change?" she continued. "What way does he want you to change?"

"Oh, you know," I mumbled. "He wants me to be less of a party-giver. And less of a party-goer. Quieter. More considerate."

"Oh, I see," she said hotly. "He wants you to be a boring fucker like him, is that right? Or else he wants you where he can keep his killjoy little eye on you. What a shit!"

She paused. And then another thought struck her.

"And what kind of idiot are you? You mean to tell me that you *believed* this crap! Can't you see that it's the oldest trick in the book?"

"In what way?" I asked. Not wanting to hear.

"He has an affair. He realizes what a huge mistake he's made. He wants you back because he really loves you—any fool can see that—but he's afraid that you'll tell him to take a hike. So he makes out that it was all your fault so you feel guilty and then you feel grateful because, even though you were an awful person, he still wants you.

"And anyway," she said, drawing breath and launching into another furious speech, "I happen to know for a fact that he's lying."

"Oh?" I said. It was about all I could manage.

"Yes," she said. "Michael told me."

Michael being Judy's boyfriend. Michael being James's friend.

"About a month ago Michael went out with James for a couple of pints, well, more like a couple of dozen pints, but anyway . . . and James got plastered and wouldn't stop talking about you. Michael says that James is bonkers about you. That he always was. And that he was always much more in love with you than you were with him. And always thought that he was going to lose you. And he couldn't handle it. So with the pressure of the baby and all that he decided to throw in the towel. And took off with Denise, who, let's face it, couldn't believe her luck to land a catch like James."

"I see," I said evenly. "That's interesting, because George told me something very similar today."

"I can't *believe* you needed to hear this from George or me. Didn't you know that James was crazy about you? And totally insecure about you?"

Judy was obviously disgusted with me.

"And he's being so manipulative," she fumed. "Taking advantage of the situation just so he can get you under his thumb. Telling you it's your fault that he left you, and that if you're not the way he wants you to be, he'll leave you again. Typical!"

"Judy," I said, "I need you to be calm for a moment. This is very important."

"Oh, er, right," she said, sounding slightly embarrassed. "Look, when I said that he was a boring fucker I didn't mean . . ."

"It's okay, Judy," I said kindly. "I know you did, but it doesn't matter."

"You know how it is," she went on. "The heat of the moment and all that."

"*Judy,*" I said. "For Christ's sake! Forget it! I need to get this straight in my head."

"Sorry, sorry," she said. "Go ahead."

"James had an affair, but he said it was my fault. Right?" I asked Judy.

"So you say," she agreed.

"He should have apologized to me, but wouldn't. Right?"

"Um, right," said Judy.

"He has convinced everyone that he loves me. Except me. Right?"

"Right."

"He has hurt me, humiliated me, confused me, compromised me, lied to me, undermined me, made me apologize for being me. Right?"

"Right."

"And he won't apologize to me or comfort me. Right?"

"Right."

"I don't need a man like that. Right?"

"Right! But . . . er . . . Claire, what are you going to do?"

"Kill the fucker."

"No, Claire, go easy now," stuttered Judy.

"Oh relax, Judy," I sighed. "I'm not going to kill him. But I'm going to hurt him real bad."

"That's okay then," she said with relief. "He's not worth going to prison for."

"Thanks for your plain-talking advice," I said. "You're right. He *is* a boring fucker, isn't he?"

"*Completely*," she said with passion.

"I'll talk to you soon," I said. "Good luck. Bye."

So now what?

I supposed I'd better wait for James to call me.

But I was no longer confused. James had made me very, very angry. And I thought it was only fair that I should let him know. In person.

James called back a short time later. He seemed delighted that I had called him.

I could barely bring myself to be civil to him. My anger kept threatening to boil over.

"Claire, lovely to hear from you," he said.

"What are you doing tonight, James?" I asked brusquely.

"Um, well nothing," he said. I like to think that he was a little bit shocked by my abrupt tone.

"Good," I said. "Be in around eight o'clock. I need to talk to you."

"Er, what about?" he asked, sounding a little bit anxious.

"You'll see," I said smoothly.

"No, no, tell me now," he said, sounding quite a bit anxious.

"No, James, wait until tonight," I said pleasantly but very, very firmly.

He was silent.

"Eight o'clock tonight then, James," I concluded pleasantly.

"Okay," he muttered.

I hung up the phone.

Still thinking about what I had recently found out.

You know, I had *known* that I wasn't as bad as James had made me out to be. And really, that wasn't just because I didn't want to believe that I was a bad person. Although I *didn't* want to believe that I was a bad person, but . . . anyway, you know what I mean. I had had a feeling that James had been lying to me, or at least exaggerating greatly when he told me what a horrible, childish, selfish, inconsiderate bitch I had been throughout our marriage.

But I couldn't see what reason he had to lie to me about it.

And I had a feeling that he had tried to cut me down to size—well, at least to a size that suited him—by telling me that I had been such a person.

He hadn't liked my confidence. He had been frightened by it. So, in a nasty cynical way, he decided to completely undermine me so that I'd be dependent on him.

What a bastard.

You know, I think I'd hated him less when I found he had been having sex with Denise. This was a worse kind of betrayal.

"Mum," I called down the stairs.

"What?" she shouted from the kitchen.

"I need you."

"What for?"

"I need you to watch Kate tonight. And I need you to drive me to the airport."

"What on earth are you talking about?"

"I'm going to London. I need you to watch Kate," I said reasonably.

"Is it Tuesday already?" she asked in confusion.

"No, Mum, today is Friday. But I'm still going to London."

"And will you be going again on Tuesday?" she asked, looking a little bewildered.

"Maybe," I said. I couldn't answer her. I didn't know myself whether I would or not.

"What's this all about?" she asked suspiciously.

"I've got some things to work out with James," I said.

"I thought you had worked things out with James," she said, reasonably enough, I suppose.

"So did I," I said sadly. "But other—what shall I call it—
evidence has come to light in the last hour or so, so I have to
go and see him."

"When will you be back?" she asked.

"Soon," I promised. "Please, Mum, this is important. I need
your help."

"Oh, all right then," she said, sounding a bit nicer. "Take
as long as you need."

"It won't be more than a day or so," I said.

"Fine then."

"I'll need to borrow money."

"Don't push your luck."

"Please?"

"How much do you need?"

"Not much. I'll put the flight on the card. But I'll need
money for incidentals. You know, subway fares, brass knuckles, the usual."

"So long as I get it back by next week, I can give you fifty."

"Fifty is plenty," I said.

Well, I hoped it would be. I had no idea where I would be
sleeping tonight. But something told me it wouldn't be in my
double bed in London with James.

Never mind. I had an ex-boyfriend or two who had never
really gotten over me. So I would at least have a roof over
my head.

As well as an erection in my back.

I dressed to kill.

I thought it would be appropriate.

But not as you might have expected, in battle fatigues, a
hard hat with a net with leaves in it and a couple of rounds
of ammo slung across my chest. Oh no, I wore a sexy, short,
black skirt with a black jacket and sheer stockings and high,
high heels. I would have worn a little black pillbox hat with
a veil if I'd had one. But luckily I didn't.

I wanted to look like a killer bitch from Hell. But in retrospect I suppose the hat would have been overdoing it.

I would just have looked like one of those glamorous wid-
ows who look beautiful at graveside but whom the townspeo-
ple hate because they suspect her of killing her husband and

inheriting the money that he had intended to leave to the town to build a new hospital.

Mum looked a little bit taken aback at my dramatic appearance as I came down the stairs but took a look at my determined, angry face and thought better of commenting on it.

"Are we ready?" I asked.

"Yes," said Mum. "I've just got to find the car keys."

I sighed. This could take *days*.

While Mum was running in and out of rooms and emptying handbags onto the kitchen table and feeling around in coat pockets and muttering to herself like the white rabbit (it *was* the white rabbit, wasn't it?) in *Alice in Wonderland*, the front door opened and Helen arrived with her usual pomp and ceremony.

"Guess what?" she yelled.

"What?" I answered. Surly. Uninterested.

"Adam has a girlfriend!"

The blood drained from my face and my heart nearly stopped beating. What was she talking about? Had someone found out about me and Adam?

"And wait until you hear!" continued Helen, sounding delighted. "He has a baby!"

I stared at her. Was she serious?

"What kind of baby?" I managed to ask.

"A *baby* baby, a girl baby," said Helen scornfully. "What did you expect? A giraffe baby? God, sometimes I worry about you!"

My head was spinning. What did this mean? When had all this happened? Why hadn't Adam told me?

"But is it a new baby or what?" I asked. I didn't even try to keep the desolation from my voice, but Helen, with her customary sensitivity, didn't seem to notice.

"No," said Helen. "I don't think so. She doesn't look like Kate. She has hair and she doesn't look like an old man."

"Kate doesn't look like an old man!" I said hotly.

"Yes, she does." Helen laughed. "She's bald and fat and hasn't any teeth."

"Shut up!" I said viciously. "She'll hear you. Babies can understand these things, you know. She's beautiful."

"Keep your panties on," said Helen mildly. "I don't know what you're so touchy about."

I said nothing.

This was all a terrible shock.

"It was hilarious," continued Helen. "Adam brought the girl and the baby into college and half my class are talking about killing themselves. And he can forget about passing any of Professor Staunton's exams. The look she gave him! I swear to God, she *hates* him."

"So, um, hadn't you met this girl before now?" I asked, trying to make sense of this. Had he been going out with her while he was leading me on? Well, he must have been. You don't just go out and buy a baby with hair in a supermarket. These things take time.

"No, we hadn't," said Helen. "Apparently they had some big fight ages and ages ago and he hadn't seen her or the baby for a long time. But now they're all reunited."

Helen began singing at the top of her voice. Some awful song about being reunited and it feeling so good. She waltzed up the stairs, still singing.

"Wait!" I wanted to shout after her. "I'm not finished. There's lots more that I want to ask you."

But she went into the bathroom and slammed the door shut behind her. I could still hear her singing, but it was a bit fainter now.

I stood in the hall, feeling desolate.

"I can't think about it now," I told myself. "I must forget it. I'll think about it some other time when everything is different. When I'm happy and things are worked out. But not now."

I forced myself to stop thinking about it. I went to the room in my brain where all my thoughts about Adam lived and disconnected the electricity and boarded up all the doors and windows, so nothing could get in or out.

Obviously it was very unsightly. There were bound to be complaints from the neighboring thoughts. But I had no choice. I was trying to sort out my marriage, one way or the other, and I could do without any distractions.

Mum eventually found the keys to the car. Kate, Mum and I piled in and we drove to the airport. We didn't speak. I could tell that Mum was itching to ask me what was going on. But thankfully she kept her mouth shut.

It was miraculous, but I really did stop thinking about Adam. I was so upset and angry about James that I suppose there just wasn't any room in my head left to worry about anything else. My worry arena was packed to capacity with thousands and thousands of thoughts worrying about James. And there wasn't even standing room left for any thoughts that might have hoped to get in and worry about Adam.

Unfair, perhaps. But it was on a first-come, first-served basis.

Leaving Kate was awful, but I had to do it. It wouldn't have been right to bring her. I believe it has a terrible effect on children if they happen to witness their mother murdering their father.

I kissed Kate good-bye at the departure area. "See you soon, darling," I said.

I hugged Mum.

"Can I ask you just one thing?" she said anxiously, inspecting my face for any imminent explosions of rage.

"Go on," I said, trying to sound nice.

"Has James gone back to that Denise woman?" she asked.

"Not that I know of." I smiled bitter reassurance at her.

"Thank God," she said, breathing out with relief.

Oh dear. Poor Mum. If only she knew. Denise wasn't a problem. But there *was* a problem. A problem that was much bigger than Denise. And, hey, that was really saying something.

Honestly, wouldn't you think that by now I might have begun to forgive and forget? Wasn't it time that I stopped being nasty about Denise?

It's just that it was so easy.

I turned on my sexy high heels and tried to march purposefully across the departure area. It wasn't easy to be purposeful when I kept colliding with all kinds of easygoing people who stood around chatting, surrounded by suitcases and bags, rest-

ing their elbows on their carts, as if they had all the time in
the world. As if this wasn't an airport at all and nobody had
a flight to catch. Certainly not one departing in the next decade
or so.

I tried briskly to reserve a flight to London.

But it wasn't possible.

The pleasant, laid-back Aer Lingus rep would only allow
me to make my reservation in a relaxed, easygoing fashion.

In between a discussion on the Russian presidency (isn't
the drink a scourge?) and a chat about the weather (let's hope
the dry spell lasts), I just happened to get myself a standby
on a flight leaving shortly for London.

There were no problems at all. Which I thought was an
awful waste because it wasn't often that I was in a filthy mood
and able to stand up for myself and insist on my rights and
cause trouble and all that and today would have been just
ideal to do it.

I was all fired up for a good fight.

But everybody was so decent and accommodating and it
all went beautifully.

Damn it.

It was ten minutes past five.

The flight was uneventful.

It would have been great if the important-looking business-
man beside me had tried to talk to me, or even better, tried to
flirt with me, just so that I could take full advantage of my
bad mood.

Honestly, I was so childish. I was just *itching* for a chance
to say something mean. I thought I might like to experiment
with a Joan Collins–type voice. You know, all posh and scary,
my words sounding like pieces of ice dropping into a glass.
And say something like, "I really wouldn't bother trying to
talk to me. I'm in a very bad mood, and I'm not sure how
long I can be polite to you."

But apart from giving me a vague "Sorry" as he fumbled
around my hips for his seat belt, he totally ignored me. He
just opened up his impressive-looking leather briefcase and in
no time at all had his nose buried in a Catherine Cookson
novel. I'm sure you know it. It's the one about the illegitimate

girl with the wine-colored birthmark, whose cousin falls in love with her, who gets scourged with a riding crop by her stepmother and raped when she is thirteen by the lord from the Big Hall and, while escaping from him, gets her foot caught in a rabbit trap and has to have it amputated and the wound cauterized by a red-hot poker while her screams echo throughout the slag heaps.

Or is that all of them?

Anyway, the man was far more interested in Catherine Cookson than he was in me and that made me a bit fidgety. I was dying to exercise my bad mood. Limber up, as it were, for the real nastiness that I'd be involved in later. But nothing doing.

And then I felt ashamed of myself and tried to strike up a conversation with him, smiling above and beyond the call of duty at him when he passed me my food tray, gently offering to open his little container of milk for him when he ran into difficulties, giving him my mint to bring home to his little girl, even though he ate his own—that kind of thing.

He turned out to be a lovely man. We discussed the book he was reading. I recommended a couple of other writers to him. And by the time we landed at Heathrow, we were on first-name terms. We shook each other's hand, said that it had been a pleasure to meet each other and warmly wished each other a safe onward journey.

Then I was on my own again. On my own with my thoughts and fears and anger.

Apart from the ninety billion other people in Heathrow I was completely alone in London.

Now if this was a film instead of a book, you'd be shown shots of red buses and black cabs passing the houses of Parliament and Big Ben, and policemen with funny hats directing traffic outside Buckingham Palace and smiling girls in very short skirts standing underneath a "Welcome to Carnaby street" sign.

But as this is a book, you'll just have to use your imagination.

Heathrow was, well . . . it was busy. That's one way of putting it.

It was totally crazy.

I couldn't believe that there were so many people. It was like a Renaissance painting of the Day of Judgment come to life.

Or like the opening ceremony at the Olympics.

People of all nationalities, with all manner of exotic outfits, rushed past me, speaking every language under the sun.

Why was everyone in such a *hurry*?

And the noise was deafening. Announcements over the loudspeaker. Small boys lost. Grown men lost. Expensive luggage lost. Patience lost. Tempers lost. Marbles lost. You name it and there was a good chance that it was lost.

I had forgotten that London was like this. There was a time when I would operate at this kind of speed with the greatest of ease. But I was now on Dublin tempo so I had slowed down and kicked back and chilled out. I stood in the arrivals area, terrified, looking like a hick from the sticks, feeling overwhelmed by the number of people, feebly apologizing as people bumped into me and tisked loudly at me.

Then I pulled myself together. This was only *London*, after all.

I mean, I could have been somewhere really scary.

Like Limerick, for example. Sorry, no, only joking.

And everywhere I looked, *everywhere*, were small clusters of businessmen. Standing around in their nasty suits, either waiting for their bags or waiting for a flight, their briefcases that were probably full of porn mags by their feet.

They were all drinking beer, out-glad-handing each other, determinedly exuding "nice-guyness" and bonhomie, having competitions to see who could laugh the most uproariously and who could make the most disparaging remark about his wife or the most vulgar remark about any of the women at the conference they had just been to or were just about to go to. "I wouldn't throw her out of the bed for farting" and "Nah, her tits are too small" and "Everyone's had her, even the guys in the mailroom" drifted over to me from the various groups.

I wonder what the collective noun for a group of businessmen is? Surely there's got to be one.

A conference of businessmen? A briefcase of businessmen? A meeting of businessmen? A polyester of businessmen? A pinstripe of businessmen?

It's no good. None of those words really conveys the *nastiness* of the little groups. How about an insincerity of businessmen? A disloyalty of businessmen? An infidelity of businessmen?

I caught a man from one of the groups leering over at me. I looked away hastily. He turned back to the four or five men he was with and said something. There was a big burst of laughter and they all started bending and stretching and craning their necks to get a good look at me.

The bastards! I wanted to kill them!

And they were all so unattractive and nondescript. How dare they be so arrogant about me? Or any woman, for that matter. They should be grateful that any woman would touch them with a stick. Fuck them! I thought furiously.

Time to leave.

I had no bags to collect. I wasn't planning on staying long enough to need them. So at least I was spared the carousel hell.

I took a deep breath, squared my shoulders, set my jaw firmly and started to push through the arrivals area. I was heading in the direction of the subway station, determinedly making my way through all the other human beings, like an Amazon explorer hacking his way through dense undergrowth.

I finally got to the station. Japan was obviously holding its national census there. After waiting for what seemed like several years while the sons of Nippon figured out how to operate the ticket machines—I thought they were all supposed to be technological wizards?—I bought myself a ticket and boarded a train for central London. Funds didn't run to a taxi. The train was full and every nation on earth had a representative on it.

I don't need to go to an Emergency Council meeting of the United Nations. I've already been there.

The journey was so crowded and uncomfortable and unpleasant that in a way it was a godsend. Even if I hadn't already been feeling totally homicidal before I got on the train, there was a good chance that I would be when I got off.

A fellow passenger was kind enough to take my mind off my forthcoming antler-locking with James by pressing his erection against me every time the train turned a corner.

And at about ten minutes to eight I arrived at my station.

thirty-four

When I came out of the station and onto the road where I lived, my stomach gave a sudden lurch. Everything was so achingly familiar, the newsagents, the launderette, the liquor store, the Indian takeout restaurant.

In one way I felt that I'd been away for light-years, but in another I felt that I'd never left. I started to walk toward my apartment, my heart pounding, my knees feeling peculiar and kind of trembly.

I was surprised. A bit shocked.

I hadn't expected to be so affected by being back in my old neighborhood. When I came around the corner and saw my apartment, the home that I had shared with James, my forehead started to prickle with sweat.

I walked slowly, reluctantly.

Now that I had arrived I didn't really know what to do.

I just wished that I wasn't there. That I didn't have to be there.

"Do I have to have this confrontation?" I asked myself wildly. "Maybe I'm wrong. Maybe James really does love me as I am. Maybe I should just turn around and go back home and pretend that everything is fine."

I stood at the entrance door to the apartment house and leaned my burning face against the cool glass. I wasn't so angry now. I wasn't angry at all. I felt afraid and so, so sad.

A taxi came around the corner. It had its light on. Hope

surged through me. I could hail it and just get out of here, I thought. I don't have to go through with this.

Let this cup pass from my lips.

Speaking of cups, I thought, my mind wandering. I really must remember to pick up some of my bras while I'm here. Now that my tits had—regrettably—returned to their normal size, all the bras that I had in Ireland were too big for me.

This momentary lapse of concentration was fatal and I watched the taxi drive past me.

I wasn't leaving, it seemed. Not just yet, in any case.

I was going to see James and find out what was going on.

Remind me again why I'm here—oh yes, I remember. Because James had lied to me. Lied about the fundamentals of how he feels about me, about the essence of our relationship.

I started to feel angry again. That was good. The whole thing wasn't quite so nightmarish when I felt angry.

I took a deep, shaky breath.

Should I ring the doorbell and give James a slight warning that I had arrived? Or should I just march on in like I owned the place? When everyone knows that I only owned half the place. But then I thought, dammit no, it's my home. I'm going to let myself bloody well in.

My hand was shaking as I fumbled around in my bag for my bunch of keys. It took me ages to get the key in the lock.

The familiar, evocative smell of the entrance hall hit me in the pit of my stomach. It smelled like home. I tried hard to ignore it—this was no time for sentimentality.

The elevator delivered me to the second floor. I reluctantly walked down the corridor to my front door. When I heard the noise of the television coming from my apartment my heart sank even further. It meant that James was home. Now there really was no getting out of it.

I let myself in and, with an attempt at nonchalance, strolled into the front room.

James nearly died of shock when he saw me.

In a perverse way I would have been glad if I had caught him up to no good. Maybe in the throes of bondage with a fourteen-year-old girl. Or even better, a fourteen-year-old boy. Or better still, a fourteen-year-old sheep.

It would have meant that I wouldn't have had to confront

him. I could have walked away from him, knowing that he was a terrible person. No room for any doubt. All neatly tied up. No loose ends.

But, contrary bastard that he was, he couldn't have looked more wholesome and innocent if he had been rehearsing all day. He was reading the paper. Even the mug beside him contained Coke and not alcohol. Clean as a goddam whistle.

"Cl . . . Claire, what are you doing here?" he gasped, leaping up from the couch. He looked as if he had seen a ghost. In fairness, it must have been a terrible shock. As far as he knew I was hundreds of miles away in another city.

But at the same time, under ordinary circumstances, he should have been a *bit* glad to see me. Surprised delighted, instead of Shocked horrified. If he really loved me and didn't have a guilty conscience and had nothing to be afraid of, or to feel ashamed about, wouldn't he have been just over the moon to see me? He looked nervous. You know, edgy, watchful. Wondering why I had come. He *knew* something was wrong.

And with a jolt I realized that I hadn't been imagining things. Something was badly amiss. I had only to look at James's face to know.

I can't be sad now, I told myself. I can let myself be heartbroken and go to pieces later, but for the moment I have to stay strong.

"Gr . . . great to see you, Claire," he said, sounding horrified. He seemed a bit hysterical.

I looked into his white, anxious face and I felt such a surge of anger that I wanted to bite him. I *wanted* to feel angry. I wanted anger to course through me.

Anger is good, I told myself. Anger keeps the pain away. Anger empowers me.

I looked around the front room. I smiled graciously at him, even though I was shaking. "The place looks nice," I told him pleasantly. I was surprised that my voice wasn't trembling. "I see you've moved your books and records and stuff back. And . . ."

I pushed past him and marched into the bedroom and flung open the closet. "I see you've moved all your clothes back also. *Very* cozy."

"Claire, what are you doing here?" he managed to ask.

"Aren't you glad to see me?" I asked, all coquettish and simpery.

"Yes!" he exclaimed, "Of course, it's just . . . I mean, I wasn't expecting you . . . you know . . . I thought you were going to call."

"I know exactly what you thought, James," I said, fixing him with a judgmental stare.

I must say, in spite of the feeling of impending doom, I was starting to enjoy this.

There was a little silence.

"Is something wrong, Claire?" he asked cautiously.

He looked frightened. From the moment James had watched me walk into the apartment, he knew that I hadn't come on a mission of love. He was acting far too guilty and scared.

Maybe he had already spoken to George and knew that I knew about his duplicity?

Maybe he had been expecting some kind of showdown?

But at least he wanted to discuss whatever was wrong.

That had to count for something, didn't it?

Maybe it was all going to be fine.

Or was I just too pathetic for words?

"Claire," he said again, a bit more urgently, "is something wrong?"

"Yes, James," I said sweetly, "something is wrong."

"What is it?" he asked, watching me warily.

"I had a very interesting conversation with George today," I said idly.

"Did you?" asked James, trying to appear unflustered. But a spasm of something—fear maybe? or could it be annoyance?—passed over his face.

"Hmmm," I said, inspecting my fingernails, "yes, I did actually." There was a pause. James stood watching me, the way a mouse watches a cat.

"Yes," I continued in a very casual tone, "and he gave me a very different version of events concerning you and me."

"Oh," said James, and swallowed heavily.

"Apparently you've always loved me," I said. "And apparently the only problem you've had with me was that you were afraid that I'd leave you."

James was silent and sullen.

"Is that right, James?" I asked sharply.

"You wouldn't want to take any notice of George," he said, recovering his aplomb somewhat.

"I know that, James," I replied smoothly, "so that's why I rang Judy. And, guess what, she told me exactly the same thing."

More silence.

"James," I sighed, "it's about time you started to tell me what's going on."

"I have," he muttered.

"No, you haven't," I corrected him loudly. "You had an affair with another woman, you left me the day I gave birth to your child, then you decided that you wanted me back. But instead of telling me that, you had to manufacture a whole pack of lies and malign me and call me selfish and childish and inconsiderate and stupid." (Voice going up several decibels here.) "And instead of apologizing for the lousy way you treated me, you made out that it was all my fault." (Voice continuing to rise.) "And you decided that you'd browbeat me into being something other than what I am. Some meek little woman who wouldn't answer you back. And wouldn't overshadow you. And wouldn't make you feel insecure!"

"It wasn't like that," he protested feebly.

"It was *exactly* like that," I shouted. "I just can't believe that I was fool enough to believe your ridiculous story!"

"Claire, you've got to listen to me," he said, sounding bad-tempered and irritated.

"Oh, no, I do not," I corrected him angrily. "Why do I have to listen to you? Are you going to try and tell me a whole lot more lies?

"Well, are you?" I shouted when he didn't answer.

I sat and looked at him, willing him to speak, willing him to make everything all right.

"Convince me," I begged silently. "I want to be wrong. *Tell* me I'm wrong. Please explain it to me. I'll even settle for an apology. Just an apology will do."

He slowly sat down on the couch with his face in his hands.

And, even though I was expecting some kind of reaction, it still gave me a little jump to realize that he was crying.

Jesus! What was I supposed to say to him?

I hate to see a grown man cry.

Actually, that's not true at all.

Usually, there's nothing I enjoy more than seeing a grown man cry. Especially if I'm the one who made him cry. That feeling of power! You just can't beat it.

If he was crying it must mean that he was really sorry that he'd been so horrible to me and that everything was going to be fine.

He was going to apologize.

He was going to admit that he was completely in the wrong.

My heart started to soften.

But then he looked up at me and I couldn't believe the expression on his face. He looked so angry! "That's just typical of you," he shouted.

"What?" I asked faintly.

"You're so bloody selfish," he yelled, all traces of the tearful man magically vanished.

"Why?" I asked, baffled.

"Everything was fine!" he shouted. "Everything was all worked out and we were going to start again and you were going to try and be mature and a bit more considerate. But you just couldn't let it lie, could you?"

"But what was I supposed to do?" I asked meekly. "George tells me one thing and you tell me something completely different. George's story is a lot more believable than yours. Especially when Judy confirmed it."

I was trying very, very hard to be reasonable. I could see how angry James was and it was frightening, but at the same time, I was trying to stand my ground. Please God, I prayed, give me the strength to stand up to him. Don't let me end up taking the blame for everything again. You know, just for once, it would be nice not to be a wimp.

"Well, of course you'd believe George and Judy," he said nastily. "Of course you want to believe nice things about yourself. You just couldn't take the truth from me, could you?"

"James," I said, struggling to stay calm, "I just want to get to the bottom of things. I just want to know why you told George that you really loved me and that you were afraid that you'd lose me, and why you told me that you could barely tolerate me. It just doesn't add up!"

"I told you the truth," he said sulkily.

"So what was it you told George?" I asked.

"George got it wrong," he said shortly.

"And did Judy get it wrong also?" I asked coldly.

"I suppose," he said offhandedly.

"And Aisling and Brian and Matthew got it wrong too?"

"They must have," he said carelessly.

"Look, James," I said earnestly, "be reasonable. They can't *all* be wrong, can they?"

"They can," he said abruptly. "They are."

"James, please, you're a logical man," I said, starting to feel desperate. "Can't you see that *someone* isn't telling the truth? And didn't you think that sooner or later the different stories would get back to me? Don't you know that my friends and I discuss everything?"

He said nothing. He sat on the couch with his arms folded and looked at me defiantly.

Jesus! It was like pulling teeth.

Right! I'd try again. No matter what happened I would stay calm. I would try not to kill him. I would try not to be angry. I would try not to hurt him the way that I wanted to. I would swallow my pride one more time. I would make it clear that I would forgive him for the affair. This was not easy, let me tell you.

Especially when, at the same time, I was trying to stand my ground and not be completely bullied by him.

I was trying to bear in mind that there was a fine line between being understanding and being a doormat, between standing up for oneself and being a crazed ax-woman.

"James," I said, miraculously managing to sound calm, "we really have to try and straighten this out. If I ask you questions, will you just answer me yes or no?"

"What kind of questions?" he asked suspiciously.

"Well, like did you lie to me when you told me that it was my fault that you left me?"

"You mean that you want to sit here and interrogate me?"

he said, outraged. "You must be joking! Who the hell do you think you are? You're trying to make me out to be some kind of criminal!"

"James," I said. I was on the verge of tears of frustration. "I'm not! Really, I'm not. I'm just trying to get you to talk to me, to tell me what you really feel, what's really going on. I want you to be honest with me. Otherwise we won't have a future."

"I see," he said nastily, "so you want me to say something like 'You're a wonderful person, Claire, and I don't know why I had an affair because you're so great.' Is that what you want to hear?"

"Yes," I thought.

"No . . ." I said weakly. "It's just—"

"You want me to take all the blame, is that it?" he said, raising his voice. "You want me to be the bad guy, the 'man you and all your friends love to hate,' is that it? After all I've done for you? Is that what you want?" he ended on a shout, his face close to mine.

"But you are the bad guy," I said, bewildered. "You were the one who had the affair, not me."

"Oh Jesus!" he shouted, *really* shouted, this time. "You'll never stop harping about that, will you? Trying to make me feel guilty about it. Well, I don't feel guilty, right? I've been so good to you always. Everyone knows that. I am not the bad person here. You are!"

Silence followed. The room reverberated with it.

I sat very still. Feeling shell-shocked.

James exhaled hard, angrily, and started pacing the room. He didn't look at me.

I realized that I was shaking.

Am I a bad person? I asked myself.

Am I really?

A little voice in my head told me not to be ridiculous. This had gone far enough. I had to hold on to what I knew to be the truth. James was the one who had had an affair. Not me. I didn't force James to have an affair. He chose to do it. James told me that I was almost impossible to love, but he told everyone else that he loved me very much.

James wanted me to take the blame for *his* affair.

As I sat there trembling, my head swimming, something became very clear to me. Something that I hadn't seen before now. James did not want to admit, would not admit, that he was in the wrong. He could not accept that he had had an affair. Well, obviously, he knew he'd had one—I'd say the memory of Denise wasn't that easy to erase—but he didn't want it to be his fault.

A little time passed. Tension hung heavy in the air.

From James's reaction I realized that he was not going to admit, not in a million years, that he had lied to me and told the truth to George.

And I happened to believe George. I was sure he wasn't making anything up—quite apart from anything else, he was too stupid! And I was sure that James didn't think for one moment that what he said to George would get back to me. He thought he was perfectly safe in telling George that he loved me very much while telling me that it was hard for him to love someone as difficult and selfish as me. I knew James hated to feel insecure about anything. He hated to be vulnerable, even about his work, not to have total control. And he wanted to feel secure around me.

I still intended to get to the bottom of the great George/Claire contradictory stories controversy but this time I decided to try a different approach. On the one hand I felt like telling James to fuck off, that he was an irresponsible, immature, emotional cripple and that a child could see that he was trying to manipulate me. But on the other hand, it was obvious that he was afraid. Or confused.

Maybe he needed someone to voice his fears, because he was too frightened to do it himself, and then I could try to put his mind at rest.

This was worth one more try.

"James," I said gently, "there's no shame in loving me, you know. It's not a sign of weakness to love someone and sometimes feel insecure. It's human. There's nothing wrong with it. And if you told George that you loved me very much, there's no need to lie to me about it. I'm not going to use it as a weapon against you. And when you came to Dublin there was no need to pretend that you barely loved me. No one's going to condemn you for loving your wife, for God's sake. And as for the affair, you made a mistake. [This was extremely hard to say, believe me, but I said it.] No one is perfect," I continued. "We all make mistakes. You can be honest with me, you know. You don't have to play games to protect yourself. We can work all this out and have a real marriage."

I finished speaking. I was exhausted.

There was a pause. I hardly dared to breathe. James sat silently, looking at the floor. Everything hinged on this.

"Claire," he finally said.

"Yes," I said, tense, terrified.

"I don't know what kind of psycho-babble crap you're talking but it makes no sense to me," he said.

So that was it.

I had lost.

"I can't see what the problem is," he continued. "I never said I didn't love you. I just said that you'd have to change for us to go on living together. I said that you'd have to grow up. I said that you were so inconsiderate—"

"I know what you said, James," I interrupted. I decided to stop him before he delivered the entire speech again. He sounded as if he was reading from a script. Or as if he was a robot programmed to say these things—press a button and he was off.

As for me, I'd had enough.

No more humiliation for me, thanks very much. No more swallowing my anger. Honestly, I couldn't manage another mouthful. But it was delicious. Did you make it yourself?

"Fine," I said.

"Fine?" he said quizzically.

"Yes, fine," I agreed.

"That's good," he said, sounding paternal and smug, "but is it really? I don't want you bringing this up every couple of months or so and throwing it in my face."

"I won't," I said shortly.

I started to gather up my bag and newspaper with a lot more rustling and fuss than was necessary. I got to my feet and started to put on my jacket.

"What are you doing?" asked James, confusion written on his face.

I affected a startled and innocent face. "What do you think I'm doing?"

"I'm not sure," he said.

"I'd better tell you then, hadn't I?" I said smoothly.

"Er . . . well, yes," said James. It gave me a cold thrill to hear him sounding a bit anxious.

"I'm leaving," I said.

"Leaving?" he hooted. "What the hell are you leaving for? We've just worked everything out."

Then he started to laugh in relief. "Oh God, sorry," he said, "for a minute there . . ." He shook his head at his own silliness. "But of course, you've got to go back. You've got to get your things and bring back Kate. But I must admit that I was kind of hoping that you'd stay the night and we might get . . . um . . . reacquainted. Never mind. We can wait a few more days. So what time on Tuesday should I expect you?"

"Oh James," I said with a mock-sympathetic little laugh, "you haven't realized, have you?"

"Realized what?" he asked carefully.

"I won't be here on Tuesday. Or any other day, for that matter," I explained nicely.

"For God's sake, what is it now?" he bellowed. "We've just worked it all out and now you—"

"No, James," I cut in icily. "We've worked nothing out. Nothing at all. *You* may have worked something out—your image of yourself as a nice guy is good and intact—but I've sorted nothing out."

"But what have we been talking about for the past hour?" he asked belligerently.

"Exactly," I said.

"What?" he barked, looking at me as if I'd gone a bit crazy.

"I said 'Exactly.' Just what the hell *have* we been talking about?" I asked him. "Because for all the good it's done me, I might as well have been talking to the wall."

"Oh, we're back to you again, are we?" asked James nastily. "It's all you care about, you and your feelings and—"

That was it!

"Shut up!" I commanded, my voice coming out much louder than I had expected.

James was so shocked that he actually did shut up.

"I'm not listening to any more of your crap about what a terrible person I am," I shouted. "*I* didn't fuck someone else. *You* did. And you're so immature and selfish that you just can't own up to it and take the blame."

"*I'm* immature and selfish?" said James in astonishment. "*Me?*" he said, dramatically pointing in disbelief to his chest. "Me? I think you're slightly confused here."

"No, I'm bloody well not," I shouted. "I know I'm not perfect. But at least I can admit it."

"So why won't you own up to being selfish and inconsiderate in our marriage?" he asked, with an air of triumph.

"Because it's not true!" I said. "I *knew* it wasn't true, but I loved you and wanted to please you so I convinced myself that it had to be true. I thought if I could fix myself that I could fix our marriage. But there was nothing wrong with me. You were just manipulating me."

"How dare you?" he said, his face red with rage. "After all I've done for you. I've been a perfect husband!"

"James," I said with icy calm, "there is no doubt that you have been very good to me over the years. I think if you look back you'll find that it was mutual. We loved each other, it was part of the deal. But you seem to have started to believe your own publicity. Having an affair with another woman is not being good to me. You cannot justify it." There was a pause. For once James didn't have an indignant answer ready. "But," I continued, "you're not the first person to behave badly, to step out of line. It's not the end of the bloody world. We could have gotten over it. But you're too interested in looking squeaky clean and whiter than white. That's the choice that you've made."

I started toward the door.

"I can't understand why you're leaving," he said.

"I know," I said.

"Tell me why," he said.

"No."

"Why the hell not?" he demanded.

"Because I've tried. And I've tried. Why should you listen now when you haven't any of the other times? I'm not wasting any more time. I'm not trying any more."

"I love you," he said quietly.

The bastard.

He sounded as if he really meant it.

I bit my lip. This was not the time to weaken.

"No, you don't," I said firmly.

"I do," he protested loudly.

"No, you don't," I told him. "If you had loved me you wouldn't have had an affair—"

"But—" he interrupted.

"And," I continued loudly, before he started his speech again, "if you loved me, you wouldn't have wanted me to change into some wimpy woman who was afraid of you. If you loved me you wouldn't have tried to manipulate me or to control me. And most of all, if you loved me, you wouldn't be afraid to admit that you're in the wrong. If you loved me you could rise above yourself and your ego and apologize to me."

"But I do love you," he said, trying to hold my hand, "you've got to believe me!"

"I don't believe you," I told him, shrugging his hand away with disgust. "I don't know who or what it is that you love, but it certainly isn't me."

"It is!"

"No, James, it isn't," I replied, ultracalmly. "You just want some kind of moron you can control. Why don't you go back to Denise?"

"I don't want Denise. I want you," he said.

"Well, that's a pity," I said evenly, "because you can't have me."

The shock was a bit much for him. He looked like he'd been kicked in the stomach. You know—a bit like the way I had looked the day he told me he was leaving me.

Not that I desired anything as crass as vengeance, you understand.

"And do you know what the worst thing of all is?" I asked him.

"What?" he said, white-faced.

"The fact that you made me doubt myself. I was prepared to try and change the way I am, change *who* I am, just for you. You made me abandon all my integrity. You tried to destroy who I am. And I let you!"

"It was for your own good," he said, but without conviction.

I narrowed my eyes at him.

"Choose your next words very carefully, you asshole. They may be your last," I told him.

He went even whiter, if that was possible, and kept his mouth firmly closed.

"I'm never going to let myself be bullied ever again," I said with determination. I like to think that I had some of the grit of Scarlett O'Hara when she gave the "As God is my witness, I'll never be cold or hungry again" speech. "I'll always be true to what I know I am," I continued. "I'm going to be me, whether it's good or bad. And if any man, even Ashley, tries to change me, I'll get rid of them so fast they'll be dizzy."

James totally missed the *Gone With the Wind* reference. No imagination.

"I never tried to bully you," he said, all indignant.

"James," I said, starting to feel weary, "this discussion is closed."

"Well, never mind the past," he said, sounding anxious and hasty. "But how about—hey . . . how about if I promise that I won't bully you in the future?"

He sounded as if he had just hit on the most innovative and novel idea. Archimedes hopping out of the bath naked would have seemed restrained and reserved in comparison.

I looked at him with scornful pity. "Of course you're not going to bully me in the future," I said, "because you won't get the chance."

"You don't mean it," he said. "You'll change your mind."

"I won't," I said with a tinkly little laugh.

"You will," he continued to insist. "You'll never last without me."

Wrong thing to say, I'm afraid.

"Where are you going?" he asked, outraged, when he saw me picking up my bag.

"Home," I said simply. If I left now I'd catch the last plane back to Dublin.

"You can't go," he said, standing up.

"Watch me," I said. And did another one of those swivels that my heels were so handy for.

"What about the apartment? What about Kate?" he asked.

Well, it was nice to know where his priorities were, the apartment being higher up on his list than Kate.

"I'll be in touch," I promised with a pleasing echo of the words he had uttered to me that awful day in the hospital.

I walked toward the front door.

"You'll be back," he said, following me out to the hall. "You'll never last without me."

"So you keep saying," I said. "But don't hold your breath" were my last words before I pulled the door shut behind me.

I managed to get all the way to the subway station before I started to cry.

thirty-five

I can't really remember much about the subway journey out to Heathrow.

The whole thing passed in a daze.

I knew I had done the right thing. At least, I thought I had done the right thing. It was just that this was real life and no decision was clearly signposted. It's not like you take the right turning and you get everlasting happiness and you take the wrong one and your life's a disaster. In real life it's often almost impossible to tell which decision is the one you should make because what you stand to gain and what you stand to lose are sometimes—often—neck and neck.

How could I really know if I'd done the right thing? I wanted someone to come up to me with a gold cup or a medal and shake my hand and clap me on the back and congratulate me on making the right decision.

I wanted my life to be like a computer game. Make the wrong decision and I lose a life. Make the right one and I gain points. I just wanted to know. I just wanted to be sure.

I kept listing the reasons why there could be no future for me and James. James wanted me to be someone I wasn't. James wasn't happy with me the way I was. And I wouldn't be happy if I changed so that James was happy. And I wasn't happy with James's saint complex. If I took him back James would be happy because then James would think that I condoned everything he did. The way he already condoned everything he did himself. It would probably mean that at the first argument I had with James in our new improved marriage everything would split wide-open all over again. James was pompous and sanctimonious and James thought that I was flighty and immature. I was sure it was for the best that the marriage really was over now. It was just that there was always room for a little bit of doubt.

You know, I wondered if I had been nicer, if I had been stronger, more gentle, more forceful, more patient, sweeter, kinder, nastier, crueler, if I had laid down the law more, if I had kept my mouth shut more, would I have saved my marriage?

I was torturing myself with these thoughts.

Because, at the end of the day, I was the one who made the decision. I was the one who said that the marriage could no longer work. I knew that James hadn't given me much of an option, much of a choice, but I was still the one who'd pulled the trigger, as it were.

I felt so *guilty*.

And then I told myself not to be so silly. What James was offering me wasn't worth the paper it wasn't written on. It was only a sham of a relationship and it would have been entirely on his terms and it wouldn't have lasted a week. And if it had lasted, it would have been at the expense of my happiness. It would have just been a Pyrrhic victory.

Around and around went my thoughts as I rocked gently on the train, my head chasing its own tail.

God! I hated this business of being grown-up. I hated having to make decisions where I didn't know what was behind the door. I wanted a world where heroes and villains were clearly labeled. Where ominous music starts playing the minute the villain comes on-screen so you can't possibly mistake him.

Where someone asks you to choose between playing with the beautiful princess in the fragrant garden and being eaten by the hideous monster in the foul-smelling pit. Not exactly a difficult one, now, is it? Not something that you would agonize over, or that would make you lose a night's sleep?

Being a victim isn't very nice, but goddammit, it takes a lot of the confusion out of things. At least you know you're in the *right*.

And I suppose I was disappointed. Very disappointed. I had loved James once. I didn't know whether I did anymore. Or if I did, it wasn't in the same way. But a reconciliation would have been nicer than no reconciliation, if you know what I mean. A reconciliation that worked, that is. Not some kind of useless compromise.

And I was sad. And then I felt angry. And then I felt guilty. And then I felt sad again. It was a bloody nightmare!

One thing stopped me from going totally crazy. I realized that there was nothing stopping me from going back to James. Right then, that *minute*, I could get off the train and cross the platform and go straight back to the apartment and tell him that I had been wrong and that we should try again.

But I didn't.

And thick and all as I was, confused, bewildered, mixed-up, distraught, that told me something.

If I'd really loved him, really wanted to be with him, I would have gone back.

So I knew I was doing the right thing. I thought.

And off I'd go again.

Heathrow had calmed down a lot. Much quieter. It was lovely. I got on a practically empty flight back to Dublin.

I had a whole row of seats to myself so I was able to sniff and cry in discreet comfort should the urge take me.

The stewardesses were intrigued.

I kept catching little huddles of them looking at me worriedly.

They probably thought that I'd just flown to London for an abortion.

When I got to Dublin it was raining. The runway was slick and shiny in the dark. And the arrivals area was deserted. I walked past the silent carousels, my sexy high heels echoing on the tile floors.

I hadn't told anyone that I was coming back, so there was no one to meet me.

There didn't seem to be anyone there to meet anyone.

I spotted a lone porter. He was busy telling some bewildered man that to miss one flight was unfortunate but to miss two was careless.

I click-clacked past all the shuttered shops, the bureaux de change that stood in darkness, the deserted car rental stands. I finally got as far as the rain-soaked entrance.

There was a single taxi waiting outside in the wet night. The driver was reading a newspaper.

He looked as though he'd been there for several days.

He drove me home in unexpected silence. The only sounds were the swish of the windshield wipers and the noise of the rain drumming on the roof of the car.

We drove through the sleeping suburbs and he eventually deposited me outside my home. It was all in darkness. I civilly thanked him for the journey. He civilly thanked me for the sum of money I handed over. We said good-bye.

It was ten minutes past one.

I let myself in quietly. I didn't want to wake anyone.

Not out of consideration for them, I'm afraid. But because I didn't want to answer any of the inevitable questions.

I was longing to see Kate but she wasn't in my room.

Mum must have thought that I wouldn't be home and moved the crib into her and Dad's room.

But I ached to hold her. I missed her so much.

I tiptoed into Mum's room to take Kate, hoping desperately that I wouldn't wake Mum.

I rustled the child successfully. And then fell into bed, exhausted. Asleep with Kate in my arms.

thirty-six

When I awoke the next morning, I felt a tiny bit better. Not healed or cured or anything of the sort, but more prepared to wait. To wait for things to get better, to wait for the pain to go.

I had made the decision not to be with James and, being "Instant Gratification Girl," I wanted to feel wonderful immediately. I had wanted the fruits of my decision to fall into my impatient lap right now.

I wanted it to be "Out with the old and in with the new!" To throw off the trappings of my previous incarnation, to have not a jot of feeling left for James, not an iota of doubt, not a crumb of indecision. I wanted an immediate, miraculous transformation. I wanted the Relationship Fairy to touch me with her magic wand, to sprinkle me with her sparkling recovery dust, and for me to instantly forget everything I ever felt for James, to forget that he even existed.

I wanted to leave my grief under my pillow and for it to be gone in the morning. I wouldn't even have cared if there wasn't any money left in its place.

But there was no magic cure, there was no Relationship Fairy. I'd realized that a long time ago.

I had to get through this on my own. I realized that I had to be patient. Time would let me know if I had made the right decision.

I still didn't know if I had done the right thing by leaving James. But to stay with him would definitely have been the wrong thing.

See if you can wrap your mind around that one.

And if you get the hang of it, would you mind explaining it to me?

James called at eight o'clock the next morning. I declined to speak to him. And at eight-forty. Ditto. And at ten past nine. And ditto once again. Then came an unexpected lull until almost eleven, when there were three calls in quick succession. Ditto, ditto and ditto. Twelve-fifteen there was another one. Ditto. Five to one, five past one and twenty past one, all saw calls. Ditto, etc. Calls remained steady for most of the afternoon, coming every half hour or so. Then a final flurry came around six o'clock. Ditto re above.

Mum very decently fielded the calls all day. I have to say it, when the chips are down, that woman is worth her weight in Mars Bars.

Dad came home from work at twenty past six and at twenty to seven burst into the room where I was sitting with Kate and all the documents relating to the apartment and roared at me, "Claire, for God's sake, will you go and talk to him!"

"I've nothing to say," I said sweetly.

"I don't care," he bellowed, "this has gone too far. And he says he's going to call all night until you come and talk to him."

"Leave the phone off the hook," I suggested, turning my attention back to the deed of the apartment.

"Claire, we can't do that," he said in exasperation. "Helen keeps hanging the bloody thing back up."

"Yes, why should my social life suffer just because you married a lunatic?" came Helen's muffled voice from somewhere outside the door.

"Please, Claire," pleaded Dad.

"Oh, all right then." I sighed, putting down the pen I had been using to make notes with.

"James," I said into the phone, "what do you want?"

"Claire," he said, sounding cross, "have you come to your senses yet?"

"I wasn't aware that I had taken leave of them," I said politely. He ignored this.

"I've been calling all day and your mother says you don't want to talk to me," he said, sounding angry and put out.

"That's right," I agreed pleasantly.

"But we've got to talk," he said.

"No, we don't," I said.

"Claire, I love you," he said earnestly. "We have to work this out."

"James," I said coldly, "We've worked out as much as we can. And now we're at the end of the line. You think you're right. I think you're wrong. And I'm not wasting any more time or energy trying to convince either of us to change our minds. Now, I wish you well and I hope we can keep this civilized, especially for Kate's sake, but there really is nothing further to discuss."

"What's happened to you, Claire?" asked James, sounding shocked. "You were never like this before. You've changed so much. You've gotten so hard."

"Oh, didn't I tell you?" I said casually. "My husband had an affair. It kind of made an impact on me."

Very unkind, I know. But I couldn't resist it.

"Very funny, Claire," he said.

"Actually no, James," I corrected him, "it wasn't funny at all."

"Look," he said, starting to sound annoyed, "this is getting us nowhere."

"That's fine by me," I said, "because nowhere is precisely where we're going."

"Very witty, Claire. Very droll," he said nastily.

"Thank you," I replied with excessive sweetness.

"Now listen," he said, suddenly sounding all official and even more pompous than usual. I could almost hear papers rustling in the background. "I have a . . . um . . . proposition for you."

"Oh?" I asked.

"Yes," he said. "Claire, I do love you and I don't want us to split up, so if it makes you feel better I'm prepared to um . . . make . . . um . . . a concession to you."

"What's that?" I asked. I was hardly interested. I barely cared.

I realized, with a shock, that there was nothing, absolutely nothing, that he could say now to make things better.

I didn't love him anymore.

I didn't know why or when I stopped.

But I had.

James continued to speak and I tried to concentrate on what he was saying.

"I'm prepared to forget all about you having to change when you come back to live with me," he was saying. "You obviously feel very strongly about having to try harder at being mature and considerate and all the other . . . um . . . things we discussed. So if it means that you'll abandon this idea that we're splitting up, I can put up with you being the way that you were in the past. I suppose you weren't that bad," he said grudgingly.

Anger surged through me. I forgot for a moment that I no longer cared. I mean, the sheer *gall* of the man! I could hardly believe my ears.

I said as much.

"Are you glad?" he asked cautiously.

"Glad! Glad?" I screeched. "Of course I'm not bloody well glad. This makes it all even worse."

"But why?" he whined. "I'm saying here that I forgive you and that everything will be fine."

I nearly exploded. I had so many things to say to him.

"Forgive me?" I said in disbelief. "*You* forgive *me?* No, no, no, no, *no* James, you have it all wrong. If there's any forgiving to be done around here, it's me forgiving you. Except that I'm not."

"Just a minute . . ." James blustered.

"And this is supposedly the reason you had the affair with that fat cow. Me being immature and selfish. But you're prepared to overlook it now, at the drop of a hat. Yet it was important enough for you to be unfaithful to me. Make up your mind, James! Either it's important or it's not."

"It is important," he said.

"Well, then you can't overlook it," I said furiously. "If you want me to be a certain way and it's important, then what kind of relationship will we have if I can't be that way?"

"All right then," he said, sounding a bit desperate, "it's not important."

"Well, if it's not important then why did you have an affair because of it?" I said triumphantly.

"Can't we just forget it?" he said. I could hear panic in his voice.

"No, James, we can't. You might be able to, but it's not so easy for me."

"Claire," he pleaded, "I'll do whatever you want."

"I suppose you would," I said sadly. "I suppose you would."

I didn't want to bicker and argue and fight with him anymore. I couldn't be bothered.

"James, I'm going now," I said.

"Will you think about what I said?" he asked.

"I will," I agreed. "But don't hold out any hope."

"I know you, Claire," he said. "You'll change your mind. Everything is going to be fine."

"Good-bye, James."

In fairness, I *did* think about what James had said. I owed it to Kate.

The arguments in favor of and against reuniting with James went back and forth in my head like a tennis ball.

But the one thing I couldn't ignore, the one thing I couldn't argue my way out of, the one thing that I couldn't convince myself was otherwise, was the fact that I no longer cared about James.

I mean, I cared about him. I didn't want anything too terrible to happen to him. But I didn't love him the way I used to. I wished I knew what had caused this to happen. But it could have been so many things. He had had an affair—much as he'd like me to overlook it. That must have done a lot to destroy my trust in him. And my getting the blame for it, well, I wasn't too happy about that. Or it could be the fact that he wasn't man enough to own up to what he had done and just apologize? That went a long way in destroying any respect I might have had for him. Even now he wouldn't admit he was in the wrong. Even though he was scaling down his requirements of me, he was still making it sound as if he was doing me a favor.

He'd betrayed me. And then compounded it by treating me like an idiot.

Or maybe I'd just lost interest in short men.

I just knew one thing, if it was dead, it was dead. No one can resurrect love once it has breathed its last.

I called James two days later and told him that there would be no reconciliation.

"You're letting your pride get in the way," he said. As though he'd been briefed.

"I'm not," I said wearily.

"You want to punish me," he suggested.

"I don't," I lied. (*Of course*, it was nice to have the boot on the other foot.)

"I can wait," he promised.

"Please don't," I replied.

"I love you," he whispered.

"Good-bye," I said.

James continued to call, maybe twice or three times a day. Checking up on me, wondering if I'd changed my mind yet— if I had, as he put it, come to my senses.

I was nice to him on the phone. It was no skin off my nose. He said he missed me. I suppose he did.

I found the phone calls a bit irritating. It was hard to believe that only three months ago I would have killed to have gotten a call from him. Now it was more likely that I would kill if the calls *didn't* stop.

Then I stopped being irritated, and all I felt was sad.

Life is a very peculiar creature.

thirty-seven

I couldn't have said that I was happy. But I wasn't miserable. Or devastated the way I had been when James first left me.

I suppose I was calm. I had accepted that my life would never be the same again and would never be the way I had planned it. The things I had hoped for were never going to happen. I was not going to have four children with James. James and I would not grow old together. Even though I had always promised that my marriage would be the one that survived, the one that didn't break up, I could now accept, without too much heartache, that it *had* broken up.

Of course, I felt sad. Sad for the idealistic me, the one who had gotten married with such high, high, expectations. Even sad for James.

I really did feel older—and how!—and wiser.

I suppose I had learned—the long, hard way—a bit of humility.

I really had control over so little. Either in my life or in any other people's.

And if I heard someone say "Everything happens for a reason" or "When God closes one door, he opens another," it was no longer too difficult to stop myself from punching them in the face. Not difficult at all, in fact.

I didn't feel that my life was totally over.

Irredeemably altered, maybe. But not totally over.

My marriage had broken up, but I had a beautiful child. I had a wonderful family, very good friends and a job to go back to. Who knew, one day, I might even meet a nice man who wouldn't mind taking Kate on as well as me. Or if I waited long enough maybe Kate would meet a nice man who wouldn't mind taking me on as well as her. But in the meantime I had decided that I was just going to get on with my life and if Mr. Perfect came along, I'd manage to make room for him somewhere.

I did all the boring legal things that I should have done weeks ago. Well, maybe I shouldn't have done weeks ago. Maybe I wasn't ready then. Maybe now was the right time.

Either way it didn't make a bit of difference. The fact is they *weren't* done then and they were being done now.

I wanted custody of Kate. James said that he wouldn't fight it if he was given plenty of access to her. I was delighted because I wanted Kate to know her father. And I knew I was very lucky that James was being so reasonable. He could have been deliberately nasty and uncooperative and, in fairness to him, he wasn't.

James and I came to an agreement about the apartment. We decided to sell it. He was going to live in it until it was sold.

That was pretty dreadful, actually. When he received the documents from my lawyer he took it quite badly. I suppose he finally realized that it was over.

"You're really not coming back, are you?" he said sadly.

And even though I had instigated the whole thing, even though it was what I really wanted, I felt so sad also. I had a pang of intense regret. If only things hadn't turned out this way. If only things had never gone wrong.

But they had.

Tearful eleventh-hour reunions are the stuff of romance novels. They rarely happen in real life. And if they do, they usually occur when either one or both parties have had a few drinks.

No one showed any interest in buying the apartment for the longest time. In a way I was glad, because the thought of anyone else living in what I still considered to be *my* home was too awful to contemplate. But on the other hand, it was a real worry because money was so tight. I like to hold James responsible. He probably nabbed any prospective buyers and bored them to death with talk of tax relief on mortgages and suchlike. They probably fell asleep before they'd even seen the bedroom. But I shouldn't be so unkind. He meant well.

I spoke to my boss and told her that I'd be back in the saddle by early August. Now if I hadn't been feeling pretty miserable before this point, the reminder that I had to go back to work was nearly enough to tip me back over the edge.

Maybe I was in the wrong job, maybe I didn't have a true vocation, maybe I was just bone lazy. Well, whatever it was I wasn't one of those lucky people (although I just think they're weird) who get great joy from their job. At best I thought of it as a means to an end, at worst a hell on earth. And I couldn't wait until I retired. Only thirty-one years to go. Unless I got lucky in the meantime and died.

No, honestly, that was just a joke.

So, in five weeks' time, it was back to the office for me. Back to administering seven hours a day, five days a week, forty-eight weeks of the year.

Jesus!

Why couldn't I have been born rich?

Sorry, sorry, I know I shouldn't complain. I was lucky to have a job. It was just that I wished that I could have someone to take care of me and Kate. I was just fantasizing. Even if I had stayed with James I would still have had to return to work. It was simply that having to go back to work reminded me of how alone I really was now. How much responsibility I had. It was no longer just me that I was working for. A child was dependent on me.

I knew that James would provide for Kate—oh yes, I knew. Believe me, I knew it. And I had an expensive lawyer to prove it! Not that James was stingy or mean in any way. Credit where it's due, etc., etc. But the days when I could spend my entire month's salary on lipstick, magazines and alcohol had gone. Long gone.

Being grown-up is not all you're led to believe it is. Not even slightly. It was too late now but I wished I'd read the small print.

I found somewhere for Kate and me to live in London.

Well, actually, Judy did.

It would have been impossible for me to find somewhere

in London while I was still in Dublin. Not unless I was willing to pay the national debt in agency fees.

Some friend of a friend of a friend of Judy's was going to work in Norway in July and needed his apartment looked after for nine months. I could afford the rent and the area wasn't too awful. Judy had seen the place and assured me that it had a roof, a floor and the full complement of walls. Then Judy lied through her teeth and told the friend of a friend of a friend that I was neat and clean and quiet and solvent. I'm not sure if she even mentioned Kate at all.

Andrew—that was his name—called me to put his mind at rest that I wasn't some kind of maniac who would douse his precious home with gasoline and set it alight before he'd even reached Terminal Two.

On the phone I was at my most prim and proper. I emphasized that I felt that cleanliness should be joined at the hip with godliness and that I was in favor of bringing back the death sentence for burglars and litterbugs.

"Well, perhaps a public flogging would be adequate. It might thrash some respect back into them," he suggested.

"Hmmmmm," I said noncommittally, because I wasn't certain whether he was joking or not.

Andrew sent me a contract and I sent him all kinds of references and bank details and, most importantly, some money. (Borrowed from Dad—would I ever grow up?)

Over the next ten days or so we had detailed phone conversations about what I was to do with his mail. And which of his plants needed to be told jokes.

He gave me all kinds of useful advice.

He warned me that the woman downstairs was crazy. "That's fine," I said unguardedly, "I'll probably like her."

"And don't go to the first Chinese restaurant," he warned. "They got caught with a German shepherd in their freezer. The one farther up the street is far better."

"Thanks," I said.

"Use up anything that's left in the cupboards or liquor cabinet," he offered.

"Thanks," I said enthusiastically.

"And if anything goes wrong," said his disembodied voice,

"then don't hesitate to call me. I'll leave you a number that you can contact me at."

"Thanks," I said again.

"I'm sure you'll be happy here," he promised, "it's a lovely airy apartment."

"Right," I said, swallowing. "Thanks." I was trying not to think of my own lovely apartment, which I had decorated and designed and made beautiful over the years. Some day I will have another one, I promised myself. When the time is right.

I felt even worse when I realized that "lovely, airy apartment" is usually what real estate agents say when they mean the windows are broken.

Oh dear.

"I'll be in London briefly in October," he said. "I hope we can meet up then."

"That would be lovely," I said.

Nice guy, I thought as I hung up the phone.

For a neo-Nazi.

I wondered what he looked like.

thirty-eight

Men.

Ah, yes, men. I suppose the issue was bound to rear its ugly head sooner or later.

Now look, I want to make one thing clear. I didn't like this Andrew guy. It's just that he sounded nice (apart from the public flogging sentiment). And I was officially a single woman again and there were some thought patterns that I just slipped back into. I couldn't help it! It was obviously genetic. Or hormonal.

Anyway, I was only curious. It didn't hurt to wonder about these things. I wasn't planning on acting on it.

And it didn't mean that I was going to jump into bed with the first man who gave me the eye.

I mean, if I was that desperate for a man, wouldn't I have stayed with James?

Although I realize that after the way I behaved with Adam there's a good chance you won't believe me.

Okay, fine, you don't have to believe me, but Adam was an exception.

Adam was special.

So you heard that Adam had a girlfriend and a baby. Well, what do you think of that? Pretty sensational, eh?

I suppose it made sense. There was always a hint that there was more to him than met the eye. But I was kind of expecting his Terrible Secret to be something like a drug habit, or a minor prison sentence, or something with a little bit of notoriety, even glamour, to it. I certainly wasn't prepared for the news that Adam was a Family Man.

It was a shock. I'd go so far as to say that it was an unpleasant shock. But when Helen broke the news to me, I wasn't able to give it my full attention and indignation. I was a bit distracted, what with being on my way out to catch a plane to London to end my marriage and all that. No, it was definitely not good news, but I was too preoccupied to look it in the face and think about how I actually felt.

And I tried not to think about it in the following weeks.

Well, I had an awful lot of things to sort out and I couldn't afford to waste time daydreaming. And Adam and I, such as it was, had been over even before I found out about his baby, so there was nothing to be gained by thinking about him. Adam was the past.

Anyway, to be perfectly frank I didn't like thinking about Adam. It didn't make me happy. It was painful. If he accidentally strayed into my head, he didn't last five seconds, a bit like an overboard sailor in the icy waters of the Antarctic. Alarms would go off and a couple of burly security guards would be sent to throw him out double fast.

If he even crossed my mind, I was lucky enough to have some kind of incredibly complicated, tedious legal document to immerse myself in.

And Helen was around a lot. She was studying for her exams and causing no end of disruption, complaining bitterly and asking questions and talking about having to have sex with all her lecturers if she hoped to pass. So she took my mind off Adam. She took my mind off everything except slow-motion fantasies of brutal murders.

But it was June and the weather had suddenly become beautiful and hot. And sometimes when I was alone with Kate in the backyard, half asleep, the sun on my face, feeling so relaxed, when maybe I should have been thinking of James, instead my mind would accidentally drift Adam-ward and I would remember how sweet he had been and how lovely he had made me feel.

And at times like that, when my guard was down, I allowed myself to miss him, to feel sad that he wasn't there. But only for a moment. I didn't like to miss him. I didn't really like to think about him at all.

Let's face it, I didn't like what Helen had told me. It was not news that gladdened my heart. Or any other of my internal organs. It's not that I felt he had two-timed me. I was hardly in any position to object, what with me being married. And from what I'd managed to piece together from Helen's garbled narrative, I was fairly sure he was estranged from his girlfriend while he had his little fling with me.

If it's even worthy of being called a fling.

If I hadn't found it so unpleasant I'd probably call it the one-night stand that it so obviously was.

I think I felt a bit, oh, I don't know, *set up*, I suppose. Fool that I was, I had been flattered by all the attention that Adam had paid me. It had been wonderful to feel so desired and admired. Especially after what had happened with James.

And now I felt that he'd only wanted me because of Kate. Not that he wanted Kate, or anything sick like that. But he wanted me because I was a mother. I probably reminded him of his girlfriend. I didn't know what the setup with Adam and his girlfriend was, but if she had run off with the child, it must have been really hard for him and maybe I was some sort of replacement.

I felt, I felt . . . a bit mortified, I suppose. I had been thrilled that Adam had chosen me. But it wasn't really me that he had chosen at all. It was my circumstances.

I was hurt.

And I felt foolish for thinking that someone as gorgeous as him could seriously be interested in someone as ordinary as me. What could I have been thinking of?

The only thing I could say in my defense was that I wasn't myself. I'd been through a lot and my sanity was an infrequent caller.

But while we're on the subject of Adam I should admit that I was angry with him.

Not very. But a bit. I was pissed off with him for playing with my feelings. For making me feel special when I wasn't. And then for giving me that sanctimonious speech about going back to James. He had no business doing that if he didn't care about me. People have to *earn* the right to make me feel guilty.

It was something that I really should try not to give away as easily as I used to.

But as time passed and I spent more time dozing in the sunny garden, my feelings began to change. I started to see the other side of the coin. In fact, I started to feel downright metaphysical about it. Not something I was normally prone to.

It might have been the excess of sun.

Maybe Adam was sent to me for a reason, I thought. Adam made me feel so good about myself, Adam restored my confidence so much, that it probably gave me the strength to stand up to James. Maybe Adam's judgmental speech was even instrumental in helping me to make the right decision about James.

It would have been nice to think that Kate and I helped Adam to deal with the pain of being separated from his child and his girlfriend. Maybe we'd helped him to realize how important they were to him, depending on whether he had left them or whether they had left him.

It was so lovely to feel the bitterness leave me. I began to feel happy that I had met Adam. I felt that Adam and I had met for a short time for a special reason. It *had* to be short-lived. And I liked to think that both of us benefited from it.

This might well be a load of mystical, superstitious nonsense. But I wasn't normally the kind of person who sees signs and portents and reasons and explanations in events. On the contrary. As I said earlier, I was always making fun of people who claimed that everything happens for a reason. Of course, I wasn't as unkind as Helen, but at the same time I was far from indulgent. Oh, existentialism, thy name is Claire.

My usual approach would have been to say something like "Adam and I had sex because we both were horny. Nothing else to it." But I just couldn't be so cynical, hard as I tried.

Very worrying, of course, but what was I to do?

But it meant that lying out in the back garden was a lot more pleasant now. Every time I thought of Adam I didn't feel as if a knife had been twisted in my gut. Some kind of peace stole over me. I didn't need to feel let down, or lied to, or humiliated or foolish. It had been a pleasure to know him for the short time that I had. Perhaps it was better that way.

You know what it's like. Sometimes, you meet a wonderful

person, but it's only for a brief instant. Maybe on vacation or on a train or maybe even in a bus line. And they touch your life for a moment, but in a special way. And instead of mourning because they can't be with you for longer, or because you don't get the chance to know them better, isn't it better to be glad that you met them at all?

There was a very discernible feeling that a chapter had ended in my life. I started preparing myself, both emotionally and sartorially, for the return to London.

I began to pack clothes. I gathered enthusiastically and spread my net widely, visiting all wardrobes in the house, especially Helen's, and leaving no drawer unopened, no hanger unexamined.

Although I continued to bicker with everyone in the family, I knew that leaving them would be awful. It would be especially hard leaving my mother. Not just because she was so handy to have around Kate. No really, I mean it. I knew I was going to miss her terribly. It would be like leaving home all over again. Worse, in fact, because when I'd first left home seven years before, I was delighted to be going, couldn't leave fast enough in my haste to capitalize on my imminent freedom.

It was different now. I was seven years older and wearier. I knew that there was no novelty in ironing my own clothes, paying my own bills.

But I had to go back to London.

After all, my job was there. And I hadn't noticed anyone in Dublin breaking down my front door to offer me a job. Although I hadn't applied for any jobs, to be fair.

But more importantly, Kate's father was in London. I wanted her to see lots of him, to know that she had a father who loved her (well, I was sure he would when he got to know her better), and to grow up with a man in her life. Because if she was looking to me to provide her with a live-in father figure, I wasn't sure that I would be able to oblige. Maybe I would meet another man someday, but I didn't feel very hopeful.

And now that I thought of it, that threw up another entirely new set of worries. What if Kate didn't like the new man?

What if she got all jealous and threw tantrums and ran away from home? Oh God!

Well, I wasn't going to worry about that yet. It was jumping the gun slightly when I already had my hands full worrying about never meeting a man again.

I didn't mean it really. I wasn't *agonizing* about never having a man again.

Just mildly concerned.

I decided that I'd go back to London on the fifteenth of July. I could move into my new apartment and give myself and Kate a couple of weeks to settle in and find a babysitter before I went back to work.

Then, in time-honored fashion, I discovered an entire new set of worries. How would I take care of Kate when I was all on my own? I'd become very dependent on having my mother around to suggest reasons why Kate wouldn't stop crying, or eating, or puking or whatever.

"You can always call me," promised Mum.

"Thanks," I said tearfully.

"And I'm sure you'll be fine," she said.

"Really?" I asked pathetically. Even though I was nearly thirty I could still behave like a child when I was around my mother.

"Oh yes," she said. "No one knows how strong they are until they have to be."

"I suppose you're right," I admitted.

"I am," she said firmly. "How about you? You haven't managed too badly in spite of all you've been through."

"I suppose," I said doubtfully.

"Really," she said. "Remember, if it doesn't kill you, it makes you stronger."

"Am I stronger?" I asked faintly, in my most childish voice.

"Jesus," she said, "when you put on that voice, I do actually wonder."

"Oh," I said, annoyed. I wanted her to be nice to me and tell me that I was wonderful and could cope with anything.

"Claire," she said, "there's no point asking me if you're stronger. You're the one who knows that."

"Well, I am then," I said belligerently.

"Good." She smiled. "And remember. You said it. Not me."

The Wednesday before I was due to go back, Anna, Kate and I were out in the garden. The weather was still beautiful. Anna was, um, how can I put it, between jobs, so the pair of us had spent the last week lounging around the garden dressed in an assortment of bikini tops and cut-off shorts, trying to get a tan.

I was winning.

I tanned easily, and Anna didn't. But then again, Anna was tiny and dainty and looked lovely in a bikini and I felt like a huge heifer beside her. I wasn't fat anymore. But she was so petite and delicate that she made me feel huge by comparison. I *liked* being tall. I just didn't like feeling like an East German Olympic athlete.

So if I was winning in the tanning war, it was really only right and just.

When the genes were distributed she got the cute little body. I got the smooth, golden skin.

She got thin legs. I didn't.

I got breasts. She didn't.

Fair is fair.

Our attention was drawn to the kitchen window. Mum had lifted the curtain and was gesturing and knocking.

"What does she want?" said Anna sleepily.

"I think she's saying hello," I said, slowly raising my head from the lounger to look at her.

"Hello," we both said languidly, and waved our arms limply. Mum continued to knock. The gestures that she made seemed to be a lot more frantic and vulgar.

"You go see what she wants," I said to Anna.

"I can't," she said. "You go."

"I'm too sleepy," I said. "You'll have to go."

"No, you go," she said, closing her eyes.

Mum came marching into the garden.

"Claire, phone!" she roared. "And the next time I knock on the window you're to come in. I don't do it for the good of my health, you know."

"Sorry, Mum."

"Keep an eye on Kate," I told Anna as I ran into the house.

"Mmmmm," she mumbled.

"And put some more sunblock on her," I shouted over my shoulder.

I stumbled into the kitchen, almost blinded by coming into the dim house after the blazing sunlight of the garden.

I picked up the phone. "Hello," I said.

"Claire," said James.

"Oh hello, James," I said, wondering what the hell he wanted. If he hadn't called to tell me that he'd sold our apartment, I didn't want to talk to him.

"How are you, Claire?" he asked politely.

"Fine," I said shortly, wishing he'd get on with it.

"Claire," he said, with great weight, "I have something to tell you."

"Well, go ahead," I cordially invited.

"Claire, I hope you don't mind, but I've met someone else."

"Oh," I said. "Well, what do you want me to say? Congratulations?"

"No," he said. "There's no need for that. But I thought I had better tell you, seeing as you made such a fuss the last time."

With monumental self-control I didn't hang up the phone.

"Thank you, James," I managed. "That's very thoughtful of you. Now, if you'll excuse me, I must go."

"But don't you want to know all about her?" he said quickly.

"No," I said.

"Don't you mind?" he asked anxiously.

"No." I laughed.

"She's lots younger than you," he said nastily. "She's only twenty-two."

"That's nice," I said mildly.

"Her name's Rita," he said.

"Nice name," I commented.

"She's an actuary," he said, sounding a bit desperate.

"How lovely," I exclaimed. "You must have so much in common!"

"What the hell is wrong with you?" he shouted.

"I don't know what you're talking about," I protested.

"Why are you acting as if you don't give a damn?" he thundered. "I've just told you I've got a new girlfriend!"

"I suppose I must be acting like I don't give a damn because I actually don't give a damn," was the only thing I could come up with.

"Oh, and James," I continued.

"Yes?" he said hopefully.

"Kate is fine," I said. "I'm sure it's just an oversight that you forgot to ask. Now I'm going. Great news! I'm delighted for you. Long may it last and all that. Good-bye." I slammed the phone down.

How pathetic can you get? What did he expect me to do? Burst into tears and beg him to take me back? Hadn't he learned anything?

I went back out to the garden. Anna had come to and was sitting up playing with Kate. She was so beautiful. Kate, that is. Although Anna was lovely too, no doubt about it. But Kate, she was more lovely. She had started to develop a little personality all of her own. When you spoke to her she made gurgly noises and laughed sometimes and made eye contact. It was almost like having a conversation with her.

Although she wasn't doing too much laughing at that moment. Her fat little face was bright pink and shiny under her yellow sunhat and she looked as if she didn't want to do any more sunbathing. "I'm hot and bored," her look said. "And I've had quite enough of talking to this flake."

"Who was it?" asked Anna.

"James," I spat, barely able to say his name.

"What's up with him?" asked Anna.

"He has a new girlfriend," I said curtly.

"Do you mind?" she asked anxiously.

"Of *course* I don't mind," I said, outraged.

"So why are you acting so cross?" asked Anna.

"Because he disturbed my sunbathing—made me get up off the lounger and *walk*—just to tell me that. I can't believe it! I really can't. What an asshole."

Never mind James. I was worried about Kate.

"You don't think she's burning, do you?" I asked Anna anxiously. "Maybe I should have used a higher factor."

"Maybe," agreed Anna doubtfully, "but I don't think they *make* a higher one."

It was true. I had smothered Kate with a sunblock that had the highest protection factor known to man. Was I being an overprotective mother? I couldn't help myself. I worried about her. I mean, after all, she was a baby and her skin was very delicate. I didn't want to take any chances.

"I think I'll bring her inside," I said, "just to be on the safe side."

"Relax," advised Anna.

"No, I'd better take her in," I said. "She might burn."

"Oh, don't go," pleaded Anna. "I'll have no one to talk to."

Just then we heard voices in the kitchen. It sounded as if a small commotion had broken out.

"Helen's home," I said to Anna, "you can play with her."

"Oh no," groaned Anna. "She'll be talking about killing herself if she fails and could she stomach having sex with Professor Macauley and asking me all these stupid questions about ancient Greece.

"I mean, what do I know about ancient Greece?" she asked, sounding wronged and very put out. "Just because I worked in a bar for six weeks in Santorini she thinks I should know about Zeus and all that crowd."

She sighed and began to gather her things. "I think I'll come in with you."

But before she could make her escape, Helen burst into the garden. She was wearing a little denim skirt and a T-shirt. Her hair was wound up on top of her head and as usual she looked beautiful.

She stopped when she saw us and stared long and hard.

"Look at them," she said bitterly. "Just look at them, the lucky bitches."

"Hi, Helen," said Anna warily.

"Lazy cows, just lying around doing nothing while I have to work my ass off studying," she continued resentfully.

I shaded my eyes with my hand to look at Helen, at her furious little face. And it was only then that I realized that Helen was not alone.

She had brought a guest.

A male guest.

A tall, handsome male guest.

A gorgeous, blue-eyed, dark-haired, square-jawed, tall, handsome, male guest who was wearing faded jeans and a white T-shirt.

One who'd gotten a tan since I last saw him.

I hadn't thought that he could get any better-looking, but it would appear that I was wrong.

The bastard!

"Hi, Adam," I said, wanting to burst into tears.

"Hi, Claire," he said politely.

I held my breath and waited for him to go back into the house. Then I realized, with horror, that he wasn't going.

"Oh shit," I thought frantically, "he's coming over."

Helen and Adam made their way over to the little oasis of chaise lounges, diet Coke, suntan lotion, women's magazines and potato chips that Anna, Kate and I had created. Adam stood for a moment, and loomed over Anna and me, prostrate on the loungers. He didn't seem too relaxed. His usual, easy charm was missing. He looked awkward, a bit unfriendly.

My heart pounded. I felt at such a terrible disadvantage. Jesus, why couldn't Helen have given me some warning that she was bringing the beautiful Adam here. I could have put on some makeup and a nice bikini. Because when I said earlier that I was lying around the garden wearing cut-off shorts and little tops, I wasn't for a moment implying that I looked like one of those sexy babes from *Baywatch*. God no! The shorts were ancient and made from really nasty brushed denim and were cut in a really weird way. They were totally unflattering and made my butt look really wide. And there was no Lycra left in my bikini top, so it was all droopy.

It was the romance novel versus real life syndrome all over again. Whenever they're caught unawares by their men they just happen to have gotten out of the shower and are covered in fragrant body lotion, their hair is in damp little tendrils which escape from their towel and they look absolutely beautiful in a totally innocent and natural way.

Enough to make you puke.

But in real life you can put money on looking at your very, very worst when the man you like/love/fancy arrives unexpectedly. Well, that's always been *my* experience. You might be a bit luckier.

I wish he wouldn't just stand there looking down at me, I thought nervously.

"Adam, you're blocking out the sun," I said, trying to make it sound like a joke. "Why don't you sit down." He sat down. It was quite amazing how a man so big and tall could make sitting down look so graceful. Sorry, I shouldn't have noticed that. I certainly shouldn't have remarked on it.

He smiled over at Anna.

"Hello," he said.

"Hi, Adam," she simpered.

"How are you?" He sounded as if he was really interested.

"Never mind her! What about me?" I nearly shouted.

"I'm fine," said Anna, smiling back shyly.

"Jesus," muttered Helen, giving Anna a "you're so pathetic" look.

Adam and Anna continued to murmur to each other.

Then Helen turned her attention to me.

"Get off that," she ordered, trying to push me off the chair. "I've just taken an exam. I need to lie down."

"That's fine," I said, getting up. "I was just going anyway."

It was important for me to let her know that she hadn't forced me into relinquishing my chair. That I was doing it of my own accord.

Power games.

I was so childish.

"Yes," said Anna hastily, her face like a tomato. "I'm going too."

"Why, where are you going?" demanded Helen.

"Inside," I said.

"Oh great," she said. She was really pissed off. "I've just taken an awful exam and I've got to learn the entire anthropology course this evening and you won't even stay for five minutes to chat and help me unwind."

"But Kate's too hot," I said.

"Go on then," she said gloomily. "Go."

She looked at Adam. "We'll start in ten minutes, okay?"

"Okay," he agreed.

"What'll we do first?" she asked.

"What do you want to do?" he replied.

Correct answer. He obviously had a good idea of how to treat Helen.

"I suppose we could do dysfunctional families," said Helen. "Seeing as you know so much about that."

She laughed nastily.

"Helen," said Anna in a shocked voice.

"What?" said Helen, all belligerent. "It's only a joke. Anyway, he *does*. Don't you?" she demanded of Adam.

"I suppose I do," he said politely.

That was enough. I was going. I picked up Kate and walked across the lawn (lawn! what a joke!) with her. The couple of yards felt like miles and miles. All I could think about was Adam's eyes homing in on my highly unattractive ass in the awful shorts.

I finally reached the safety of the kitchen.

I realized that I had left my magazine in the garden. Well, it could stay there! You wouldn't catch me going anywhere near Adam of my own volition.

Oh dear!

I was very upset. Because, over the past few weeks, I had begun to suspect that maybe Adam hadn't been that attractive at all. That in my recently deserted state, my judgment had been impaired. Perhaps I had been so grateful for the attention from him that I had managed to convince myself that he was gorgeous.

But no. It wasn't true. The bastard was gorgeous. I hadn't imagined it. I hadn't been deluded.

And he looked even nicer with a tan. And his arms were so big and muscley in that T-shirt.

Jesus! It was too much to bear, what with my being celibate for close to five months, not counting that one night with Adam.

Actually, it was a lot longer than that, because James wouldn't touch me with a stick in the last four or five months of my pregnancy.

Anyway, what was Adam's problem? Why was he all cold and unfriendly to me? Surely that was a bit unnecessary? Was he afraid that I was going to attempt to jump on his bones?

That I wouldn't be able to restrain myself? Did he feel that he had to keep me at bay?

Well, he needn't worry, I thought. He was safe. I wouldn't attempt to come between him and his girlfriend. I wasn't as stupid as I used to be. I recognized a no-win situation when I was looking it in the face.

"Isn't it weird?" I thought as I carried Kate upstairs. "The last time I saw Adam I had just gotten out of his bed. We had been as intimate as two human beings could possibly be. And now we're acting like polite strangers."

thirty-nine

Kate was a lot happier inside. All smiles and gurgles and kicks when I put her into her crib. I held her hot little feet and cycled her legs—she loved that. Well, at least I hoped she loved it because I enjoyed it immensely—when I heard the knock on my bedroom door.

What was going on? *No one* knocked in our house.

The door opened and Adam loomed into the room. Every-thing instantly looked much smaller, like a doll's house.

"Oh Lord," I thought, going into shock and abruptly aban-doning Kate's little legs. "What does he want?"

Maybe he wasn't able to believe how awful my shorts were and was coming for a second look.

"Claire," he said sheepishly, "can I talk to you for a moment?"

He stood there, so big, so beautiful, an anxious look on his handsome face.

I looked at him and something happened inside me (no not that!), something wonderful.

My heart lifted and a surge of *gladness* rushed through me so strong it nearly knocked me over. I was suddenly filled with hope and gladness and happiness. That elation when you thought all was lost and then you realized that everything was going to be fine.

You know the one I'm talking about. The one that only happens once or twice in a lifetime.

"Yes," I said, "of course."

He came over and shook Kate's foot and then sat down beside me on the bed. The mattress nearly hit the floor, but never mind that.

"Claire," he said, looking at me beseechingly with his blue, blue eyes, "I'd like to explain about my girlfriend and my baby."

"Oh yes?" I asked, trying to sound brisk and businesslike. As if he wasn't having a very unsettling effect on me.

His bigness and nearness were a bit overwhelming. As I said before, the first thing I had ever noticed about him was his manliness. And now it was as if he had doused the bed with testosterone. Or as if he'd walked around the room with one of those incense dispenser things that the priests wave around at Benediction, except, instead of incense, his dispenser thing was filled with Essence of Man.

I couldn't *help* it if I thought about having sex with him. I was only human. If you prick me do I not bleed? If you stick a gorgeous man under my nose, do I not want to rip the clothes off him?

I mean, *I* don't make the rules.

It was imperative that I got myself under control. Adam was not here to offer me his body. He was here, well, at least I hoped he was here, so we could untangle whatever was happening in our lives when we met each other. Then maybe we could be friends.

I realized that I'd really, really like to be friends with him. He was so interesting and entertaining and sweet. He was a lovely person to be around. Special, you know. Whoever this girlfriend of his was, she was one lucky woman.

"Claire," he said, "thank you for giving me this chance to explain."

"Oh God," I said, "get a grip. Stop sounding so humble."

"It's just . . . I don't know." He faltered. "It must have been a bit of a, a . . . *surprise* when Helen told you about me having a child."

"Yes, it was a . . . surprise," I said with a little smile.

"Okay, okay," he said. He ran his hand through his lovely, silky hair. "Maybe *surprise* is the wrong word."

"Maybe," I agreed. But in a nice way.

"I should have told you," he said.

"Why?" I asked. "It's not as if we were going out with each other or anything."

He stared at me. He looked sad.

"Well, even if we weren't going out with each other, I still felt that I should have told you," he said. "But I was afraid that I'd frighten you off," he continued.

"That was hardly likely, considering my circumstances," I replied.

"But I thought you'd wonder what kind of guy I was that I wasn't allowed to see my own child. I wanted to tell you. I nearly did try to tell you lots of times but I always lost my nerve at the last minute."

"And why are you telling me now?" I asked.

"Because it's all fixed," he said.

"Well, wasn't it a stroke of luck that Helen invited you here today and that I just happened in?" I asked a bit tartly.

"Claire," he said anxiously. "If you hadn't been here today I would have called you. I thought you'd gone back to London ages ago. Otherwise I would have been in touch sooner.

"No, *honestly*," he assured me when he saw the skeptical look that I gave him.

"All right," I conceded. "I believe you."

"So tell me all about it," I suggested, forcing myself to speak gently. Trying to keep the urgent curiosity out of my voice.

I always enjoy a good human interest story, even if I happen to be peripherally involved.

A series of peculiar, gurgly type noises came from Kate's crib. Oh please don't cry, darling, I hoped desperately. Not right now. I *really* want to hear this. It's important to Mummy.

And would you believe it? She quieted down again. She'd obviously inherited something good from her father.

But sshush now, ladies and gentlemen, Adam was going to explain all.

"I had gone out with Hannah for—" he began.

"Who's Hannah?" I interrupted.

It's always good to sort out who all the main characters are before the story begins.

"The mother of my child," he explained.

"Fine," I said, "go on."

"I had gone out with her for a long time, about two years," he said.

"Yes." I nodded.

"And it ended," he said.

"Oh," I said, "that sounds a bit abrupt."

"No, no, it wasn't," he said. "What I mean is neither of us ran off with someone else or anything like that. It had just run its course."

"Yes." I nodded.

"So we split up," he said.

"Yes," I said. "I'm with you so far."

"But I was still really fond of her," he said. "I missed her. But every time we saw each other it was awful. She'd cry and ask why hadn't it worked and could we try again and that kind of thing."

"Yes," I said. This was all very familiar.

"And we always ended up going to bed together," he said.

He looked a bit embarrassed when he said this. I didn't know why. I mean, *everyone* does that when they split up with someone they once loved and still do in a way, don't they?

It's the rule.

You split up, you say you'll still be friends, you meet up a week later for your first "friendly" drink, you get drunk, you say how weird it is not being able to touch each other even in an affectionate way, you kiss each other, you stop and say "No, we mustn't," you kiss again, you stop and say "This is ridiculous," you kiss again, you say "Maybe just this once; it's only because I miss you so much." You get the bus back to his place, you practically have sex in someone's backyard when you get off the bus, you get to his house, everything is so familiar and you cry because you know you don't belong there anymore. You have sex, you cry again, you go to sleep, you have horrible dreams where one minute you're back together and the next you've split up again and you wake up the next morning wishing you were dead.

Everyone knows that rule. It's one of the first principles governing the end of a love affair. Adam must be very naive if he thought it's only ever happened to him.

"Anyway, Hannah got pregnant," he said.

"Oh dear," I said sympathetically.

He looked at me a bit sharply. He thought that I was being sarcastic. I wasn't, honestly.

"We talked about it and we considered everything. She wanted to get married. I didn't want to, because I thought it was a stupid thing to do. I didn't see the point in getting married to give the child a stable home if its parents didn't love each other anymore."

"Mmmmm," I said noncommittally. I mean, technically he was right. But as one woman to another, my heart went out to the misfortunate Hannah.

"I suppose you think I'm a total bastard," he said, looking a bit wretched.

"No, not really," I said. "I agree with you that getting married achieves nothing in that situation."

"You *do* think I'm a bastard," he said, "I can tell."

"I *don't*," I said, exasperated. "Get on with it, would you."

There was far too much developing of the characters and not enough action in this story for my taste.

"We thought about her having the baby and putting it up for adoption but Hannah didn't want to do that. Then we talked about her having an abortion."

I flashed a quick look at Kate. I couldn't help it. I just felt so incredibly lucky that I hadn't had to consider an abortion when I found out that I was pregnant.

"Anyway, an abortion seemed like some sort of solution," he said wearily. "But neither of us wanted to do that."

"I'm sure you didn't," I murmured, trying to sound like I believed him.

But I wondered to myself "Is this guy for *real*?"

I'd always suspected that most men thought that abortion was almost a sacrament, a gift generously bestowed on them by Heaven to make their lives uncomplicated and pleasant. To deal with nasty little nuisances, like children, which might interfere with their life of gay bachelorhood.

Of course there's always the crowd who get all sanctimonious and self-righteous and say that abortion is murder. You'll find that the men who are quite happy to say this are the ones whose girlfriends aren't pregnant. But the minute their women have an "accident" and are with child, it's usually a very different story.

They're often the very first to tentatively suggest that maybe now is not the right time to have a baby and that there's nothing to an abortion, really. That it's easier than having a tooth out. And that in most cases you don't even have to stay overnight. And there's no need to feel guilty because, at this stage, it's not even a child, just a few cells. And that they'll come with her and pick her up afterward. And maybe in a few weeks they'll go away for a weekend to help her get over it. And then, before the woman knows what's happening to her, she's lying on an operating table in an expensive "clinic" wearing a paper gown that opens all the way up the back, with a needle stuck in her arm, counting down from ten.

Sorry, sorry! I got a little bit distracted there.

As you may have noticed, this is something I feel very strongly about, but maybe now isn't the time to go into it. Suffice it to say that Adam had me convinced that he wasn't one of those men.

But just one more thing and then I'll shut up. Show me a man who's pregnant, penniless and partnerless and *then* invite him to stand on the soapbox and tell me that he still thinks abortion is completely wrong. Hah!

Anyway, back to Adam the feminist.

He was still explaining, all anxious and earnest, staring at me with a beseeching look in his beautiful eyes.

D'you know, he had the most gorgeous eyelashes? Really thick and long and . . . sorry.

Ahem.

"I said that if she had the baby, I'd do whatever I could to help," he said. "I promised I'd support her financially and that I was happy for the baby to live with me. Or with her. Or we could share. Whatever Hannah wanted. I wanted her to have the baby but I knew that at the end of the day the decision was hers. I couldn't decide for her and I didn't want to put pressure on her to have the child because I knew she was scared. She was only twenty-two."

"Oh dear," I said, "that's very sad."

"It was," he said miserably. "It was really awful."

"And then what happened?" I asked.

"Her parents got involved. And when they found out that we'd discussed her having an abortion, they went crazy. Fair enough, I suppose. And they took her away, from my supposedly evil influence, to their house in Sligo."

"Jesus," I said, imagining Hannah being locked up in a tower in the middle of nowhere like the princess with the long golden hair. "How awful. It's barbaric! Like something out of the dark ages."

"No," he said quickly, eager to put me right, "it wasn't that bad. They meant well. They only wanted the best for the baby. After all, it was their grandchild and they wanted to make sure that Hannah didn't have an abortion. But then they wouldn't let me talk to Hannah any time that I called. And they said that when the baby was born, I was to leave them alone."

"Are you serious?" I said, outraged. "I've never heard anything like that. Well, I suppose I have. But only about uncivilized, crazy people. And then what happened? Didn't this Hannah have any mind of her own? Didn't she tell these parents of hers where to get off? I mean, she was a grown woman!"

"Well," he said awkwardly, "then Hannah didn't want to see me either. I went to Sligo and she spoke to me and told me that she didn't want anything further to do with me and she didn't want me interfering when the baby was born."

"But why?" I cried.

"I don't really know," he said unhappily. "I think she felt very bitter that I wouldn't marry her. And she was angry with me for getting her pregnant. Her parents had convinced her that I must be the son of Satan to have thought about an abortion."

"I see," I said, "so what happened next?"

"I got legal advice to see what I could do. And, do you know what? I've got almost *no* rights at all. Practically none. But even if I could have insisted on my right to see my child, I didn't want it to be a vicious legal battle. I really couldn't believe that Hannah would do that to me. It was terrible."

He was silent for a few moments.

Kate was being suspiciously quiet, I thought in alarm. But she *looked* fine.

"The worst time of all was when the baby was born," Adam went on. "I didn't even know if it *had* been born or not.

I didn't know if it was healthy. I didn't know whether it was
a boy or a girl. Then I called her house and her father told me
that it was a girl and she was fine. And that Hannah was fine
too. But he said she didn't want to speak to me."

"Isn't that awful?" I breathed.

"Yes, it was. And for a whole year I heard nothing," he
said. "It was a nightmare. I was totally powerless."

My attention was distracted from Adam's sorry plight by
the sound of feet pounding up the stairs. Then Helen burst
into the room. She stared from me to Adam and back again.
"What's going on here?" she asked in astonishment.

I went totally dumb. I couldn't speak. I didn't know what
the hell to say to her.

Adam, in time-honored fashion, came to the rescue.

"Helen," he said gently, "would you mind giving me a few
moments with Claire."

"Yes!" she said truculently. "I would mind."

A pause while she wrestled with her curiosity. Then she
demanded, "Why?"

"I'll explain later," he said with a kindly look.

She stood at the door for a while, suspicion and jealousy
written all over her exquisite little face.

"Five minutes," she said, throwing me a poisonous look as
she flounced from the room.

"Oh God," I said, "you'd better go."

"No," he said, "she's already pissed off with me. I might
as well stay and finish what I'm telling you."

"On your head be it, in that case," I said nervously, marvel-
ing at his courage.

"Fine," he said, unbothered. "Well, as I said, I didn't hear
from her for a whole year—I was just starting to come to terms
with it. And then about a month ago she turned up out of the
blue. I couldn't believe it! And she brought Molly with her."

"Who's Molly?" I interrupted. "Is that your baby?"

"Yes," he said. "Isn't it a terrible name for a baby?"

"I like it," I said huffily. I suppose I'm a bit defensive because my baby's name isn't the most glamorous one you could
imagine either.

"Maybe," said Adam, "but you'd have to see her. She's

gorgeous. She should be called something beautiful. Like Mira-belle or—"

"Isn't that a restaurant?" I interrupted. I didn't like the direction this conversation was taking. Especially with Kate within earshot. I didn't want her to get a complex. God knows, the cards were stacked against her enough as it was. I was afraid that in thirty years' time when she was a drug addict and an alcoholic and bulimic and addicted to shoplifting, that I'd get the blame. That she'd say that it was all my fault for not calling her something pretty and girlie.

"Look, don't worry about your child's name," I said. "Keep going with the story."

"Okay," he said. "Well, anyway, we made up, I suppose. She said she was sorry that she hadn't involved me from the beginning with Molly. But she wanted to know was it too late to start now?"

"And?" I asked.

"Well, at first I really wanted to tell her to fuck off," he said.

Jesus! I nearly gasped. I could hardly believe that Adam was acting so *normal*.

Hold the front page. Shocking new headlines—"Adam holds grudge!"

"But then I realized that I'd be cutting off my nose to spite my face," he continued.

How disappointing, I thought. For a moment there I thought he was going to act immature and childish. Well, never mind. There's always another time.

"So we've come to a civilized agreement about Molly's cus-tody. Hannah and I are friends again—well, at least we're working on it," he said.

"Oh!" I said, startled. "Oh."

What did "friends" mean? I wondered. Did it mean that they had sex at every available opportunity or did it really mean just "friends"?

Only one way to find out. I took a deep breath.

"Um, so does that mean that you and Hannah aren't, you know, going out with each other?" I asked, trying to sound very casual.

"No." He laughed, giving me a "Haven't you been paying attention to *anything* I've been saying" look.

("Thank God!")

"No," he said. "I thought that was obvious. That's the whole point. That's why this is all so great. I can be involved in my child's life without having to be romantically involved with her mother.

"But at the same time I can be friends with Hannah because I respect and admire her," he added hastily, always anxious to be good and decent.

"Are you really happy about seeing your child?" I asked gently.

He nodded and looked as if he might cry.

Oh, please don't, I thought frantically. I think I'm sick of all this new man business. *Stop* being in touch with your bloody emotions. Keep away from your feminine side! If I catch you near it I'll slap you.

A little voice in my head prompted, "Ask him!"

"Fuck off," I muttered back to it.

"Go *on*," it said again, "ask him. What have you got to lose?"

"*No*," I said, feeling very uncomfortable. "Leave me alone."

"You're dying to know," reminded the voice. "In fact, you deserve to know."

"Just shut up," I said through gritted teeth. "I'm not going to ask him anything!"

"Well, if you won't," said the voice, "then I will."

And to my horror I found myself opening my mouth and a voice came out and asked Adam, "So was that why you liked being around me? You know, because of Kate? Because I had a baby?"

I was mortified!

I couldn't believe that I had found the nerve to ask it.

You couldn't take my subconscious *anywhere*.

"No!" said Adam. Well, he didn't so much say it as shout it. "No, no, no. I was so afraid you'd think that. That you'd go all Freudian on me and think that I liked being with you just because I was looking for some sort of replacement for my lost child and girlfriend."

"Well, you can hardly blame me, can you?" I asked. But not in a nasty aggressive way.

"But why would I need some kind of bait to want to be with you?" he asked. "You're wonderful!"

I said nothing. Just sat there, feeling half embarrassed, half delighted.

"Seriously," he went on. "You've got to believe me. What kind of self-esteem have you got? You're amazing. Don't tell me you didn't know that?

"Well, didn't you?" he asked again when I didn't answer.

"No," I muttered.

"Look at me," he said. He put his hand gently on my cheek and turned my face up to his. "Please listen to me. You're so beautiful. And kind and smart and funny and lovely and a laugh. *They're* some of the reasons that I like being with you so much. The fact that you had a child was neither here nor there."

"Really?" I asked. Blushing like a beacon and going all girlie and shy.

"Really." He laughed. "I would have liked you even if you hadn't had a baby."

He smiled.

He looked beautiful.

Oh God! I was melting.

"Honestly," he said.

"I believe you," I said.

I smiled too. I couldn't help myself.

We sat on the bed smirking at each other like morons.

After a while he spoke again.

"So you took my advice in the end," he said, gently teasing.

"About what?" I asked. "Oh, you mean about James. Well, I didn't go back to him after all, but it wasn't because of anything *you* said."

"Fine, fine." He laughed. "I'm just glad you changed your mind. It doesn't really matter who changed it for you. You deserve a lot better than someone like him."

"Can I ask you something?" I said.

"Of course," he replied.

"What does Hannah look like?"

He gave me a knowing look and laughed slightly before

he spoke. "She's got long curly blond hair. She's about the same size as Helen or Anna. She's got brown eyes."

"Oh," I said.

"Happy now?" he asked.

"What are you talking about?"

"That she looks nothing like you? That I wasn't trying to replace her with you?"

You had to hand it to him. You couldn't say he wasn't perceptive. I was satisfied that this Hannah was nothing like me. But now I was all jealous because she sounded tiny and beautiful.

Jesus! Was I never satisfied?

I started to laugh. I was being ridiculous. "Yes, Adam, I'm happy that you weren't trying to replace her with me. But right now, you'd better get back to Helen," I said.

I stood up.

Then he stood up, instantly making me feel tiny.

There we stood, not really knowing what to say. I just knew that I didn't want to say good-bye.

"You're a very special woman," he said. And he pulled me to him and tightened his arms around me.

And fool that I was, I let him.

Big mistake. Huge, colossal, *enormous* mistake.

I hadn't been too bad until we made physical contact. But the minute I was in his arms all hell broke loose on the emotions front. Longing and yearning and lust (yes, even more!) and loss and a warm fuzzy feeling. Being in his arms reminded me of how he had made me feel. I thought I had forgotten how wonderful it was to be with him. But it all came rushing back.

My head was buried against his chest. I could feel his heart beating through the thin material of the T-shirt. The same beautiful hint of soap and warm male skin that I remembered.

I wanted to stay there forever, safe, pressed up against his beautiful hard body, his arms holding me tenderly.

I pulled away from him.

"You're not so bad yourself," I replied. For the life of me I couldn't understand why I had tears in my eyes.

"Be happy," he said.

"You too," I replied.

I wriggled out of his arms.

"Well, good-bye," I sniffed.

"Why good-bye?" he asked, smiling.

"Because I'm going back to London on Sunday, so I probably won't ever see you again," I said. I felt as if I was going to burst into tears. And wondered what the hell he was smiling at. Who gave him the right to look so smug and happy? Had he no sense of occasion? This was no laughing matter! On the contrary.

I couldn't believe how wretched I felt. This was so painful. I wished he would just *go*!

"Won't you ever go out again?" he asked. "Can't you get a baby-sitter?"

"Of course I will," I said sadly. "But I still won't be able to see you. Not unless you jet over to London now and then for an evening out. And I can't see you doing that."

"No," he said thoughtfully. "You're right. There would be no point jetting over to London for an evening out when I'm already there."

For a moment I thought I'd misheard him. But I looked at him, at his smiling face, and knew that I hadn't.

Hope rushed through me, such a feeling of something wonderful that I thought I might burst from it.

"What are you talking about?" I asked, barely able to breathe.

I had to sit down.

"Um, I'm, er, moving to London," he said quietly. He sat down beside me on the bed. He was trying to look very serious but a smile kept breaking through.

"Are you?" I squeaked. "But why?"

And then a thought struck me.

"Hey, don't tell me. You've nowhere to stay and you were wondering, just wondering if you could sleep on my floor. Just for a couple of nights, a year max. Is that right?" I said bitterly.

He burst out laughing.

"Claire, you're so funny!" he said.

"Why?" I asked, annoyed. "What are you laughing at?"

"You!" he said, still in hysterics. "I've *got* somewhere to stay. I'm not stupid enough to be nice to you just so I can ask you if I can stay with you. Do you think I have a death wish? I know you'd kill me."

"Good," I said, slightly mollified. At least he had a little bit of respect.

"Is that why you think I came up here to talk to you?" he asked, a lot more seriously. "Maybe I'm the stupid one here, but I thought I'd made it clear how much I like you and care for you. Don't you believe me?"

"Well, you can't blame me for being suspicious," I said sulkily.

"No," he sighed. "We'll just have to work on convincing you how wonderful you are and that I have no ulterior motives for wanting to be around you. I don't want you for your child. I don't want you for your apartment. I just want you for you."

"Do you want me?" I whispered, suddenly feeling very alive and sexy. So powerful, so aware that I was a woman and that he was a man and that unavoidable physical attraction pulsed between us. His eyes darkened, the blue almost turned to black, and he looked and sounded very serious.

"I want you very much," he said.

The room suddenly went quiet and still. Even Kate wasn't making a sound. You could have cut the sexual tension with a knife.

I broke the mood before one or both of us combusted spontaneously.

"Let me get this straight," I said, trying to be businesslike. "You're coming to London. What for? Why?"

"I've got a job," he said, as if it was the most reasonable explanation in the world.

"But what about college?" I asked, bewildered. "Are you giving it all up?"

"No," he said, "but it's going to be different. I'll study at night."

"Why?" I asked, still not really understanding. "Why are you doing this?"

"Because I've got to work now that I've got a child to support. And there aren't any jobs in Dublin. And my dad was able to get me into some merchant bank in London. And I'll still be able to get my degree. It'll just take longer."

"But what about your baby?" I wailed. "You've just gotten

to know her and now you'll have to leave her again. That's awful!"

It was his turn to look bewildered.

"But Molly's coming with me," he said, sounding a bit baffled. "I'm taking Molly to London."

"Jesus," I said in hushed tones. "Don't tell me that you're abducting her? I've heard of fathers doing that."

"No!" he said, exasperated. "Hannah *wants* me to take her. Hannah wants to go around the world; she's had enough of being responsible for a while. I suppose it's no coincidence that she was suddenly overcome with remorse about not letting me see Molly when she suddenly realized that she needed a baby-sitter for a year."

"Golly," I said. "It hardly sounds ideal. What about poor Molly? And why didn't Hannah's parents insist on taking care of her?"

"Oh, Hannah had a major falling-out with them when she decided that she was going off on vacation for a year," explained Adam. "And Molly will be fine, I hope. I'll get her into therapy as soon as she's able to talk.

"I'm only joking," he said when he saw my horrified face. "I know it's not the perfect upbringing for a child. To be uprooted from her home and for her mother to run away for a year and to be landed on a father who doesn't even know her. But all I can do is my best."

"And what about when Hannah comes back and wants to take Molly back to Ireland?" I said, racked with worry.

"Oh, Claire," he said gently, taking my hand in his. "Would you relax? Who knows what's going to happen in a year's time? I'll worry about that when I come to it. Can't we just live in the now for a little while?"

I said nothing.

I was thinking.

He was right, I decided.

When happiness makes a guest appearance in one's life, it's important to make the most of it. It may not stay around for long and when it *has* gone wouldn't it be terrible to think that all the time one could have been happy was wasted worrying about when that happiness would be taken away?

"So, if I could get to the main point of my visit," he continued, suddenly very brisk. "May I ask you something?"

"Of course." I smiled.

"If I'm being too forward, please stop me," he said, all self-deprecating charm. "But do you think it would be possible for us to meet each other some time in London? Perhaps we could share a baby-sitter? And, of course, any time you need a baby-sitter, I'll be only too happy to oblige."

"Thank you, Adam," I said politely. "I would love to see you in London. And, of course, if you too should need a baby-sitter, please don't hesitate to ask."

"Seriously," he said, his voice dropped several octaves. "This is very important to me. Will we really be able to see each other in London?"

"Of *course*," I said, laughing. "I'd love to see you."

I looked up and caught his eye. When I saw the look on his face—admiration, like, almost certainly lust. In fact, there might even have been love—the smile froze on my face.

"Oh, Claire," he breathed as he bent to kiss me. "I've missed you."

It was at this point that Kate decided that she'd had enough of being ignored and started up like a police siren.

At the same time Helen burst through the door and stopped abruptly when she saw us. She took in the pair of us sitting on the bed. Adam holding my hand, my head raised for Adam's kiss, and she said slowly, "I don't fucking believe it."

I braced myself for the onslaught.

Retribution would be both swift and terrible.

I looked at my feet and I was horrified to hear her crying. Helen? Crying? Surely some mistake. It was unheard of!

I looked up at her, filled with remorse and compassion. I was almost in tears myself.

And then I realized that she wasn't crying.

The bitch was laughing!

She laughed and laughed. "You and Adam," she said, shaking her head, tears of laughter pouring down her face. "The *shame* of it."

"Why?" I demanded, all annoyed compassion and remorse quickly forgotten. "What's wrong with me?"

"Nothing." She laughed. "Nothing. But you're so old

and . . ." She stopped, unable to speak, she found it all so funny. "The look on your face! You looked terrified. And I thought he liked *me!*" she exclaimed, and she was off again. It was all so hilarious that she couldn't even stand straight. She leaned up against the wall and then doubled over.

I sat and stared coldly at her while Kate wailed like a banshee.

Adam looked slightly bemused.

If there was something funny, then I certainly couldn't see it.

I picked up Kate before she burst a blood vessel and nodded to Adam. "Talk to Helen," I suggested.

Adam unfolded himself and left the room after Helen.

I rocked Kate in my arms and tried to soothe her. She was a lovely child, but, I swear to God, sometimes her timing was so off.

I could hear Helen laughing all the way down the stairs.

And a while later she arrived back in.

"You fucking bitch," she said cheerfully, sitting down on the bed beside me. "You had us all fooled. Pretending to be totally heartbroken about James and all the time you had the hots for Adam."

"No, Helen . . ." I protested weakly. "It wasn't like that."

She ignored me. She had more important things on her mind.

"What's he like?" she said, drawing conspiratorially nearer to me and dropping her voice several decibels. "Has he got a big one?"

"What kind of a question is that?" I asked, pretending to be horrified.

"I won't tell anyone," she lied.

"Helen!" I said, my head swimming slightly. I think I would have preferred it if she had been furious with me. Now I'd have to put up with her being my best friend so that she could find out what Adam was like in bed so that she could tell everyone.

"Where is he anyway?" I asked her.

"In the kitchen sucking up to Mum. But never mind that," she said enthusiastically. "I think he loves you."

"Oh, Helen, go away," I said, starting to feel exhausted.

"No, really, I do," she promised.

"Really?" I asked tentatively. I was such a sucker. I shouldn't have listened to anything she said. At my age I really should have had more sense.

"Yes," she said, sounding unusually serious.

"Why?" I asked.

"Because he had a huge hard-on when he was talking about you just now." Then she screamed with laughter. "I really got you going there, didn't I?"

"Oh, go away, would you?" I said.

I'd had enough for one day.

"Sorry," sniggered Helen. "No, I am, I promise. I do think he loves you. I really do. And let's face it, if anyone's an expert on men being in love, it's me."

She had a point.

"Do you love him?" she demanded.

"I don't know," I said awkwardly. "I don't really know him well enough to say. But I like him a lot. Will that do?"

"It'll have to," she said thoughtfully. "I hope you do love each other. I hope you'll be happy together."

"Gosh, thank you, Helen," I said, really touched. Tears sprang to my eyes. I was overwhelmed by her good wishes.

"Yes," she said vaguely. "I've a bet on with that cow Melissa Saint that she won't get a date with him before the end of the summer. I was actually starting to get a bit worried but this is great. A godsend. She hasn't a hope now because you'll keep him well out of her way.

"That's the easiest bet I ever won," she said, rubbing her hands together gleefully. "Yes," she continued, sounding very pleased. "I must say this has all worked out very well. Very well indeed."

acknowledgments

I'm thrilled to be published in the U.S., and I'd like to thank all those who made it possible. Thanks to my agents Jonathan Lloyd and Russ Galen for introducing me to Avon Books. And thanks to all at Avon for their enthusiasm and hard work on this edition of *Watermelon*. Special thanks to my editor, Jennifer Hershey, for her vision, enthusiasm and meticulous, sensitive editing.

There seemed to be a direct link between how difficult it was to get to a fortune-teller's house and how good their reputation was. The more inaccessible and off-putting the venue, the higher the quality of the predictions, was the widely held view.

Which meant that Mrs. Nolan must have been brilliant because she lived in some awful, faraway suburb on the outskirts of London.

On Monday, at five on the dot, Megan, Hetty, Meredia and I assembled on the front steps of our place of work. Hetty went and got her car from where it was parked, several miles away—because that was parking in central London for you—and in we got.

The journey was a nightmare. We spent hours either stuck in traffic or traveling through anonymous suburbs, then we went onto a highway. After driving for ages more, we turned off an exit and finally turned into a housing project.

And what a neighborhood! It was downright apocalyptic. The neighborhood I'd grown up in was pretty poor, but not this bad!

Two huge gray blocks loomed like watchtowers over what seemed like hundreds of miserable little gray box houses. A couple of stray dogs roamed aimlessly, half-heartedly looking for someone to bite.

There were no plants, no trees, no grass.

In the distance there was a small concrete row of shops. It was nearly all boarded up except for a sandwich shop and a bookie's office and a liquor store. It was probably just my over-active imagination but through the evening gloom I could have *sworn* I saw four horsemen loitering outside the sandwich shop. So far, so good—Mrs. Nolan was obviously better than I had already realized.

"My god," said Megan her face twisted in disgust. "What a dump!"

"Yes, isn't it?" Meredia smiled with pride.

In the middle of all the grayness was a small patch of ground that some urban planner had obviously anticipated would be a little oasis of abundant greenness where laughing families would play in the sunshine. But it looked like it had been a long time since grass had grown there. Through the twilight gloom we could see a group of about fifteen children gathered. They were clustered around something that looked suspiciously like a burned-out car.

Even though it was a bitterly cold March evening, none of them was wearing coats and, as soon as they saw us, they paused from whatever criminal activity they were up to and ran toward us, whooping loudly.

"Good God!" cried Hetty. "Lock your doors!" All four locks snapped shut as the children swarmed round the car, staring at us with their old and knowing eyes.

What made them look even more scary was that they were smeared with black stuff, which was probably only oil or charred metal from the burned car, but it looked like war paint.

They were mouthing something at us.

"What are they saying?" asked Hetty in terror.

"I think they're asking us if we've come to see Mrs. Nolan," I said doubtfully.

I opened the window a fraction of an inch and through the babel of childish voices established that that was indeed what they were asking us.

"Phew! The natives are friendly," smiled Hetty, making a great show of wiping the sweat from her forehead and breathing deeply with relief.

"Talk to them, Lucy."

Nervously, I opened the window a bit more.

"Er . . . we've come to see Mrs. Nolan," I said.

A cacophony of shrill voices answered us.

"That's her house."

"She lives over there."

"That's the one."

"You can leave your car here."

"That's her house."

"Over there."

"I'll show you."

"No, I'll show you."

"No, *I'm* showing them."

"No, *I'm* showing them."

"But I saw them first."

"But you got the last lot."

"Fuck you, Cherise Tiller."

"No, fuck *you*, Claudine Hall."

A vicious fight broke out between four or five of the little girls while we sat in the car and waited for them to stop.

"Let's get out." Megan sounded a bit bored. It took more than a crowd of semisavage children to frighten her. She opened the door and stepped over a couple of children wrestling on the pavement.

Then Hetty and I got out.

As soon as Hetty put foot outside the car a wiry, skinny little girl with the face of a thirty-five-year-old cardsharp began tugging at her coat. "Hey, me and my friend'll guard your car," she promised.

Her friend, who was even more skinny, nodded silently.

"Thank you," said Hetty, her face a picture of horror, trying to shake the little girl off.

"We'll make sure that nothing happens to it," said the wizened little girl, a bit more threateningly, still holding on to Hetty's coat tightly.

"Give them some money," suggested Megan in exasperation. "That's what she's really saying."

"Excuse *me!*" said Hetty, outraged. "I will not. That's blackmail."

"Do you want the wheels to be on your car when you get back or don't you?" Megan demanded.

The little girl and her friend patiently watched the exchange with folded arms. Now that a sensible streetwise woman like Megan was on the case, they knew that the outcome would be to their liking.

"Here," I said, giving the thirty-five-year-old little girl a pound.

She accepted it with a grim nod.

"*Now* can we please go and have our fortunes told?" asked Megan impatiently.

Meredia, the big wimp, had cowered in the car during the entire exchange with the Children from Hell. She waited for them to drift away before levering herself out.

But the minute they saw her emerging from the car they returned at high speed. It wasn't often that they got a two-hundred-pound woman dressed head to toe in crimson crushed velvet, with matching hair, in their neighborhood. But when they did, they knew how to make the most of it. The screeches of laughter that emerged from the children were bloodcurdling.

Poor Meredia, her face as crimson as the rest of her, lumbered the short distance to Mrs. Nolan's front door like the Pied Piper, with swarms of horrible brats running and dancing after her, laughing and shouting insults. A carnival atmosphere prevailed, as though the circus had come to town, while Hetty, Megan and I jostled protectively around Meredia, making half-hearted attempts to shoo the children away.

Then we saw Mrs. Nolan's house. You couldn't miss it.

It had double-glazed windows and a little glass porch stuck onto its front. All its windows had scalloped, lacy net curtains and elaborately looped Austrian blinds. The windowsills were crammed to capacity with ornaments, china horses and glass dogs and brass jugs and little furry things on little wooden rocking chairs. Evident signs of prosperity that set it apart from all the other houses around it. Mrs. Nolan was obviously a bit of a superstar among tarot readers.

"Ring the bell," Hetty told Meredia.

"No, you do it," said Meredia.

"But you've been here before," said Hetty.

"*I'll* do it," I sighed, reached over and pressed the button.

When the first couple of verses of "Greensleeves" began chiming in the hall, Megan and I both started to snigger.

Meredia turned and glared.

"Shut up," she hissed. "Have some respect. This woman is the best. She's the master."

"She's coming. Oh my god. She's coming," whispered Hetty in hoarse excitement as a shadowy shape moved behind the frosted glass of the porch.

The door opened and instead of an exotic, dusky, psychic-looking woman, an unfriendly-looking young man stood there. A small child with a dirty face peeped out from between his legs.

"Yes?" he said, looking us over. His eyes widened with mild shock as he registered Meredia in all her crimsonness.

None of us spoke. Hetty gently nudged Meredia and Meredia elbowed Megan and Megan elbowed me.

"Say something," hissed Hetty.

"No, you," muttered Meredia.

"Well?" enquired the creepy-looking man again, none too civilly.

"Is Mrs. Nolan here?" I asked.

He eyed me suspiciously, then apparently decided that I could be trusted.

"She's busy," he muttered.

"Doing what?" demanded Megan impatiently.

"She's having her tea," he said.

"Well, can we come in and wait?" I asked.

"She's expecting us," volunteered Meredia.

"We've come a long way," explained Hetty.

"We were led by a star from the East," sniggered Megan from the back.

All three of us turned and frowned at her.

"Sorry," she muttered.

The young man looked mortally offended at the disrespect shown to his mother or granny—or whatever Mrs. Nolan was to him—and began to close the door.

"No, please don't," pleaded Hetty. "She's sorry."

"I am," called Megan cheerfully, not sounding a bit of it.

"All right then," he said grudgingly and let us into a tiny hall.

There was barely space for the four of us.

"Wait here," he ordered and went into another room. It must have been the kitchen, judging by the smoke and the clinking of teacups and the smell of fried eggs that emerged when he opened the door and disappeared when he shut it again.

There was hardly an inch of wall space in the hall that wasn't covered with pictures or barometers or tapestries or horseshoes. Meredia moved slightly and knocked a photograph of a very large family off the wall. She bent down to pick it up and brushed against ten other pictures that went tumbling to the floor.

We loitered in the hall, totally ignored, while sounds of talk and laughter came from behind the closed door. The minutes ticked by.

"I'm *starving*," said Megan.

"Me too," I agreed. "I wonder what they're having for tea."

"This is stupid," said Megan. "Let's go."

"Please wait," said Meredia. "She's wonderful. She really is."

Eventually Mrs. Nolan finished her tea. I couldn't help feeling disappointed when I saw her—she looked so ordinary. There wasn't a red head scarf or a gold hoop earring in sight.

She had glasses and a short perm and was wearing a beige sweater and sweat pants and, worst of all, *slippers*. And she was *minute!* I wasn't very tall myself but she barely came up to my waist.

"Right girls," she said, brisk and businesslike, in a Dublin accent. "Who's first?"

Meredia went first. Then Hetty. Then me. Megan wanted to wait until last to see if the rest of us thought it was worth the money.

When it was my turn I went into what was obviously the family "good room." I barely got past the door because the room was so crammed with furniture and stuff. An embroidered fireguard stood next to a huge mahogany sideboard, which groaned under the weight of yet more ornaments. There were footstools and nests of tables everywhere you looked and a sofa and chairs in brown velvet. They still had their plastic covers.

Mrs. Nolan was sitting on one of the plastic-covered chairs and she gestured to me to sit on the other.

As I fought through the furniture to get to the seat, I began to feel nervous and excited. Although Mrs. Nolan looked like she would be more at home on her knees scrubbing Hetty's kitchen floor, she had obviously earned her wonderful reputation as a fortune-teller, *somehow*. What would she tell me? I wondered. What was in store for me? "Sit down, me dear," she said.

I sat, balanced on the edge of the plastic-covered chair.

She looked at me. Shrewdly? Wisely?

She spoke. Prophetically? Portentously?

"You have come a long way, me dear," she said.

I gave a little jump. So accurate! Yes, indeed I *had* come a long way from my working class childhood. "Yes," I agreed tentatively, quite shaken by her perception.

"Was the traffic bad, me dear?"

"*What?* The *hat*? Er . . . oh . . . the traffic? No, not really," I managed to reply.

Oh I see. She had only been making conversation. The reading hadn't started yet. How disappointing. Well, never mind. "Yes, me dear," she sighed. "If they ever finish that bloody bypass it'll be a miracle."

"Er, yes." I nodded.

But then it was straight down to business. "Ball or cards?" she shot at me.

"S . . . sorry?" I asked politely.

"Ball or cards? Crystal ball or tarot cards?"

"Oh! Well, let's see. What's the difference?"

"Five pounds."

"No, I meant . . . never mind. The tarot cards please."

"Right," said Mrs. Nolan and with that she started shuffling the deck with the finesse of a riverboat poker player.

"Shuffle them, me dear," she said, handing me the cards. "And whatever you do, don't drop them on the floor."

It must be bad luck to drop them on the floor. I nodded knowingly.

"I have a bad back," she explained. "The doctor said no bending."

"Now, ask yourself a question, me dear," she advised. "A

question that the cards will answer for you, me dear. Don't
tell it to me, me dear. I don't need to know it"—a little pause,
meaningful eye contact—"me dear."

I could have chosen one of several questions. Like, would
there be an end to world hunger? Would they find a cure for
AIDS? Would there be peace on earth? Will they manage to
fix the hole in the ozone layer? But interestingly enough, the
question that I wanted to ask was the "Will I ever meet a nice
man?" one. Funny.

"Have you decided on the question, me dear?" she asked,
taking the deck back from me.

I nodded. She started flinging cards on the table at high
speed. I didn't know what any of the pictures meant, but I
thought that they didn't look very promising. There seemed
to be a lot of them with swords, and surely that couldn't be
good? "Your question concerns a man, me dear?" she said.

Even *I* wasn't impressed with that.

I mean, I was a young woman. I had few concerns in my
life. Well, actually, I had plenty. But the *average* young woman
would only seek guidance from a fortune-teller for two reasons—her career and her love life. And if she was having problems with her career, she would probably do something
constructive about it herself.

Like sleep with her boss.

So that just left the love life option. "Yes," I answered wearily. "It concerns a man."

"You have been unlucky in love, me dear," she said
sympathetically.

Once again, I refused to be impressed.

Yes, I had been unlucky in love. But show me a woman
who hasn't.

"There is a fair-haired man in your past, me dear," she
said.

I suppose she meant Steven. But I mean, who *hadn't* got a
fair-haired man in their past? "He was not the one for you,
me dear," she continued.

"Thanks," I said, a bit annoyed, because I'd already figured
that out myself.

"But waste no tears on him, me dear," she advised.

"Don't worry."

"For there is another man, me dear," she said, giving me a big smile.

"Really?" I asked, delighted, leaning closer to her, the plastic covers squeaking against my thighs. "Now you're talking."

"Yes," she said, studying the cards. "I see a marriage."

"Do you really?" I demanded. "Whose? Mine?"

"Yes, me dear," she said. "Yours."

"Really?" I said. "When?"

"Before the leaves have fallen on the ground for the second time, me dear."

"Sorry?"

"Before the four seasons have rolled by a time and half a time again," she said.

"Sorry, I'm still not sure what you mean," I apologized.

"In about a year," she snapped, sounding a bit annoyed.

I was slightly disappointed. In about a year, it would still be winter, and I'd always seen myself getting married in the spring. On the rare occasions that I could see myself married at all, that is. "You couldn't make it a bit longer than a year, could you?" I asked.

"Me dear," she said sharply. "I do not ordain these things. I am simply the messenger."

"Sorry," I muttered.

"Well," she said, in a nicer tone, "let's say up to eighteen months just to be on the safe side."

"Thanks," I said, thinking that was very decent of her. So I was getting married, I thought. Momentous stuff. I would just have settled for a boyfriend.

"I wonder who he is?"

"You must be careful, me dear," she warned me. "At first you may not recognize him for who he truly is."

"You mean I'll meet him at a costume party?"

"No," she said ominously. "At first he may not be who he appears to be."

"Oh, you mean he's going to lie to me," I said, understanding. "Well, fair enough then. Why should this one be any different?"

I laughed.

Mrs. Nolan looked annoyed.

"No, me dear," she said irritably. "I mean that you must

take care not to wear cupid's blinkers. You may have to seek
this man out and look at him with clear and fearless eyes. He
may not have money, but you must not humble him. He may
not have looks, but you must not humble him."

Oh great, I thought. I might have known! A deformed
pauper.

"I see," I said. "So he's going to be poor and ugly."

"*No*, me dear," said Mrs. Nolan, in exasperation and dropping her mystical language. "I just mean that he mightn't be
your usual type."

"I *see!*" I said.

If only she'd said that to begin with. Clear and fearless
eyes, indeed! "So," I continued, "when Jason, the seventeen-
year-old with all the pimples and those awful baggy clothes,
meets me at the photocopier and asks me out, I shouldn't
laugh in his face and tell him that I'll see him ice-skating in
hell?"

"That's the idea, me dear," said Mrs. Nolan, sounding
pleased. "For the flower of love may flourish in the most unexpected of places, and you must be ready to pluck it."

"I understand," I nodded.

All the same, I'd want to be pretty desperate before Jason
would have any kind of chance. But there was no need to tell
Mrs. Nolan that.

Anyway, if she was worth her salt, she already knew. She
started pointing briskly at cards and barking out staccato sentences, thus indicating that the audience was nearing its end.
"You will have three children, two girls and a boy, me dear,"
and "You will never have money, but you will have happiness,
me dear," and "You have an enemy at work, me dear. She is
jealous of your success." I had to laugh—slightly bitterly—at
that one. She would have laughed too if she knew how menial
and awful my job was.

Then she paused.

She looked at the cards, then she looked at me. Something
like concern was on her face.

"There has been a cloud over you, me dear," she said
slowly. "A darkness, a sadness."

Suddenly, to my horror, I had a lump in my throat. A dark
cloud was exactly how I described the bouts of depression that

I sometimes got. Not the usual "I wish I owned that suede skirt" type of depression—although I suffered from *that* kind of depression too. But since I had been seventeen, I had had bouts of actual clinical depression.

I nodded, almost unable to speak.

"Yes," I whispered.

"For many years you have carried this," she said quietly, looking at me with great sympathy and understanding.

"Yes," I whispered again, feeling my eyes fill with tears.

"You have carried it almost entirely alone," she said gently.

"Yes," I nodded, feeling a tear make its way slowly down my cheek. Oh my God! It was awful! I thought that we had come for a laugh. But instead this woman, who was almost a complete stranger, had seen through to the essence of me, had touched me in a place where few human beings had ever been.

"Sorry," I sniffed, wiping my face with my hand.

"Don't worry, me dear," she said, handing me a tissue from a box that was obviously there for this very reason. "This happens a lot."

She waited for a few moments while I recovered my composure and then she began to speak again.

"Okay, me dear?"

"Yes." Sniff. "Thanks."

"This can get better, me dear. But you must not hide from people who wish to help you. How can they help you if you won't let them?"

"I don't really know what you mean," I mumbled.

"Maybe you don't, me dear," she agreed kindly. "but I hope that you will learn."

"Thanks," I sniffed. "You've been very nice. And thanks, you know, for the guy and me getting married and all that. It was nice to hear."

"Not at all, me dear," she said pleasantly. "Now that'll be thirty pounds, please."

I paid her and launched myself out of the crackling plastic.

"Good luck, me dear," she said. "And will you send the next young lady in?"

"Who's next?" I wondered. "Oh it's Megan, isn't it?"

"Megan!" exclaimed Mrs. Nolan. "Isn't that a lovely name? She must be Welsh."

"Australian, actually," I smiled. "Thanks again. Bye now."

"Bye, me dear," she nodded, smiling. I went back out into the tiny hall, where the other three fell on me with urgent questions. "Well?" and "What did she say?" Megan asked, "Was it worth the money?"

"Yes," I told her. "You should go."

"I'll only go if you all promise not to tell anything until I'm back out and we're all together," said Megan sulkily. "I don't want to miss anything."

CONTEMPORARY ROMANCE
from
Mary Alice Kruesi

*One
Summer's
Night*

81433-1/$5.99 US/$7.99 Can
A yound woman is awakened to the power of love
in this evocative, modern-day fairy tale.

*Second
Star
To The
Right*

79887-5/$5.99 US/$7.99 Can
A poignant and unforgettable story about the healing power
of love—and the heart-soaring realization that dreams
really can come true.